NEW YORK TIMES AND *USA TODAY* BESTSELLING AUTHOR

RACHEL VINCENT

PREY

"COMPELLING AND EDGY, DARK AND EVOCATIVE, *STRAY* IS A MUST READ!" – *NEW YORK TIMES* BESTSELLING AUTHOR GENA SHOWALTER

Look for the first book in a brand-new series from *New York Times* bestselling author

RACHEL VINCENT

Kaylee Kavanaugh just wants to enjoy having caught the attention of the hottest guy in school, but a normal date is tough to come by when your classmates start dropping dead, and only you know who'll be next....

MY SOUL TO TAKE

SOUL SCREAMERS

THE LAST THING YOU HEAR BEFORE YOU DIE

ISBN-13: 978-0-7783-2913-8

HARLEQUIN TEEN

MRV0709IFC

Praise for the novels of
***New York Times* bestselling author**

RACHEL VINCENT

"Compelling and edgy, dark and evocative, *Stray* is a must read! I loved it from beginning to end."
—*New York Times* bestselling author Gena Showalter

"I liked the character and loved the action. I look forward to reading the next book in the series."
—*New York Times* bestselling author Charlaine Harris

"Her first-person perspective, dialogue, descriptions, and even her sound effects are phenomenal (I heard the noises, I swear it!).... I think Vincent has a hit on her hands."
—*Romantic Reader at Heart*

"The second installment of Vincent's urban fantasy series (after *Stray*) features a well-thought-out vision of werecat social structure as well as a heroine who insists on carving her own path, even if it means breaking some of her society's most sacred taboos."
—*Library Journal* on *Rogue*

****½ "Vincent's smart, sexy sequel to *Stray* continues in the same vein, but this story has more emotional resonance. Faythe's as sassy as ever, and her first-person observations add greatly to the reader's experience."
—*RT Book Reviews* on *Rogue*

Also by New York Times *bestselling author*
Rachel Vincent

The Shifters

STRAY
ROGUE
PRIDE
PREY
SHIFT

And coming in October 2010

ALPHA

And from Harlequin Teen

Soul Screamers

MY SOUL TO TAKE
MY SOUL TO SAVE

And coming in June 2010

MY SOUL TO KEEP

T

PREY

MIRA®

Recycling programs for this product may not exist in your area.

ISBN-13: 978-0-7783-2913-8

PREY

For questions and comments about the quality of this book please contact us at Customer_eCare@Harlequin.ca.

www.MIRABooks.com

Printed in U.S.A.

For Matrice, my editor, without whose amazing suggestion this story would not exist in its current form. Thanks for your patience, and for nudging my creative compass back to true north.

ACKNOWLEDGMENTS

Thanks first of all to #1, who handled almost every single detail of our recent move, so I could finish the rough draft I was working on, as well as the line edits for *Prey*. Without you to keep track of the details, I would live in utter chaos.

Thanks to Elizabeth Mazer for all her hard work behind the scenes, to the MIRA art department for the amazing cover (my favorite so far!) and to the entire production staff, for turning my little story into an actual book.

Thanks to Miriam Kriss, who handles all the business so I can bury myself in other worlds. To Vicki Pettersson, who kept me accountable during the revisions. And to Jocelynn Drake, who lets me complain.

And thanks most of all to my critique partner, Rinda Elliot, for all the hours spent helping me sort this one out. You keep me working. You keep me writing. You keep me sane.

One

"You planning to get there sometime this century, Vic?" I glanced at my watch, my foot tapping an anxious beat on the floorboard.

Victor Di Carlo shot me a long-suffering smile, then turned back to the road. "Speed limit's seventy-five, Faythe. I'm doing eighty. But if you think you can get there faster on foot, be my guest."

But of course, I couldn't. Not even on four paws. A cheetah can run sixty-five miles an hour, but can't sustain that speed for long. And I'm no cheetah. So I was stuck drumming my stubby nails on the passenger-seat armrest in Vic's Suburban as it stubbornly maintained a speed I considered unacceptable.

"Relax." Vic flicked on the left blinker, then moved the SUV smoothly out of the right lane to pass a lumbering semi. "We'll get there on schedule, and Marc will be waiting."

I nodded, locking and unlocking the passenger-side door until he glared at me. "Sorry."

"Jeez, Faythe, you act like you haven't seen him in weeks," Ethan said, and I twisted in my seat to see him roll his eyes from the back row, his usual good-humored grin firmly in place. He was the youngest of my four brothers—only two years my elder—and the one most likely to beat me up in training, then bring ice for my bruises. "How long has it been?"

I stared out my window at empty fields and winter-bare trees growing dim in the late-afternoon light. "Nine weeks, tomorrow." A lot had happened since Marc had been exiled, and the most notable example lay sleeping in the seat behind me.

Manx's baby. Des. The two-week-old was fastened into a reclined, backward-facing car seat on the bench next to his mother. Who somehow managed to look disarmingly beautiful, even with drool trailing from her open mouth. Since the baby came, she caught her *z's* when she could. Whenever he was quiet. As did the rest of us.

It turns out sensitive cat hearing comes with a serious downside.

In the past two months, Manx had given birth, and Kaci—the wild teenage tabby we'd taken in—had mostly settled into life at the ranch, though so far she'd refused to Shift. November had blown leaves from the trees, December had brought a rare Texas snowstorm, and the eighth day of January had crowned it all with an even less common and more beautiful layer of thick ice, which had yet to fully melt.

But I had not seen Marc. Not even once, in all those weeks.

Vic grinned at me for a moment before turning back to the traffic. "And I suppose it's the stimulating *conversation* you miss, right?"

"La-la-la!" Ethan sang. He slouched in his seat and stuffed earbuds into his ears to block out the response he might not want to hear from his sister.

"Right now, I'd listen to anything he has to say, so long as I get to hear it in person." Sighing, I snatched a paper cup from the drink holder and downed the last of my 7-Eleven coffee. It was cold. As I dropped the cup into the trash can wedged between the seats, Vic's cell phone rang. He leaned to the right and dug it from his left hip pocket, then flipped it open without swerving an inch. I probably would have put us in the ditch.

"Hello?"

"Vic." It was my dad. We could all hear him perfectly well, except for Manx, who was now snoring delicately, if such a thing was possible. "Your father came through for me. I wanted you to be the first to know."

Vic's sigh was audible, and his face suddenly drained of tension I hadn't even realized it held. He smiled as the Suburban soared past another eighteen-wheeler. "I never doubted it." But the relief in his eyes said otherwise. He'd been worried. We all had.

Springs squealed over the line—Greg Sanders leaning back in his desk chair. He'd probably called as soon as he got the news. "Remind Faythe to deliver my message to your family, please," he said, and I rolled my eyes.

"I know, Daddy."

My father chuckled. "Drive carefully, and let me know when you get there."

"Will do." Vic was still grinning like a clown when he hung up, and I doubted he'd even heard what he was agreeing to. Fortunately, I had.

"So, that's three now, right?" I twisted in my seat to look at Ethan, who'd turned off the music and was no longer feigning sleep.

The backseat groaned as he searched for a more comfortable position. "Yeah. Uncle Rick and Ed Taylor." Whose daughters both owed their lives to our Pride. I'd freed my cousin Abby after we were both kidnapped by a jungle stray intending to sell us as breeders, then we'd caught and killed that same stray before he could snatch Carissa Taylor. Their fathers were understandably loyal to mine. "And now Bert."

Umberto Di Carlo—Vic's dad—was one of my father's oldest friends. We'd been counting on his support, but were far from sure we'd get it. After all, politics could uproot entire family trees, to say nothing of friendships.

Nine weeks ago I'd been acquitted—*barely*—of infecting my college boyfriend and then killing him in self-defense. On the last day of my trial—the day after Marc was exiled—Calvin Malone had made a formal challenge to my father's leadership, petitioning to have him removed as head of the Territorial Council. Though he remained our Alpha, my dad had been temporarily suspended from his position of authority over the other council members, pending an official vote by all ten Alphas. That vote was scheduled for the first of February—two weeks away.

Since his suspension, my father and Malone had been fighting—figuratively—for a commitment of support from each of their peers.

My uncle had thrown his weight behind us immediately, and Edward Taylor had followed suit a week later. But our Pride's other allies had asked for time to consider. To weigh their options. Their hesitance stung, but it made sense. However they voted, their decisions would have an irreversible effect on the council, and on the werecat community at large. After all, most of them had sons serving in Prides on both sides of the conflict. Brothers living in territories loyal to Malone. Daughters or sisters married to toms participating in the coup. I was lucky that three of my brothers—Michael, Owen, and Ethan—had no loyalties to anyone else. As for my brother Ryan, well, the less said about him the better.

The waiting was hard on Vic, but it was nothing compared to the effect the whole thing was having on our fellow enforcer Jace, whose stepfather had organized the attempt to unseat my dad. Jace felt personally responsible for Calvin Malone's betrayal, though he could have done nothing to stop it.

"What about Malone?" I asked, doing a mental tally of the other Alphas.

Ethan pulled his earphones from his ears and wound them around one hand. "Last I heard, he has three votes, too. Milo Mitchell, Wes Gardner, and Paul Blackwell."

Mitchell's son, Kevin, had been kicked out of our Pride four months earlier for repeatedly helping a stray sneak into the south-central territory. Gardner was irate over our "failure" to avenge his brother Jamey's death at Manx's hands. And as far as we could tell, Paul Blackwell was siding against us because he legitimately objected to my father's equal-opportunity approach to leadership. Apparently the saying about an old dog's inability to learn new tricks held true for old cats, as well, and though Blackwell—unlike Malone—didn't seem to hate women and strays, neither did he envision a place for them among the community's leaders.

That left only two undecided Alphas: Nick Davidson and Jerald Pierce—another fellow enforcer's father. And with both sides now scrambling to claim those votes, one thing was clear: the fight was about to get ugly.

"Parker's dad will come through." Vic sounded much more confident than I felt. "That'll give us four." But we needed Davidson's vote, too. Four votes would only lock the proceedings in a tie, and we needed a clear victory. Otherwise, even if my father managed to hold on to his position, the peace would never last.

"How much longer?" I asked, my hand clenched around the car door handle.

"Our exit's up next." Vic nodded at the sign ahead, advertising food and gas in one mile.

About time! After hours on the road and too many cups of coffee to count…

I turned in my seat to see Ethan sitting up straight now

and shrugging into his jacket. Manx was still asleep, her long black ringlets draping the back of the seat and the front of her blouse. She was the very picture of peace and happiness, of maternal bliss, in spite of very little rest and the unpleasant reason for our trip.

Des was born on the last day of 2008, which would have given Manx an extra tax deduction for the year—if she were a U.S. citizen or a legal immigrant. But she was neither, which also meant she couldn't board a plane. Which is how Vic, Ethan, and I wound up driving her from our ranch in eastern Texas to the outskirts of Atlanta, where Vic's dad—and my father's newest ally—was hosting Manx's hearing.

I'd volunteered for the transport—normally a very dull assignment—because we had to drive through the free territory to get to Atlanta. Marc was in the free territory.

And in minutes, he'd be in my arms.

"Manx, wake up!" Leaning over the armrest, I shoved the bottom of the center bench seat hard enough to jostle the tabby, but careful not to brush her leg. She didn't like to be touched. Considering the abuse she'd suffered, I couldn't blame her.

Her eyes fluttered open, and in a single blink she banished the sleep stupor from her expression, replacing it with an instant alertness I envied. Followed by an initial, panicked search for her child, as if someone had stolen him while she slept. And that's exactly what she was afraid of.

When she was still pregnant, we'd all heard her scream at night, crying in her sleep. The first few times, my mother had tried to wake her, but my father insisted she stop before she got a broken nose for her efforts. Fortunately, the dreams had ended when the baby came, and Manx insisted he stay in the bed with her. She said he slept better like that, but I couldn't help thinking *she* was the one who really benefited. As did the rest of us, from the peaceful silence.

Manx relaxed when her eyes found Des, still asleep in his car seat. She pushed hair back from her face and looked up. "This is Mississippi?"

"Yup." Vic flicked the right blinker on and veered onto the off-ramp as I settled back into my seat. I ignored the restaurants we passed, focusing on the Conoco station at the end of a strip of convenience stores.

By all accounts, Marc had settled into his new life as well as could be expected. He'd found a job and an isolated rental house, and was slowly carving out an existence for himself in the human world—a world that no longer included me. At least in person. But we spoke on the phone almost daily, and I'd even talked him through a partial Shift a month earlier. Though I'd only been ordered to teach my fellow Pride cats the partial shift, I was proud to say that Marc Ramos, my favorite stray, was the first tom to accomplish it.

Evidently he held more than enough suppressed anger to trigger the facial transformation. Not a surprise.

My eyes scanned the crowded lot. We'd scheduled a rest stop at Natchez, just beyond the Mississippi border, where Marc was supposed to join us and escort us across the entire free territory, including an overnight stay in the middle of Mississippi. But I didn't see his car. Disappointed, I clenched my hands in my lap until my fingers ached.

Vic turned right into the parking lot, then pulled into an empty space at the rear. I started to get out and look for Marc inside the store, but Vic laid one hand on my arm as soon as I got the door open. "Can you stay with them for a minute? I have to pee."

I glanced at Vic, then back at Ethan. Normally, my youngest brother would have been enough security for one postpartum tabby and an infant. But the free zone was unregulated, and Manx was skittish at best, even when she *wasn't* about to be tried for murder, so we were trying to give her double coverage at all times. "Yeah, I'll stay. But hurry up." He smiled in thanks as I closed my door, then shut his own and made his way to the front of the building.

Des made a mewling noise behind me, and I twisted in my seat to see Manx bring the baby up to one exposed breast, where he latched on eagerly. The mewling became a soft sucking sound as he began to nurse. Again. Did that kid ever do anything but eat? Even with his androgynous baby face, I could tell the little monster was a boy by his appetite alone.

Still, I couldn't help but smile as I turned to scan the parking lot out the driver-side window. The little guy was a true survivor. Just like his mother.

"Looking for me?" Something tapped on the glass behind me, and I jumped, then whirled fast enough to hit my head on the sun visor. Marc stood outside the window, looking warm and welcoming in a worn brown leather jacket and an old pair of jeans. His smile widened as I fumbled for the door handle. But in my excitement I couldn't find it, so he opened it for me, nearly ripping the door from its hinges.

My feet never hit the ground. One moment I was in the front seat, the next I was in his arms, my legs wrapped around his waist, his mouth soft but insistent beneath mine. People stared—I saw them over Marc's shoulder—but then they smiled and went about their business, except for a few kids, who giggled at our display.

Evidently reunions look much the same in any species.

"Your hair grew," Marc whispered, and the warmth of his breath against my ear gave me chills that had nothing to do with the ice half coating the parking lot.

"You cut yours." I ran my hand through cold, short curls.

He put me down, but still held me close. "Yeah, I figured with the new life, why not try a new look? What do you think?"

Grinning, I stepped back for a better look. "Not bad." Marc would look good in an orange clown wig, if he decided to wear one. Still, though he'd only lost two inches, I couldn't help missing the rest of his hair. But nowhere near as badly as I'd missed *him.*

I was threading my arm through his when a familiar scent caught my attention. A stray scent, and—oddly enough—one I knew.

Daniel Painter.

I froze, and my grip tightened around Marc's arm as my pulse raced. I scanned the parking lot for the stray who'd ratted Manx out in exchange for a chance to join our Pride. If he could keep his nose clean in the free zone for a year.

Keeping his nose clean did *not* include picking a fight with a delegation of Pride cats as soon as we crossed the border. And there was no way in hell that his presence in that particular parking lot was a coincidence…

Two

"What's wrong?" Marc's gold-flecked brown eyes darkened as he frowned, glancing around in search of whatever had set me on edge.

"Dan Painter's here." My fingers brushed his leather-clad arm as I turned, trying to glance around the parking lot inconspicuously.

A flicker of annoyance flashed across Marc's expression. "I know. I can't shake him."

I felt my eyes go wide and gave up the search for Painter to stare at Marc. "He's *tailing* you?"

"Sort of." Marc flushed, and I knew there was more to the story than he wanted to tell me.

"And you're just…letting him?"

He sighed and rolled his eyes. "He's not actually causing any trouble, so I don't feel justified pounding on him. He just hangs around and asks questions about the Pride, and the way we—you guys—do things. Where we come from, how we control bloodlust, why there are so few tabbies, why there aren't any strays in the Pride. Well, not anymore, anyway."

Marc was a stray—a werecat born human, and later infected through a bite or scratch from a werecat in feline form—and he remained the only stray ever admitted into a Pride. Even if he was no longer officially a part of that Pride.

"The guy never shuts up. Seriously, he talks *all day long.*"

I smiled. Kaci had a very similar habit, and as much as I liked her, I'd started to value long-distance assignments simply for the peace and quiet. Surely his job provided the same relief. "At least he can't bug you at work, right?"

Marc's flush deepened. "He joined my crew last month. We frame houses together now. Every day."

I couldn't help laughing. "That's so cute! You have a *sidekick.* A little mini-me." Though if memory served, Painter wasn't much smaller than Marc.

"Whatever. Forget about Painter." His gaze flicked behind me to the back passenger-side door, which my brother had just opened and stepped through. "Hey, Ethan, how's monogamy treating you?"

For the first time in his life, the family Casanova had been dating the same girl for four straight months. Our mother was thrilled, and for once she was fantasizing about a wedding that *wouldn't* involve me in a veil.

"It's like eating white rice for every meal," Ethan said, right on cue.

Marc grinned. "Hey, if you're eating every day, I'd say you're a lucky man." His words were for Ethan, but his eyes were on me. Apparently he missed my…rice.

Ethan shrugged, unmoved. "I guess. How's the construction business treating *you?*"

Marc scruffed one hand through his newly shorn curls. "It's like swinging a hammer eight hours a day for minimum wage." And just like that, they were all caught up.

Still in the SUV, the baby hiccuped, and I glanced over my brother's shoulder to see Manx buttoning her blouse. Then she climbed out of the car and lifted Des from his seat, wrapping him gently in a blue knit blanket.

"How are you, Manx?" Marc stuffed his hands into his pockets to show the tabby he had no intention of touching her. We'd discovered that approach—especially coming from the toms—kept her fairly relaxed.

"Good, thank you." Her exotic accent—she was Venezuelan by birth—made her statement sound striking, rather than common. She beamed a brilliant smile at him and held the baby slightly away from her body, wordlessly inviting him to peek.

"Wow." Marc's eyes went softer than I'd ever seen them as he stared at Des, and I wasn't sure whether I should be amused or worried. "Do I get an introduction?" he finally asked.

Manx's smile widened. "This is Desiderio. He is my heart's desire."

"We call him Des," I added, ever helpful.

"He's beautiful. May I?" Marc pulled one hand from his pocket and mimed stroking the baby's cheek.

Manx hesitated, and her smile froze for an instant. Then she took a deep breath and released it slowly. "Of course."

Marc ran the back of one rough finger down the child's face. When he reached the corner of Des's mouth, the baby turned toward his touch, lips pursed and ready to suckle. Marc laughed, and I couldn't help but smile.

"I see you've met our latest addition," Vic said, and I looked up to see him walking toward us from the convenience store, a white plastic sack in one hand.

"He's amazing," Marc said, and on the edge of my vision, Manx's posture relaxed a little more.

"Yeah, he is." Vic set his bag on the front passenger seat and glanced at the baby with that gaga look most toms assumed when confronted with members of the next generation. Yet more proof that propagation of the species was indeed their biggest goal in life.

Vic shut the car door and embraced his former field

partner in a masculine, back-thumping greeting. Then he stepped away and glanced from me to Marc as Ethan settled a long coat over Manx's shoulders, careful not to touch her. "You're not going to believe who I ran into inside." He tossed his head toward the building.

"Dan Painter." I grinned.

Vic huffed. "You smelled him?"

I nodded. "He and Marc have…*bonded*."

Vic's brow rose in amusement, but a dark look from Marc kept him from pressing for details. "This cold can't be good for the baby," he said instead, still grinning at Marc. "Let's get done here and get on the road."

Marc and I flanked Manx on the way into the building, where he waited outside the ladies' room while she and I went inside. She changed the baby's diaper on a fold-down table while I made use of one of the stalls. Then she asked if I could hold him while she relieved herself.

"Oh, I don't know." My heart thudded in panic. I'd literally never held a baby, and whatever idiot had said all women possessed some kind of maternal instinct was *wrong*. "Can't you just…put him down for a couple of minutes?"

"On the *ground?*" Manx glared at me, and I shrugged helplessly. She rolled her eyes. "Fine. I will ask one of the men."

I sighed heavily. "Give him here." I could *not* let Marc know I was…*hesitant* to hold a baby. He'd never let me live it down. "What do I do with him?" I held my arms out football style, as I'd seen my mother do often enough over the past two weeks.

Manx placed the baby gently in my arms, settling his little head securely into the crook of my elbow. "Nothing. He is sleeping. Hold him for just two minutes."

I nodded, afraid to move anything but my head for risk of waking Des.

Manx hesitated, her hand on the swinging metal door. Then she shot me a smile that couldn't quite relieve the nervous lines spanning her forehead and stepped into the stall.

I stared at the baby, taking in each detail up close for the first time. He was *unbelievably* small. Like a doll, but more fragile. His cheeks were round and red, his nose sprinkled with tiny, colorless bumps. His hands and feet were wrapped in the blanket, but a wisp of straight black hair showed above his forehead.

I saw no trace of Luiz in him, thank goodness.

But then, I saw no trace of Manx, either. I saw only a baby, cute in a red, squirmy kind of way, and perfectly tolerable when he was sleeping.

"Thank you." The stall door swung open and Manx stepped out. She washed her hands, then took her baby back, and only then did the worry lines fade from around her mouth.

On our way through the store, we passed Dan Painter in line at the counter, holding a big bag of chips, a handful of Slim Jims, and a two-liter of Coke. I tapped him on the shoulder as I passed, and when his eyes met mine, he nearly choked on the chunk he'd already torn from one of the meat sticks.

I laughed. He obviously remembered our first meeting, when I'd knocked him unconscious with one swing. I like to leave a good first impression.

In the parking lot, Manx buckled Des into his car seat in the SUV, which Vic had already refueled and warmed up. Ethan had claimed the front passenger seat, which was fine with me. I was riding with Marc.

Squeezing into his tiny, low-slung car felt weird after weeks of riding in Vic's Suburban, but it was a good kind of weird. Familiar and easy. And sorely missed.

We pulled from the lot first, and Vic followed as the last rays of daylight deepened to a dramatic red and orange. Then darkness descended, and Marc and I were together—and alone—for the first time in months.

Unfortunately, we were also on the road, which made anything more than conversation impossible. Or at least impractical.

"So, how's your dad holding up?" Marc twined his hand around mine on the center console as outside, small buildings and restaurants gave way to open fields, then long stretches of woods.

"Okay, I guess." I shrugged. "He's pretty quiet lately. I don't think he wants anyone to know how hard this whole sucker punch from Malone has been on him. The council's completely fractured. Manx's hearing should be interesting, considering the current coup-in-progress." And though I would never admit it aloud for fear of sounding like a coward, I was greatly relieved that my responsibility to Kaci meant I couldn't stay for the trial. Hanging out in a room full of angry Alphas did *not* appeal to my sense of adventure. Or my survival instinct.

Marc changed lanes, and I watched in the side-view mirror as Vic followed his lead. "Who's on the tribunal this time?"

"Taylor, Mitchell, and Pierce." Fortunately, that particular combination of Alphas gave Manx a decent shot at a fair trial. Taylor had thrown his weight behind my father, Mitchell was firmly in place behind Malone, and Parker's dad was still sticking to his Switzerland routine. But on the downside, getting those three to agree on anything—much less a verdict—would not be easy.

"And Wes Gardner's going to be there, of course." Because his brother was one of Manx's victims.

"I assume Michael's going in a professional capacity."

"Yeah." While werecat law didn't mirror human law exactly, as an attorney, my oldest brother was by far the most qualified to assist Manx in her defense. He'd be flying to Atlanta the following day, shortly after his wife—a human woman and honest-to-goodness runway model named Holly—left for a photo shoot in Italy. Michael was lucky his wife traveled so much, and that she stayed too busy to ask many questions. She knew nothing of our werecat existence. Theirs was definitely an odd marriage, but it seemed to fit them both well.

Marc glanced in the rearview mirror, then briefly at me before turning his eyes back toward the road. "How's Kaci? Still refusing to Shift?"

"Yeah. I'm starting to really worry about her. She's tired all the time, and listless, and she only perks up when I let her watch me spar. She seems to think if she learns to defend herself in human form, she'll never have to Shift again."

"What's the doc say?"

I sighed. "Her symptoms are similar to chronic fatigue and depression. And if she doesn't give in to her feline form soon, her body will start shutting down a little at a time, until she's too weak to move. He says refusing to Shift will eventually kill her. And by 'eventually,' he means *soon.*"

"Damn." Marc looked surprised for a moment, then concern dragged his mouth into a deep frown.

"I know. I feel like I'm failing her." I loosened my seat belt and twisted in the bucket seat to face him. "I mean, I'm supposed to be taking care of her, and instead I'm letting her wither up and die. She deserves better than that, but I can't convince her to Shift. She won't even listen when I bring it up anymore."

"So what are you going to do?"

I shrugged, scowling out the window at the ice-glazed power lines running along the highway. I couldn't get used to that question; until recently, I was rarely allowed to make my own choices, much less someone else's. But Kaci wasn't old enough or mature enough to choose to suffer. She was my responsibility.

"I don't know. But I'm not going to let her waste

away. She's fought too hard for survival to give up now. Especially over something as simple as this."

Unfortunately, Shifting wasn't simple for her. The last time she'd been in cat form, she'd killed four people, including her own mother and sister. But that kid was *strong*. And stubborn enough to make sure nothing like that ever happened again, even if she had to kill herself to prevent it.

The rest of the Pride was counting on my strength and stubbornness to override hers. In the beginning, I'd thought it would work. But after nine weeks with no success, I wasn't so sure.

"Dr. Carver said to call him if she hasn't done it by this time next week. He's going to try to force her Shift." With an intravenous cocktail of adrenaline and a couple of other drugs.

Marc's head swiveled to face me, eyebrows high in surprise. "*Into* cat form? Is that possible?"

"We're not sure. In theory, it shouldn't be much different from forcing someone into human form." Which we had to do occasionally, in order to question uncooperative strays, or stop them from shredding anyone who came near. "But in practice…well, no one's ever tried it. I hate to experiment on a child, but she's really leaving us no choice."

"Have you told her?"

"Yeah." I rubbed my forehead, fighting off frustration. I hadn't seen Marc in months, and I wanted these few hours together to pass *pleasantly*. "But she doesn't think we'll do it. She says she'd rather be tired for the rest of her life than risk hurting someone in cat form."

"Yeah, but would she rather be *dead?*"

I closed my eyes and let my head fall against the headrest. "Honestly, I think she would. She's horrified by what happened last time, and we still can't get her to talk about it. But I'm hoping that if I can—"

My eyes flew open as Marc's car jerked beneath us and started to sputter.

"What's that?" I sat straight in my seat, staring out the windshield at nothing but darkness, broken by two overlapping cones of light from the headlights.

He didn't answer, but his hands tightened around the already misshapen wheel—a casualty of many past temper fits—and his frown deepened.

The car sputtered again, then began to shake, like it was trying to die. Steam rolled from beneath the hood, white as snow against the cold, black night.

Marc veered slowly onto the right shoulder, glancing back and forth between the windshield and the rearview mirror. I twisted to watch as Vic came to a stop behind us. We got out, crunching on a layer of ice, and Vic joined us at the front of the car, where Marc pulled a penlight from his pocket and popped the hood. He shined the light on parts I didn't recognize, grunting in frustration. Then he knelt and shimmied under the car, in spite of the frigid concrete at his back.

Seconds later he emerged, scowling. "My radiator hose is slashed."

"Son of a *bitch!*" Vic muttered, as Ethan stepped out of the SUV, followed by Manx, clutching the bundled baby to her chest. "You can't drive long like that. No more than ten, fifteen miles. Had to've happened at the gas station."

Marc nodded in agreement, then his eyes met mine, his face lit unevenly by the headlights. "We'll pile into Vic's SUV with everyone else, and I'll have mine towed."

Obviously, that wasn't how I'd intended our reunion to go, but it could have been much worse, especially considering that some asshole had sabotaged Marc's car. What if they'd cut the brake line instead?

Pissed now, I jerked open the passenger-side door

and leaned in to grab the sodas Marc had bought at the Conoco. And that's when I saw them. Two pinpoints of red light in the trees across the street. Those lights went out, then appeared again a second later.

Eyes. *Cat* eyes, reflecting the little available light. Someone was blinking, and whoever it was, he wasn't alone. Several more sets of eyes appeared in the trees, each pair at least ten feet from the next.

My stomach twisted in on itself, churning around my road-trip munchies in fear. We hadn't just been sabotaged. We'd been fucking *ambushed.*

Straightening slowly, I sniffed, wincing when the frigid air pierced my nose, throat, and lungs with a thousand microscopic shards of ice. Fortunately, one good whiff was enough.

Strays.

"Um…guys?" I hissed as the first dark form slunk out of the woods and into the moonlit night, uncommon confidence in each silent step.

"We see them," Marc whispered, and I glanced over the roof to find him backing slowly toward the trunk of his car.

"Three strays at your six o'clock, Faythe," Vic said, anger threading a cord of danger through his voice as he stared over my shoulder. "No, make that four."

At my back, too? *Damn it!* "Five more straight ahead." I nodded at the trees across the street and stepped to the side so I could close the car door.

Gravel crunched on my left, and my brother spoke from his position near the passenger side of the Suburban. "This makes no sense. Strays are loners."

Yet several had united to fight us in Montana two months earlier. This new trend made me nervous. As did the cats creeping slowly toward us—from all directions. Each in cat form. At a glance I counted eleven of them now, and there were only five of us, even if Manx could fight holding a baby. Which she could *not.*

"Manx, get in the car with Des," Marc ordered. Manx climbed through Vic's rear driver-side door without a word and shoved it closed.

Okay, make that four *of us.*

"Faythe?" Marc had his trunk open now, and he held something out to me. I inched toward him with my arm extended, sliding for a moment before I could steady myself on the thin layer of ice beneath my boots. Something long, cold and hard hit my palm—a shovel, still caked with dried dirt.

I arched one eyebrow at him in question, and he gave me a grim smile. "We don't stand a chance unarmed." And there was clearly no time to Shift. I shivered from the cold, but knew I'd soon be sweating from exertion.

Marc tossed a second shovel to Vic, who caught it one-handed, then he pulled a small ax from the trunk and wrapped both hands around the twelve-inch rubber grip. He hefted it briefly, as if considering, then handed it to Ethan, who'd come to a stop on his left.

"You ready for this?" Marc asked, pulling a crowbar from the trunk for himself before slamming it shut.

"Looking forward to it." Ethan removed his earphones from around his neck with his free hand. He wound them around his MP3 player and slid both into his front pocket, then gave the ax an experimental swing. "What, no samurai?" He swung the ax again, then shrugged, green eyes glinting in bleak humor. "I guess this'll do."

"Okay, let's go." Marc stalked toward the SUV and stopped at the driver-side door. "Manx?" He tapped on the window, and her head appeared between the seats. "Don't come out, no matter what."

She nodded.

Marc checked to make sure the keys were still in the ignition—they were—then turned to me, his features severe in the harsh, reddish glare of his own taillights. "If this goes bad, get them out of here. Don't look back, just drive straight to the ranch." I started to protest, but he ignored me. "I'm serious, Faythe. Get them back safely. I'll haunt your ass till the day you die if you let something happen to that baby."

I nodded, more alarmed by the tone of his voice than by the cats, the nearest of which was now only a couple of feet away, slinking across the near lane eight feet to my right. Two serpentine puffs of air floated from his nostrils with each breath. Moonlight shone on his glossy fur. Rage glinted in the reflective surface of his eyes.

Marc stepped closer to the hood and tossed his head, telling me to scoot toward the rear door. "Keep your backs to the vehicle and make them come to you."

And that's when the first cat pounced.

Three

The furry bastard flew at Marc, claws bared, hissing through a mouthful of pointy feline teeth. He ripped four jagged slashes in the sleeve of Marc's jacket. Marc slammed the rounded corner of the crowbar into the side of the cat's head on the upswing. I swung my shovel like a golf club and hit the stray's right flank. A hideous yowl splintered the frigid night. An instant later, Marc buried the short end of the crowbar in the top of the cat's skull.

The body hit the ground at Marc's feet. He wrenched the crowbar free with a wet sucking sound and was already swinging again when the next cat approached, screeching in the back of his throat, fur standing on end.

Another stray leapt at me head-on. My shovel met him in midair. His skull rang the metal blade like a cymbal, and he scampered back to regroup, whimpering, claws scraping the ice-slick concrete with each step.

A series of grunts, growls, and hisses on my left told me Ethan was holding his own, and from the rear of the Suburban came the crunch of a shovel hitting pavement, as Vic kept two more strays occupied.

After the initial surge, none of us had a chance to help anyone else. The cats had us outnumbered three-to-one, and only the car at our backs kept us from being surrounded and dispatched in short order—right there on the side of the road, in plain sight, should anyone happen upon us.

And no sooner had that thought passed through my head than two broad beams of white light appeared on the road, in the direction we'd come from. Headlights. Humans were coming. The fight was about to get unbelievably, irreversibly bad.

But instead of racing past—which I assume most humans would do when confronted with a pack of big black cats attacking a group of stranded motorists—the car slowed as it approached, nearly blinding us with the glare from its headlights.

I blinked and swung wildly as my eyes watered, missing my target completely. Sharp teeth sank into my left arm, and I kicked out blindly. My steel-toed boots connected with an underbelly, bouncing off what could only have been a rib. I clenched my jaw to keep from screaming as the cat tried to back away without letting go of my arm.

Grunting with effort, I swung the shovel one-handed. It thunked into something hard, and the stray released my arm. A secondary dose of relief came when the car pulled forward, removing his high beams from my retinas. But he didn't take off. Instead, the driver pulled onto the shoulder in front of Marc's car and killed his engine.

What kind of dumbass human is *this?* I thought, batting at the next cat, though my hands were so cold I could barely grip the shovel. The stranger would either come out with a gun and start shooting, or he'd get himself killed. Maybe both. Either way, those of us who survived would have one hell of a mess to clean up.

A car door slammed, and footsteps crunched into ice and loose rocks on the side of the road. "What the *fuck* is *this?*" Dan Painter shouted over the cacophony of yowls, hisses, and snarls. He stomped toward us carrying the biggest hammer I'd ever seen, and suddenly I understood: Marc's sidekick had followed us. And for once I didn't mind being tracked.

"Where's Manx and the kid?" Painter demanded as he passed the trunk of Marc's car, thus far completely unmolested by the other strays.

"In the Suburban." Marc grunted, swinging the crowbar hard enough to sink the business end into the side of an unfortunate stray, just below his rib cage. "You just gonna stand there?" He ripped the metal free and the cat snarled, lashing out with a paw full of unsheathed claws.

"Just figurin' how best to jump in." An instant later Painter exploded into motion, swinging the hammer like a baseball bat. His first blow hit the rump of the cat Marc was fighting, and sent him sprawling. His second shot knocked the legs out from under the cat who'd replaced the first one. Then two more strays jumped Painter, and he was fighting alongside us, full force.

"What the hell kind of hammer is *that?*" I asked, panting from exertion as I swung for another blow.

"FatMax Xtreme framing hammer," Painter said, posing for a moment like a salesman in an infomercial, as the cat in front of him collapsed. "Precision balanced—feel the difference." With that, he took aim at another stray's leg. Bone crunched and the unfortunate knee bent *backward.* The cat collapsed, screeching nonstop on the slick pavement.

I swung my shovel again and again, but no sooner had I knocked one cat back than another stepped up, snarling and slashing at me. Three cats lay unmoving on the side of the road by then, but more had replaced them—there were at least fifteen strays still up and slashing. Where the *hell* were they coming from, and why were they working together? I'd never *heard* of such a large band of strays, and a unified attack against Pride cats was completely unprecedented.

Well, except for that time in the Montana mountains…

I braced my feet for another blow and sent one cat sprawling. Another pounced at me before I could reset my swing, and his claws tore through denim and into my thigh, just above my right knee.

Pain ripped through my leg, and I knew from the powerful scent and the disturbing warmth that my blood was flowing freely. I kicked instinctively with my left leg, and followed that with another blow from the shovel, this one powered by anger, as well as fear. And to my extreme satisfaction, *that* bastard hobbled away from me with a dislocated shoulder, mewling like a newborn kitten.

Meow, meow, motherfucker.

But then the previous cat was back. I swung my shovel. He ducked, plastering himself to the concrete. I heaved the shovel over my head, preparing to use the blade like a giant ice pick. But he lunged forward before I could bring it down. His jaw snapped closed over my right ankle, and he pulled. I fell on my ass, and my teeth clacked together. The cat tugged again, and I slid several inches across the icy asphalt. I screamed, shock and pain momentarily washing not only logic, but training from my mind.

Then Des screeched from inside the car, and my focus came roaring back. I sucked in a deep, painfully cold breath and fumbled over my head for the driver-side door handle with my empty fist, praying Manx had locked it. She had. My new grip halted my slide across the concrete.

Finally stable, I kicked the cat's skull with my free foot. Then I smacked him with the shovel. The stray released my leg, and I scrambled to my feet using the shovel as a crutch. I kicked him again, this time in the jaw, already caked with my blood. Then I settled my weight onto my good leg and resumed fighting, ignoring the pain as best I could.

On my left, Ethan dropped to one knee, swinging his ax up. The blade caught a stray beneath his jaw, and almost cleaved the cat's head from his neck. The body hit the ground with a nauseating two-part thud—first the torso, then the nearly detached skull—and Ethan was in motion again. I would have been impressed, if I'd had time to think about it.

But I didn't, because Vic screamed on my brother's other side, near the end of the car. Then he stumbled into view and fell to the gravel on his rump. The cat he'd been fighting pounced, driving his shoulders to the ground.

"Ethan!" I shouted in midswing, because my brother was closest. He glanced at me, then followed my gaze to Vic.

"I'm on it." He lunged to the left, swinging even as he dove for Vic's shovel. His blow glanced off the nearest cat, but he came up with a weapon in each hand. Swinging wildly now, Ethan knocked the cat off Vic with the shovel, then threw the ax end over end so fast I could hardly trace it. The blade thunked into the side of another cat, who dropped to the ground, chest heaving and pouring blood.

Ethan picked Vic up and nearly tore open the rear door of the Suburban—that one was unlocked, thankfully. Then he shoved Vic into the cargo compartment and slammed the door. As soon as he turned, another stray was on him.

"Marc!" I shouted, aiming my shovel at an anonymous feline torso. "Vic's hurt."

"I know." He knocked his opponent out with a blow to the head, then kicked a cat about to charge me. There were only half a dozen strays left standing now, and most of those were hurt. We'd won, even outnumbered and in human form. Or so I thought.

A deep bleating roar from the woods across the road caught my attention. Reinforcements. We were exhausted, and the fucking *strays* had backup. From the sound of it, the troops were still a mile away or so, but when they arrived, we'd be screwed. Or worse—dead.

Determined to take my break while I could, I set my shovel on the ground and leaned against the side of the car, frigid against my back, even through my jacket. My sore arms hung at my sides and I took several deep breaths, letting the cold reinvigorate me. The air smelled like blood and pine, an oddly festive combination.

My arm throbbed where that bastard had bit me, and though frozen blood crusted the rip in my pants, my leg had stopped bleeding. But it hurt with every move I made.

Marc watched me inspect my wounds, his eyes shining in the glare from the Suburban's headlights. He glanced from me to the woods, where the reinforcements presumably raced toward us. "Faythe, get in the car," he said over the disharmonious yowls of the injured cats. His eyes never left the trees, though he was breathing hard and bleeding from countless gashes. "With you and Manx gone, they'll have no reason to keep fighting. Ethan, get them out of here. Painter and I will clean up, and I'll call you when we leave."

"I'm not leaving you behind!" I shouted, and only when my breath puffed up in front of my eyes did I realize I could no longer feel my fingers. Or my nose. I'd cooled down too quickly after that first round and was now getting stiff.

Marc nodded to Ethan, who sidestepped an injured but still hissing cat and pulled open the driver-side door. He shoved me inside before I could protest, then climbed in after me.

"Buckle up," he ordered, already sliding the gearshift into Drive. "If you go through the windshield, I'm not stopping for you." He swerved around several motionless feline forms glinting with moonlight and blood. We slid for a moment on ice, and I whacked my head on the window, then gravel crunched when we pulled off the shoulder and back onto the road. As we drove away, I saw Marc and Painter walking backward toward the trees on our side of the road, each pulling two dead cats by the tails.

"We can't just leave them," I insisted, as Manx crouched over Des in the car seat behind me.

Ethan sighed, eyes on the rearview mirror. "They're moving bodies, not storming the Bastille. They'll be on the road in a couple of minutes."

"We should have helped," I snapped, turning to stare through the rear window as Marc went back for another corpse. How many had we killed? "And what the hell do you know about the Bastille?"

He shrugged, squinting into the patch of road illuminated by the headlights. "Angela wrote a paper on the French Revolution."

"And you *read* it?" My tone conveyed more than adequate skepticism. Angela, his girlfriend, was a college senior. It was an odd pairing, to say the least, but their "relationship" had outlasted my most conservative estimate by nearly three months.

No one had won the office pool.

"I *am* literate. And no, we should *not* have helped Marc and Painter. We should get Manx and the baby to safety." Ethan wiped a dark smear from his forehead with the back of one palm. "Not to mention Vic. He's bleeding pretty badly."

Oh yeah.

The crinkle of plastic drew my eyes to the third row, where Vic was spreading black plastic sheeting across the seat, to catch his own blood. Even injured, he was trying to protect his upholstery. Must have been a guy thing.

But my brother was right—a decidedly odd turn of events. So I took one last look at Marc and Painter and made my way to the back of the vehicle to see what I could do for Vic. Then we did what I couldn't remember any Pride cat ever doing before: we ran from the strays.

We'd been driving for about ten minutes when Marc called my cell phone.

"You guys okay?" I asked by way of a greeting, as I fiddled with the vent above the rear bench seat. I'd bandaged Vic as well as I could, then stayed in the back to keep an eye on him.

Over the line, Painter's crappy old engine protested as he accelerated. They were on the road, too. "All scratched up, but I've been worse," Marc said.

"Me, too," Painter spoke up, his voice slightly muffled from distance to the phone.

"What happened?" Des started to fuss behind me, and I looked up to see Manx dig a capped pacifier from a pale blue diaper bag.

Marc exhaled deeply over the phone. "After you guys left, their motivation faded. We dragged the dead ones into the trees. Same with the unconscious ones."

"What about the rest?"

"The strays who could walk hobbled off on their own. We knocked the rest of them out and moved them into the trees with the others."

"How many bodies?" Vic called from behind me, his excitement obvious, even through the pain in his voice. I'd never heard of Pride cats facing foes in such great numbers before, and we'd more than held our own. The news would travel fast, and surely even my father's opponents would be impressed. How could they not be?

"Six dead," Marc said. "Five unconscious. Seven more injured, but awake until we fixed that oversight. At least three got away."

Ethan whistled as he changed lanes, and I did the math in my head, gasping at the total. "Twenty-one strays, all working together?"

My brother huffed. "Plus however many would have been in the second wave." The very thought of which made me shudder.

"What do you think they wanted?" I said into the phone, staring out the window at the passing darkness. After the ambush, my imagination was working overtime, and I kept thinking I saw eyes staring out at me from the woods.

"Well, they weren't dressed for conversation," Marc said. In fact, they weren't dressed for anything, which was his point. It was impossible to negotiate—or even make demands—without human vocal cords.

The strays had come to kill. But why?

"We need to call Dad." Ethan flicked off the high beams when headlights appeared on the road in front of us.

"Already have." Soda fizzed and Marc gulped in my ear, and I pictured him drinking directly from Painter's two-liter of Coke. "He's sending a crew to take care of the bodies." He paused for another drink. "There's a Holiday Inn just off the Meadville exit. Check in and get several adjoining rooms. Preferably on the back side. We'll be there in half an hour."

Adjoining rooms would make it easier to keep an eye on Manx and the baby, and parking in the back would help hide our vehicles, in case the second wave of strays came looking for us.

"Got it. See you in a few." I hung up the phone and immediately wished I'd told him I loved him, especially considering how close we'd all just come to dying. "How you holding up, Vic?" I twisted again to look at him in the constant ebb and flow of the highway lights, now that we were on an actual highway, instead of some dark, two-lane back road.

"The bleeding's slowed," he said, accompanied by the crinkle of plastic. "But my arm stings like a bitch."

"Don't worry, we'll get you all fixed up."

Forty-five minutes later, I sat in the center of the left-hand bed in the hotel room Vic and Ethan would share. Their room was connected by a currently open set of back-to-back doors to another room, where Manx sat in a wheeled desk chair, nursing Des. Again.

Marc and I had our own room, next to Manx's, but not connecting. A little privacy was all we'd be able to salvage from the botched transport/reunion. That, and dinner together, if Ethan and Painter ever returned with food.

"Okay, let's take a look at the damage," Marc said from the end of the other bed. He clenched the shoulder of Vic's T-shirt and pulled. Seams split with a rapid-fire popping sound, and the detached material slid from Vic's arm to the floor. We'd learned through experience that the torn-sleeve approach was much easier than making the patient pull his shirt over his head with an injured arm.

I sucked in a deep breath at the sight of Vic's gored arm, and my fist clenched around the hideous orange-and-yellow-print comforter. But Marc didn't even blink. He'd seen worse. Hell, he'd *been through* worse.

So had I, come to think of it. I fingered the healed slash marks on the left side of my abdomen as I stared at Vic's arm. My scars were ten weeks old, and still pink, a permanent reminder of Zeke Radley and his Montana band of loyal/crazy strays—which had just been dwarfed by the gang we'd faced an hour earlier.

"What do you want for the pain?" Marc asked, angling Vic's arm into the glow from the lamp on the bedside table. *Why don't hotel rooms ever have overhead lights?*

Vic grimaced. "Whiskey."

"You're in luck." Marc smiled as he lifted a white plastic sack from the floor; he and Painter had made a supply run on the way. He pulled two bottles from the bag. One was Jack Daniel's, the other hydrogen peroxide. But the clink from the sack as he set it down told me Marc was prepared for Vic's second and third choices, too.

For the next twenty minutes, I watched Marc clean and stitch Vic's wounds, grateful that they were shallow, if long and ugly.

I was next. We'd decided the bite marks on my arm could simply be bandaged, since they hadn't torn. But my leg needed stitches, and apparently that fact was nonnegotiable.

Marc held my arm to stabilize me as I hobbled across the dingy carpet to the cheap dinette, wearing only the tank top and snug boy-shorts I usually slept in. My pants had gone the way of Vic's shirt and the remains were now draped over the unused chair on the other side of the table.

Marc knelt next to me and ran one hand up my bare leg, ostensibly inspecting the gashes above my right knee, and neither of us even pretended I was shivering from cold, or from shock. He hadn't touched me in months, and the pain of my injuries couldn't trump the feel of his hand on my skin. Squeezing. Stroking. Lingering…

I clamped my jaws shut on a moan of both pain and pleasure, unwilling to embarrass either of us with my lack of control.

"You ready?" Marc asked, and I nodded hesitantly. In spite of many past injuries, I'd never had homemade sutures, and had *certainly* never surrendered to them with nothing more than Tylenol for pain. Well, Tylenol and whiskey—*not* my drink of choice, but apparently sitting for stitches wasn't a margarita-sippin' kind of event.

He smiled sympathetically and lifted my leg to slide a clean white towel from the bathroom beneath my thigh. "Take a couple of drinks while I get you cleaned up."

For once, he didn't have to tell me twice. On the table sat two glasses. One Manx had half filled with whiskey, the other with Coke and ice from the vending machine in the lobby. I picked up the first glass and made myself gulp twice before chasing the contents with half the cup of Coke. I barely felt the sting of peroxide on my thigh because of the flames of whiskey in my throat.

Marc laughed and poured more soda. Then he picked up the thin, curved suture needle.

The hardest part was holding still. The needle didn't hurt much more than the gashes themselves. So as long as I didn't look, I was mostly okay. Even so, within minutes I'd finished both glasses, and Vic crossed the room to refill them for me with his good arm.

We were both half-drunk, and probably looked pretty damn pathetic. The alcohol would wear off quickly, thanks to our enhanced metabolism, but I had a feeling the pathetic part would last a while. And leave scars.

Like I didn't have enough of *those* already…

By the time Marc had sewed up my thigh, and cleaned and bandaged both my ankle and my arm, Ethan and Painter were back with dinner: five large pizzas, three more two-liters, and two dozen doughnuts.

Manx refused to leave Des, even with him asleep in the middle of the bed in the next room, with the connecting doors open. So she took a paper plate full of pizza back to her room. The rest of us spread out on the floor of Vic and Ethan's room, pizza boxes open, plastic cups filled with one combination or another of soda, ice and alcohol. I had more Coke, with Absolut Vanilia, which Dan had picked up because he thought it might go down easier for me. He was right. If I held my nose while I swallowed, it tasted like Vanilla Coke.

Sort of.

"So, how is the kid?" Dan asked, a slice of pizza poised to enter his mouth, point first. "She any closer to Shifting?"

I shook my head. "She won't even talk about it. And when you try to make her, she puts on her earphones and turns her music up loud enough to damage her own hearing."

Vic grinned at Ethan, and spoke with his mouth full. "Michael says you should never have given her that damn thing."

"Whatever." Ethan tossed his crust into a half-empty pizza box and grabbed another slice. "She's not turning up her music because she doesn't want to Shift, or because she doesn't want to *talk* about Shifting. She's turning up her music 'cause she's a teenager. And because she doesn't want to hear any more of that psychobabble bullshit you all spout at her 24/7."

"We're not spouting psychobabble, we're trying to keep her healthy," I insisted, sipping from my cup. "But you're right. Michael's full of shit." My brother grinned, so I continued. "Listening to that MP3 player is the closest she's ever going to get to a normal teenage activity. Well, that and ignoring the advice of her elders."

"You'd know."

"Bite me," I snapped. But Ethan was right, of course. I'd recently begun seeing things from the far side of the generation gap, and the view from the adult side *sucks.*

"How long's it been since she Shifted?" Dan asked, reaching for another piece of pizza.

"More than two months."

He frowned. "Has anyone ever gone that long without Shifting?"

I searched my memory, but came up blank as Marc shook his head. "No one I can think of."

"I wouldn't know." Ethan grinned. "I'm not one to deny my animalistic urges."

I'd probably never heard a more truthful statement.

"Speaking of which, any idea what that whole ambush was about?" I asked, around a mouthful of Meat Lover's. "I've never seen *anything* like that before. Not even from Zeke Radley and his *Pride.*" I raised the cup again and drank deeply that time. I was more relaxed now that the alcohol had kicked in, and was determined to enjoy my buzz while it lasted. "I thought strays were mostly loners."

Painter sat straighter as all eyes turned his way for verification from our resident *expert.* "Yeah, for the most part. But strays'll come together if they have a good reason to, just like anybody else."

"Like a common enemy?" I asked, trying to ignore the sinking feeling in the pit of my stomach. How had we become that common enemy?

"Yeah. Or somethin' they wanna know." His cheeks flushed. "Like how to fight. To take care of themselves, you know? Like Marc's been teaching me."

And Marc was a fine instructor, if his protégé's performance that night was any indication. Painter was damn talented with a hammer.

"So, did you know any of those toms we fought?" Vic asked, and I heard a thin thread of tension in his voice, though his expression seemed amiable enough.

"Not friendly-like." Dan took another bite, but then his chewing slowed to a stop as the reasoning behind the question sank in. He swallowed thickly. "I had *nothin'* to do with that. I fought *with* you guys."

So he had, greatly strengthening our odds. And he could easily have been killed.

But Marc's eyes had gone hard, and his expression sent a chill up my arms, in spite of the hotel heater and my alcohol-induced flush. "Dan, did you tell anyone we were coming through tonight?" His voice had gone deep and scary, and no one was chewing anymore.

Painter shook his head, eyes wide. “Just Ben. He’s interested in Pride politics and wanted to meet you guys. I told him I’d introduce him. But he never showed up.”

“Damn it, Dan!” Marc stood in a lightning-fast, fluid motion and kicked an unopened bottle of soda across the room. It crashed into the door and rolled away. “You may as well have handed us over bound and gagged. The whole damn ambush was your fault!”

Four

Painter's face flushed, and he shook his head vehemently. "Ben wasn't there tonight." The stray stood uncertainly, backing away from Marc out of instinct even a human would have understood. "He wasn't with the toms we fought."

"That doesn't mean he didn't cut my hose, or tell someone else where we'd be," Marc growled, advancing on him slowly as we watched. "You need to understand something, Dan. You will never be a Pride cat if you don't learn when to keep your mouth shut!" With that, he grabbed Painter by the arm, ripped open the hotel door and tossed him out into the parking lot.

Before the door swung shut, I caught a glimpse of Dan as he stumbled across the sidewalk and reached out to steady himself on the hood of the Suburban. He looked shocked, and as disappointed as an orphan at Christmas, still clutching a half-eaten slice of Supreme in one hand as the door slammed in his face.

"Will he be okay out there?" I asked, as Marc threw the dead bolt and stomped across the carpet toward us.

"Who cares if he isn't?" Marc folded his legs beneath himself as he dropped to the floor at my side. But his glance at the door gave away his conflict.

Painter was a friend, and he clearly hadn't betrayed us intentionally.

"Well, I guess that explains why the strays didn't attack him until he took a swing." Ethan wiped a smear of pizza sauce from the corner of his mouth with the back of one hand. "He's their source."

"Yeah, but he *did* take that swing, and he didn't feed them information on purpose," I insisted, glancing from one stony male face to another. "He fought alongside us, and even if the strays were inclined to spare him for further use, they won't be *now.* And they're probably still out there..." I let my sentence fade into silent censure, aimed pointedly at Marc.

"He'll be fine." Marc grabbed another slice of pizza and tore into it, speaking again only once he'd swallowed. "If getting rid of him were that easy, I'd have done it weeks ago. He's probably in the front office right now, renting the room next to ours."

The rest of the meal passed as Marc and the other guys got caught up after more than two months apart. After dinner, I checked on Manx to find her curled up asleep with the baby, both of them fully clothed, a paper plate scattered with pizza crusts on the floor beside the bed. I pulled a blanket from the empty bed to cover them, then closed the connecting door on my way out.

Ethan and Vic were already arguing over the remote control, so Marc helped me into my jacket and ripped pants, and we took one half-full box of pizza back to our room.

The door closed at my back, cutting off the biting January cold, and Marc's hands were all over me, warming me everywhere my skin was exposed. Then exposing even more.

My hand opened, and the pizza box thumped to the table. His fingers slid beneath my jacket, pushing it gently down my arms and over the bandaged bite marks.

The jacket hit the floor and I stepped over it, then winced and nearly went down when my full weight hit my injured leg.

Marc caught me, then lifted me. I wrapped my legs around his hips and pulled his ripped, bloodstained shirt off one arm at a time, while he supported my back with first one hand then the other. His shirt hit the floor. I nibbled on his collarbone. Four steps later he set me on the edge of the bed, and I let him pull my ruined pants off. His followed quickly as I pulled my tank top over my head and squirmed out of my underwear.

And finally, after months apart, we were alone, with nothing between us but memories and need…

Later, I lay next to Marc on the bed farthest from the door, propped up on my right elbow, my chin in my hand. I was bruised all over, and I ached from head to toe after the fight, but I pushed my discomfort aside, determined to focus on Marc for what little time we'd have together.

"You hate it, don't you?" My left index finger traced the long-healed claw-mark scars that had brought him into my life fifteen years earlier, when he was infected by the werecat who'd killed his mother. My parents felt responsible for him because he was orphaned and infected in our territory, so my mother nursed him through scratch fever, then my father made him the first and only stray ever accepted into a Pride.

"Hate what?" His chest rose and sank beneath my hand with each breath, and our mingled scents surrounded me with an almost physical presence. It was intoxicating, just being near him, but the knowledge that his company was only temporary kept me from being truly content.

I ran my fingers over each hard ridge of his stomach. "Living here. Surrounded by humans." Marc had lived with us for half of his life—for *all* of his life as a werecat—until my father had been forced to choose between us. Marc was exiled as part of the under-the-table deal that eliminated execution as a possible sentence at my hearing.

Marc went willingly. He would do nothing to endanger my life, even if it meant living without me. But that was proving every bit as hard as we'd known it would be. Marc hadn't lived among humans since the day he was scratched, and had, in fact, ceased thinking like one around the same time. He no longer knew how to relate to humans, which probably frustrated him even more than it would a Pride cat, considering he'd been born among their ranks.

He shook his head slowly, as if considering. "I don't hate it. It does no good to hate something you can't change."

"How very Zen of you." I smiled skeptically at his unusual display of composure, because we *could* change his location. As soon as my father's position on the council was secure, I would do whatever it took to get Marc back into the south-central Pride.

But in the meantime… "Have you made any friends? Other than Dan Painter?"

"I don't need friends," he insisted, turning his head to grin up at me. "I just need you to visit more often."

Unfortunately, we both knew that was impossible, especially now.

My father had hired Brian Taylor—Ed Taylor's youngest son, and Carissa's brother—to help pick up the slack when he'd been forced to exile Marc. Brian was a year my junior, which made him the youngest enforcer on the payroll. But he was also a quick learner, and eager to impress his new Alpha and earn the respect of his fellow toms. In short, the kid had real potential.

Still, he didn't have anywhere near the experience Marc

had, so while we weren't technically shorthanded, neither were we truly running at max capacity. I'd been temporarily paired with Vic, my father's right-hand man now that Marc was gone, and we were always working. *Always.* Patrolling the territorial boundaries, chasing down trespassers, teaching my fellow enforcers the partial Shift—after Marc mastered it, Jace and Vic picked it up quickly—and working with Kaci during every spare moment.

But this *particular* moment was mine. *Ours.*

"I'm here now." I laid my palm flat on Marc's chest, so I could feel as well as hear his heart beat in sync with my own.

"So you are…" He rose to kiss me, and I lay back on the pillow, sighing when his delicious weight pressed me into the mattress. I arched my neck and let my hands wander his torso as his mouth trailed over my chin and down my throat. Every hard plane on his body was as familiar to me as my own face. I knew how he'd gotten each scar, and at one time or another I'd tasted them all.

"Maybe we could take an extra day," I murmured into his ear, rubbing his thigh with my knee as I wrapped my good leg around him. "Surely full-scale attack and a slashed radiator hose warrant a bit of a delay…."

"Somehow I doubt the council will see it that way." His right hand slid up the back of my thigh, then cupped my rear, shifting me gently into position.

"*Screw* the council—" I whispered, not surprised to hear my voice go hoarse with all-new need. One romp wasn't enough to alleviate the ache of a two-month absence. That would take many, many…

Three brisk knocks on the door drenched the moment like a dunk in an ice-cold pond.

Marc sighed, and collapsed on top of me for a moment before rolling off to search for his pants. "Hang on!" he growled, as the knocking started again.

"Don't let me interrupt..." my brother called through the door. "I'll just stand out here and freeze my balls off while you two get reacquainted. No hurry."

"Damn it, Ethan!" I stepped into my underwear, one hand on the pressboard bedside table for balance as I favored my injured leg. Then I pulled my tank top over my head and tugged it into place, already hopping toward the entrance as Marc zipped his pants. He settled onto the end of the bed with a sigh, and motioned for me to go ahead.

I slid the chain free and twisted the dead bolt, then jerked open the door to find my youngest brother grinning at me, hands stuffed into the pockets of a jacket much too thin to ward off the biting January cold. "I swear, you two have no self-control. You're like animals."

"Asshole." But I couldn't summon real malice, knowing he wouldn't have interrupted us without a good reason. I tried to step aside and let him in, but I wasn't fast enough. Ethan brushed past me into the warmth of the bedroom, and I stumbled back. My weight hit my injured leg and I hissed, then fell on my ass with all the poise of a hippo en pointe.

Ethan just kicked the door shut and hauled me up by one arm, even as I heard Marc rise from the bed behind me. "Way to go, Grace." Then my brother frowned as his gaze settled on the three parallel rows of stitches on my thigh, and the bandages still circling my ankle. "Why haven't you Shifted? You should be half-healed by now."

"I'm fine." I hopped along as he led me toward a chair. "And I *will* Shift. I just...haven't had a chance yet." I snuck a glance at Marc and smiled. Shifting into cat form can accelerate healing by as much as several days, as the body tears itself apart, then puts itself back together in another form. But Shifting while injured is far from comfortable, and it wasn't at the top of my to-do list, especially considering all the other, more pleasurable ways to amuse myself in Marc's company.

"Uh-huh." Ethan rolled his eyes—like he was one to criticize—and turned from me to Marc, who watched us solemnly, waiting for whatever news the messenger bore. "Jace and Brian just loaded *eight* dead cats into the back of the van, and left seven more still unconscious."

They would drive the corpses back to the ranch to be destroyed in the industrial incinerator—the type most farmers used to dispose of dead livestock.

We used it to get rid of evidence. Though we'd never had quite so much to dispose of at once before.

Marc arched both brows. "Only seven unconscious? Several must have wandered off on their own." And two more had died since we'd left them.

"Sounds about right. Damn, that was some brawl."

"It was a fucking *ambush.*" Marc dropped into the chair opposite mine and pulled the bottle of Absolut forward. "In the ten years I worked for your dad, I never *once* saw that many strays in league. This gang was several times the size of Radley's, and they meant business."

Ethan flipped open the pizza box and picked up the largest remaining slice. "So you think they were after Manx?"

Marc glanced at me before nodding, and his eyes lingered on mine in concern as he twisted the top from the bottle. "And probably Faythe, too. Did you see her ankle? One of them tried to drag her off in the middle of the fight."

A growl started in the back of my throat, and my hands clenched into fists in my lap. It was always the same old song and dance with most strays, and frankly, I was getting pretty damn tired of the whole snatch-and-grab routine.

Marc gulped from the bottle, not bothering with a

chaser. "I mean, how often do two tabbies travel through the free territory together? We may as well have painted a target on the back of the Suburban."

"It's not like we had another option." I chose a slice of cold pizza at random. "Manx can't fly, and avoiding the free zone would have added several *days* to the trip." And I would never have even gotten a *glimpse* of Marc that way.

"I know." Marc sighed. "Where're Jace and Brian?"

Ethan swallowed his bite and twisted the lid from a half-empty two-liter of Coke. "Covering the cargo in the back of the van of a thousand corpses."

Which meant Jace wasn't up for seeing me and Marc half-naked together. He could accept how I felt about Marc—grudgingly—but drew the line at seeing it in person. Which we all understood.

Ethan closed the soda and met my eyes, his own oddly solemn. "Mom can't get Kaci to cooperate with you gone, so I'm going to drive the van back with Jace, and Brian will go on with you guys." Which was no doubt why they'd risked driving the corpses back *into* the free zone. "Okay?"

"Sure." Other than me, Kaci was most comfortable with Jace and Ethan. For some reason, the wonder twins could always make her smile, even when I would have sworn she didn't have the strength. "Tell Kaci I'll call her tomorrow. And *please* be careful. What would happen if you two got pulled over with eight bodies in the back of the van?"

Ethan grinned, green eyes sparkling. "We hope the cop's a cat lover." He took another bite, then gestured with the crust of his pizza. "But we won't get pulled over. It's not like we've never driven home with a body in the back before."

Unfortunately.

Two short, sharp knocks sounded on the door, and we

all turned as Ethan yelled, "Come on in, Jace. They're not doin' it. Yet."

That was my brother. Mr. Sensitivity.

Jace opened the door and stepped inside, then quickly shoved the door closed and leaned against it, pushing brown waves out of his bright blue eyes. "Hey, how's life on the outside?" he said, greeting Marc first out of respect, even though he no longer had any rank within the Pride. Most other toms wouldn't have done that, especially considering that I'd chosen Marc over Jace. But Jace was a good guy. My father didn't hire any other kind.

"Can't complain." Marc stood to shake Jace's hand with just a hint of formality. "How's everything at the ranch?"

"Not the same without you, man," Jace said, and I smiled as Marc exhaled deeply, and nodded in acknowledgment.

"Thanks."

I knew better than anyone else how much that sentiment meant to Marc, and I could have kissed Jace for it—if that wouldn't have made everything infinitely worse.

Finally, Jace's eyes found me, and concern washed over his face as he stepped forward. "Your dad didn't say you were hurt."

"I don't think anyone's told him yet." I clutched the arm of my chair to keep from self-consciously touching my wounds. "I'm fine, though. One Shift should take care of the limp."

"Well, do it soon," Jace said, then turned to Ethan, his jaw tight with whatever he was not saying. "You ready?"

"Yeah." Ethan took one last gulp of Coke and snatched a slice of pizza for the road. "You guys be careful." He pulled me up and into a bear hug. "Mom will never forgive any of us if her only daughter comes home disfigured."

I twisted out of his grip when the hug got too tight. “After tonight, she ought to be grateful I’m coming home at all.”

“Can I be there when you tell her that?” Ethan asked, still grinning as he headed for the door.

“Yeah, I’m considering a rephrase.” I followed him, hobbling along with my arm intertwined with Marc’s. “Seriously, though, will you tell Kaci I’m fine? We’re all fine. And we’ll be home in a couple of days, good as new.”

“Will do.” Ethan followed Jace outside, to where my father’s van was now parked next to Vic’s Suburban. “Mom said she fell asleep playing PS3 after dinner.”

I frowned, shivering in the sudden cold as I gripped the door frame. “I’ll talk her into Shifting when I get back. One way or another.”

Ethan opened the passenger-side door as Jace started the engine. “I know.” My brother grinned one last time as Jace backed my dad’s ancient van out of the parking space. Then they were gone.

I closed the door and twisted to find Marc watching me with a new heat in his eyes. So we picked up right where we’d left off….

Six hours later, my cell phone rang out from the dark. I sat up, blinking, and reached over Marc to feel around on the nightstand, aiming vaguely for the bouncing, glowing mound of plastic.

I couldn’t reach it, so I levered myself over Marc with my elbow in his chest. He grunted and his eyes flew open, and I gasped when my bad leg twisted beneath me, because I still hadn’t found a chance to Shift. But then my fingers closed around the phone and I eased my weight back onto the mattress, flipping the phone open without reading the name on the display.

"Faythe?" It was my dad, and he sounded infinitely more alert than I was. Which was probably a very bad sign.

"It's five in the morning, Daddy." I shrugged when Marc rubbed sleep from one eye and mouthed, *What's wrong?*

"I know what time it is," my father snapped, and his tone brought me instantly awake. "Ryan's gone."

Five

"*What?*" I said, as Marc sat up and clicked on the lamp on the nightstand.

I'd expected to hear that Kaci had Shifted, or that Jace and Ethan had arrived home safely with the bodies. Or even that they'd been pulled over on the way home and arrested on some weird murder and illegal-corpse-disposal charge. But I didn't quite know how to react to the news that my middle—and least favorite—brother, Ryan, had pulled a Houdini. "How?"

"I honestly don't know. I was up tending the incinerator, and went down to the basement for spare flashlight batteries, and he was just gone. The cage door was standing wide open, and the lock was missing."

Damn. But why would he take the lock?

Ryan had spent the past six and a half months locked up in our basement prison cell, as punishment for playing the role of spy and jailer in a scheme to kidnap several U.S. tabbies—including me—to be sold to Alphas in the Amazon. When we'd caught him, he was thin and weak. But he'd grown healthier in captivity, eating my mother's cooking, despite the lack of sunshine, fresh air and exercise.

But that did not explain how he'd escaped. The cage

was built to stand up to toms in the prime of life, fueled by rage and fear. He should not have been able to break the lock on his own, and he had access to nothing with which to pound it off.

"Any idea how long he's been gone?" I asked, rubbing my forehead in frustration.

"Owen took his dinner down at seven, and everything was normal. So it could have been anytime in the past ten hours." The weariness in his voice spoke volumes, and had little to do with the early hour or lack of sleep. With my father's position on the Territorial Council so tenuous at the moment, Ryan's escape was a blow he really couldn't afford. Malone would use that as just one more piece of evidence that my father was an incompetent Alpha. Which was *not* true.

"Did he leave a trail?" Marc ran one hand through short curls he'd probably forgotten he'd sheared.

My father sighed over the line. "Yes, but it did little good. Owen tracked him for about a mile and a half, then lost the trail shortly after he found his clothes. It looks like Ryan Shifted and took to the trees."

Cats can't track animals like dogs can, and the same holds true for werecats. We use our keen sense of smell to scavenge and to identify one another, and our eyes and ears to find prey during an active chase. However, we lack the necessary instinct to follow a cold trail on scent alone, and once Ryan was in the trees—no doubt walking the limbs like a splintered forest path—he was beyond our immediate grasp. Which probably infuriated Owen, my third brother.

"So what do you want us to do?" I sipped from the cup of lukewarm water Marc handed me from the nightstand.

"There isn't much you *can* do." My father's desk chair squealed in my ear, and I could easily picture him sitting in his office in his blue striped robe, glaring at the empty room. "Just ask Marc to keep his eyes and ears open. I'm pretty sure Ryan's headed your way."

Because Mississippi was the closest free territory to the ranch, thus the easiest for Ryan to reach. In theory. Unfortunately, we now knew there was an exceptionally large band of very angry strays roaming near the border, and one whiff of Ryan's Pride-cat scent would likely set them off again.

My idiot brother had jumped out of the frying pan and into the fucking *volcano,* and I had a sudden bleak certainty that the next body we buried might break my mother's heart.

Marc exhaled heavily and scowled. He and Ryan hadn't exchanged two civil words since June, and Marc no longer officially worked for my father. But he would never say no to my dad. "I'll be looking for him," he said, well aware his former Alpha could hear him, even several feet from the phone.

"Thanks." My father ordered us to get some sleep. Then he hung up.

We didn't sleep.

After the ambush, injuries, and Ryan's escape, sleeping seemed like a waste of time, especially considering that Marc and I only had a matter of hours left together. So we made other, better use of the predawn hours.

When the first direct rays of daylight glinted through the gap in the faded motel curtains, I squeezed my eyes shut, hoping that if I didn't see it, it didn't exist. But morning would not be ignored.

Marc sighed and kissed my jaw, just below my ear. "You hungry?"

I shook my head on the pillow, but he only laughed and tossed the covers back. Werecats were *always* hungry. "Why don't you Shift while I grab some breakfast. Then I'll take another look at your leg."

"Oh, fine." I sat up naked in bed, hoping to tempt him into putting off the food run. No such luck. His eyes lingered, but the rest of him did not. Ten minutes later he was showered, dressed and headed toward the IHOP across the street.

Alone, I knelt on the floor to Shift.

The usual pain of the transformation was intensified in my leg, especially the flesh over my thigh, which burned and throbbed with an acute agony. The skin pulled and stretched, and for a couple of minutes I worried that the stitches would pop. But when the Shift was complete, my leg felt much better. Still tender, but fully functional.

I stretched with my forepaws extended, rump in the air, tail waving lazily. Then I sat up and groomed the fur over my left shoulder until it lay properly. After that I explored my surroundings. I'd never been in a hotel room in cat form, and everything looked and smelled very different with my feline senses. Which was not necessarily a good thing.

As a human, I'd been blissfully unaware of the traces of whoever'd had the room before us, but as a cat, I couldn't ignore the lingering stench of strangers' sweat, stale coffee, old takeout, and seafood-scented vomit in one corner of the bathroom. I was afraid to get too close to the bed, for fear of what I'd smell there.

After a mere five minutes in cat form, I'd had enough. I Shifted back and stepped into the shower, glad I'd brought along my own shampoo—a familiar scent to help wash the others from my memory.

I was drying my hair when a cold draft around my ankles announced Marc's return. The scents of bacon, eggs, syrup and fruit told me he'd ordered nearly the entire IHOP menu. I was halfway through my first pancake when his cell rang out.

Marc dug in his right pocket and pulled out his cell phone—one I hadn't seen before. New job, new house, and a new phone, since my father no longer picked up the cellular bill. Everything had changed.

"It's your dad," he said after a glance at the display, then flipped his phone open. "Hey, Greg, what can I do for you?" As if he were still on the clock.

"I spoke to Bert Di Carlo this morning and reported last night's ambush. With both Vic and Faythe injured—" Ethan and Jace had obviously reported my condition "—Bert and I would feel much better about this trip if you'd accompany the delegation for a bit longer than we'd planned. You have permission to go as far as Birmingham. If you're interested."

Marc grinned and glanced at me. "Of course I'm interested."

"Good." I pictured my father nodding, signaling the end of the discussion. "Put Faythe on the line, please."

Marc handed me his phone, still smiling as he speared a link of sausage with a plastic fork. I was grinning like an idiot, too, thrilled by the prospect of a couple of extra hours with Marc, even if we'd be stuck in Vic's car along with the rest of the delegation.

"Hi, Daddy." I dipped a slice of bacon in a puddle of syrup and bit into it, covering the mouthpiece to keep from crunching into his ear.

"How's your leg?"

"It's fine. Just three slashes above my right knee, and bite marks around my ankle. I Shifted this morning, and the wounds have closed nicely. I'm not even limping."

"Ethan said you handled yourself very well. I'm paraphrasing, of course."

I grinned and speared a tangle of hash browns, more pleased by the compliment than I would have admitted. "So did he. The boy swings a mean ax."

My father chuckled. "Call me when you get to Bert's place."

"I will."

My dad said goodbye and hung up, and I handed the phone back to Marc, still smiling.

Twenty minutes later we were on the road. Vic drove, and Brian took the passenger seat, with Manx and the baby in the middle row. Marc and I sat in the back, his arm around my waist, my head on his shoulder. His scent and warmth, along with the rhythmic jostle of the van around us, lulled me into a peaceful trance, and I was almost asleep when Vic spoke up from the front, eyeing us in the rearview mirror.

"Hey, Marc, isn't that Painter's car behind us?"

Marc twisted, and I turned to look with him. Sure enough, there it was—a grimy white Dodge Daytona, with a fist-size dent in the front bumper.

Marc scowled. "I *told* you he wouldn't be that easy to lose."

"What should I do?"

"Nothing. Let him follow us." Marc's jaws bulged in irritation. "I'll need a ride back from Birmingham anyway."

The rest of the trip was blessedly uneventful. Even with several bathroom and breast-feeding breaks, the winter sun was just past its zenith when we pulled into a Shell station off the highway, a couple of miles south of Birmingham. While Vic pumped gas, I made myself say goodbye to Marc.

We'd planned for him to drive me back across the free zone—the guys would stay with Manx for the duration of the trial—but after the previous day's ambush my father wouldn't *hear* of another trip through Mississippi. So I'd be flying back.

"It's not forever," Marc insisted softly. But it may as well have been.

My hand lingered on his chest, his on my waist, and only when Dan Painter pulled up behind us in his sick-sounding car did Marc let our foreheads touch. He whispered goodbye and kissed me. Then he pulled open Vic's passenger-side door, pushed me gently onto the seat and closed the door again.

I rolled the window down and stole one more kiss, then he smiled and turned away.

"Need a ride?" Painter asked, one arm hanging out his car window.

Marc scowled. "Do you think you can resist announcing our whereabouts to any future opponents we may encounter?"

"Dude, I *told* you that was an accident. I had no *idea* some asshole was gonna round up the posse and come out guns a-blazin'. What do you want, a formal apology?"

"A little silence would suffice," Marc snapped, stomping around the car. He jerked open the door and slid onto the seat, just as Vic emerged from the convenience store. Marc waved to him, then turned to Dan. "Let's get out of here before someone gets a whiff of you. No one gave you permission to leave the free zone."

With that, Dan stomped on the gas and they roared out of the parking lot and back onto the highway.

The rest of the drive was much less pleasant, but peacefully dull. And if not for several crying spells from Des, I might have made up for the sleep I'd missed the night before. But when the Atlanta skyline came into view, Manx began to fidget. Her foot bounced on the floorboard. Her nails tapped on the armrest. She stared out her window and didn't seem to hear Des when he began to fuss, waving tiny red fists in the air.

"Manx, you okay?" I leaned over the bench seat with my chin resting on my folded arms.

She never looked away from the window. "That is Atlanta?"

"Yeah. See that big round building? That's a hotel. I stayed there once with Sara. Her mom took us for a weekend downtown after she graduated from high—" I fell silent when I noticed Vic watching me in the rearview mirror, his eyes brimming with pain and full of nostalgia.

Sara Di Carlo, his only sister, had been raped and murdered seven months earlier by the jungle stray Ryan had fallen in with. Days later, his younger brother, Anthony, died during our attempt to capture Sara's killers.

The Di Carlo family's wounds were still fresh, and the tragedy didn't end there. With no tabby to bear its next generation, their family line would die along with Vic and his brothers, and with no descendants, they would eventually lose control of their territory.

Which was why my father hoped that, if all parties were amenable—and if she survived her trial—Manx might join the southeast Pride. She could never replace Sara, of course. But she could help the Di Carlos hold on to their territory. Help them reclaim their future. If she were willing.

But at the moment, Manx didn't look very happy to be in Georgia.

"So, we are close?" she asked, and I thought I saw her chin quiver.

Manx was one of the toughest tabbies I'd ever met in my life. Tougher than my mother, who'd once kept the Alphas in line single-handedly, and who'd saved my life only months earlier. Tougher than me, by far. And maybe even tougher than Kaci, who had to live every day of her life knowing what she'd accidentally done to her family. Manx had survived abduction, brutal beatings, the loss of her tail, serial rape, and the murder of two infant sons. Somehow, she'd come out of a living hell stronger than ever, and determined to hunt down the bastard who'd both sired and murdered her children.

But now Luiz was dead, and she was on trial for

multiple counts of murder. If she was convicted and sentenced to death, the son she'd fought to save would never even know his mother.

After years of torture and months of running and fighting, *now* Manx was scared. And it almost broke my heart.

"About forty more miles." Vic flexed his injured arm stiffly, his free hand still on the wheel. "Mom has the guest room all fixed up for you and Des. She even dug up Sara's old crib. It's ancient, and I think it's pink, but it'll give him somewhere comfortable to nap."

The sun had just dipped beneath the horizon when we pulled into the Di Carlos' long, arched driveway, beyond which their beautiful, old Italianate house was lit by several strategically placed floodlights.

Vic's family lived outside of Canton, Georgia, in the house they'd bought when Vic was still a toddler, and had been renovating ever since. It looked like a big white-framed box, lined in black-shuttered windows and crowned with four redbrick chimneys. As the SUV bounced over the gravel driveway, headlights illuminated an elaborate porch, complete with columns and latticed arches, lined in evergreen shrubs.

The property sat in the center of a broad, flat lawn that was green in the summer, but brown and crunchy in the middle of January.

In back of the main house stood a large detached garage, above which sat the former servants' quarters. But the Di Carlos had long ago enclosed the garage and turned the entire building into an apartment, where their enforcers now lived.

Beyond the apartment were several acres of private woodland, a necessity for any large group of werecats. It was a place for them to run, play, and hunt, without being bothered by the surrounding human population.

Since the trial would begin the following morning, I'd

expected the driveway to be full, cars parked in rows out back, even. But there were only three vehicles ahead of our van, all of which probably belonged to Vic's family.

"Where is everyone?" I asked, pushing open the car door. The temperature had dropped when the sun went down, and I pulled my jacket tight around me, shivering in spite of the layer of leather.

Vic stepped onto the driveway, boots crunching on gravel. "The guys park around back. They're probably in the apartment, lying low."

Which I could easily understand. Large Alpha gatherings made me nervous, too.

"My mom and dad are both here." Vic eyed the two cars parked closest to the house. "But I don't recognize that one." He nodded to the beige sedan we'd parked behind.

I bent to read the sticker on one corner of the rear windshield. "It's a rental. Michael must already be here." *Thank goodness.* I didn't want to be the only one representing my family, even just for a few hours. As much progress as I'd made in the think-before-you-speak department, slip-ups still happened, at the worst possible times, and Alphas Gardner and Mitchell were already angry *enough* with the south-central Pride.

"My dad said the Alphas all took rooms in town, so they probably won't show up until tomorrow morning," Vic said, as if he'd read my mind. Or my expression.

"Oh." *Good.*

At the back of the van, Brian was stacking luggage on the ground. I zipped up my jacket and grabbed two suitcases, then followed Vic up the sidewalk toward the house. We were halfway there when the door creaked opened and a tiny woman in creased jeans and a dark blouse appeared on the porch.

"Victor!" Donna Di Carlo raced down the steps and stood on tiptoe to hug her son, heedless of the bags he held, or the cold that must have blown instantly through her thin shirt. She looked older than when I'd last seen her, the lines on her face deeper, her hair grayer. Losing two children was likely the hardest thing she'd ever endure, but Vic's mother was strong; she hadn't let it kill her.

In that respect, she reminded me of Manx.

"Why does it take a tragedy to get you to visit? Just once I'd like to see you when nothing's wrong. When you just came home to say, 'Mom, I love you.'"

"Mom, I love you." Vic grinned, but there was pain beneath his pleasant expression. He hadn't seen his parents since Sara and Anthony's funeral, and I suspected he wouldn't see them again for quite a while. Because being home made him remember.

"That's much better. Now go put those bags in the front hall before they freeze out here." Vic did as he was told, and his mother turned her eagle-sharp eyes on me. "Faythe Sanders, I'd say it was nice to see you, if you didn't look so thin. Has your mother stopped cooking?"

"No, ma'am, and I haven't stopped eating, either." I smiled. "But I burn a lot of energy on the job."

"Job?" She looked confused for a moment, hands propped on hips that flared from her tiny waist. "Oh, yes. You're enforcing for your father. Hardly a proper line of work for a young woman, but if you're going to fight like a man, I can certainly feed you like one." Her smile softened the sting of her censure. "Come on in. We're about to sit down to a big pot of gumbo. You like gumbo, don't you?"

"Yes, ma'am." I followed her up the porch stairs and into the long central hallway, where I dropped the bags I carried next to those Vic had abandoned before he'd disappeared.

"Bert, come on out and say hi," she said, taking the jacket I shrugged out of.

But before Umberto Di Carlo appeared, soft footsteps clicked on the hardwood behind us, and I turned to find Manx standing in the doorway, a blanket-wrapped bundle clutched close to her chest. Her gray eyes were wide, her cheeks flushed from the cold beneath her smooth, olive complexion.

"Well, you must be Mercedes." Mrs. Di Carlo propped her hands on her hips again and stepped forward boldly to inspect Manx, who towered over her by at least six inches. "My, aren't you a beauty. I'll have to warn my boys to keep their distance."

Whether she was thinking of Manx's fear of being touched, or her status as a serial killer, I wasn't sure. Either way, her greeting obviously wasn't what Manx had expected. The tabby stared at Vic's mother and clutched the baby tighter.

"Well, come on in before you let out all the heat." Mrs. Di Carlo ushered Manx into the entry, and Brian slipped inside carrying two more suitcases before she could close the door. "And who is this little gentleman?" Mrs. Di Carlo leaned over to peer at the baby's face, the only exposed part of his tiny body.

"This is Desiderio Carreño." Manx's eyes went soft as her gaze fell on her baby. "He smiled just this morning."

"Did he!" Mrs. Di Carlo beamed, clearly thrilled by the news, though she'd barely even met the child. "Well, this *is* a pleasure. We haven't had a baby in the house in such a long time. I'll show you to your room."

Manx and Brian trailed our hostess up the central staircase, and they'd no sooner vanished from sight than a door opened down the hallway, admitting Umberto Di Carlo into the entry. His wide-set brown eyes brightened the moment they landed on me.

"Faythe! Come in and warm up. Your brother and I were about to indulge in a predinner drink. Join us!" He turned without waiting for my reply, and I followed him through an arched doorway into a room filled with overstuffed furniture, dark woods and thick rugs. On the far side of the room, facing a cozy arrangement of couches and chairs, logs blazed in a stone fireplace, casting jumping shadows on the warm, wood-paneled walls.

Michael stood when we entered, frowning in concern the moment his eyes found mine. "Dad told me about the ambush. Are you okay?" He took my arm before I could protest and pushed my sleeve up carefully to expose the half-healed bite marks I hadn't bothered to rebandage that morning.

"I'm fine. None of us was seriously injured, which is a miracle, considering how badly we were outnumbered."

Michael looked half relieved and half jealous to have missed the excitement.

"Sit!" Vic's father ordered pleasantly, after a glance at my new scars. His footsteps thundered as he crossed the room toward a small cherry bar in one corner. "What can I get you to drink?"

"Scotch?" Michael sank onto the left-hand sofa beside me, and Bert nodded in approval.

"Just like your father." He pulled a half-empty bottle of Chivas Regal from beneath the bar and poured an inch into two short glasses, then looked up at me. "Faythe?"

"I'm fine, thanks." I'd had enough alcohol the night before to last the rest of the month, at least.

He nodded and crossed the room to hand one glass to Michael. Then he sat on the sedate green couch opposite us, resting a thick hand on the scrolled arm. "So, how are things at the Lazy S?"

"A little tense right now," I admitted, scuffing the toe of my boot on the red and gray rug.

Michael cleared his throat. "I can't tell you how much

my father appreciates your support, especially at a time like this."

Di Carlo nodded gravely, and I could see that his decision to back our dad hadn't been made lightly. "The council's going to hell in a handbasket, Michael, and if someone doesn't stand up to Calvin Malone, it's only going to get worse. But I'm afraid this one won't be won easily."

"Nothing worthwhile ever is." Michael frowned sagely, and I knew the conversation would turn quickly to unpleasant politics. If I didn't deliver my message soon, I'd lose my chance.

"Mr. Di Carlo…"

"Child, call me Bert." He grinned, and leaned toward me conspiratorially. "I saw you streak through your father's office in the buff when you were no higher than my knee. I'd say that makes us friends."

I flushed, but nodded. "Bert, my father has an idea he wanted me to mention to you. About Manx. Mercedes. Assuming the tribunal finds in her favor… Well, she's lost her whole family, and you've lost your daughter…" I broke off, unsure how to continue. Saying it aloud made it sound like I was trying to restructure the Di Carlo family—sticking my nose in where it *definitely* didn't belong.

But Bert finished the thought for me. "Your father thought we might want to keep her?"

"Well…" I wouldn't have phrased it quite that way, but… "Yes. Assuming she gets along with everyone. And wants to stay, of course."

Bert nodded and sipped from his glass. "I have to admit I've had similar thoughts. Your father assures us that her crimes were the result of *severe* physical and emotional trauma…"

"Of the worst sort," Michael interjected solemnly.

"…and that she's no longer dangerous. Do you agree with his assessment?"

I *really* wished he hadn't asked me that. But sure enough, the Alpha was looking at me, rather than at my older, wiser brother, and I wasn't going to bullshit one of my father's few sworn allies.

"Mr. Di Carlo—Bert—Manx has survived things I can't even *imagine* suffering. Horrors no one should ever have to experience. For years, she was never touched by a man who didn't hurt her. *Years.* And the very thing that pulled her through—an iron-hard survivalist instinct—is what led her to kill those toms. They touched her. She thought they were going to hurt her, or her unborn baby. So she defended herself. Preemptively."

I hesitated on the next part, then finally leaned forward to let him see how earnest I was. "Is there a possibility it could happen again? Yes. Unfortunately, I think there is. If she feels threatened, I think she would lash out in self-defense. Or baby-defense. But she's been with us for four months now and has never raised a hand to anyone. I think if you give her a chance to get used to your family, and to the idea that no one here means her any harm, she'll come around eventually. I think she *wants* a normal life, and it won't take too much effort to convince her that you can be trusted."

For a moment, the southeast Pride's Alpha only stared at me, still processing my blunt speech. As was Michael. "I see," Di Carlo said finally. Then he smiled. "Well, I suppose it's worth a shot. Assuming the tribunal sees fit to let her live."

And I knew from personal experience just how big an *if* that really was.

Six

"Well, this looks nice." *Once you get over all the pink.* I ran my hand along the crib railing and nudged one of the mobile's lace butterflies into motion. Vic said his parents had set up a crib for Des, but he hadn't mentioned any of the other stuff. My gaze took in a white wicker rocking chair, some kind of bouncy seat with stuffed bumble bees suspended over it, a changing table piled high with accessories and necessities, and a dirty-diaper storage…contraption…*thing.* Which I was pretty sure hadn't even been invented when Sara was born.

The Di Carlos had gone shopping for Manx's baby.

"Very nice," Manx agreed. But tears stood in her eyes, and in spite of the room full of furnishings, she still clutched the baby to her chest, as if he were the only thing keeping her above water in a swirling, churning whirlpool of fear and confusion.

"What's wrong?" I asked, then immediately regretted the question. What *wasn't* wrong? "Do you want to… maybe… put him down while you get settled in?" I gestured awkwardly toward the crib, and Manx glanced at the baby bed as if seeing it for the first time.

But instead of moving toward it, she met my gaze, her gray eyes magnified by tears. "What will happen to me, Faythe? The truth. Vic says all will be fine. What do you say?"

Well, shit. I picked up a stuffed lamb from one corner of the crib and played absently with the soft, curly wool. "Manx, I honestly don't know. This is kind of unprecedented." I was the only other tabby who'd ever been on trial in the U.S., and my case wasn't much like hers, in spite of the surface similarities. The charges against her were more serious—three counts of murder to my one count each of murder and infection—yet her chances of getting off were much greater than mine.

Which was probably exactly what she needed to hear.

"Okay, on the bright side, I don't *think* they'll vote to execute." I glanced at Manx, then at the door open into the hall. Everyone else was downstairs, and none of the tribunal members had arrived yet, but I wasn't taking any chances. "Why don't you sit? I need to explain something to you."

Manx's beautiful lips thinned in dread, but in the end her curiosity won out. While I closed the door, she laid the sleeping baby in the crib, then collapsed into the rocker as if it were a massage chair. I settled cross-legged onto the bed.

"Okay…" In the absence of my own punching pillow, I had to make do with a frilly sham from Manx's temporary bed. I pulled it onto my lap and traced the lacy pattern as I spoke. "You're on trial for killing three toms, but that's not all this hearing is about."

Her forehead knit into several thin lines. "What does that mean?"

I wasn't sure how much my mother had already explained to her, so I started at the beginning. "It's political." From what I'd gathered, the South American Prides' council held much less authority over individual Prides than ours did, so our political struggles were largely foreign to her. "You know my dad was suspended as head of the Territorial Council a little while ago, right?" I asked. She nodded. "Well, his enemies will probably try to use your trial to manipulate more Alphas into siding against my father. This is as much about him and the way he dealt with your... *crimes* as it is about you."

Her frown deepened. "I do not understand."

I exhaled slowly, struggling with how best to explain. "Some people think my father should have punished you for killing Jamey Gardner. Jamey's brother Wes is Alpha of the Great Lakes Pride, and Wes is pushing for the death penalty for you."

Manx nodded, but her hand began to tremble on the arm of the rocker. She'd known execution was a possibility, of course, but knowing something and hearing it spoken aloud were two entirely different animals. To which I could personally attest.

"But like I said, I don't *think* they'll do that. You *are* a tabby, and we really don't have any of those to spare." Which was probably the only reason I was still breathing.

The tribunal had threatened me with execution, too, but that threat had merely been a bargaining chip meant to force Marc out of the Pride and me into a marriage with someone else. Someone they considered a more appropriate match for me than a stray.

They'd gotten rid of Marc—for the moment—but I'd rather *die* than let someone else decide who I would marry. Or that I would marry at all. That decision was all *mine,* and if the council thought otherwise, they could happily go *fuck* themselves.

Regarding Manx's trial, my best guess was that they would spare her life because, unlike me, she was obviously willing to bear desperately needed children. But there was a catch. She was *not* willing to be touched by a man. *Any* man, other than Dr. Carver, whom she'd shown no attraction to. And that would seem to make any future children from her pretty damn hard to come by.

Fortunately, Michael had come to Georgia in a professional capacity, and would no doubt emphasize to the tribunal that Manx was still severely traumatized, but that with time, she would recover and hopefully go on to live a normal life. Including a husband and more children.

Though I personally thought that husband would have to be a brave soul indeed…

"So…if they save me? What then?"

"Oh, *now* you're asking the tough questions." I smiled, trying to relax her. And to avoid mentioning that whatever happened after her trial would depend heavily on her sentence. "But the way I see it, you have a few options. You can come back to the ranch and stay with us. Everyone would love to have you. Though I don't think the council will let you stay in Texas forever."

With both me and Kaci on the ranch, the south-central Pride was already estrogen-heavy, and the other Alphas would never let my father "keep" three fertile tabbies.

"If you don't eventually join another Pride, I suspect our Territorial Council will choose one for you." Which meant she would be claimed by the Alpha who wielded the most power. "And they would probably expect you to marry one of their sons."

And if, by some catastrophe, Calvin Malone wound up in charge of the council, Manx might live the rest of her life as his daughter-in-law, which probably wouldn't be much better than life in captivity with Luiz.

I'd only avoided a similar fate myself because my father was reluctant to force me into a marriage, and because he remained convinced that I would eventually marry Marc on my own. But all of Manx's close family members had died in a hostile takeover by a neighboring Pride, shortly after she had been kidnapped by Miguel and Luiz. In fact, her disappearance was probably what had weakened her father's hold on his territory—without her, he could promise his members no heir.

So Manx and her son were alone in the world and, as with me, my father was the only thing standing between her and an unwanted marriage.

Manx's eyes widened, and the blood drained from her face as that fact sank in. "They would force me to…"

"No!" I started to take her hand, then thought better of it and snatched mine back. "Not like Luiz did. The council would never stand for that."

But was forcing her into marriage any less reprehensible than what Miguel and his brother had done? Sure, she wouldn't technically be raped, and neither Manx nor her children would be in any physical harm. But she'd be expected to submit on her own, night after night, to a man she didn't love, so that she and Des would have a safe place to live.

Because if Manx ever refused to bear the next generation, her life would cease to have value, and there would be little motivation for *some* members of the council to keep her alive. Which was exactly what I'd been told during my own trial.

My blood boiled just thinking about it. The North American Prides were no more civilized than our neighbors to the south! We just dressed up barbarism better, cloaking injustice and oppression—and hell, *prostitution*—in pretty words like *duty* and *honor.*

What a *load* of *shit!*

Part of me wanted to march downstairs and demand every cat in the house join me in a protest, pushing for a tabby's right to chose her own future. *Fighting* for it, if necessary. But the other, wiser, more logical part of me knew that merely *demanding* change would accomplish nothing. And fighting would only put me back on the stand next to Manx.

If I wanted to change the system, I'd have to do it from

the inside. Jace had told me that, and he was right. I could see that clearly now. And I also knew that it wouldn't happen quickly. Not in time to save Manx. To keep her out of Malone's household, we'd need a more immediately accessible alternative.

Fortunately, we might have one…

My throat ached with all the angry words I was holding back to keep from scaring the crap out of her. So I took a deep breath and slowed my pulse, hoping that if I stayed composed, she would, too. Then I forced a comforting smile and launched into the alternative.

"Or, if you like the Di Carlos and they like you, there's a good possibility that you could stay here." I glanced down to find my hands twisted around a handful of satin and stuffing, and had to swallow past the lump in my throat in order to speak. "Last summer, they lost their daughter, Sara, shortly before her wedding. Miguel killed her. They're hurting pretty badly, so if you decide not to stay here, I'd ask you to please break it to them very gently. The last thing they need is more pain."

"Vic misses her."

Surprised, I looked up to see that Manx's tears had actually fallen. "He talks to you about Sara?"

She nodded slowly, wiping moisture from her cheeks. "She was smart, and beautiful, and strong. She spit in Miguel's face."

"Yeah." I laughed and blinked moisture from my own eyes. "That was Sara. She was halfway through a degree in economics, and planned to finish before having kids." A decision I'd greatly respected.

But now she was dead, and the Di Carlos had no heir, and no way to hold on to their territory once Umberto retired. Or died.

"They're good people," I said, looking around at the room they'd fixed up for Manx and Des. "And who knows? You might decide you actually *like* Vic or one of his brothers. So maybe just think about it?"

"I will." Manx nodded earnestly, blotting her long, dark lashes with a tissue from the changing table. "If I live."

I wanted to tell her that she would. That everything would be okay, one way or another. But I couldn't *swear* to it, and I wasn't going to lie to her. And she seemed to respect that.

"Faythe, I need a… um…" Manx paused and closed her eyes, probably searching for the right word in English. "A favor." She met my eyes again, and the depth of her gaze alone emphasized the importance of whatever she was about to say.

"Yes?" I held my breath, and could hear both our hearts beating. No, all *three* of our hearts.

"If I die, will you take Desiderio home? To your mother? I have not asked her, but I think she will take him."

For a moment I was so horrified by the necessity of such a question that I couldn't answer. I'd known arrangements would have to be made for Des, just in case. But Manx making those arrangements herself, less than twelve hours before the start of her trial?

I could barely even conceive of that kind of courage.

"Please," Manx whispered, misinterpreting my silence, her eyes deep gray pools of despair.

"Of course I will," I assured her. Relief washed over Manx, and she slumped against the back of the rocker, as if now that we had that out of the way, she could finally relax.

I couldn't remember ever seeing anyone look quite so pleased when contemplating her own death.

That night after dinner, I tried my hardest to keep Donna Di Carlo from putting me up in Sara's bedroom.

But she wouldn't take no for an answer, and I stopped arguing when I realized she might take my refusal as an insult.

I didn't mean it as one. Sara's pictures still topped the dresser, and her old stuffed animals reclined on the bed. Her room looked like a shrine, and I didn't want to disturb it. But her mother was tired of seeing it sit empty and clearly wanted me to get some use out of it.

So I lay down in Sara's bed just after eleven o'clock—and was still awake three hours later. I couldn't sleep with her staring down at me from the walls, asking me wordlessly why I saved Abby but couldn't save her.

Her eyes haunted me.

Finally, around two-thirty in the morning, I snuck out of her room and down the hall to Vic's, where I climbed into bed with him. He barely even noticed. He just scooted over to make room, then went back to snoring softly.

I would never have gotten in bed with Jace, because Marc would never have forgiven either of us. He knew that Jace and I had made a real connection, and that Jace would be happy to revive it. But Vic and Marc had been partners for years, and Marc trusted him completely. Mostly because Vic had never shown any interest in me sexually. He was a friend, and one who would understand why I couldn't sleep in his dead sister's bed.

In minutes, I was asleep, but I woke up with the first rays of sun and crept back into Sara's room to keep from hurting her mother's feelings.

I dressed and showered early, and after breakfast I said goodbye to Michael, Manx and Brian. Then Vic drove me to the airport in Atlanta. My plane landed in Dallas just before noon, and I made my way to baggage claim, where Jace waited, his blue eyes sparkling in the fluorescent glow from overhead. Kaci stood at his side, chestnut waves in a ponytail behind one ear. She had her hands stuffed into the pockets of a faded pair of jeans, her jacket unzipped over her favorite long-sleeved tee.

She hadn't seen me yet, and was anxiously scanning the crowd. Then Jace tapped her shoulder and pointed me out.

Kaci's hazel eyes found mine, and her face lit up with relief and excitement. She took off through the throng, hair trailing behind her, moving at human speed because of her weakened state. And hopefully in consideration of the people around her. Even so, Jace panicked the moment she left his side. I could see it in his eyes. He'd lost sight of her in the crowd, and was seconds from seriously losing his cool.

I caught his eye and shook my head calmly; I could see her.

A second later she collided with my midriff, but lacked the strength to even push me back. "I thought you weren't coming back," she mumbled into my jacket, and her arms tightened around my waist.

"What? Why wouldn't I come back?" I dropped my bag and put both hands on her shoulders, prying her away gently until I could see her face. She was panting from the brief exertion, and her face was flushed with effort beneath the sickly pallor of her skin—a recent development.

But I smiled to reassure her, and she grinned back, evidently convinced I was real.

Kaci stepped back and took my bag in both hands, already turning toward Jace when she spoke. "Greg said you were hurt, and I thought you'd stay in Georgia till you got better."

I took the bag from her, afraid she'd keel over with the additional weight. "I'm fine, Kaci. See?" I stomped my right foot on the floor, demonstrating my own sturdiness. "Not even a limp. And you know why?"

"Why?"

"Because I *Shifted.*" I switched to a whisper in concession to the presence of so many humans. "Shifting can heal injuries in a *fraction* of the time it would have taken if I stayed in human form."

"Well, good for you." Kaci shrugged and headed for Jace, dismissing my less-than-subtle hint with an easy toss of her hair. "*I'm* not injured."

I growled beneath my breath. Two months earlier, I would never have believed a thirteen-year-old could be harder to deal with than an infant. I guess that's why nature starts most women off with babies and lets them grow into teenagers.

Jace took charge of my bag, and I gave him a quick hug. "How's the leg?" he asked, eyeing me carefully when I pulled away.

"Just a little sore. But these make me look badass, huh?" I pushed back my sleeve to show off my new battle scars, and he whistled in appreciation, then laughed. "Where's Ethan?" I asked, tugging my sleeve back into place.

Kaci grinned, pulling her MP3 player from her front pocket. "He's trying to hook up with the girl at the Starbucks counter."

I scowled. "*Hook up* with her?" I wasn't sure whether I should be more bothered by Kaci's too-casual phrasing, or my brother's obvious disdain for the concept of monogamy. Guess he was getting tired of white rice.

Kaci nodded sagely. "Yeah, but I don't think he's really after coffee."

Jace grinned sheepishly at me over her head, and I rolled my eyes. "Let's go home. And no more hanging out with Ethan. You're supposed to be under the supervision of your *mental* elders."

We retrieved my brother from the food court, where he sat in front of a tall cup of something slathered with whipped cream, across from a girl in a green Starbucks apron. He grinned all the way to the car.

During the three-hour drive from the airport, Kaci fell asleep against the car door, her earbuds in place, blasting the latest teen-angst anthem. I watched her breathe, amazed by how peaceful she looked, all things considered.

Because Kaci Dillon had not led a peaceful life. Not even for a werecat.

Kaci wasn't born into any Pride. In itself, that wasn't incredibly unusual, as the ever-growing population of strays might suggest. But Kaci wasn't a stray. She was a rare genetic anomaly—a werecat born to two *human* parents.

And so far, she was the only one of her kind we'd ever found.

We'd only known for about six months that, in spite of generations of belief to the contrary, it was indeed possible—if unlikely—for a werecat and a human to procreate. The children of such rare unions were humans whose DNA contained certain recessive werecat genes. Those genes would have no effect on the child unless they were one day "activated" by a bite or scratch from a werecat in cat form.

Normal humans can't survive a werecat attack. Their bodies fight the "virus" and eventually they die of the infection. So all strays were once humans who already had the necessary werecat genes *before* they were attacked.

Kaci's parents both carried those recessive genes, though they never knew it. Their unlikely pairing resulted in one daughter who didn't inherit any werecat genes. And in Kaci, who got them from both sides. She was a full-blooded werecat, born of two humans, and she'd had no idea until puberty brought on her first Shift.

I can't even imagine what that must have been like. So much unexplainable pain and an unfathomable transformation. In the height of her pain and terror, completely ignorant of what was happening to her, she accidentally killed her mother and sister. And in the process, she'd temporarily lost most of her sanity.

Kaci had wandered on her own for weeks, stuck in cat form because she had no idea she could Shift back, much less how to do it. She did what she had to do to survive, mostly out of instinct, but when we found her and showed her how to regain her human form—and with it, her sanity—she was horrified by what she'd done on four paws.

So horrified that she'd sworn never to assume her feline form again, convinced that if she did, she would hurt someone else.

But by refusing to Shift, she was only hurting herself.

Watching her sleep, I was shocked to realize Kaci was nearly as thin now as she'd been when I first saw her. She was slowly killing herself, and I had to do something to stop it. To help her help herself.

It was nearly four in the afternoon when we pulled through the gate onto the long gravel driveway leading onto my family's property. The Lazy S ranch lay before us, winter-bare fields on both sides of the driveway. Deep tire ruts cut into the eastern field at an angle, leading to the big red barn, quaint with its gabled roof and chipped paint. And at the end of the driveway lay the house, long and low and simple in design, in contrast to the buildings my father designed in his professional life.

Jace parked behind Ethan's car in the circular driveway, and the guys disappeared into the guesthouse, where my brother Owen was setting up a Rock Band tournament.

I grabbed my bag and headed for my room, not surprised when Kaci followed me. My mother had fixed up the bedroom Michael and Ryan once shared for her, but the tabby did little more than sleep there. She spent most of her time shadowing me, convinced that if she could learn to fight well enough in human form, she'd never have to Shift again. And no matter what I did or said, I couldn't convince her otherwise.

In my room, I dropped my duffel on the bed, and Kaci plopped down next to it on her stomach, her legs bent at the knee, feet dangling over the backs of her thighs. "Hey, you wanna go see a movie tonight? Parker gave me twenty bucks to vacuum the guesthouse a couple of days ago, and I've barely been off the ranch all week."

Groaning, I unzipped the bag and pulled my shampoo and conditioner from an inside pocket. "Kaci, don't clean for the guys! They're perfectly capable of picking up their own messes, but if you act like a maid, they'll treat you like one."

She frowned, her feelings hurt by my reproach, and I cursed myself silently. It should not be so hard for me to talk to one little girl. But then, I'd never expected to be someone's mentor. Hell, I'd probably never even be anyone's *aunt.*

I grinned to lighten the mood and took another shot. "Besides, if you feel like vacuuming, there are plenty of perfectly good floors in the main house. Like mine, for instance." I made a sweeping gesture at my beige Berber carpet, which could certainly use the attention.

Kaci laughed, and all was well. "So, what about the movie? You buy the tickets, and I'll buy the popcorn."

I walked backward toward the bathroom, hair products in hand. "It's a school night."

She swirled one finger along the stitches in my comforter. "I don't go to school."

"You *could....*" I left that possibility dangling and turned into my private bathroom, the only real advantage to being the sole daughter out of five children. Kaci pouted at me through the open doorway as I set the shampoo and conditioner on the edge of the tub. "You know how to make that happen."

The original plan had been for Kaci to start eighth grade in Lufkin, at the beginning of the second semester. My father had acquired the necessary documentation—birth certificate and shot records under the name Karli Sanders—and she would be his niece, recently orphaned and left to our care. She'd picked out a new haircut and color—long, dark layers—and we were relatively sure that with those precautions taken, no one would ever connect Karli Sanders with Kaci Dillon, who'd disappeared from her home in southern British Columbia during an attack by a pack of wild animals.

Of course, it helped that Kaci's family was no longer looking for her. She was presumed dead in the same attack that had killed her mother and sister. Her father had erected a memorial headstone for her months earlier, and by all accounts seemed to be trying to come to terms with his loss and grief.

But in the end, none of that mattered because by the time the spring semester had started a week earlier, Kaci was too weak to go. She got winded just walking to the barn, and took several naps a day. Her skin was pale and sometimes clammy, and she got constant migraines and occasional bouts of nausea.

She couldn't go to school until she'd Shifted and regained her strength. Until then, my mother was homeschooling her in the core subjects.

Neither of them was enjoying it.

"I can't do it." Kaci's frown deepened as she rolled onto her back to stare at my ceiling, rubbing her forehead to fend off another headache.

"Yes, you can. I can help." I went back to the bag for my toiletry pouch and hair dryer, still talking as I set them on the bathroom counter. "Dr. Carver says that once you're Shifting regularly, you'll get better very quickly. Then you can go to school like a normal kid."

"Normal!" She huffed and rolled her head to the side to meet my gaze. "What the hell is that?"

I groaned at her language. How the *hell* had she managed to pick up all of my bad habits and *none* of my good ones? "You know you can't talk like that in front of the Alpha, right?"

Kaci rolled both big hazel eyes at me. "*You* do."

Damn it!

From somewhere near the front of the house, my mother laughed out loud, having obviously heard the entire exchange. She'd always said she hoped I had a kid just like me, but neither of us had expected that to happen quite so soon.

But Kaci was right, of course. I sank onto the bed with a frustrated sigh, and she rolled onto her side to look at me, her face in one hand, her elbow spearing the comforter. "Kaci, you do *not* want to model your life in this Pride after mine. A *smart* girl would learn from a few of my mistakes, instead of choosing to repeat them all just for the experience."

She frowned and stared down at the comfortor. "My dad didn't let me cuss, either."

My heart jumped into my throat. Kaci hardly *ever* mentioned her father, or anything else from her previous existence, as if it were easier not to talk or even think about them. Though I understood that, I also knew that ignoring her problems wasn't the healthiest way to deal with them.

But before I could encourage her to go on, she changed the subject with a sudden shake of her head. "Besides, you look like you're doin' okay to me."

"But *you* could do better. You could do anything you want. Starting with public school."

Kaci sighed and flopped back over to stare at the ceiling, her hands folded across her stomach. But I could see wistfulness in her eyes. She wanted to go to school, no matter what she said to the contrary. I'd been in her position—aside from the whole refusing-to-Shift thing—and knew exactly how badly it sucked to be stuck in one place, under constant, nagging supervision.

At the end of the bed again, I dug in the duffel and pulled out my bloody, ruined jeans, tied up in a white plastic Wal-Mart sack.

"What's that smell?" Kaci rolled onto her stomach and sniffed the air with a spark of interest as I dropped the bundle on the floor. That night I would have to fire up the industrial incinerator behind the barn and toss the whole mess inside.

Hmm. I wonder if it's still hot from the recent mass cremation....

"You're probably smelling the stray who slashed through my jeans," I said, glancing at the bag in irritation. "That was my favorite pair."

"No, that's not it." She stuck her nose into my duffel and sniffed dramatically, and when she rose, the zipper pulled several strands of thick brown hair free from her ponytail to hang over her cheeks. "It's Marc." She shoved the loose strands back from her face. "Your underwear smells like *Marc!*"

I flushed and pulled my bag off the bed. When I was thirteen, there was no older woman around for me to ask about guys, other than my mother. And I wouldn't have asked *her* about sex if the future of the species depended upon my understanding of the process.

Which, according to my mother, it did.

Caught off guard by the questions I could practically feel her forming, I crossed the room to upend the rest of the duffel into my regular hamper, a purple ribbon-trimmed wicker thing my mother had put in my room when I was twelve.

I stared at the hamper critically, suddenly perplexed by its presence. *What kind of enforcer's hamper has ribbons threaded through it?* I needed something else. Something utilitarian. Something big and sturdy, and not at odds with the blood- and sweat-stained clothes it would be holding.

Like, a big metal trash can. Or a *barrel.*

I turned toward Kaci, intending to ask her if she wanted the girlie hamper, but she was already talking before I could get the question out. "So, how long have you been with Marc?"

"Um…we were together for my last two years of high school, then we broke up for about five years. And we got back together last summer."

"Why did you break up?"

Because I'm an idiot. I tossed my empty duffel into my closet and kicked the door shut. "It's complicated, Kaci. Things get weird when you grow up. Enjoy being a kid while you can."

"Whatever." She rolled onto her back again. "Being a kid sucks. People tell you when to get up, when to go to bed, when to eat, what not to wear…"

I glanced up from my dresser, onto which I'd been emptying my jeans pockets, to see her watching me in obvious—and incredibly *misplaced*—envy. "Have you *met* my parents? In case you haven't noticed, they still tell me what to do. *All the time.*"

"Yeah, well, at least you get paid for it."

"Not *this* year." Enforcers drew a small salary, in addition to free room and board. But as part of the "community service" sentence handed down to me from the tribunal in November, in addition to teaching my fellow enforcers to do the partial Shift, I had to forgo my salary for an entire year. All I had now was what little money I'd saved since college and the business credit card all my father's enforcers had. And that could only be used for official enforcer business. Which apparently did *not* include a pint of New York Super Fudge Chunk. Or a trip to Starbucks.

Oops.

"You love Marc, don't you?" In the mirror, Kaci's reflection stared at me, one cheek pressed into the comforter.

Surprised, I turned from the dresser to find her watching me in undisguised curiosity, as if my life served no other purpose than to entertain her. Yet I wasn't irritated, as I would no doubt have been if my mother were the one interrogating me, because Kaci had no ulterior motive. She wasn't trying to talk me into anything, or manipulate me. She just wanted to know…*everything.*

Sighing, I crossed my bedroom and sat facing her on the bed, my legs folded beneath me, yoga style. "Do I love Marc?" I repeated, and she nodded, sitting up with her back against my headboard. I pulled my fluffy pink punching pillow into my lap—if I was going to voluntarily engage in girl talk, I might as well be properly armed.

"Yes, I love Marc." *So much that it* hurts *not to see and touch him every day.*

"What about Jace?"

My chest tightened, and my heart seemed to be trying to beat its way free. "What about him?"

"He likes you. Like *Marc* likes you."

"What makes you think that?" I gave her my best blank face.

"He watches you. *All* the time. If you need something, he brings it to you. And when he looks at you, his heart beats *really* hard. I can hear it." She smiled slyly, and her big hazel eyes glinted. "Like yours is doing right now."

Damn it. I resisted the urge to close my eyes, or otherwise betray my frustration, which she would probably notice, like she had my heartbeat. "Kaci, that's really… complicated."

"Because you don't like him like that?" Bald hope flooded Kaci's features, and suddenly I understood. This wasn't about me and Marc. It was about *Jace.*

Kaci had a crush on Jace.

Oh, shit.

An interest in boys was a nice, normal development for a girl her age, and might go a long way toward convincing her to Shift, so she'd be healthy enough to start dating—with several huge, protective chaperones. But Jace was nearly twenty-five, and Kaci was only thirteen. She needed a boy her *own* age to crush on.

Yet another reason to get her enrolled in school.

But as for her actual question… "Kaci, I'm with Marc."

"So, Jace is single, right?"

Kaci frowned again and glanced at my open bedroom door. Then she turned back to me, and when she spoke, her voice was a barely audible whisper. "How old were you when you and Marc first…"

Mayday, mayday!

Alarms went off in my head, and my eyes snapped shut in denial. I was *not* ready to have this conversation with Kaci. And somehow we were back to her looking at my life as a blueprint for her own. I didn't want that kind of responsibility! I wanted the freedom to mess up and know that my mistakes wouldn't screw up anyone's life but my own.

Unfortunately, I'd kind of given up that privilege when I became an enforcer.

"Whoa, Kaci, back up a bit." I shook my head and made myself meet her frank gaze. "You're waaaay too young to be thinking about sex."

She rolled her eyes, and the gesture was eerily familiar from my own adolescence. Okay, also from what little of my adulthood I'd survived so far.

"I was talking about *kissing,*" Kaci said, in that exasperated tone she usually saved for my mother, during homeschooling. "I just meant, how old were you when you first kissed Marc? But since you brought up sex…"

Her eyes glinted with a spark of mischief. "Same question."

Damn it! "Way older than you are." My head was throbbing and pain was shooting through my chest. I was having a panic attack. The little whelp was giving me an aneurism!

I was a firm believer in telling the truth, but some of my truths weren't suitable for such young ears, and I did *not* want to screw up someone *else's* kid!

I had to redirect. Change the subject. Turn the conversation back onto her before my mother decided to step in. But Kaci was still talking…

"Was it your idea, or his?"

Oh, shit. But she wasn't done yet.

"Does it hurt? 'Cause I heard…"

Okay, this has to stop.

I threw up one hand, palm facing her, in the universal sign for *halt!* Then I took a deep breath and glanced at the open door again, this time thinking of escape, rather than of being overheard. But that was the coward's way out. If I could stand against multiple strays in cat form, wielding only a shovel, surely I could face a single thirteen-year-old and her birds-and-bees inquisition.

And, if not, I could procrastinate with the best of them.

"You're throwing an awful lot of questions at me all at once, Kaci. And asking for a lot of very personal information."

Her face fell, and she tugged aimlessly at the frayed cuff of her jeans. "You're not going to tell me anything, are you?"

I sighed. Answering her questions—at least some of them—might go a long way toward getting her to truly trust me. Which might help me convince her to Shift. But no true compromise was one-sided. "I tell you what. I will answer three of your questions—any three you want…"

Her eyes lit up in expectation.

"…*after* you Shift."

Kaci scowled. Then she stood, more color draining from her already pale face, and stomped across my room and through the open doorway.

"I take it that's a no?" I called after her.

She slammed her bedroom door in reply, and I flinched.

Well, that *went well…*

Seven

"Again!" Ethan wrapped both bare arms around the heavy punching bag to steady it, and I shot him a look meant to scorch him from the inside out. Or at least to shut him up. "Harder this time. And a little higher. Hit his knee from the side, and he'll go down. Then it's all over but the beatin'."

"He doesn't *have* knees," I snapped, wiping sweat from my forehead with an equally sweaty forearm. There was a clean, dry towel hanging over a folding chair near the bathroom, but I was too tired to cross the basement for it. "He doesn't even have *legs.*"

"Oh, you got *jokes?*" Ethan grinned amiably, his green eyes flashing in challenge. He dropped his arms, then stepped around the bag, his sneakers sinking into the thick blue mat with each step. "If you've got energy to be funny, we're not working you hard enough. Right, Kaci?"

"Right." The young tabby tucked her legs up onto her folding metal chair and sipped from a covered mug filled with hot chocolate. Then she grinned at me and set her drink back on the bench press serving as an end table. The night before, she'd officially forgiven me for pushing the Shifting issue so hard. Still, she didn't seem to mind watching Ethan kick my ass.…

Little traitor.

Our basement was unheated, but was naturally insulated by the earth surrounding it, so the slight chill seeping in from the high windows was no problem for me or Ethan. After only half an hour of moderate lifting, he and I were both covered in sweat, even wearing only light workout clothes. In fact, he'd shed his shirt several minutes earlier.

But Kaci shivered beneath long sleeves, jeans, and a light blanket. She didn't have enough energy to exercise with us, and she lacked the body fat to keep herself warm, but no amount of begging, coercing, or threatening on our part could convince her to go back upstairs, where my mother waited with more cocoa and an algebra textbook.

I could probably have *made* her go up, but I'd decided not to push the issue because she was still mad at me over the unanswered sex questions. Besides, we'd be heading up for lunch soon anyway.

"You're not *working* me at all." I reached up to catch the towel Ethan tossed me. "You're practicing *with* me, not *on* me. Or do you need another reminder?"

"What I need is an actual *challenge,* smart-ass." Ethan winked at Kaci, who grinned, enjoying our banter. "Think you can manage that?"

"Oh, you're asking for it n—" Before I could finish the sentence, Ethan charged.

I lunged to the right, but I was too slow. His shoulder clipped my arm, knocking me off balance. I hit the thick pad on my hip and rolled out of the way. He slammed into the mat where I'd been, but I was already on my feet.

I dropped onto his back and planted my knee in his spine. Ethan howled and bucked. I straddled him for stability. My hand closed around his flailing right arm and I dug in the pocket of my workout pants for my cuffs.

Ethan's left hand brushed my leg, then closed around

the back of my knee. He tugged me forward. I leaned back to counter and snapped one cuff over his right wrist. He pulled harder, and I slid onto the mat with my left leg folded beneath me.

My brother tossed his weight over me, and we rolled. His elbow hit my ribs. His skull slammed into my right cheekbone, but I held on to my cuffs. Dizzy now, I stuck one knee out to halt our roll. We stopped with him facedown, me straddling his back again, and this time I didn't hesitate. I pulled his left arm back and snapped the other cuff closed over his wrist.

Then I stood and backed away, waiting for the sparks. Waiting to gloat as he ranted and raged, demanding to be let loose.

Instead he shook with laughter.

I stared at Ethan for a moment, a little disappointed, then turned when I heard Kaci giggling behind me. "That was *awesome!*" she yelled, on her feet now, the cocoa forgotten.

"I agree." Ethan's words were muffled with half of his face pressed into the mat, and I turned to find him watching me, now lying on his right shoulder. "That was damned impressive." He smiled, looking almost as pleased as he would have been had our positions been reversed. "But let's not tell anyone, 'kay? We'll keep this a private victory, just between the three of us."

"No way!" Kaci shouted, grinning so hard her cheeks were flushed with excitement. Or maybe with the cold. "Faythe *owns* you! I wish I had a camera. Wait till Jace—"

Ethan's phone rang, Puddle of Mudd singing "She Hates Me."

I laughed. I couldn't help it. "Whose ring is that?"

He let his head hit the mat. "Angela's."

Kaci glanced at the bench press, where two cell phones lay, alongside her hot chocolate and two bottles of water. She picked up his phone and glanced at the display, her eyes shining in mischief. "You want me to tell her you're all tied up?"

"No!" Ethan shouted, scooting awkwardly across the mat on his side. "Don't answer it. She wants to 'talk about our relationship.' I've been dodging her calls all week."

I rolled my eyes and dug my handcuff key from one side of my sneaker. "Wouldn't it be easier to just tell her you're no longer into white rice? Or that you're moving to Yemen? Or whatever you tell those poor girls when your attention span turns out to be smaller than your—" I hesitated, censoring myself on Kaci's behalf "—*IQ,* and you get bored with them?"

"No." Ethan went still as I freed his hands, then he sat up, rubbing his wrists as Puddle of Mudd played on. "It's easier to avoid her calls until she gets the picture on her own. That way, no one gets dumped. Really, I'm doing her a favor."

"You're an ass." I was seriously considering answering his phone myself. But then the ringing stopped, and Kaci dropped the phone onto the padded bench next to mine. "And just for that, I'm not letting you up next time."

Ethan had barely regained his feet when I rushed him. My shoulder slammed into his chest. I drove him backward onto the mat again, and his breath exploded from his chest in a massive "oof."

"Yeah!" Kaci shouted, and I twisted to see her standing again, her smile almost as big as mine.

But I shouldn't have looked.

Ethan grabbed my left shoulder and rolled me over, sitting on my thighs. "So much for a challenge," he taunted.

I retorted with my fist.

My first blow landed on his ribs, and I shoved him off

me. But before I could flip him onto his stomach and go for my cuffs again, more music rang out from the bench next to Kaci.

Papa Roach, singing "Scars." That was my phone. Marc's ring.

I was halfway to the bale of hay when something hit my back, fast and hard. I fell face-first onto the mat, Ethan's weight pinning me.

"You're too easily distracted," he scolded. "Are you going to ask the bad guys to stop beating on you for a minute so you can answer your phone?"

I twisted beneath him but couldn't get any leverage; he'd pinned my arms to my sides. "Get *up!*" I shouted, as loud as I could with his weight constricting my lungs. "That's Marc!"

Ethan slid off me reluctantly. "You don't see me going all starry-eyed when my girlfriend's on the line," he huffed.

"You're not even taking her calls." I glanced at Kaci and held my right hand up, palm cupped. "Toss it here, please."

Her aim was good, but mine wasn't. The phone flew past my hand and landed on the mat behind me. Ethan dove for it, an impish grin lighting his whole face. But I was faster. My fingers closed around the plastic just as his closed around my arm, and I put the phone in my other hand, flipping it open as Ethan groaned in defeat.

The look on his face was so comical that I was laughing when I spoke into the receiver.

"Hello?"

"Faythe? Is that you?" At first I didn't recognize the voice, either because I was expecting Marc's, or because the speaker sounded so panicked. But understanding didn't take long. "This is Daniel Painter." He huffed into the phone like he'd just run a marathon.

My heart stopped beating for a moment, even as my

pulse tripped so fast the surge of adrenaline actually hurt. "What's wrong?" I shoved Ethan when he tried to snatch the phone from me, still playing around. But my tone froze him in place, and the smile drained from his expression. He glanced at my phone, and I knew he was listening in.

"Marc's gone, and there are two dead toms in his living room." Painter's words all ran together and at first I thought I'd misunderstood him. I *must* have misunderstood him. "Some of the blood is theirs, but lots of it is his, too…."

There was blood?

My heart seemed to burst within my chest, flooding me with more pain and confusion than I could sort through at once. I fell off my knees onto my rump and could barely feel the mat I sat on. My hands tingled as if they were on hold, waiting to receive signals from my brain, and I was afraid I'd drop the phone.

Painter was still talking in my ear, babbling words I couldn't understand. Phrases that wouldn't sink in. *Bastards. Dead. Blood. Missing.* I could barely hear him over the static in my head, the ambient noise of my own denial.

"Faythe!" Ethan muttered. I blinked and shook my head, then forced my eyes to make sense of his face. "Slow him down. Make him give you the facts."

Right. The facts.

And just like that, the world hurled itself back into focus around me, the entire barn tilting wildly for a moment before everything seemed to settle with an eerily crisp clarity. I met my brother's eyes, thanking him wordlessly for the mental face-slap. "Take Kaci upstairs and get Dad. I think he's in the barn."

By the time I'd gotten a deep breath, Ethan was on the bottom step, one hand beckoning Kaci to follow him, the other flipping open his own phone, because he could call the barn much faster than he could get there, even with a werecat's speed.

"Faythe?" Dan was shouting now and I took a moment to be grateful that I got a strong signal in our basement. "Are you there?"

"I'm here. Calm down and explain it to me slowly." I stood, and almost lost my balance when one foot hit the concrete floor and the other sank into the thick mat. "Marc is gone, but you smell his blood. Is that right?"

"It's everywhere," Painter said, with no hesitation, and I pictured him nodding, though I couldn't see the gesture over the line. "There's a thick trail of it leading across the carpet to the front door. Like someone dragged him off."

Oh, shit. Oh, noooo!

Stop it, Faythe. He's lost a lot of blood, but that doesn't mean he's dead. Marc would be fine. We just had to find him.

"Where does the trail go?" I asked, struggling to keep my voice calm and even. If I panicked, Dan might panic, and we'd lose valuable time that would be better spent looking for Marc. "Does it continue out the front door?"

"Yeah. Across the front stoop, down the steps and over the grass. That's how I knew something was wrong when I got here."

"So, it ends in the grass?"

"On the edge of the driveway." Painter paused, and I heard a metallic groan, as a screen door creaked open. "It looks like they put him in a car and took off with him. There're big ruts in the gravel from where they peeled off too fast." He hesitated again, then asked the question I hadn't even posed to myself yet. "Do you think he's dead?"

My eyes closed, and I inhaled deeply. Then exhaled slowly. "I don't know." I sucked in another breath and forced my concentration back to the work at hand, and away from thoughts I couldn't bear to entertain. "Did they take his car?"

"No. It's up next to the house. Along the south side, where he always parks it." The screen door slammed shut with a horrid tinny screech, and Painter's voice echoed slightly, now that it had four walls to bounce off again.

"Should I go look for Marc, or start cleaning up the mess?" Painter inhaled deeply, obviously trying to calm himself. "And the *bodies…?*"

I wanted to tell him to forget about the bodies and start driving around town on the lookout for Marc. Or into the forest, keeping an eye out for fresh tire tracks. But the truth was that if there were enough of them to take Marc down, there would be too many for Painter to handle on his own. Assuming he found them.

My mind was flooded by the possibilities. Maybe they'd taken him alive. But if so, why? And where?

Maybe they'd killed him, and had left to dispose of the body. My eyes watered, and my fist clenched around the phone, the nails of my opposite hand biting into my flesh. No. That's not what happened. If they'd killed him, why not dispose of all three bodies at once? Why leave the others?

Unless the killers drove a compact…

"Okay, let's take it one thing at a time." My feet moved as I spoke, and I found myself on the aisle formed by two rows of weight-lifting equipment. "The other bodies. Are they strays? Do you know them?" I thought about going upstairs, but didn't want Kaci to overhear anything that might upset her.

"Yeah, they're strays. I recognize the scents, but don't know the names."

"There are two of them, right?" I ran my hand over the leg press, cursing silently when a flake of paint slid beneath my fingernail. "And they bled on the carpet?"

"Yeah." Floorboards creaked, and I pictured Painter

leaning over the bodies. "The carpet, themselves, each other. The biggest one has a huge gash on the top of his skull. Near the back. And the coffee table's broken and covered in his blood. Looks like he fell and hit it. Or else someone hit him *with* it."

Yeah, that sounded like Marc. An odd pang of pride and pain rang through me, as I hoped fervently that he was still alive to repeat that performance someday.

"What about the other one?"

"Side of his head's caved in. Looks like someone took a rung-back chair to 'im."

"Okay, now I need you to sniff around. Concentrate. Do you smell any scents that don't belong to either Marc or the dead strays? Did anyone else bleed in there recently? Or sweat? Or touch anything? Sniff the doorknobs first, then anything that might have been used as a weapon. Did you touch the doorknob?"

"Only from the outside of the door." There was a pause on his end, and I thought I heard floorboards groan as he knelt. Or stood. "Yeah, there's another scent on the front door. The wood and the knob. It's another stray, but no one I know."

"Good." I was walking again, my feet whispering on concrete, my hand trailing over the long bar on the bench press. That scent belonged to the last person who'd touched the doorknob—presumably whoever had taken Marc. "Don't touch the knob. We'll need to smell that scent."

I didn't hear what he said next because of the footsteps thundering toward me from the kitchen. My dad jerked open the door and jogged down the steps, breathing deeply from exertion, his eyes wide with alarm. I'd rarely seen him so flustered, and it meant the world to me that Marc meant so much to him.

My father wore no coat other than his usual suit jacket, and only once I noticed that his cheeks were flushed from the cold did I realize that I was completely covered with chill bumps, and that I was actually shivering.

Now that I was done exercising, my sweat had dried to leave me cold in the basement chill.

"What happened?" Moving briskly, my father stepped over the corner of the mat and snatched the blanket from Kaci's chair.

"Hang on a second, Dan," I said into the mouthpiece, while my father draped the blanket over my shoulders. "Daniel Painter found two dead strays in Marc's living room. Marc's missing, and a trail of his blood leads out the house and to the driveway, where it looks like he was loaded into a car. At least one other stray was there, based on the scent on the doorknob."

My Alpha's expression grew bleaker with each word I spoke. "How much blood did he lose?"

"I don't know," I answered, just as Painter said, "A lot." My heart thumped harder, *aching* within my chest at the thought of how much blood he'd lost, and my father motioned for me to sit in the chair Kaci had vacated.

"Are these dead strays in cat form or human form?" he asked, knowing Painter would hear him.

"Human form." Painter sighed, and when springs squealed over the phone, I pictured him sinking wearily onto Marc's couch. A couch I'd never sat on, or even *seen*.

My father frowned, and I shared his confusion. Why would werecats attack someone they obviously meant to kill, based on the earlier ambush, without the use of their best weapons—claws and canines? For that matter, why attack Marc at all? Weren't Manx and I the original targets? Wasn't the objective the usual: kidnap the women and kill the men? If so, why go after Marc when Manx and I weren't even there?

My phone was getting hot, so I switched to my other ear.

"Are the dead men carrying anything?" My dad dug in his inside coat pocket and pulled out his own cell phone, scrolling through the menu as he spoke. "Wallets? Checkbooks? Phones? Anything that might identify them?"

"I don't know." More springs groaned as Painter stood again. "Want me to search 'em?"

Instead of answering Painter, my father turned to me with his free hand outstretched. "Give me the phone."

I hesitated, even though my father—not to mention my Alpha—had given me a direct order, because handing over my phone felt like giving up my link to Marc. Or at least to the man currently in the best position to help him. But after a second, I obeyed.

"Painter?" my father barked. His concern came through as gruffness. But then, that's how most of his strong emotions sounded. "This is Greg Sanders, Alpha of the south-central Pride. Thank you for alerting us. Can you stay there until my team arrives?"

"Yeah, sure," Painter said, and I pictured him nodding eagerly, pleased to be needed, in spite of the circumstances.

My concern for Painter paled in comparison to my fear for Marc, but I still didn't want him to get hurt, especially trying to help us. "What if they come back to clean up the rest of their mess?"

My dad tilted my phone so that the mouthpiece slanted away from his lips. "Hopefully, he'll get a good description." To Painter, he said, "Lock the door and turn off the lights. Then Shift." Because it would be easier to defend himself that way, should the need arise. "And if they come back, go right out the front door and call Faythe."

"How's he supposed to call me in cat form?" I asked, frowning.

My father shrugged, and spoke into the phone, though he was still watching me. "Autodial. If you keep Faythe's number up on the display, you can call her with the press of one button, using a toe pad, or a claw. I've done it before."

He had? I thought about asking, but decided I didn't want to know.

"Faythe and her partner will be leaving immediately." My father eyed me with both eyebrows raised, and I nodded, relieved that I wouldn't have to argue with him on that point. "Is there any trouble with the neighbors? Did anyone hear or see anything?" He began to pace back and forth across the straw-strewn dirt floor. "Or call the police?"

"Oh. Nah. The nearest neighbor is 'bout two miles away, and I doubt they coulda heard anything."

I might have guessed Marc wouldn't want any close neighbors. He'd lived on our compound for half of his life, and typically wanted little to do with humans.

"Good." But my father's face showed no real relief. With Marc missing and likely gravely injured, the news that there had been no witnesses was decidedly bitter-sweet.

My dad handed my phone back to me. "Thanks, Dan," I said, suddenly eager to be off the phone and on the road. "I'll be there as soon as I can." I started to say goodbye, but then something else occurred to me. "They broke in the front door, right?"

"Yeah. It's still on the hinges, but the lock's busted." He seemed to know where I was headed with that question.

I sank onto the padded, duct-tape-patched seat of the bench press. "Can you move something in front of the doors? That way if they come back, you'll at least have some warning before they get in."

"Um, just a sec." Painter's breathing changed as he

stood, and footsteps over the line told me he was on the move. "I can push the couch in front of the front door. And the back one looks fine. I'm locking it up now." A chain rattled, and metal scraped wood softly as he slid the dead bolt home.

"Good, but can you put something in front of that one, too? Just in case?"

"Sure. I'll see if he's got anything heavy in the other room."

"Thanks, Dan." I hesitated, wishing my gratitude for him wasn't overshadowed by my fear for Marc. But it was. "I'm leaving now, and it'll take me about five hours. Call me immediately if anyone shows up."

"I will."

I flipped my phone closed and turned to find my father watching me from one corner of the exercise mat. Owen, Ethan, Jace and Parker stood at the bottom of the stairs, breathing hard and waiting for orders.

"Faythe, Parker, get packed." Parker and I nodded in unison, and my father continued. "Take enough for two days, just in case. But I can't spare you any longer than that. Not with everything else going on."

I found myself nodding, but knew in my heart that I wouldn't leave the free zone before we'd found Marc. Not conscious and walking upright, anyway.

"Sniff around and see what you can find out about the dead strays. Get me names, and I'll get you addresses. Play it safe, and play it smart. Do *not* go wandering off through the woods looking for a needle in a haystack. And don't go anywhere alone. For all we know, this is a trap designed to get you back into the free zone. Check in three times a day. Got it?"

I nodded again, and Parker mimicked me. We were itching to get going.

"And, Faythe?" My father eyed me sternly.

"Yeah?"

"I don't have any extra backup to send with you, so it's just you two and Dan Painter. Be careful."

"Of course," I said, as if his common warning meant no more this time than it ever had. But that wasn't the case. Always before, *we'd* had the advantage of larger numbers, and I was distinctly uncomfortable with having the tables turned.

"Okay, go!" my father ordered. And we went.

Eight

When I got to my room, Kaci was waiting on my bed, propped up on my pillows, and the sense of déjà vu was inescapable as I packed. She'd watched me *un*pack less than a day earlier, looking much happier than she did at the moment.

She pulled my punching pillow into her lap as if for comfort. But then I was almost amused to see her clench it in both fists, as if she might rip it in two. It was scary sometimes, how much she and I had in common. "What happened?" The tabby's smooth, beautiful features were twisted in an odd combination of fear and irritation. "No one will tell me anything."

"Marc's been abducted, and he lost a lot of blood in the process." I snatched my duffel from the floor of my closet and dropped it on the end of the bed, and when our eyes finally met, the shock in hers took me completely by surprise.

Maybe I shouldn't have been *quite* so blunt. Was this one of those truths kids weren't supposed to hear? What was I supposed to do, *lie* to her?

I was pretty sure that even if I tried to gloss over the facts, she'd see the truth in my eyes. Then she'd never trust me again.

I wanted to sink onto the bed next to Kaci and hug her. Then slowly, carefully, explain that sometimes bad things happen to good people, and those good people aren't always okay afterward. But surely she knew that better than anyone, and I didn't have time for slow and careful. I had to find Marc, to make sure he didn't become one of those people who wasn't okay.

Like Kaci herself.

Shit. She needed reassurance from me almost as badly as Marc needed to be found and treated. I'd have to talk while I packed.

"Kaci, hon, I don't know how this is going to end." I turned from her as I opened my top dresser drawer, to keep her from seeing just how terrified I was. She needed to see me as a rock. As someone she could depend on, no matter what happened. She did *not* need to know that a hit on Marc was the one punch I wasn't sure I could roll with.

When I had my expression under control, I met her eyes again as I stuffed a handful of underwear into the bag. "But I'm going to *find* Marc, and make sure that whoever took him lives to regret it. For a few minutes, anyway."

She only blinked at me, and I turned back to the dresser for some shirts. "How did it happen?" Kaci asked as I pulled two long-sleeved tees from the second drawer.

"It looks like some men broke into his house and beat him up, then took off with him."

"Somebody beat *Marc* up?" Disbelief was thick in her voice, and my pride for Marc and his reputation swelled, even under the circumstances.

"It was at least three against one." No need to mention that the weapons were pieces of his broken furniture, or that he was in his own *home* at the time. "And he got two of them," I said after a moment's hesitation, hoping she wouldn't ask me what "got" meant.

I was a little conflicted about how much to tell her. On one hand Kaci was a werecat now, a fully integrated member of our society, and she needed to know how life worked for us. Sheltering her would do little to help her adjust. But on the other hand, even though she wasn't scratched or bitten, her entry into our secret world was heralded by violence, and I wasn't eager to remind her of what she'd done. She needed to move past that if she was ever going to truly settle into her new existence.

"Were they werecats?" she asked, as I shoved the shirts into the bag.

"Yeah." But the real question was whether any of the men who'd attacked Marc this time were in on the ambush two days earlier.

From the bathroom, I grabbed my hair dryer, toiletries, and what little makeup I wore on a semiregular basis. Kaci watched as I dropped it all into the duffel bag, the dryer cord dangling over one side.

"Were they in cat form?" she whispered, and dread sifted through me at the quiet horror in her voice. She wound the cord around my hair dryer, then tucked it neatly into one end of the duffel, nestled between my shampoo and makeup bag.

"No." I started to zip the bag, but stopped when I noticed that her eyes were shinier than usual. They were standing in tears. "Kaci, no, honey, they were in human form. This had *nothing* to do with what form they were in. These are bad men, and they'd be bad on either four legs or two. Just like you'd be good in either form."

"But I *wasn't* good as a cat!" she insisted, and the silent tears began to fall.

Well, hell… Sympathy squeezed my heart to the point of pain, but her timing could not have been worse. I'd been waiting months for an opening into her psyche—to get her to talk about what she'd gone through during and after her first transformation—and when the breakthrough finally came, I didn't have time to stay and listen. To help her work through it.

But she was crying. I'd have to *find* a minute with Kaci, then make up for it on the drive to the free zone.

I shoved my duffel aside and climbed over the footboard onto the end of the mattress, as close to her as I could get. Werecats are very physically demonstrative, and I was hoping the contact might help calm her.

"Kaci, you were *great* as a cat!" I put one arm around her shoulders and squeezed, pulling her even closer. "You're so strong. So *amazing*. What happened when you first Shifted, that wasn't your fault. Not Kaci-the-person's fault, and not Kaci-the-cat's fault."

I let go of her shoulders and gently turned her face toward mine, staring into big hazel eyes magnified by tears. "That wasn't *anyone's* fault. It was just a tragedy. A horrible, devastating tragedy, and I know you're dealing with it the only way you know how, but we have to figure out some other way for you to handle this, or you're going to wind up hurting yourself. You're nearly there now."

"I know." She wiped tears from her cheeks with both hands, then clenched my punching pillow as if it alone anchored her to her human form. "But I don't think I can do it. I don't think I can *control* it."

"Yes, you can." I twisted on the comforter to face her more directly, hoping my conviction was contagious. "Kaci, when I first met you, you were in cat form, and you didn't hurt me. You didn't even come near me. And that's when you were terrified and in a strange place. It will be different this time. We can do it in the barn. Just you and me, if you want. And if you're worried about losing control, I'll close the doors so you can't get out. All you need is one good Shift to prove to yourself that you can do this. That your inner cat isn't some rabid tiger looking for its next meal. It's just another part of you. A part you're going to *have* to come to terms with."

Her forehead crinkled. "But what if I hurt you?"

I laughed out loud, letting her see my genuine amusement. "Honey, you couldn't hurt me if you tried. I've faced down bigger and badder cats than you under much worse circumstances. That's my job, and I'm pretty damn good at it. You'll be fine. I won't let anything happen to either of us."

For the first time, I saw belief in her eyes. And trust. She was coming around. And if I didn't have to leave immediately, she might have been willing to give it a try right then.

But I *had* to go. I had to find Marc, and each minute I spent on the ranch when I should have been out looking for him weighed on my mind like a pile of bricks, threatening to crush me.

"I tell you what." I swung my legs over the side of the bed. "You think about it for the next couple of days. Get yourself ready mentally. Then, when I get back, we'll do it together. It'll be fine, and you'll feel so much better. And then you can go to school—finally get out of this house. Okay?"

She nodded, but looked unconvinced, and I knew I might have to repeat my little pep talk when I got back.

I gave her another reassuring smile as I dug through my bag to make sure I wasn't forgetting anything. And I was. Pants.

Groaning over my own oversight, I whirled toward the dresser and pulled a pair of jeans from the bottom drawer.

"I probably already know what you're gonna to say, but can I come with you?" Kaci held the duffel open while I shoved my pants inside, then tugged the zipper shut. "I wouldn't get in the way. And I could help look for Marc."

I smiled to soften the coming blow. "I'm sorry, Kaci, but this is way too dangerous."

The frustration and disappointment in her eyes were achingly familiar. Even with my father's liberal stance on a woman's place in the Pride, I'd spent much of my childhood being left out of things for my own safety. I'd even heard that line a time or two since becoming an enforcer, though staying behind had yet to actually keep me out of the action. But that didn't change anything for Kaci. At the moment, she wasn't well enough for a brisk walk through the woods, much less a risky trip across two states and a desperate hunt…wherever Marc's trail should lead us.

"This is a job for enforcers, Kaci. You're not old enough, and you don't have any training."

"Can I be an enforcer someday?" she asked, as I dropped my bag on the carpet near the door.

I couldn't resist a grin. "Absolutely. You can do anything you want. But first, you have to get healthy. And enforcers do a lot of their work in cat form, so you have to get used to Shifting. We'll work on that when I get back, 'kay?"

This time when she nodded, she didn't look quite as hesitant, and I took that as a very good sign.

"Okay, I have to go, but I hear my mom messing around in the kitchen." Pots clanged together at the front of the house, as if to punctuate my claim. "Why don't you go see what she's making for lunch."

Kaci went reluctantly, and I changed quickly into a fresh pair of jeans and a dark green sweater with a cowl neck and too-long sleeves, then hurried outside to throw my bag in the backseat of Parker's car. When I came back in, Kaci sat at the bar in the kitchen, sipping the broth from my mother's homemade chicken soup. I ignored the rumble of my own stomach and headed into my father's office to tell him Parker and I were ready to go.

The office door was closed, but I barely noticed in my hurry to get on the road. I twisted the knob and walked in. My father stood in front of his desk, facing the glass display case against the wall. He clutched the phone to his ear, face flaming in rage so consuming he hadn't even noticed my entrance. Which he probably hadn't heard over his own shouting.

"…a child, and I will *not* hand her over just to satisfy some scheming, underhanded Alpha's selfish political ambitions!"

Whoa…

My hand tightened on the doorknob in surprise, and my father heard the creak. He whirled to face me fully, one hand on the edge of his desk, and slammed the cordless phone onto the receiver. "Didn't I ever teach you to knock?" he demanded, eyes flashing in fury.

I should have apologized and meekly backed out of the room. But the sick feeling twisting my stomach wouldn't let me. "What was that about?" I asked from the doorway, not daring to come any farther into the office.

If my father had taken his phone call in any other room of the house, we all would have heard his side of the conversation, and likely most of the other side. But the office was a special room, designed for privacy in a house whose occupants all had supernatural hearing. The walls were solid concrete, without so much as a window for sound to leak through. The door was a panel of solid oak, and while not as soundproof as the walls themselves, it held a definite advantage over the hollow interior doors in the rest of the house.

My father sighed, and in that moment he looked a decade past his fifty-six years. "Come in and close the door." He propped one hip on the corner of his desk next to the phone and waved me inside, lowering his voice to a weary whisper. "I'm going to tell you what happened, before your imagination kicks into overdrive. But you will *not* tell anyone else. I'll make the announcement myself, when the time is right."

Nodding, I hesitated a moment—I really needed to go after Marc—then stepped into the office and pushed the door shut, twisting the lock to keep someone else from walking in, like I had. I had no doubt that if my father had been expecting the call he'd just fielded, the door would have been locked before.

The flimsy twist-lock wouldn't stop a werecat who really wanted in, but it wasn't supposed to. It was merely a signal that my father required a little privacy, and the lock would be respected for its intent rather than its strength.

"Who was that?" I sank onto the edge of the couch nearest the desk, acutely aware that every passing second was another one-second delay in getting to Marc. But I had to know…

My father gripped the edge of the desk he sat on. "That was Milo Mitchell." Kevin Mitchell's father, who was currently in Georgia for Manx's trial. Kevin had been expelled from the south-central Pride for accepting bribes to sneak a stray into New Orleans. "Milo claims he represents a 'concerned faction' of the Territorial Council, but I have no doubt he's working with Calvin Malone."

"And they want Kaci?" That sick feeling in my stomach grew to encompass most of the rest of me, and I was suddenly sure I would be violently ill right there on my father's Oriental rug.

"Yes. Mitchell says several of the Alphas are worried, in light of Malone's claims, that I'm acting against the best interest of the council. They want me to relinquish custody of Kaci to the council at large, which will then appoint a guardian for her. But you know exactly where she'll wind up."

"With Malone." I scowled so hard my face hurt. The bastard was scheming to get control of both Kaci and Manx, just like we'd feared he would.

My father nodded solemnly and rose from the desk to sink into his armchair on my left.

"So, what are you going to do?" Even if I hadn't just heard him refuse to give up Kaci, I knew my dad would never bow to threats from another Alpha. Much less hand over a mostly innocent child to be used as a political pawn.

Malone wanted control of Kaci for the same reason he'd tried to strong-arm me into marrying one of his sons—to put more territory under his misogynistic, bigoted, politically ambitious metaphorical thumb.

My father shrugged. "At this point it's a simple request, and I'm within my rights to refuse. But they'll come back with a formal demand, and our response at that time will have to be much more…civil."

Ha! I'd show them *civil.* I would tell the council exactly where it could shove its "civil" requests. Which my badass Alpha had just done.

"Daddy, I'm *this* close to talking Kaci into Shifting." I held my thumb and forefinger less than an inch apart. "I think I could get her to do it today, if I had the time. But she's *never* going to Shift for someone she doesn't know and trust, and she hates Calvin Malone almost as much as she hates her own cat form." Which was partly my fault. She'd heard everything Jace and I had to say about his abusive, narrow-minded, ass-wipe of a stepfather and now the tabby was firmly aligned with our Pride against him.

"I know." My father sighed and suddenly looked very tired. "I won't let this happen."

The last time he'd said that, he'd been talking about my possible execution, and he'd been as good as his word. Unfortunately, to take the death penalty off the table, he'd had to exile Marc.

I couldn't help but wonder what we'd have to give up to keep Kaci.

"So, what's the plan?" I fingered a figurine on the end table on my left—a pewter cat reared to pounce. Then I forced my hands into my lap when I realized I was betraying my extreme impatience.

"*You're* going to find Marc. I can handle Kaci, and I don't want you worrying about this until he's back and healthy. There's nothing you can do about it, anyway. This is *my* battle, Faythe. I may not be young anymore, but there's a fight or two left in me still. Don't count your father out just yet."

"I haven't, Daddy." And I never would. But Kaci was as much my responsibility now as I ever was his. We'd *both* fight for her.

Just as soon as I was sure Marc was okay.

"I'm calling in reinforcements from the rest of the Pride, so we'll have some extra bodies on patrol." He went to the desk and pulled open the top drawer and removed a bulging three-ring binder, which he dropped on the blotter with a thunk. "With all that stray activity going on so close to the border, we need to know immediately if they try to cross over."

"Good." With Michael, Brian and Vic still in Georgia, and me and Parker off looking for Marc, my father would need all three of his remaining enforcers to protect the home and hearth. But he could hardly ignore the threat posed by our suddenly aggressive neighbors.

I hated that we were so crippled by circumstance, but incredibly grateful that we had resources to call on in our time of need. The other members of our Pride would be called into active duty, a possibility they'd agreed to upon joining the south-central Pride. And if I knew my father, he'd pair the less experienced toms with those who'd once served as enforcers.

They'd take sick days, vacation days, unpaid workdays, or whatever it took to get off work when they were called. And in a matter of hours the Mississippi border would be crawling with south-central cats. They would patrol in human form until dusk, then on four paws once darkness descended to blend with their fur.

"With any luck, by the time you get there, several toms will be within an hour's drive should you need them," my father continued. "Do not hesitate to call them in. There are no bonus points for bravery on this one, Faythe. The only way to win is to get Marc back then get all three of you home in one piece. Understand?"

"Of course, Daddy." I didn't even roll my eyes, because for once I was pretty sure he wasn't being over-protective just because I was a girl. He was being regular-protective, because I was one of his enforcers, and that felt good. Really good. Almost as good as him letting me go in the first place.

Nine

Four and a half hours later, Parker and I turned onto a long, tree-lined gravel driveway beside a house I knew without a doubt to be Marc's, though I'd never been there or seen any pictures. And though Painter's directions had been about as clear as swamp water.

The setting sun shone on a large lot, open in front and wooded in the back. The house was isolated; Marc's nearest neighbor was two and a half miles down a dirt road—and a good six miles from Rosetta proper. And if the Homochitto National Forest didn't actually adjoin the property, it came damn close.

The only detraction I could see was the house itself, which had to be at least eighty years old and had definitely seen better days. But in my opinion, and no doubt in Marc's, the benefits far outweighed any material discomfort caused by outdated wiring, insufficient insulation, or peeling paint and crooked shutters.

I was out of the car the instant it stopped, long before Parker actually shut down the engine, and for a moment, the below-freezing windchill—a relative rarity for the South—stole my breath from my lungs. My boots crunched across gravel briefly before landing on dead, brittle grass. Relieved to see that the ice had melted in

Mississippi, I raced over the lawn—then skidded to a halt about a foot from an ominous, dark trail slicing across one corner of Marc's front yard. The stain was dry, and no longer bright red as it must have been hours earlier, but it stood out starkly against the dull, colorless lawn.

And the scent was unmistakable.

Blood. *Marc's* blood. He'd been dragged over the very spot where I now stood.

At my side, my hands clenched into fists so tight my fingers cramped instantly, and only when ice crystals formed on my cheeks did I realize I was crying.

My jaws clenched, I wiped frigid tears from my face and forced myself to step over the trail of Marc's blood. Then my gaze followed it up the stairs and across the uncovered concrete stoop to where it disappeared beneath the scuffed front door.

He wasn't there. I already knew that. But I couldn't stop myself from racing alongside that grisly trail, careful not to actually touch it, and up one side of the steps to the porch. I turned the knob and pushed, but the door gave less than an inch before bumping against something heavy.

Dan Painter had barricaded himself inside, just as I'd instructed. In fact, through the small gap I'd created, I could see him, standing completely still but for his nose, which twitched even as a warning rumble leaked from his throat.

"Dan, it's me. Faythe," I said, as Parker's steps clomped up the steps behind me. There wasn't room for us both to stand comfortably on the tiny stoop, so he stopped on the third step, balanced precariously to avoid stepping in Marc's blood. "Parker and I are coming in now. We need you to go ahead and Shift back, okay?"

For a moment, Dan only blinked at me and sniffed some more, and I had to remind myself that he couldn't see as much of me through the crack as I could see of him, and that his cat brain—especially under such stressful circumstances—probably wasn't thinking very clearly. But then his nose verified what I'd told him and he stood down, his growl fading into silence as he sank onto his haunches near an ancient kitchen table with spindly aluminum legs.

Taking that as permission to enter, I made room for Parker on the stoop and we pushed the door open, forcing back the heavy bureau and chest of drawers Dan had braced it with. Obviously, if we could get in, so could the bad guys, but the furniture was only intended to give Dan a chance to get out before they broke through, not to keep them out entirely.

Dan didn't begin Shifting back until we'd forced our way in, and I couldn't really blame him, so while he writhed on the floor in the grip of his transformation, we knelt to examine the bodies growing cold and stiff on Marc's floor.

Both were strays, and both were dead. But that's where the similarities ended.

The first was tall and thin, with a mop of unmanageably wavy pale brown hair. He'd probably enjoyed strength and power as a werecat that he'd never had in his human life. Not that it mattered now. Death was the great equalizer.

The skinny stray'd had the side of his head bashed in, likely by the bloodstained chair leg lying two feet from his body. Across the room lay the rest of the chair, splintered where its missing limb had been detached.

The other stray was shorter and thicker, bigger than his buddy in every respect but height. He'd likely proved more of a challenge to Marc than his gangly friend, but evidently that old saying was true: the bigger they were, the harder they fell.

This particular big bastard had fallen—probably in response to a blow from Marc—and hit his head on the coffee table now smashed to bits half under him. The gash in the back of his skull was wide enough for me to put my middle finger into. Not that I tried. There were splinters of bone in the wound, and probably even more lodged in his brain.

The entire house reeked of blood. The carpet was soaked with it, and it squished beneath my boot when I stepped in part of a puddle. And, though it horrified me no end, all I could think as I stared at the dead strays was, *At least he took two of them with him.*

No, I decided, before the first thought was even fully formed. *Marc's not dead. He sent these assholes on ahead....*

Motion to my left drew my eye as Dan Painter stood, finally human and fully nude. "Hey."

"Hey." I rose from my crouch next to the second body. "No trouble since we spoke?"

He shook his head, pulling a pair of boxers from the seat of an ancient, wobbly kitchen chair. "It's been quieter 'n a graveyard." I didn't much like his analogy, but I had to admit it was apt. "So…what's the plan?"

I wiped my hands on my jeans, though I hadn't gotten any blood on them. They just felt dirty. "We find Marc."

"What can I do?" He stepped into the shorts, then into a pair of jeans. "I want to help."

I nodded, accepting his offer, touched by the simple honesty in his statement. "Obviously we can't track him physically. So we'll have to track him by other means." Even if we'd had a scent to follow—which we didn't, thanks to the bad guy's car—we were back to that whole cats-don't-hunt-or-track-with-their-noses thing, like dogs do. We have the biology but lack the instinct. Fortunately, our particular breed of cat was gifted with human logic. Most of us, anyway. "We have to ID the one who got away. When we find him, we'll find Marc."

Parker nodded silently, and his look of confidence in

me meant more than I could have imagined. He'd been enforcing much longer than I had, and if he'd had a better place to start, he would have said so. His silence said I was getting it right. So far.

Dan clenched his cotton T-shirt in both fists and continued to watch me, waiting for his orders.

"Is the doorknob the best scent source for the guy who took Marc?" I asked him, glancing around at the ruined carpet and broken furniture. "I don't suppose you've found any of his blood in this mess?"

Dan put his arms through the sleeves of his tee and paused with the material gathered in both hands, ready to go over his head. "It's mixed with Marc's in several places, but there's one spot over by the window that's just his." He nodded his head toward the north-facing window, then pulled the shirt over his skull. "There ain't much of it, but it might help."

"Thanks." I bent to get a good whiff of the doorknob, then stepped carefully toward the window, where I knelt to compare the scent of the vaguely hand-shaped carpet stain to that on the knob. They were from the same tom. "Okay, Dan, I need a box cutter, or a sharp serrated knife and a plastic sandwich bag." Dan headed into the kitchen and I turned to Parker, who'd begun to stack pieces of the broken furniture in a pile near the door. "I'm gonna call in a report, then I'll help with the cleanup."

He nodded and continued cleaning as I dug my phone from my pocket and autodialed my dad.

"Faythe?" my father said into my ear.

"Yeah, it's me. We're here and we're safe, at least for the moment." His sigh of relief was brief but real; I'd put to rest his fear that we'd been ambushed again, or that we'd walked into a trap. "We're going to clean up the worst of the mess then go talk to a few strays and see if we can identify the one who got away with Marc."

"Faythe—"

"Dad, I know what I'm doing. We'll be careful. I'm not going to sit here licking my fur while Marc's out there suffering who knows what." *At least, I hope he's still out there,* some soft, traitorous voice whispered from deep in my mind.

But not from my heart. My heart knew he was still alive, no matter how much blood he'd lost.

Springs creaked as my dad leaned forward in his chair, two hundred fifty miles away. "Faythe, you don't have enough experience interrogating—"

"We won't be interrogating, we'll be *interviewing*..." That's like interrogating without throwing punches.

"And Dan Painter doesn't have any."

"But we have Parker, and he's been with you for years. We'll be fine." I squatted next to the wall and dug my fingertips beneath the baseboard, heedless of the grime that lodged beneath my nails.

"No. I'm bringing Brian home on the next flight from Atlanta—"

"Brian has no more experience than *I* do!" Irritation fueled me as I jerked the board away from the wall. Wood splintered, and a two-foot length of trim broke off in my hands.

Technically Brian Taylor been enforcing for his father for a couple of years before coming to work for mine. But I was on the fast track toward Alphadom, and he hadn't yet moved beyond working with his fists. "He's never even *seen* an interrogation!"

"Which is why he's coming home," my father continued, and I cursed myself silently for interrupting. My dad was upset, too, but he never let grief or worry impede his logic. "I'm sending you one of the wonder twins. Do you want Jace or Ethan?"

I had to think about that for a moment. They were both great fighters, and I'd trust either with my life. But Ethan had more experience with interrogation—despite what

I'd told my father, I had a feeling it might come down to a few thrown punches—and while I knew Jace would do everything he could to help us find Marc, his presence in Marc's house would be uncomfortable for both of us. For all three of us, once Marc was back.

"Ethan. But, Dad, it'll take him hours to get here. We can't wait that long." Especially considering that Marc had already been missing—and bleeding—for five hours.

"You can, and you *will.*"

Fear washed over me, disguised as anger, and my arm shot out before I could stop it. The detached strip of wood flew across the room and lodged in the Sheetrock over Marc's couch.

Oops.

My father sighed again. "Do I even want to know what that was?"

I ignored his question and twisted to put my back to Dan and Parker, who were watching me in a mixture of surprise and worry. "Do you *want* Marc to die?" I demanded, forgetting to think before I spoke as fear and frustration crested inside me.

"I'm going to pretend I didn't hear that." My father's voice had gone hard, but it was a brittle hardness, as if one more word from me might shatter his composure. That rare glimpse into my Alpha's psyche scared me, as if I were seeing something I shouldn't. A weakness.

I made myself take a deep breath. A long one. My dad was just as worried about Marc as I was. But he had to think about the rest of us, too.

"Faythe, if he can't hold on for a few more hours, there's nothing we can do for him." The weariness in his voice told me exactly what it cost him to admit that. "Clean up the mess and bury the bodies." Because our incinerator was a couple hundred miles away and we couldn't spare anyone to pick up the corpses. "Get me a list of the strays you want to talk to, and I'll get you any information we have about them. By then, Ethan will be there."

"Dad…"

"That's final, Faythe," he said. My hands curled into fists, but I resisted throwing anything that time.

"Fine." The concession tasted bitter on my tongue, and I couldn't spit it out fast enough.

The chair springs squealed again, slowly, and I knew my dad was leaning back in his chair now, probably with his free hand over his eyes. "We'll get him back."

"I know." But I *didn't* know that. Not for sure. Nor did I know how to handle the next few hours of not searching for Marc.

I said goodbye to my father and Alpha, closed my phone and slid it into my pocket. Then I looked up to take the steak knife Dan offered me, handle first. "What's it for?" he asked, and it took me a moment to realize he meant the knife. It takes a brave man to hand an angry werecat a knife. Especially when he doesn't know what she plans to do with it.

"It's for the scent sample." I dug at the edge of the carpet, now exposed by the missing section of baseboard, and pulled it up from the floor. At first, I only got slack, but another tug pulled a large section of carpet out from under the remaining boards, so that I could roll it back like a tortilla.

I plunged the serrated blade into the raised bit of carpet and began to saw, perversely satisfied when the thick, matted weave resisted me, because that meant I could saw harder, pretending my blade sank into my enemy's flesh with each vicious stroke.

Several minutes later I'd removed an uneven square of carpet, containing most of the hand-shaped bloodstain. Parker held the plastic bag open for me, and I dropped the sample in, then pressed the seal to close it.

"Is that for your lab?" Dan asked, vague excitement edging the fear in his eye as he stared at the morbid package balanced on my palm.

"Lab?" I stood and set the carpet sample on top of the bureau once again blocking the front door.

Dan picked up the knife and crossed the living room into the tiny, galley-style kitchen to drop it in the sink. "Marc said you guys have your own lab up in Washington State, where this doctor's trying to figure out why you don't have more girls."

"Ohhh." I knelt to pull a photo of myself from a ruined frame and dropped the mangled wood and glass into the trash bag Painter held out. The picture was from my senior year in high school. It was definitely time to have some new ones taken. "You mean Dr. Eames."

John Eames was a geneticist belonging to one of the northwestern Prides. For the past few years, he'd used his resources and his spare time to try to bridge the gap between the number of male and female babies born into the American Prides. But in the process, he'd discovered everything we now knew about werecat genetics and the ability of a werecat to procreate with humans. So I could see why Dan might be confused.

"Unfortunately, the lab isn't actually ours. Dr. Eames just uses it for his own purposes—*our* purposes—after hours. And I don't think his skills would do us much good without another, identified sample to compare this one to." I tossed my head toward the square of carpet. "Fortunately, we have all the equipment we need right here." I tapped my nose and smiled grimly at Dan.

He raised one eyebrow. "We're going to sniff it?"

I frowned, until I realized he was joking. "You're going to make a list of every stray you know and we're going to take the sample around and let *them* sniff it, until someone can give us a name to go with the scent."

"What if no one recognizes it?"

"That won't happen." Parker stood on the couch and braced one hand against the wall while he pulled the baseboard I'd thrown from the Sheetrock it had lodged in. Then he turned, gesturing with the oak strip as he spoke. "You guys may not be as community oriented out here in the free zone as we are in Pride territory, but you wouldn't have survived so long on your own without keeping an eye on your rivals. There will be *someone* out here who can tell us *exactly* who this blood belongs to." At his last word, he dropped the wooden board into a heavy-duty trash bag and tied it off.

Dan bent to haul the busted coffee table from beneath the heavier of the dead strays. "What if they won't talk to us?"

I met his eyes boldly, to leave no doubt about my meaning. "They won't have that option."

Dan nodded without a word and sat down at the table to start his list, and while he was writing, Parker and I got started on the living room.

I'd never seen a bigger or bloodier mess than the disaster in Marc's living room, and with any luck, I never would. I memorized the names and addresses of the dead strays before wrapping their wallets—including all their money, credit cards and ID—up in plastic with the corpses. We stacked them in the kitchen, where they took up easily half of the available floor space.

By then Dan was done writing. He waved me over to the table and slid a sheet of notebook paper toward me, and I frowned down at it. "This is it?" There were five full names on the paper and four more last names.

We'd been attacked by more than *twenty* strays in the ambush, and there were even more we'd heard but hadn't seen. How could he know so few of them?

He must have seen the suspicion on my face, because he rushed to explain. "These are the only ones I've got names for. I know a bunch more by scent, though."

"So do we," I snapped, thinking of all the scents I'd smelled during the ambush. Parker frowned at me, and I nodded, huffing in frustration. I knew Dan was doing his best. But his best wasn't good enough for Marc. Still…I shrugged. "It's a place to start." I sank into a chair and pulled my phone from my pocket to report the names to my father.

When I hung up, we went back to cleaning. All the living room furniture was broken, except for the couch, and since the sun had truly set by then, we tossed piece after piece into the backyard to be disposed of later.

The living room carpet was ruined. It took all three of us to pull it free from the carpet tacks running along the walls and roll it up, then haul it through the kitchen and out the back door. Fortunately, beneath the blood-soaked padding was the original floor: tough, lacquered hardwood, which looked better than ever after we'd ruined two sponge mop heads cleaning it.

When the house was in fairly good order—if mostly bare—we hauled the plastic-wrapped bodies into the woods behind Marc's house and buried them in a single grave, a task I hated only marginally less than wrestling with rank, blood-soaked carpet.

It was nearly ten o'clock by the time we finished the late-night burial. Marc only had one bathroom, and the guys were nice enough to let me shower first. When I was dry but for my hair, I put two frozen pizzas into the oven, and when Dan emerged from the bathroom, he sat down with his list and tried to think of any names he might have forgotten. Without much luck.

As I was bending to take the first pizza out of the oven, headlights flashed in the front window and my cell phone rang out from my pocket. I set the pizza on the counter and answered my phone.

"It's me," Ethan said into my ear. "Let me in."

The guys pulled the furniture away from the front

door while I removed the second pizza, and when I kicked the oven door shut and turned around, Ethan was there, his arms already open for a hug.

In my brother's arms, I could no longer resist the tears I'd held back. I cried on his shoulder, trying not to drip snot on his shirt while he rubbed my back. "We'll find him, Faythe."

I nodded and pulled from his grasp, wiping my face with a rough paper towel from the counter. "Damn right."

Ethan cut the pizza and tossed uneven slices onto four paper plates while I dug several cans of Coke from the fridge. "Eat fast."

While the guys chewed, I called my dad to tell him Ethan had arrived safely and to give him a report. "The house is clean. We had to pull up the carpet, but the floor beneath it is in pretty good shape. Marc's landlord should thank us. The bodies are buried, but we'll need to dispose of the broken furniture, as well as the carpet and padding."

"Take the furniture to the town dump. You can bring the rest of the mess with you when you come home, and we'll burn it. Fortunately," my father continued, as I popped open my can and drank from it, "with the temperature so low, it shouldn't start to smell for at least a couple of days."

I wanted to ask what would happen if we hadn't found Marc in a couple of days, but I didn't, because I already knew the answer. If we hadn't found him by then, we wouldn't find him alive.

"Okay, about these names…" A pencil tapped against paper, and I knew my dad was staring at the list I'd given him. "Michael's given me addresses for two of them, but we have no record of the other three." Which wasn't much of a surprise. We tried to keep up with the strays living near our territory, but our lists became outdated fairly quickly, as strays were killed in skirmishes and others popped up to replace them. "And I can't do much with the partials."

"I figured." I sighed, already tired of dead ends. "Just give me what you have, please." I scribbled as my father spoke, then thanked him for the information.

"Ground rules," he began, before I could hang up gracefully, and I glanced around the table to make sure the guys were all listening. "Talk to them one at a time. Strays are loners, so that shouldn't be too hard. But then again, things seem to be changing in the free zone, so you never know. But if you can't get a stray by himself, don't approach him. Just follow him until he is alone. Got it?"

"Of course," I said, and all around the table, the guys nodded silently.

"You can do the talking, but Ethan and Parker are in charge if *persuasion* proves necessary."

I pouted a bit over that one. I'd never played bad cop, and couldn't think of a more appropriate time to start. But if I argued, my dad would pull me off the case, regardless of my relationship to Marc. Because if that relationship got in the way of my work, it would put us all in danger.

"And keep me updated."

"We will."

Again, I started to say goodbye, but again my father interrupted. "Ethan?"

"Yeah?" my brother said in the general direction of my phone, around a mouthful of pizza crust.

"Make sure she eats something."

I rolled my eyes, but Ethan grinned and washed his bite down with half a can of Coke. "No problem."

I said goodbye to my father and slid my phone into my pocket, then snatched a slice of pizza from my untouched plate, saluting my brother with it to demonstrate my cooperation. "Let's go."

Parker grabbed his keys while Dan shrugged into his jacket, and they all followed me out the front door, Ethan carrying the rest of my dinner for me. But I couldn't think about food, and knew I would have no appetite until we'd gotten Marc back. Alive.

And eliminated the sorry bastards who'd taken him.

Ten

"So, who *is* Ben Feldman?" I leaned forward from the middle row, resting my elbows on the back of the passenger seat, inches from Dan's head. Parker was driving, because it was his car, and Dan won shotgun by default, because he was the one with the directions.

Feldman was the only stray on the list whose address Dan knew without consulting the information my father had given us.

The stray turned slightly in his seat to face me and Ethan, who sat on my left. "Feldman got bit about seven years ago. That makes him kinda old for a stray, right?"

I shrugged. "I guess." Dr. Carver claimed that because of their typically violent lifestyle, the average postinfection life span for a stray was under three years. I didn't know if that was true, but Dan didn't seem to doubt it. He'd probably heard those figures from Marc, who'd already lived far beyond that average.

Ben Feldman... Why did that sound familiar? "Would this be the same Ben you told about us coming through the free zone on Friday night?"

"Uh, yeah." Dan glanced at Ethan, then back at me. "Before I met Marc, everything I knew about werecats I got from Ben Feldman."

I leaned back in my seat and stared out at the dark road, thinking for a moment. "Was Feldman one of the cats who ambushed us the other night?"

"No, but I couldn't swear he wasn't in with the second wave."

Which we'd never actually seen.

"So, are we assuming this is related to the ambush?" Parker glanced from me to Ethan in the rearview mirror.

"Until we find evidence to the contrary, yes." I nodded, crossing my arms over my chest. "It's too much of a coincidence, otherwise." Feldman *had* to be connected to the ambush, because he was the only one Dan had told about our stop in Natchez.

"I can't see Ben being mixed up in any of this. He's a good guy." Dan loosened his seat belt and twisted even farther in his seat, as if showing us his earnest expression would convince us. "Out of all the guys on that list, he's the one I'd guess would help us out. He's big and he's got a temper, but he's smart and he knows what's right."

"Oh, good!" Ethan's green eyes brightened with mock mirth. "Maybe instead of throwing empty beer bottles at us when we wake him up in the middle of the night, he'll show us in and serve hot tea!"

Dan glared at him, but Ethan's good humor couldn't be stifled. Even at midnight, on a strange highway in the free zone.

Unfortunately, after nearly an hour of driving, we got neither empty bottles nor hot tea, because Mr. Feldman—our best shot at peaceful information, in Dan's opinion—wasn't home. So we moved down the list to Hooper Galloway, because he lived the closest to Feldman.

Galloway lived in a tiny rental house crowded into a street already packed with dozens more just like his. There was no front yard to speak of, and standing on his porch in the middle of the night made me nervous. I was sure some nosy, insomniac neighbor was peering through a dusty set of miniblinds at that very moment, wondering why a young woman and three large men were knocking on the Galloway boy's door at nearly one in the morning.

But as thoroughly as I scanned the darkness, I could detect no one watching. The streetlight in front of the house was busted, and human eyes wouldn't have been able to see much of us at all.

When Dan's first, polite knock got no response, Parker took over, pounding on the door with a volume and tempo which could not be ignored. We were assuming Galloway was home, based on the car parked in the driveway, which reeked of stray. So I nodded when Parker asked me with a mimed knock whether or not he should give it another try. But that proved unnecessary, as uneven footsteps thumped toward us from within the house.

The white-painted steel front door opened, leaving only a storm door between me and Hooper Galloway. Who obviously wasn't yet fully awake. "This better be—" he began, voice rough with sleep. Then his gaze found me briefly before flicking to the three large toms at my back. Galloway's eyes widened when his gaze landed on Dan, whom he clearly recognized, but he did *not* invite us in.

"Hooper Galloway?" I asked, and his eyes narrowed, nostrils finally flaring to confirm my species. Most strays would live and die without ever laying eyes on a tabby, and I knew from his own scent that Galloway had not been among the toms who'd attacked us three nights before.

"Who the hell are you?" Spoken like a man who has no idea that a screen door isn't enough of a barrier between himself and the serious trouble I was dying to unleash on someone.

But I kept my temper in check; his voluntary cooperation would get us information much faster than having to beat it out of him. As much fun as that might have been, under the circumstances. "My name is Faythe Sanders, and I'm an enforcer for the south-central Pride. As are two of the gentlemen behind me. We'd like to ask you a few questions. May we come in?"

Galloway only blinked at me, and I could almost see comprehension slide across his features as my words sank in. One by one, evidently. Fear glinted in his eyes, but it was pigheaded stubbornness that tightened his grip on the screen door handle. As if that would keep us out.

I raised both eyebrows and let a wry smile turn up one corner of my mouth. "Whoops. I phrased that as a question, didn't I? My mistake." I stepped back and Ethan wrapped one hand around the door handle—one of those old, flimsy metal ones with a button at the top for your thumb—and pulled it right out of the door frame with a single tug. Metal screws squealed as they tore free from the wood, and Ethan stepped past me holding the door with both hands.

I could have done that myself, of course, but I was supposed to be playing the good cop, which meant I didn't get to break stuff unless the whole thing went downhill and we went for plan B: bad cop/worse cop.

"Now, Mr. Galloway, you have two choices. You can either step aside and let us in, or you can hold your ground and be forcibly removed, just like your door."

He moved back faster than I could catch more than a whiff of his fresh fear.

"Thank you." I stepped past Galloway into his living room, flipping the switch as I went. Dim light flooded the room from a cheap ceiling-fan fixture overhead, and I made myself at home on the ratty futon serving as his couch while the guys followed me inside. Parker was the last one in, and he bolted the still-functioning door while Ethan propped the storm door against a bare, white wall.

"What's…uh…going on?" Galloway shrugged nervously, addressing his question to Dan, the only one of us he might—almost—trust.

"You know Marc Ramos, right?" Dan sat next to me on the futon and gestured for Galloway to sit in the only chair, while Ethan and Parker remained standing—a constant and obvious threat.

Galloway nodded hesitantly, sinking into a decent-looking overstuffed armchair—easily the nicest piece of furniture in the room. And probably in the house. "That big Mexican tom who got kicked out…" His own words seemed to sink in, and his voice faded as his gaze traveled over us again. "You're looking for Marc? What did he do?"

I raised one eyebrow over his assumption that we were trying to *apprehend* Marc.

"He disappeared." I glanced at Ethan, unsure how much to tell the stray before asking our questions. But Galloway's expression had shifted from fear to genuine eagerness and curiosity. This was a man *looking* for information, rather than hiding it.

Ethan shrugged, leaving the decision up to me, so I turned back to the stray. "Do you have any idea where Marc is, or who he's with?"

Galloway appeared confused. "Why would I? He's *your* friend. And rumor has it you two are *more* than just friends."

I started to roll my eyes and ignore the implication—accurate though it was—but stopped when I recognized an opportunity to drive home my determination. "That's right. And I'd do *anything* to find him, and the bastard who took him."

"Whoa, someone *took* him?" Galloway sat straighter in his chair and ran one hand through shaggy black hair as he glanced at Dan for confirmation. "I thought you meant he'd skipped town or something."

"No." I leaned forward to underline the importance of what I was about to say. "He was taken by force, and we'll get him back the same way, if necessary. Did his abduction have anything to do with the attack on our caravan on Friday?"

"What attack?" Galloway scrunched his forehead in an exaggerated look of confusion, and his heart beat just a little bit faster. Which gave me a baseline. His reaction said he knew something about the ambush, but his *lack* of a reaction earlier said that he truly knew nothing about what happened to Marc.

Either that, or he was a *really* good actor. I wasn't prepared to give Galloway that much credit yet.

"You were in the second wave of the ambush, weren't you?" I pinned him with my gaze, and I *swear* the tom actually squirmed in his chair. *There goes the good-actor theory....*

"I don't know what you're—"

But I'd already moved on. "We thought you were after the tabbies," I said, still watching him as if I could read his mind just by looking into his eyes. "But you were after Marc, weren't you? Why?"

Galloway's gaze flicked quickly from me, to Ethan, to Parker, and back again, and he began to fidget with a loose thread on the arm of his chair. "Look, I'm not the one you want to talk to about this—"

"But you're the one who's *here*." Parker took a menacing step forward, arms crossed over his chest. "So go easy on yourself. Tell us what the hell you guys want with Marc."

"They don't *want* Marc, they want him *dead*." Galloway sighed, as if giving up the information had somehow tarnished his badge of honor.

It had bruised my soul.

Terror clenched around my heart so tightly that at first it refused to beat. They wanted Marc dead, and now he was missing, all except for several pints of his blood. Had they gotten what they wanted?

No. I couldn't make myself believe it. Not while there were still questions unanswered by that theory.

If they'd killed Marc, why take his body and leave the others?

I took a deep breath and nodded to Ethan's questioning gaze to tell him I was all right. Then I turned back to Galloway and forced myself to focus. "They?"

"Well, it wasn't *my* idea! I just do what I'm told."

"By whom?" I scooted to the edge of the futon, when what I really wanted to do was stand up and pace. Pacing helped me think. But I sat still, because the stray would likely read my pacing as aggression—like a caged cat. Not a good impression coming from the "good" cop.

He glanced at Dan, as if for permission, or an opinion about what he was about to say, but Dan could only shrug, clearly at a loss. "Pete Yarnell."

The name sounded familiar. Dan nodded on the edge of my vision, and I turned to him. "You know Pete?"

"I met him a couple of times. His name's on the list."

Oh, yeah. He was the only tom my father hadn't been able to find an address for.

"Man, you made them a *list?*" Galloway looked both shocked and impressed by Dan's nerve. "You better watch it. They'll be after you next."

My head swiveled in his direction so fast I got an instant headache. "Next, after whom? Marc? Why are they after Marc?"

Galloway closed his eyes briefly, then met my gaze reluctantly, as if already ashamed by what he was about to admit. "I don't know who took your boyfriend, or what they want. But it wasn't one of us. At least, not that I know of. On Friday, we were trying to take him out of the picture, but that obviously didn't work. And I haven't heard anything about a second attempt."

"Why was there a *first* attempt?" Ethan stepped closer to me for a better view of our new informant.

"Because he's a fucking *traitor!*" Galloway sat straighter, his courage evidently bolstered by what he saw as the unblemished truth. Then he turned to Dan. "And they won't be very happy with *you,* either, when they find out you're picking up where Marc left off."

Frustrated almost beyond rational thought, I turned to Dan. "What the *hell* is he talking about?"

He sighed. "Pete thinks Marc's still working for your dad."

I shook my head; comprehension wouldn't come. "Why would he think that?"

"Because nobody really believes he got kicked out in some kind o' political squabble." Dan hesitated, clearly preparing to say something I wasn't going to like. "You have to understand how it looks to them. To the strays that don't know Marc." He gestured at Galloway as an example. "Marc's a legend. A stray living with the Pride cats, bangin' one of their princesses—no offense—" I waved him on, and he continued "—doin' the messy jobs so the Pride cats don't have to get their hands dirty."

"That's not true!" I snapped. "We're *all* out there getting our hands dirty. Enforcers fight nearly every day to protect and defend our territory—not to mention the entire *species*—from trespassers stomping all over our land and rogues out there making no attempt to hide their existence from humans. We're trying to keep everyone safe. Both Pride *and* stray."

Dan rolled his eyes. "I get it. You're the National Guard and the fuckin' ASPCA all rolled into one. But what *they* see is a hired gun that's been pickin' them off one by one for the last decade or so. And now he's livin' here *with* them—"

"Still picking us off one at a time," Galloway finished for him.

I frowned at him. "What does that mean?"

"Rumor has it he's here to clean house for the Prides," Dan said. "To rid the free zone of strays, once and for all."

"What?" I felt my eyebrows arch halfway up my forehead, and my fellow Pride cats looked just as upset as I was by that little nugget of information. "Why the *hell* would they think that?" I demanded. "Marc's a stray, just like everyone else here."

"He's a stray, but *not* like everybody else," Painter insisted, clearly surprised that I couldn't see his point. "He's got training and knowledge and connections. He's a threat. And everyone here knows where his loyalties lie, and it ain't with every common stray that crosses his path."

I laughed bitterly at the irony, and looked at Ethan. "If they only knew."

"Knew what?" Galloway glanced back and forth between us. If he were in cat form, his eager ears would have swiveled in my direction.

"The Prides don't want Marc." I spit the vile truth, hating each word as I said it. "My father's the only Alpha who ever accepted a stray into a Pride, and he's paying for that right now." I made myself stop because I wasn't sure how much Dan and Galloway knew about my father's political problems. Or how much they *should* know, considering Dan's habit of sharing information with our enemies and Galloway's tendency to work for them. "Marc's about as welcome in most of the Prides as he is here."

Painter shrugged, a gesture that was starting to look habitual. "Well, at least the Pride cats aren't trying to kill him."

Not so far, anyway.

"So, wait..." Parker said to Galloway, drawing me back on track. "What do you mean, Marc's picking you off one at a time?"

Galloway shrugged. "Just what I said. Guys are going missing. Just…gone. And everyone knows it's Marc. He's killing them, for your dad."

"No, he isn't!" I shouted, as Ethan said, "Whoa, how do they know it's Marc?"

"And how many have gone missing?" Parker asked.

"I don't know. Three? Four?" Galloway looked to Dan for confirmation, but he just shrugged.

"I wasn't keeping count."

I rubbed my forehead, wishing desperately for a painkiller strong enough to work on werecats for more than an hour at a time. "If you haven't found any bodies, how do you know they're dead? And what makes you think Marc's responsible?"

"Because this wasn't happening before he came here. And if they aren't dead, where the hell are they?"

"Okay, one fact at a time," I said, trying to sort it all out in my head. "Have you talked to their employers? Or landlords? Did any of the missing toms quit their jobs, or leave a forwarding address?"

Galloway frowned. "I have no idea. I don't even know if anyone's tried any of that. I just know that no one's seen them in a while."

And that basically summed up the structure of werecat life in the free zone. There were no Alphas to keep track of everyone, and no enforcers to keep everyone safe. If you were killed, it might be days, or even weeks, before someone noticed—*if* anyone noticed—because for the most part, strays were loners. They didn't see each other on a regular basis, and had no obligation to check in or to contribute to the society.

"So, the truth is that you don't *know* they're dead. Or even that they're actually missing. You just know you haven't seen them in a while." I couldn't quite control the patronizing quality of my voice.

"They're gone," Galloway insisted. The firm line of

his mouth told me how serious he considered the situation, and the fact that Marc had been attacked twice now told me the other strays were taking it just as seriously.

Figures. It *would* take disaster to draw strays together.

"How long has this been going on?"

Galloway glanced at Dan again for help. "A month?"

Dan nodded, but I was unconvinced. "Marc's been here for more than two months," I snapped. "Your theory's about as watertight as the *Titanic.*"

"All I know is this wasn't going on *before* he got here." Galloway shrugged, unbothered by my skepticism.

"So, you guys think Marc's behind this series of disappearances, so you tried to kill him." But something was nagging at the back of my mind. "Why do it with all of us around? He's here alone day after day, but you waited to attack until he had serious backup."

Galloway huffed in frustration. "Pete said it would make a statement. You and your boys were supposed to be there as witnesses, to go back and tell your dad that we're not going to be messed with anymore. That if there's power in numbers, we have it now, too. But that kind of backfired on us."

Damn right.

Ethan sank onto the futon next to me, now that it was clear that Galloway posed no threat. "So, you guys admit to trying to kill Marc. But not to taking him?"

Galloway rolled small, dark eyes. "Because we *didn't* take him. If one of us had done this, they'd have left the body. That message, again."

But I was following Ethan's logic, even if our unwilling host wasn't. "Well, I can guarantee you that Marc isn't behind those other disappearances. So doesn't it stand to reason that whoever took those other toms probably took Marc, too?"

Dan nodded, and after a second to think it over, even

Galloway looked half-convinced, if startled by the possibility. "But why?"

"Good question. And I have an even better one." I turned to Parker with one hand outstretched. "Let me have the sample."

Parker pulled the plastic bag from his bulging back pocket and handed it over. I opened the seal and leaned forward to hold the bag in front of our host's face. "Do you recognize this scent?"

Galloway leaned forward and sniffed dramatically, and recognition showed clearly on his features. For a moment, I thought he might resist answering again. But then he simply met my gaze and nodded. "Adam Eckard. Where did you get this? Is he dead?"

"No, but these two are." I handed the sample to Parker and leaned back on the futon to dig a scrap of paper from my right hip pocket, then gave it to Galloway, who unfolded it and read with a blank expression. "Did you know them?"

"Not personally," he said, handing the paper back. "Why?"

"Two hours ago, we dragged their corpses from Marc's living room floor. That's his carpet soaked in Eckard's blood."

Galloway blinked at me while he processed the new information. "*They* went after Marc?"

I nodded. "These two died in the fight." I held up the scrap of paper. "And Eckard dragged Marc across his own lawn and shoved him into a car, then drove off with him. That surprises you?"

"Yeah." Galloway nodded, and his forehead furrowed with confusion. "They were all three with me in the second group on Friday night. We were stationed farther down the road, because we weren't sure where the car would actually break down. But we were supposed to kill Marc in front of you. Not *take* him. I haven't heard anything more about any of it since then. And I have no idea why they'd take those other toms." Which we all now seemed to believe was the case. "They're strays, just like the rest of us."

I believed him. I didn't *want* to, but he was too tired, too stressed and too bad an actor to lie his way out of this one.

"You have a pen?" I asked Ethan. My brother pulled a wallet-size pen from his pocket and handed it to me, along with a mini-notepad. I gave them both to Galloway. "I need the names of the other missing toms."

Galloway took the pen and paper without argument. "You guys took down fifteen or so of us on Friday night, and rumor has it Marc got off with little more than a scratch from the whole thing." He met my eyes, his own dulled by bleak fear. "So if they can get Marc, what's to stop them from getting any one of the rest of us?"

I gave him a grim smile as he sat with his pen poised over the paper. "We are."

Eleven

I called my dad on the drive back to Marc's house, both to give him the requested update, and because Galloway hadn't known Adam Eckard's address.

"Hello?" my father croaked into my ear, as Parker turned left onto a small country highway.

"It's me. Did I wake you up?"

"I was just dozing." Leather creaked, and I pictured my father sitting up on the sofa in his office. "You have a report?"

"Yeah. We just spoke to Hooper Galloway, at the address you gave us."

"Good." He sounded more awake now, and his socked feet brushed softly against the floor. "Injuries?"

I grinned, though only Ethan could see my face in the passing glow from a streetlight. "Nothing but Galloway's pride."

"Collateral damage?"

"One storm door." Ethan returned my grin.

My father sighed, and springs groaned over the line as he sank into his desk chair. "I guess it could have been worse. What did you find out?"

"We took a sample of blood from the stray who got away with Marc, and Galloway says it belongs to a tom named Adam Eckard. He's not on our list, so we need whatever you can find out about him. Specifically, his address and anything you can get on his car. Same for the two dead toms, if you can. We're not sure who was driving, and neither of the corpses was in possession of a set of keys."

"I'll put Owen on it as soon as I hang up," my father promised. "Anything else?"

"Yeah." I braced myself with one hand on the back of Dan's seat as Parker took a sharp turn. "We misunderstood the motive for the ambush. Manx and I weren't the target. Marc was. Galloway says they were supposed to kill him in front of us, to send a message."

My father growled softly into my ear. "Sounds like they're trying to pick a fight."

"*They* think they're trying to end one. Several strays have gone missing in the area over the past month. They're presumed dead, and Marc is presumed responsible. But it looks to us like Eckard and the dead toms are to blame. Though I wouldn't be surprised to find out they're working *with* or *for* someone else."

"You have names for the missing strays?" A drawer squealed open over the line, and something smacked lightly onto the surface of my dad's desk. Probably a legal pad.

"Yeah." I read him the list of three names Galloway had given me, along with the question mark at the bottom of the list—Galloway was sure there had been a fourth, but couldn't remember his name.

"I'll call you in the morning with whatever we can dig up. Though Michael could probably dig a lot faster." But Michael was in Georgia and couldn't be spared until Manx's trial was over. My dad's palm scratched against the receiver, stifling his yawn. "I want you all to get some sleep. There's nothing more you can do tonight, without an address."

I thought about arguing—I wasn't sure I could sleep

with Marc missing in action—but for once I was too tired to bicker. So I changed the subject. "How's Kaci?"

"Exhausted." Concern echoed in his voice and probably in his posture. "She's going to be seriously ill soon if she doesn't Shift."

"I know." I sighed and stared out the window as a series of bare, frozen fields flew by in the dark. "We were really close this afternoon, though. I'm hoping I can talk her into it as soon as I get back."

"Good." He paused and yawned again, triggering one of my own. "Get some sleep."

"I'll try."

It was nearly three in the morning when we got back to Marc's house. Dan crashed on the couch, and Ethan, Parker and I curled up together on Marc's bed, like a pile of lions. I honestly don't think I could have slept surrounded by Marc's scent in his absence, if not for the shared warmth and the steady, comforting beats of two familiar hearts. And as it was, I didn't sleep *well.* I was haunted by images of Marc, lying dead in a bare hole in the ground, in a congealing pool of his own blood, while scavengers picked the flesh from his bones.

I woke up in a cold sweat, with tears still damp on my face. Ethan's arm lay over my shoulder, as if he'd tried to comfort me in my sleep.

It was still dark outside. The alarm clock read five forty-five. I was awake for good.

Ethan and Parker were still sleeping, so I snuck out of bed and tiptoed to the front of the house in my socks, only pausing to grab my cell phone from Marc's nightstand. To my surprise, Dan Painter sat at the kitchen table, holding a can of Coke, damp with condensation, in spite of the chill in the poorly insulated room. His cell phone lay on the table in front of him.

"What are you doing up?" I padded past him into the kitchen in my thick, fuzzy socks.

"Tetris." He held up the phone so I could see the colored bricks stacking up across his screen. "Couldn't sleep."

"Me, neither." I pulled the empty carafe from the coffeemaker and ran water into it from the sink. "Wouldn't you rather have coffee?" I asked, eyeing the cold can.

"I was afraid it'd wake you up."

I gave him a small smile, thanking him for the courtesy. Then I reached overhead and started opening cabinets, looking for the coffee and filters.

"Second from the left, on the bottom shelf."

Damn it. Dan Painter knew where Marc kept his stuff, and I didn't. For about the thousandth time in the past few days, frustration raged through me, intensifying my fear and anger on Marc's behalf. Being separated from him sucked. But not knowing whether he was dead or alive was *torture.*

I grabbed a filter and a bag of ground coffee from the bottom shelf and dumped a generous pile of the latter into the former. When the coffee was brewing, the very scent gifting me with rational thought in spite of my exhausted, emotionally drained state, I pulled out the chair opposite Dan and dropped into it. "Why can't you sleep?"

Dan stared at the can he twisted on the cracked table surface. "Guilty conscience."

My heart beat harder in sympathy. "Dan, this is not your fault."

He shrugged, still avoiding my eyes. "If it was me instead of him, this never woulda happened. He woulda stopped 'em."

I sighed. He was probably right—after all, we were talking about *Marc*—but his guilt was totally misplaced. "You weren't *there,* Dan. There was nothing you could do."

He looked unconvinced, but before I could think of a more convincing argument, my phone rang from the pocket of my pj pants and I stood as I answered it, padding to the cabinets in search of coffee mugs.

"Did I wake you?" my father asked, his voice rough with exhaustion.

"No, I'm up. Did you find anything?"

"Owen found Eckard's address, but we had to call Michael to find out what he drives. I have no idea how he gathers information like that so quickly."

"He has friends in the Dallas PD, and serious computer skills." The first cabinet held only paper plates and a case of Coke, so I moved on to the next one.

"Do you have something to write with?"

I glanced around the tiny kitchen and found a pad of Post-it notes in a magnetic case stuck to the fridge, and a chewed-up pencil in the silverware compartment of the otherwise empty dish drainer. "Yeah, go ahead."

I wrote as my father read Adam Eckard's address, then noted that he drove a black 2001 Ford Explorer. "Thanks, Dad. We'll be on the road before the sun comes up."

"It's a bit of a drive, and if he works a normal nine-to-five, you probably won't catch him before work."

I shrugged, though he couldn't see me. "If not, we'll check out his place."

My father sighed. "Be careful, Faythe."

"I will." Finally, the third and last cabinet yielded three coffee mugs and a half-empty bag of powdered sugar. There was no creamer, because Marc took his coffee black.

The sugar was for French toast, his favorite breakfast. He ate half a loaf at a time.

After I hung up, I poured myself a mug of coffee with extra sugar—trying to make up for the lack of creamer—and took my mug into the bathroom along with shampoo and a change of clothes from my bag. I'd wake the guys up *after* my shower, because otherwise, they'd use all the hot water before I got a shot at it.

When I got out of the shower, my coffee was cool enough to drink—if not quite sweet enough—and I emerged from the bathroom ten minutes later with mostly dry hair and an empty mug. All three guys sat at the table, Ethan and Dan drinking from Marc's last two mugs, while Parker cradled a white foam cup he'd found in one of the cabinets.

"You guys get showered and dressed." I poured the last of the coffee into my mug and turned to face them, leaning against the countertop. "Dad came through with Eckard's address, and that's our first stop."

"We know." Ethan waved the Post-it I'd scribbled on.

Parker stood and drained his cup. "I'll make breakfast if you'll start some bacon while I shower."

"Deal." I wasn't much of a cook, but even I could handle throwing a few strips of meat into a skillet.

Twenty minutes later, Ethan—the last to shower—emerged from the bathroom barefoot and shirtless, a strand of black hair plastered to his forehead. He slid into the fourth chair just as Parker set down two paper plates piled with a dozen fried eggs. Ethan snatched a strip of bacon from another plate—we'd cooked two pounds—while Parker went back for twelve pieces of buttered toast and a jar of grape jelly.

Marc didn't have milk or juice, so I was on my third cup of bitter black coffee. It was nasty, but after only two and a half hours of sleep, it was also necessary.

We left the house before seven in the morning, but it took us nearly an hour to get from Rosetta to Fayette, where Eckard lived. Plus another twenty minutes to find his house. Adam Eckard lived in the right half of a duplex, and shared his driveway with the left half of the duplex next door. His side of the driveway was empty, except for several oil stains, but we knocked on the door just in case. Or rather, I knocked on the door.

Since we couldn't force our way inside in broad

daylight, the guys watched from the car as I stood on the double front porch alone. I was confident I could take a single stray on my own, if I needed to, considering that unless he knew to sniff my scent immediately, Eckard probably wouldn't realize I was a werecat.

And the guys were confident they could get to me very quickly, in case I was wrong about that. But in the end, it didn't matter. Eckard wasn't home.

"You lookin' for Adam?" The screen door to the other half of the duplex swung open on my left as I turned toward the car, and I whirled around to find a little boy watching me, one hand still on the door handle. He was no older than eight and, in spite of the temperature, he wore only a pair of worn-out jeans and a faded short-sleeved T-shirt, his feet bare on the cold concrete. His cheeks were flushed and his eyes glassy with fever, and a single whiff of his scent told me he was sick. Some kind of infection, which had no doubt kept him home from school.

Behind me, the back door of Parker's car opened, and I glanced over my shoulder to tell Ethan I was fine. He nodded but jogged down the cracked walkway toward me, rather than getting back into the car.

"What's your name?" I asked the boy, as my brother's footsteps slowed to a stop just behind me.

"Jack," the child said, his eyes widening as Ethan knelt at my side, putting himself roughly even with the boy's line of sight. My brother smiled, but Jack only stared, neither intimidated nor frightened by the presence of two strangers.

"Jack, are your parents home?" I asked, and his fever-dull eyes rolled up to meet my gaze.

"My mom's still sleepin'."

I stifled a flash of irritation with the mother who should have been awake, giving the poor kid some Tylenol and making sure he stayed hydrated. "We're looking for your neighbor. Mr. Eckard," I said, answering his earlier question. "Do you know him?"

"I seen him." Jack blinked listlessly at me.

"Today?" Ethan asked, and the boy's head swiveled in his direction.

"Yesterday."

"Do you know where he went?" I didn't really expect an answer, and sure enough, Jack shook his head.

"He left with his friends, but I don't know where they was goin'."

Ethan glanced up at me with both eyebrows raised, and I nodded. "What did his friends look like?"

"One was tall and skinny, and the other guy was shorter. But he was more muscley."

This time I smiled at Ethan. Jack had seen the dead strays before they were dead. "What did they do when they were here?"

"Nothin'. Adam went in, and the other guys stayed in the car. Then he came back out and they left."

"And that was the last time you saw them?"

Jack shook his head slowly. "Adam came back later, but the other guys wasn't with him."

I glanced at Ethan again, my heart pounding unevenly against my sternum. "What did he do? Did he have anyone else with him?"

"Nuh-uh." Jack let the screen door close and shoved cold-reddened hands into the pockets of his jeans. "He was just by himself. He went in and changed shirts. Then he came back out and put the shovel in the backseat."

My pulse spiked so hard and fast my vision went dark for one interminable instant. "He had a *shovel?* Did he say why?" *It wasn't for Marc. It wasn't for Marc. Marc's still alive. I'd know if he were dead.*

I'd know. Wouldn't I?

"I asked him. He said it was for the deer. He hit a deer with his car, and was gonna bury it." The boy sniffled and wiped his runny nose with the back of one bare arm. We were surely worsening his fever by keeping him out in the cold, but I had to know about Marc. We'd send him back in shortly.

"Did you see the deer?" I asked, then held my breath until he answered.

Jack shook his head again. "He said it was in the trunk. My daddy ties deer to the roof when he goes huntin', 'cause they never fit in the trunk. Adam musta hit a real little one. Prob'ly a doe. Or a baby. And he got all covered in blood puttin' it in the trunk. That's why he had to change shirts, I guess."

I didn't realize I'd stopped breathing until Ethan elbowed me in the ribs, then pulled me to my feet. Adam Eckard had shoved Marc into his trunk, then swung by home to change clothes and grab a shovel. And I could only think of one use for a shovel…

"Thank you. You've been a big help." Ethan scuffed the boy's hair and knelt beside him again to feel the child's flaming cheek with the back of his hand. "You've got a fever, Jack. Has your mom given you any medicine?"

Jack shook his head.

"Okay, I want you to go inside and get yourself a big drink of water. Then go wake your mom up and tell her you need some Tylenol. Okay?"

But before Jack could respond, light footsteps creaked from within the house, and a woman's hoarse voice called out. "Jack? Get your ass in here and close the damn door. You're lettin' out all the heat!"

Ethan nodded to encourage the boy, and Jack went back inside and closed both doors. "Some people should never be parents," my brother spat.

For a moment, anger on the boy's behalf peeked through my surging terror, a bookend to Ethan's blatant disgust. But then fear for Marc washed over me again, and I staggered on my feet.

I don't remember walking back to the car, but I'm pretty sure Ethan pulled me down the sidewalk, then pushed me across the bench seat to make room for himself. I didn't really wake up until Dan turned toward me, frowning after one glance at my face.

"What did he say?"

I blinked at him, and Ethan glanced at me, trying to decide whether or not to answer for me. But I shook my head. I was fine. "Adam went out with the strays Marc killed. Then he came back alone, covered in blood, just long enough to change clothes and grab a shovel."

"Fuck!" Parker's fist slammed into the right half of his steering wheel, and fury tightened the line of his jaw—what little I could see of it in the rearview mirror.

"It's okay," I insisted softly. "He's alive."

"How do you know?" Dan eyed me sharply, like he was looking for hope he could borrow.

"Because Marc doesn't lose, and he never gives up." I stared out the window as Parker pulled slowly away from the curb, my gaze glued to the front window of Adam Eckard's half of the duplex. "He's still alive, and we're going to find him."

"We need to know where he works." I took the lid off my coffee and dropped it on a paper napkin, then reached into the box for another chocolate-cake doughnut hole. "Let's go back and ask Jack." I'd been too stunned and horrified to think of that before we left Eckard's house.

"Why?" Dan asked, around a mouthful of apple fritter. On his right, Parker sat chewing in livid silence, his free hand clenched into a fist on the table. But his carefully blank expression couldn't quite hide the grief in his eyes, and that was really starting to piss me off. Marc was still alive—I *knew* it!—but Parker had already written him off. He was gearing up to *avenge* Marc's death, while I was determined to *prevent* it.

Some small, traitorous part of me insisted Parker was just being realistic. That he was drawing conclusions based on solid facts. But the rest of me didn't care. He'd given up on Marc, and for one tiny, fleeting moment, I hated him for that.

Behind Parker and Dan, the door opened to admit a family of five, as well as a blast of frigid air. Two of the three children—the two big enough to walk—took off immediately for the counter to peer through the glass at an assortment of sugary breakfast treats.

"Because then we can go *find* Eckard and *beat* him until he tells us where Marc is," I said in response to Dan's question. *And I am* not *playing good cop this time.*

Parker and Ethan exchanged a pained look across the table. "Faythe…" Parker began, but I shook my head vehemently, my hair flying out to smack my brother in the face.

"Don't say it," I snapped, glaring at him like I could burn the thought from his mind. "He's not dead, but he might be soon, and we're *not* going to sit here all day stuffing our faces, waiting for answers to fall into our laps."

"Why don't we just do a thorough search of his house, like you said?" Ethan suggested, appealing to me to be reasonable with one raised eyebrow. "Something in there might tell us where he took Marc."

I rolled my eyes, trying to get a grip on the rage scalding my insides. "You think he left a big flashing *arrow* pointing to a filing cabinet labeled 'Evidence Here!'? He's a stray, Ethan, not Wile E. Coyote!"

"I don't know what he left, but there has to be something," my brother insisted, standing up to my enraged outburst, the lines around his bright green eyes reminding me I wasn't the only one scared for Marc. "And if not, we can wait until he comes home, *then* beat it out of him. See? You still get to beat on him." He shot me a good-humored smile, trying to placate me, but I only scowled. I didn't want to be placated.

I wanted Marc back.

"We don't have time to wait." I spit the last word like the profanity it tasted like, and this time all three of the guys stared down at their food, refusing to meet my eyes.

I sighed. "Look, I know you think he's dead. I know Dad probably agrees with you." His heavy silence during the latest update had spoken volumes. "But I don't. And your lack of faith doesn't really change anything. If he's dead, are we just going to let him rot in the woods somewhere, where any scavenger is free to snatch a bite?"

"Of course not." Ethan frowned, and I got another glimpse of his own carefully hidden anger and anguish. "We love him, too, you know, and we'll make sure he gets a proper burial. But..."

But if he's dead, there's no real hurry. We could wait until Eckard got home from work. Until the sun went down and we gained the cover of darkness. He didn't have to say it. I could see it in his eyes.

I took another doughnut hole from the box and made myself chew, though I had no appetite. Eating gave me something to do, other than avoiding thoughts I couldn't bear to think. When I swallowed, and finally felt calm enough to respond, I looked up. "Fine. If you want to search Eckard's place, we'll try that first. That's probably the easiest way to find out where he works, anyway."

Ethan sighed and glanced again at Parker, who nodded. We'd reached a compromise.

On the way out of the doughnut shop, I snatched a handful of powdered creamer packets and stuffed them into my pocket for later. Something told me there would be lots more black coffee in my future.

An hour later, Dan, Ethan, and I stood in Adam Eckard's living room, staring at the mess we'd made ransacking his apartment. We'd snuck in through the back—Ethan broke the doorknob lock with one sharp twist—and had left Parker in the car a block away to cut down on our chances of being spotted breaking and entering in broad daylight.

And so the getaway car would be ready to go, just in case.

We'd searched every drawer and cabinet in the apartment, and though we had found an employee name tag and several check stubs—Eckard sold TVs at a local electronics store chain—we'd found nothing to indicate where he might have taken Marc.

"Okay, back to plan A," I said, kicking a couch cushion out of my way, as Dan pilfered through a desk drawer. "Let's go meet Eckard for lunch."

Ethan picked up a cracked video-game case and turned it over to glance at the title. "I still have doughnut glaze between my teeth, but what the hell. I could eat again." He snatched a half-eaten bag of Doritos from Eckard's desk and stuck his nose inside to sniff the contents. Then he considered the scent for a moment, shrugged and shoved a chip into his mouth.

"Eww, Ethan. Is there anything you won't eat?"

He answered by crunching into a second bite, then turned to follow me out the way we'd come in. But I'd only gone a couple of steps when a shrill telephone ring sliced through the near silence. An actual, plugged-into-the-wall phone; not one of our cells.

I turned, glancing around for the source, and saw Dan rooting through a pile of old newspapers on a table near the door, in search of the phone. Ethan dropped the chip bag to lift a series of dingy pillows, stained couch cushions and unwashed articles of clothing. I found the phone beneath a discarded pair of jeans, on the floor next to the steel-and-glass computer desk—an obvious place to keep one's phone, right?

"Should I answer it?" I asked, as Ethan retrieved his snack. But before either of the guys could reply, a mechanical voice spoke up from the overturned answering machine next to the phone.

"Eckard?" said an unfamiliar voice after the beep. "Where the hell are you? If you're not clocked in in twenty minutes, don't come at all. I'll put your last check in the mail." The machine clicked as the caller hung up, and I knelt to turn it over. On the digital display, the number two blinked in bright red.

Well, there goes plan A. Eckard wasn't at work, and it didn't sound like he *would* be anytime soon.

"There's another message," I said, as Dan shoved his hands in his pockets and my brother devoured another handful of the rogue's corn chips.

He shrugged. "Let's hear it."

I pushed Play and stood as a new message filled the room, irritation lending a sharp edge to the familiar voice. "Adam, where the hell *are* you? I sent Pete in this morning to clean up after you, and he said the whole house was already clean and reeking of Pride cats. Sounds like Greg's boys are in town, so stay away from Ramos's place, and keep your eyes open. And charge your fucking cell phone. It's kicking me straight to voice mail."

The message ended with a click, and Ethan's snack bag hit the floor at the same time as my rump. I looked up to find him staring at me in an odd mixture of surprise and rage. He recognized the voice, too.

Kevin Mitchell.

Twelve

"Are you *sure* it was Kevin Mitchell?" Parker asked for the third time, pulling into a parking spot near the front of the small shopping center in what passed for downtown Rosetta. After we'd given my father another update, the guys had insisted we go for a supply run while we waited to hear back from our Alpha on Kevin's current address and vitals, like his place of employment, phone numbers and vehicle description.

There were more shopping options in Fayette, near Eckard's duplex, but Rosetta was only minutes from Marc's house, so we stood a much better chance of getting our frozen food into the freezer before it thawed.

But I did not want to be there. Like eating, shopping felt like an abominable waste of time. Time Marc couldn't afford for us to squander. My hands clenched and unclenched, and my right foot tapped rapidly on the floorboard, my eyes darting swiftly over everything I saw through the windshield. My impatience was as obvious as Marc's absence.

"Yes, we're sure." I climbed out of the front passenger seat—I'd *finally* claimed shotgun—and slammed the door, rolling my eyes at Parker in exasperation. "I couldn't forget that voice if I tried."

"I know. It just doesn't make any sense." He and Ethan rounded the car and all four of us cut across the lot for a quick trip to the hardware store before hitting the Save-A-Lot. "Why would he kill Marc? I know they didn't get along, but that hardly seems motive for murder."

"Yeah, well, *none* of this makes any sense to me. Except for Pete. I'm assuming this Pete that Kevin sent to Marc's house is the Pete Yarnell whom Galloway mentioned. Right, Dan?" I glanced at him as I stepped over a concrete tire bumper. "The same Pete who organized the ambush?"

Dan shrugged. "I only know one stray named Pete, and that's him."

"And they're obviously in this together." I jogged ahead, trying to rush everyone on, but Ethan caught up with me as I stepped onto the sidewalk.

"You know, there's nothing more we can do until we know where to find Kevin, and we *need* supplies."

"I know." But nothing could quash the sense of urgency driving me, the adrenaline flooding my body in mass quantities, insisting that I do nothing else until I'd found Marc.

"Who's Kevin Mitchell?" Dan asked from Parker's other side as they caught up with us, and I glanced at him in surprise before remembering he hadn't been with us during the Kevin fiasco several months earlier.

"One of our former Pride members. He's been living in the free zone since my dad kicked him out back in September."

"Like Marc?" Dan asked, and we stared at him like he'd just desecrated the American flag.

"No." I stepped through the glass door Parker held open for me and nodded in response to the cashier who greeted us, then rushed us toward the back of the store, speaking to Dan in a hushed voice. "Marc was sacrificed to the political machine. My dad had no choice." Though it had taken me a while to truly understand that. "Kevin was kicked out for breaking the rules. Repeatedly. He accepted money to sneak a stray—one of the toms Manx later killed—over the territorial border into New Orleans on a weekly basis for some male bonding at a local strip club."

"And that's where Manx found the tom?" Dan concluded, as we passed a display of artfully arranged toilet bowl plungers. He looked angry on behalf of the slaughtered stray.

"Exactly."

Since he'd been expelled by my father, Kevin was officially considered a wildcat—a natural-born werecat living in the free zone, whether by choice or not. Of course, if we could prove his involvement in the attack on Marc, he'd also be a considered a rogue, by virtue of his criminal behavior.

Wildcats, like my brother Ryan, typically lived even more isolated lives than strays, who hated them for the birthright they no longer possessed. So it was quite a surprise to hear Kevin's voice coming from Adam Eckard's answering machine. They were clearly both implicated in what had happened to Marc—and to whatever had become of the other missing strays—and I couldn't help but wonder how an unlikely partnership like that had formed.

And who else was involved.

There were very few toms on the face of the planet I respected less than Kevin Mitchell, not just because of his betrayal of our Pride, but because of the way he'd always treated Marc, as if our Pride's "token stray" wasn't good enough to lick Kevin's paws. Marc had broken Kevin's nose after a comment to that effect a few months earlier, and I'd never cheered harder on the inside.

At the back of the hardware store, I fidgeted with a display of doorknobs while Parker selected three different locks—two for Marc's front door and one to reinforce the bolt on the back door. After hearing that one of Kevin's "men" had been at Marc's house, we were determined to give ourselves as much warning as possible, should someone else show up.

We also picked out a good-quality air mattress, inflatable pillows and blankets.

Next we hit the grocery store. Marc's fridge was far from empty—he was a tom, after all—but he had nowhere near enough food to sustain four full-grown werecats.

I hurried the guys through the aisles while they piled the cart with enough to feed the Dallas Cowboys for a week, and nothing that took much trouble to prepare. Pizza, frozen lasagna, family-size bags of frozen pasta, and all the usual snack stuff.

While Ethan and I paid for the food, Dan and Parker ran next door for some staples from the liquor store.

I stared at my phone all the way to Marc's house, willing it to ring. Willing my father to come through with the information we needed to find Kevin. Who could hopefully tell us where to find Marc.

With any luck, he'd make us beat it out of him.

Parker and Dan installed the locks while Ethan and I put up the other supplies and stuck two party-size boxes of frozen enchiladas in the oven for a late lunch. I carried the blow-up mattress into the empty front bedroom, autodialing my father as I went.

I pressed my phone between my ear and my shoulder as I unrolled the mound of vinyl and hooked up the virtually useless plastic hand pump.

"Hello?" my father said into my ear, sounding both distracted and frustrated.

"Anything on Kevin yet?" I probably should have

opened with a salutation, considering that I was speaking to my Alpha as well as my dad, but I'd reached the end of my patience. The beating of my own heart felt like a second hand ticking away the last moments of Marc's life, and I couldn't stand the thought that he could be dying while I sat in his house, pumping air into a stupid inflatable mattress!

"We have an address on file for him," my dad said, and I stopped pumping so I could hear him over the hiss of air. "But he's not there anymore. His cell phone's been disconnected, too. Owen's looking for more current information, but we're not having much luck so far. We'll keep trying, though."

Damn it! I resumed pumping with determination fueled by anger and frustration.

"Faythe, are you okay?" my father asked gently.

I made myself take a long, deep breath, and my hand went still on the pump. "No. Fortunately, we have another lead. There's another stray who might know where Eckard took Marc, but I'm gonna need Michael's help finding him. Will they let him answer his phone during the trial?"

"I'm sure he can take a break." He paused, and I heard Owen clacking away on a keyboard in the background. "Let me know what you find out."

"I will." I hung up the phone and plugged the hole in the mattress, though it was only half-inflated. "Hey, Dan?" I called, heading down the hall toward the living room.

"Yeah?" He sat in a chair in front of the open front door, patiently installing a new dead bolt with a flat-head screwdriver.

"Are you sure you don't know where Peter Yarnell lives?" It would be so much easier if he did, and we could leave immediately, instead of having to wait for Michael to dig up an address.

Dan sat up and met my gaze, the screwdriver held loosely in his lap. "I'm sure. It's not like we get together to play poker or anything. I've only met him a couple of times. But he's definitely the one you want. His scent's right here." Dan pointed one callused finger at the knob on the outside of the door, and I knelt for a whiff.

Sure enough, the faint scent of yet another stray clung to the aluminum knob, though I smelled it nowhere else.

"He must not have touched anything else," I ventured, glancing around the living room and kitchen at all the things that didn't carry his scent.

"I'm guessin' he broke in and saw that we'd already cleaned up, then hightailed it outta here."

I nodded, already distracted. "Thanks, Dan."

The stray's head bobbed in acknowledgment, and he bent over his work again.

I dialed Michael on my way into the kitchen to check on the enchiladas. The phone rang in my ear as I opened the oven door and flipped on the tiny lightbulb. And while I closed the door and took a chilled soda from the fridge. And while I popped the seal and gulped from the can. And still the ringing continued.

Just when I thought Michael's voice mail would pick up, he answered his phone and snapped softly into it, "This better be important, Faythe. We're in the middle of a *hearing*."

Oops.

"It won't take long." Since I'd already interrupted him anyway…

"Fine. Hold on." His shoes squeaked on the Di Carlos' stone floor and a door closed. Then his voice gained its normal volume. "What's wrong?"

"Oh, just about everything." I set my can on the counter and lifted the chewed-up pencil, which had somehow made it back into the empty dish drainer. "The short version is that Marc's still missing, and Kevin

Mitchell's mixed up in it somehow." I exhaled slowly, and tapped the eraser end of the pencil on the faded Formica. "I don't think he has much time left, Michael. It's twenty-nine degrees outside, and we don't know how or where he's injured, but we know he's lost a lot of blood."

"I'm so sorry, Faythe...." he began, but I cut him off, tears standing in my eyes.

"He's not dead, Michael. And I need your help to find him."

"What can I do?" That was my big brother. Always ready for the bottom line. But this time his voice was pinched with concern, which warmed my heart just a little bit, and I forgave his lack of faith. I loved it that the rest of my family loved Marc as much as I did.

"Do we have anything on a stray named Peter Yarnell?" We kept track of as many cats in the free zone as we could, to make our job easier, and because Michael kept the records, he always had the most up-to-date information.

"Hang on and let me check my spreadsheet." His footsteps echoed on the floor again, and another door creaked open. "Who is Peter Yarnell?"

"He's the stray Kevin sent to Marc's house this morning, to dispose of the bodies. Which we'd already done, of course. I'm hoping, since he's obviously in on this, that he'll know where Eckard took Marc."

"Okay, just a minute." Springs groaned softly as Michael settled into a chair, probably in front of the laptop he kept running all day, every day. "Um...yes. As of May of last year, Peter Yarnell was living in Gloster, Mississippi." His fingers tapped rapidly over the keys, then he spoke again, before I could ask. "That's about half an hour from Rosetta."

"What's the address?" I wrote on Marc's notepad while Michael read information from his obsessively organized spreadsheet. "Do you have a phone number?"

"Yes, but I wouldn't suggest warning him before you show up."

I rolled my eyes. "Thanks, Michael. What would I ever do without the benefit of your wisdom?"

"You're welcome," he said in response to my sarcasm. Then he read me the number.

"Thank you. Hey, while I have you on the phone, how's the hearing going?" I asked, taking another sip from my soda.

"It's not looking good, Faythe."

My heart pumped harder in sympathy for Manx. I'd really been hoping for some good news to balance out the most miserable thirty-six hours of my life. "Why not?"

"Because Manx claims she killed those toms in self-defense, but they've already gotten her to admit she was in no immediate danger at the time. And the council doesn't recognize any kind of temporary insanity defense."

Which was a real shame, because most of the councilmen had considered me crazy for most of my life.

After I spoke to Michael, I called my father and gave him another update while I finished blowing up the mattress. He gave us permission to go interrogate Peter Yarnell at our earliest convenience—the very words I'd been hoping to hear.

In the kitchen, I opened the oven and pulled out both trays of enchiladas, setting them on top of the burners. Then I grabbed a pile of paper plates from an upper cabinet and a handful of mismatched forks from the top drawer. "Lunch!" I yelled, pulling three more sodas from the fridge. Footsteps stomped toward me from all directions, and in seconds the three toms had converged around the stove, scooping sloppy servings onto flimsy paper plates.

"Eat quickly," I ordered, pleased to hear my father's no-nonsense tone coming from my own mouth. "We're leaving for Gloster in ten minutes."

I filled the guys in while they shoveled huge bites of chicken, cheese and tortilla into their mouths, and I picked at my plate, only actually eating when Ethan frowned at me or nodded at my food.

Then I put on my steel-toed boots and led the way to Parker's car, a foam cup of coffee in one hand.

Twenty minutes later, we drove into downtown Gloster, past a row of quaint storefronts and several residents ambling down the sidewalks, presumably to or from work at one of the local businesses. After another mile and a couple of turns, Parker stopped at the first—and only—gas station we saw to ask for directions to Peter Yarnell's street. We found it quickly after that, and slowly cruised past house after house in the calm, middle-class neighborhood, in search of the address I'd written down.

It turned out to be the last one on the block, before the street ended in a dead end and a rough circle of asphalt. Yarnell's house blended perfectly with the rest of the neighborhood. Redbrick with black shutters. Tall windows; small, neat lawn. The two-car garage was closed, but parked in front of it was a conservative dark blue SUV.

Looks like Mr. Yarnell's home. He'd probably taken the day off from some white-collar pencil-pushing job to clean up Eckard's mess. Too bad for him…

Parker turned around in the circle, then parked on the edge of it, facing the house. "What's the plan?"

"I knock on the door and flirt my way inside. You guys stand out of his line of sight, then follow me in. And try not to look too thuggish. This kind of neighborhood's probably full of bored stay-at-home moms just itching to press the panic button."

"What if he knows who you are?" Parker asked, scanning the hushed street.

"Then we go in as quickly and quietly as possible." Just because we didn't see the neighbors didn't mean they couldn't see us.

"Who gets to do the honors?" Ethan asked, his usual smile dim beneath the weight of recent grim responsibility. He'd been picking up a lot of Marc's former duties, including interrogation, and the strain was starting to show on him.

I do. "We'll play it by ear."

Ethan nodded and opened his door, letting in a frigid draft. I started to follow him, but before anyone could get out of the car, Dan cleared his throat, drawing our attention. "Guys, I don't know Pete Yarnell real well, but I know him by sight, and he's…a pretty good size."

"Size isn't everything." I pushed my door open but remained seated. "Anyway, compared to me, you're all huge, and I've never had any trouble taking Ethan down."

My brother's expression lightened, and he stuck his tongue out at me, but Dan wasn't done. "I don't know if you could tell from that little bit of his scent on the doorknob, but Pete was there that night. Durin' the ambush."

I closed my door again and twisted to face Dan directly, a spike of anger quickening my pulse. "No, I couldn't tell." I'd only fought a few of the strays we faced that night, and there were too many personal scents floating around for me to concentrate on any one of them. "That settles it, then. If Mr. Yarnell doesn't start talking pretty damn quickly, this is gonna move beyond chitchat. Everybody ready?"

Dan nodded and stepped out of the car, and the rest of us followed.

On the way across Yarnell's tidy, winter-brown yard, a fluffy miniature pooch of some kind barked at us with his head sticking out of an igloo-shaped doghouse in the neighbor's side yard. I snarled, and the dog turned a tight circle and cowered at the back of his house, whimpering like a scared…well, puppy.

Damn right.

From Yarnell's front porch, I heard television violence and the soft hum of a central heating unit. I made a motion to the guys, and they stepped back against the front wall of the house, where Yarnell wouldn't be able to see them from the door. Hands stuffed into their pockets for warmth, they tried to look casual, in case we were being observed by any of the neighbors. I thought they looked guilty as hell, but then, I knew what we were up to.

I took a deep, calming breath, then knocked on the door and struck my clueless-motorist pose. When no one answered, I knocked again, and that time the TV went silent, then the door swung open to reveal a tall, bull-necked man, separated from me by nothing more than a decorative storm door.

"Can I help you?" Yarnell's voice was deep, as was his scowl, until his gaze landed on my face, then quickly traveled south.

"Hey!" My breath puffed from my mouth in a cold white cloud, and I arched my brows in fake excitement and relief. "I'm lost and my cell's dead. Could I maybe come in and borrow your phone? Please?" I cocked my head to look harmless and vaguely stupid, mentally crossing my fingers in hopes that he wouldn't think to check my scent.

He didn't. He never got past the view of my cleavage, easily visible through my unzipped black leather jacket. I honestly hated playing the boob card, but I'd have done almost anything for a few private moments of Pete Yarnell's time.

"No problem. Come on in." Yarnell pulled open the

screen door and stepped back, one thick, extended arm welcoming me into his home.

"Thanks!" I stepped into the large, warm living room, past a gas fireplace and a huge television, and when Yarnell tried to close the door behind me, Parker's broad palm was there, holding it open.

"What the hell?" Yarnell's initial reaction was to push back, and I couldn't help but admire his instinct—answering with aggression in the face of a threat. If he weren't a bad guy—and easily distracted by cleavage—he might have made a good enforcer.

Clued in now, Yarnell sniffed the air, and his eyes darkened in outrage as the line of his jaw tightened.

Ethan followed Parker into the room and waved one hand at the couch. "Have a seat, Pete." He grinned amiably at his own rhyme—*dork*—then nodded at me in acknowledgment. "Good work, sis."

"Thanks." But I barely glanced at him. My attention was focused on Yarnell, who'd backed toward the couch to put some space between himself and the sudden crowd in his living room, but had yet to sit.

Yarnell scowled, staring over my shoulder at Dan, the last arrival. "What the *fuck* are you doing here?" Apparently he remembered Dan.

"These are Marc Ramos's friends." Dan spoke softly, his voice heavy with quiet anger, and I glanced over my shoulder to find him watching Yarnell calmly, a formidable, silent threat in his steady gaze. Marc had taught him well. "Just answer their questions, and we'll go away."

"Like *hell*. You can't just walk in here and start asking—"

"There are four of us, and only one of you." Ethan pulled the drawstring on the blinds covering the living room windows, and they slid down, darkening the room and shielding us from potential Peeping Toms. "So right now, we can do just about any damn thing we want."

I glared at my brother over my shoulder. No wonder most of the free zone thought we were a bunch of elitist tyrants. But Marc's safety was more important than our reputation, so I turned back to our host, now flanked by both Dan and Parker.

"Mr. Yarnell, I'm a big fan of civil rights, so normally I'd agree with you. But today we're here under the authority of the south-central Pride, in search of information we have reason to believe you can give us. And honestly, until I know that Marc Ramos's well-being is secure, I don't give a flying fuck about yours. Consider that your one and only warning."

Ethan grinned at me, radiating pride. Fortunately, he was professional enough to do it where Yarnell couldn't see.

With everyone in place—Dan and Parker flanking our host, ready to restrain him if the need arose, and Ethan on the edge of the room, my visible backup—I saw no reason to circle the proverbial bush. "Where's Marc?" I met the potential informant's gaze, hopefully showing fortitude in the strength of mine.

Yarnell pressed his lips together and smiled at me. The arrogant bastard!

I growled deep in my throat, and stepped within his immediate reach to show I wasn't scared of him, in spite of the six inches and at least sixty pounds he had over me. "We know Kevin sent you to clean up Eckard's mess. So just tell me where they took Marc, and we'll get out of your fur."

"I'm not telling you shit, bitch." Yarnell's pale brown eyes sparkled; he enjoyed pissing me off.

"Last chance." My hands curled into fists at my sides, and the motion drew his gaze downward. "Tell me where they took him, or we're going to find out which breaks first—your face or my fist."

In the past, the thought of beating information out of

a witness—even a hostile one—had made me sick to my stomach. Though I'd often seen Marc do that very thing, my most frequent offensive weapon was my mouth, rather than my fists, so I was mildly surprised by my own steady stance. Rather than nausea or nerves, I felt only desperate fear and rage, both growing by the second. They swallowed my weaker emotions, diverting all energy to the task at hand.

Thank goodness.

But Yarnell could not be shaken. He watched me steadily, silently daring me to act.

I crouched, and my foot flew, hard and fast. The motion was a blur of denim and black leather. The steel toe of my boot slammed into his left side. He staggered to his right, absorbing the force of my blow, and I actually heard his rib crack.

Yarnell dropped to the floor in front of the couch, one hand pressed to his side, but his lips were stubbornly sealed against a cry of pain, as if to show that he was stronger than me.

"Pick him up." I was surprised by the cold, commanding quality of my voice, and so was Parker. He eyed me with lifted eyebrows while he hauled Yarnell to his feet, then let him go. "Where's Marc?"

"Bitch, you think you scare me?" The stray sucked in a breath and flinched at the pain, but dropped his hands, as if by denying the injury he could deny the pain. "You can kick me all night long, but I'm only going to say this one thing—Marc Ramos is a murderer, and a fucking traitor, and he got what he damn well deserved."

"I don't have time to convince you otherwise." I pivoted on one foot this time, throwing all my rage into a sloppy-but-strong roundhouse. My boot caught him near the same spot, and dimly I heard another snap.

Yarnell's face went pale, and he hunched over in pain, but his smile never faltered. Dan stepped forward to catch him in case he fell, but Yarnell slapped his hand away. "You want to know where Marc is?" he spit, glaring at me, fists clenched at his sides.

I nodded, not daring to hope he'd actually answer.

"He's in a *hole,* four feet deep in the frozen ground. Your boyfriend's *dead.* And like I said, he got *exactly* what he deserved."

Stunned, I staggered back a step, choking on a cry of anguish until my throat burned. But the pain went much deeper than that. It hurt all the way through my heart and into my soul.

No! He was lying. Trying to throw me off. He had to be.

For a moment, I could do nothing but breathe through the shock and pain ripping into me like a full-body cramp, ending in a bolt of agony in my throat, and behind my eyes. Ethan reached for me. I sucked in a deep breath and forced my head upright, knocking his hand away. I was *fine.* And so was Marc.

Yarnell came into focus before me, the browns and blues of his clothes oddly muted. But I only had eyes for his face, that leering grin, those smug eyes fueling my rush of rage.

A feline growl tore free from my throat and I rushed him, fists flying. His hands shot up in defense, but mine landed first. My right fist hit his chin, followed by a left to the ribs. Then another right, and another left.

He swung at me, but he was hurt and I was too fast, and it took most of his energy to block my fists. Only one of his blows landed, on my left side.

I roared in fury and slammed my knee into his groin. Yarnell hit the carpet, one hand clutching his crotch, the other protecting his head, and still I swung at him.

Hands grabbed my upper arms from behind, lifting me off him. So I kicked instead. My right foot hit his left side, then my left slammed into his thigh, and his whole leg spasmed.

"Faythe!" Ethan dragged me backward, wrapping his arms around me from behind, pinning me to him as I struggled wildly. Tears poured down my face, though I had no memory of crying. "Faythe, stop kicking!"

I went still—limp in my brother's arms. He set me on the floor, then turned me to face him, wiping my cheeks with his bare palms. His eyes searched mine, then widened in surprise, and that's when I realized mine had Shifted. "You okay?"

"No." I wiped the damp spots he'd missed, and vaguely noted that my voice was oddly deep and rumbly. My throat had Shifted, too, at least in part. "But thanks."

He nodded, and I turned back to Yarnell, who lay on the floor with blood dripping from his nose and smeared across a cut on his cheek. "Pick him up."

Parker glanced at me in surprise over the sound of my voice, then leaned down to oblige me. But Dan hesitated. "Faythe, I think he's had enough."

"I'm not going to hit him." *Yet.* My jaws ached from being clenched, and my knuckles were bruised. "Just pick him up."

Dan and Parker lifted Yarnell and set him on his feet. He stood hunched over in pain, but his eyes were clear, focused on me in rage rivaling my own. Though he didn't seem to have noticed my subtle demonstration of the partial Shift the stray community had surely heard about, he was conscious and coherent. *Good.* Because I had something to say.

I stepped forward until my face was inches from his, his blood tainting every breath I took. And when I growled, his eyes widened, flickering with the first sign of fear, and of comprehension of my partial Shift. "Marc is *not* dead," I whispered, fury echoing in each soft syllable. "I'd know if he were dead, because a part of me would have died with him. So you tell *me* where the hell he is, or I'll break every fucking bone in your body."

Thirteen

Parker gaped at me, and Dan looked…scared. Any other time, that might have amused me, but at the moment I had neither the time nor the patience for anything but finding Marc, even if I had to stomp Pete Yarnell into the ground to do it.

And hopefully, I'd made that crystal clear.

"You ready to play nice?" I stood my ground, well within Yarnell's personal space, and for a moment, I thought he'd clam up again—thought he'd actually rather die than tell me what I wanted to know. But then he spoke, eyes flashing in fury, face tensed against pain. His every movement spoke of injury, and I'd never in my life faced anyone who truly hated me until that moment.

Don't get me wrong. I piss a lot of people off. But beneath the anger, everyone else I'd ever met had *wanted* me for something. Even Andrew, the human I'd accidentally infected. Beneath the murderous fury I'd witnessed in the last moments of his life, there was a heartbreaking familiarity in his eyes, a sense of my betrayal, which had fractured some crucial part of his humanity. Part of him—*most* of him, probably—had wanted me dead. But there was still that small kernel of hope deep inside him, hopelessly smothered by devastating rage, that wanted me to save him. To take it all back and give him peace.

I saw none of that in Peter Yarnell. He harbored only hatred for me, and would have tried to kill me that very moment, if not for the three other toms in the room.

"Well?" I asked, and finally Yarnell opened his mouth.

"Fuck you."

"You'll have to stand in line for that one, and frankly, you don't look up to the challenge." I launched my left fist into his chest as hard as I could—an opportunity I rarely allowed myself—and was rewarded with a soft snap as a third rib broke. That southpaw practice was really paying off.

"Bitch!" Yarnell wheezed, hunching over violently before forcing himself upright. "I told you, he's dead."

Fresh rage shot up my spine, but I tamped it down, focusing on the immediate goal. "I'll believe that when I see his body. Where did they bury him?"

"I don't know." Yarnell gave me a bloody grin, arms crossed protectively over his battered chest, and I knew from his bearing that he was telling the truth. But I also knew that he was pleased to have no information to give me. The bastard.

"Did you see him?" I demanded, ducking to recapture his gaze when too deep a breath made him flinch in pain.

"Didn't need to," he gasped, then licked a drop of blood from his lip.

My pulse spiked, sending a painful jolt of adrenaline through my heart. "Wait, you didn't see the body?" I glanced at Dan to see surprise plain on his features. "Then how do you know he's dead?"

"Because that idiot Eckard accidentally killed him." Yarnell was talking willingly enough now that he thought his information would hurt me. But in truth, he'd just gifted me with more hope than I'd ever thought to feel again.

"Accidentally?" Ethan asked from behind me, and Yarnell's gaze flicked his way. But the bloodied stray refused to answer. He wasn't going to give us anything that might help us. Not on purpose, anyway.

"Where did Eckard take him?" I repeated, recapturing Yarnell's attention.

"I told you—I don't know."

"Think harder." I lurched into motion again, and this time my foot hit his upper rib cage, snapping two fingers on the hand that shielded it.

"Fuck!" Yarnell clenched his broken hand to his chest and glared at me, wiping blood from his nose with the sleeve of his opposite arm.

"Did Kevin tell Eckard where to take Marc?" I demanded. Yarnell shrugged, examining the last two digits on his right hand, which were already swelling and turning blue. "Is there somewhere you guys usually bury bodies? A regular dumping ground?"

Yarnell shook his head, but his posture stiffened, and he avoided my eyes. He was lying.

"Where do you take them?" I repeated, ducking again to draw his eyes, as Parker stepped closer on the stray's right. I growled, an impressive sound with my partially Shifted voice box. "Tell me, or I'll break your other hand. Gonna be kind of hard to wrap your ribs with two broken hands."

Yarnell's teeth ground in fury. "You bitch. The next time I see you, I'll *kill* you…."

I rolled my eyes. "It's a date," I said, almost amused now by the gruff quality of my voice. "Now, your answer, or your hand?" I crossed my arms over my chest, holding his gaze. "Where do you bury your bodies?" And the thought of how many there might be was enough to make me shudder.

"Two places," Yarnell spat. "In the woods north of Highway 563, south of Rosetta."

I glanced at Ethan, to see if he'd caught that, and he nodded, scribbling on the notebook he kept in his back pocket. Then I turned back to Yarnell. "Where else?"

"Why does it matter?" he demanded, obviously riding a new surge of rebellion. "He's dead. You need to dig him up to believe it?"

"Yes." I didn't hesitate. He could say it once every second for a year, but I wouldn't believe Marc was dead until I'd touched his lifeless body with my own hands. I needed to see their burial site so I could prove to the others that Marc *wasn't* in it. "Where's the second site?"

"In the woods east of White Apple."

Ethan's pencil scratched on paper behind me, and Yarnell's eyes flicked his way. "But you'll never find either of them. The roads are pissy little dirt paths, and the woods are dense. You won't find his grave, but you'll never find *him,* either." The stray's eyes flashed with renewed, vigorous anger, and he lunged at me. Parker and Dan caught him by both arms, but still he strained forward. "You'll live the rest of your life never knowing what happened to him. You'll wake up crying, empty inside from not knowing. From *never* knowing…"

I threw one last punch, and it landed squarely on the left side of his chin. Yarnell's head rocked back, and he let it hang there for a moment before meeting my gaze. "Maybe," I had to admit, though the very thought killed some small, vulnerable part of me. "But if you ever come near me or Marc again, we'll all know *exactly* what happened to *you.*"

We left Yarnell bleeding in his living room, and on the way across his front lawn, Ethan threw one arm over my shoulder. "Damn, boys, my sister is *badass!*"

I forced a small smile, knowing he was trying to cheer me up. But I couldn't forget the fact that, though I was sure he wouldn't be there, we were about to embark upon a search for Marc's *body.* There was no good cheer in me to be found.

I slid into the front seat of the car again and concentrated on reversing my accidental partial Shift. Then, as Parker drove off, I grabbed the atlas from the pocket on the back of my seat and twisted in my seat so I could see everyone. After flipping a few pages, I found a map of Mississippi. Unfortunately, there was no close-up of the Rosetta area, so I couldn't see the smaller roads. "Okay, White Apple is ten or twelve miles north of Rosetta, off of State Highway 33. We'll go back to Marc's and split up. Parker, you and Dan head toward White Apple, and Ethan and I will go south on 563. Keep your eyes open. There will probably be a break in the woods wherever they usually enter, but it'll likely be faint."

I paused, and closed my eyes while I uttered a silent prayer for Marc. Then I looked up to find Parker alternately staring at me and the road. "What?"

He hesitated. "Do you really think we'll find him either of those places?"

"I certainly hope not." I spent most of the rest of the drive giving my dad another, somber update, pretending I didn't hear hopelessness in his every exhale.

At Marc's house, I used the restroom and traded my leather jacket for a heavier coat I found in his closet, then grabbed a box of protein bars and several bottles of water from the fridge. As I split the supplies among two backpacks, I heard voices speaking softly from the front yard.

Through the front window, I saw Ethan and Parker standing side by side, each stuffing something into the backs of their respective vehicles. Rolls of black plastic. Ethan held an unopened roll of duct tape, and the handle of a shovel stuck up over the backseat of Parker's car when he closed the back hatch.

I was hoping for the best, and they were preparing for the worst.

Sighing, I blinked unshed tears from my eyes and kicked the kitchen cabinet closed, then joined them outside, where Dan stood on the porch, both hands stuffed into the pockets of his own light coat.

"I think you're right," he said, steadily holding my gaze. "I think Marc's still out there somewhere, alive. But you can't blame them for bein' ready, in case we're wrong."

"I don't blame them." I handed one of the loaded packs to him. "But we're *not* wrong."

I waved goodbye to Parker and Dan as we pulled out of Marc's driveway, a better map of Mississippi on my lap, the heater blowing full blast into my face.

"You okay?" Ethan glanced at me briefly, then back at the road.

"No."

He sighed, lips pressed together, hands gripping the wheel so hard his fingers had gone white with tension. "Faythe, I know you want to believe Marc's still alive. And I hope to hell you're right. None of us can handle losing him. But you need to be prepared for the possibility that he's really gone. Or that Yarnell's right, and we may never find him."

"That won't happen." I clenched my hands in my lap to keep from putting a fist-shaped indentation in his glove compartment. "I'd know if he were dead, Ethan."

"How?"

I closed my eyes and ground my teeth together. *Damned logic...* "I just would. Wouldn't you know if something were wrong with Angela?"

Ethan chuckled. "Yeah. She'd call every five minutes, like she's done all day long."

"Your phone's on silent?" I couldn't resist a grin.

"Vibrate. Twenty-two missed calls."

I raised one brow in amusement. "Maybe you should call her back."

"I will. Once all this is over." Ethan frowned. "She's so…normal, I can't talk to her about relationship stuff while I'm on Pride business. It feels too strange. Does that sound weird?"

"Yes, but I know what you mean." *That whole worlds colliding thing…*

Ethan glanced my way again, bright green eyes shining with insufferable sympathy, and I realized I hadn't gotten away with changing the subject. "I just want you to be prepared for the worst, Faythe."

Clearly we were done talking about Angela.

"Fine. I'm prepared." I crossed my arms over my chest and stared out the window. "End of subject." My brother frowned again but didn't push the matter.

I loved him for that, almost as much as I loved him for being there with me, considering what he thought we'd find.

Dense forest raced past in a blur, casting long shadows on the highway. The clock on the dashboard read four-thirty. The sun would set in less than an hour, and we'd be hiking through the woods in the dark, in below-freezing temperatures.

But at least I had a coat. In the twenty-eight hours Marc had been missing, the temperature hadn't yet risen above freezing, and he didn't even have *that* much. I knew that for a fact because his coat was draped across the backseat behind me. I'd been hauling it around all day, along with his own ironically unused first-aid kit, just in case we found him.

I sat in silence until Ethan turned from Highway 33 onto 563, headed south toward Wilkinson, at which point my heart started thumping in my chest and I sat straight in my seat, scanning both sides of the highway. We'd find a break in the trees soon. We had to.

In a three-mile length of two-lane highway, we came across two cars abandoned on the side of the road, where they'd slid off the pavement during the ice storm several days earlier. Wrecking crews had been working overtime for days to haul off all the deserted vehicles, but they obviously hadn't made it this far out of town yet.

But other than the roadside wreckages and turnoffs onto several small roads, I saw nothing of note in the tree line. I'd just decided to have Ethan turn around when we got to the next town, so I could scan the other side of the road, when my gaze caught on another stranded vehicle and my heart jumped so hard it lodged in my throat.

"Stop!" I shouted, startling Ethan so badly he jerked, twisting the wheel toward me. The car lurched to the right, but he corrected quickly, stomping on the brake in the process.

"What?!"

"What did Dad say Adam Eckard drives?"

"A black Explorer."

"Like that one?" I pointed out the windshield toward the vehicle stopped on our side of the road, about two hundred feet ahead.

Ethan squinted. "Are you sure that's an Explorer?"

"An older one, but yes." My eyes are better than his. That's been well established.

"Eckard's is a 2001." Ethan drove us slowly past the SUV, and I noticed two things immediately. First, it was empty—no sign of either Marc or Eckard. And second, when the Explorer had slid off the road—which it had clearly done—it had smashed head-on into a trunk on the edge of the tree line.

"He went off the road!" I shouted, too excited to manage a calm volume. "Marc's not dead, he's just lost in the woods." And bleeding. And freezing.

But what had happened to Eckard? Neither his boss nor Kevin had seen him, and we'd found his wrecked car abandoned on the side of the road. Could he and Marc both be lost in the woods?

"Faythe, don't get your hopes up…." Ethan warned. "Marc lost a lot of blood, and it's twenty-eight degrees outside. If he's still…out there, why didn't he come back to the car for shelter? Or call someone?" He made a sharp U-turn, drove us back past the Explorer, then turned again and brought us to a stop on the narrow shoulder, behind the Explorer.

"Because he knows that if he got away, they'd send someone else after him. It's not safe in Eckard's Explorer." I was out of the car before he'd even turned off the engine. "And he didn't call because he doesn't have his phone. Dan called me from it, remember?"

"Faythe, wait!" Ethan's door slammed shut, but I was already at the Explorer, peering through the back hatch. "Best-case scenario, he's out there somewhere, injured and freezing, and probably still bleeding. And for all we know, Eckard could be chasing him. We should Shift—"

"No." Since cats can't track by smell, there wasn't much point in Shifting. Though we *could* hear much better with cat ears… But in the end, I shook my head. "I can't help him without hands, Ethan."

"Fine. But the worst-case scenario isn't—"

"Nooo!" I moaned, my face pressed into one of the rear windows, one hand up to shield my eyes from the crimson glare of the setting sun. The cargo area was too shadowed for me to see much of, but the backseat was well lit. And draped across it was a ratty blanket, covered in blood. "No!"

Ethan pulled me back and glanced through the window. He sucked in a sharp breath, then regained control and turned toward me, taking me by both arms. "It might not all be his," he insisted, peering into my eyes. "If Marc fought him, some of that could be Eckard's."

Please, please *let some of that be Adam Eckard's blood.* Most *of it.* Because there was surely too much for one man to survive losing. There was so much blood soaked into that blanket and the cloth-covered seats that if we'd been in cat form, we would have smelled it, even with the car doors shut and the windows rolled up.

I jerked on the rear door handle, desperate to get inside. To identify the blood and prove to myself that Marc could still be out there. But the door was locked, so I moved on to the front door. It was locked, too. They all were. Why were they locked?

Whatever had happened there the day before, someone had left the vehicle with the presence of mind to click the locks.

"Here, wait a minute." Ethan pulled me away from the Explorer and slammed his elbow backward into the rear window. The glass shattered, shot through with a thousand icelike webs, but remained in place. One more blow knocked the entire cracked pane into the backseat, where it slid onto the stained floorboard.

I didn't bother opening the door. I just stuck my head in the window and sniffed.

The scent of Marc's blood was everywhere. It couldn't have been stronger if I'd been *wading* in it, and my heart throbbed, my lip trembling in devastation. But then I sucked in another breath through my nose, and a fainter scent caught my attention, a morbid mercy.

Adam Eckard's blood. Not much of it, but it was there.

"It's not all his." I whirled to face Ethan, searching his face for the hope I needed to see.

He smiled hesitantly and inhaled through his nose. Then he nodded. "I'm not sure there's enough of it, but it's definitely there. Either Eckard was still bleeding from his injury at Marc's, or Marc hurt him again."

"Come on, he's still out there!"

"Faythe..." Ethan's warning look was in place again as he backed slowly toward his car for the pack.

I rolled my eyes, reluctant to take his warning seriously. "I know, don't get my hopes up. He's lost a lot of blood, and it's freezing."

"And it's been more than twenty-four hours."

Yeah, there was that, too. While he got his pack and added two flashlights from the glove box, I called Parker and told him what we'd found. He was almost as excited as I was at first, but then the facts sank in, and caution crept into his voice as he listed the same warnings Ethan had.

I told him to leave the pessimism in White Apple and haul ass in our direction. Because I wasn't leaving the woods until we found Marc.

The sun went down half an hour later and we got out the flashlights, still tramping through the woods. We were exhausted and freezing, but spurred on by the occasional smudge of blood on the trunk of a tree, or splattered on frost-covered leaves. Unfortunately, since the blood was frozen and sparse, it carried almost no scent, and we couldn't tell which drops belonged to whom. Still, a picture formed in my mind as we went.

"He thought Marc was dead," I said, shining my flashlight on another few drops of blood, standing out starkly against a frost-covered brown leaf. "Eckard probably drove him into the middle of nowhere for an emergency, midafternoon burial. And if Marc was unconscious after losing that much blood, I can kind of understand the mistake."

Ethan smiled, and I could see the effort in the lines around his eyes, heavily shadowed in the glare from my flashlight. He didn't buy my story, but he wasn't going to argue. Bless him.

"At some point, obviously, Marc woke up. Maybe he fought with Eckard in the car, running them off the road." I shrugged. "Or maybe he woke up when the car hit the tree." I wasn't sure on that point yet. But they'd both obviously torn through the woods, though who was chasing whom, I couldn't have said.

"Eckard could have been carrying Marc," Ethan ventured gently, and I had to agree that that was possible. If unlikely.

"Why would he have bothered?" I wiped moisture from my forehead, surprised that I'd worked up a sweat in light of the temperature. "If Marc were dead, wouldn't Eckard have just dragged him, like he did in Marc's yard?"

Ethan had no response to that, and I smiled smugly, content to let us search in silence for a little while.

A few minutes later, my phone rang, and I dug it from my pocket with cold-numbed fingers. It was Parker, calling to tell me they'd parked behind Ethan's car and would catch up with us soon. I gave him our heading, because that would be faster than making him hunt out the same sparse trail of blood we were tediously following, then hung up, my impatience revived by the phone call, as well as the knowledge that we had to be getting close to something.

Surely both toms couldn't have run very far in the woods. Not injured and underclothed.

And fifteen minutes later, that theory was proved true, when my flashlight skirted over something much too pale to be a dead leaf, or even an exposed root.

My frozen left hand shot out, curling around a handful of Ethan's coat, bringing him to an abrupt halt. "Look." I nodded toward the end of my trail of light.

"What the hell…"

"It's a hand," I whispered, my voice hoarse with shock and dread. I sniffed, and to my horror, I smelled both Marc and Eckard, which meant they'd both spilled enough blood to retain the scents, in spite of the extreme temperatures. "I can't look." My hesitation had nothing to do with any girlie impulse or squeamishness. I ate raw venison on a regular basis, in cat form. But in that moment, as I stared at a motionless, frost-covered human hand in a pile of dead leaves, my certainty that Marc was still out there somewhere—alive, if not well—was awfully hard to cling to.

Ethan's beam of light joined my own, and he stepped slowly forward as my heart pounded in my ears, putting himself between me and…whoever lay dead in the woods. He knelt, and my pulse spiked as I heard leaves rustle.

Then my brother stood and spun to face me. I couldn't see his smile in the dark, but I heard it clearly in his voice. "It's not him. Faythe, it's not him."

I exhaled, unaware until that moment that I'd been holding my breath. Then I crashed through the leaves toward him, and in less than a second I was kneeling on the frozen ground at his side, staring at the back of a dead man's head.

I inhaled deeply through my cold, stuffy nose, taking the scent all the way into my lungs, grateful for once for the freezing temperatures, which had kept the corpse from decomposing. So far.

"It's Eckard," I confirmed, relief coursing through me in spite of the fact that I smelled Marc's blood, too. "Marc won." Joy spiked through my veins, and my whole body tingled, head to toe. "He's *alive,* Ethan."

Ethan smiled cautiously, his eyes sparkling like emeralds in the edges of my flashlight beam. "At least he was when he was here. And it looks like he found some extra clothes."

I followed the beam of his flashlight far enough to see that Eckard was naked from the waist up. Ethan was right. Marc now had an extra shirt, and hopefully a coat. Even with the massive blood loss, he could have made it with warm clothing. Right?

"What's that?" I frowned, squinting at a quarter-size spot of blood on Eckard's upper back.

"The death blow?" Ethan suggested, obliging my curiosity with his light.

I shook my head. The crunchy, frozen blood beneath my boot said that Eckard's neck had been ripped open. And the back wound hadn't bled much, which meant Eckard's heart hadn't been pumping when he came by the injury. The back wound was probably postmortem. I edged closer for a better look.

There, between Adam Eckard's shoulder blades, just to the left of his spine, was a small cut, with neat, straight edges, as if the flesh had been precisely sliced.

"What the hell…?" I asked, but Ethan could only shrug. "Marc sliced open his back. Why the *hell* would he do that?"

Fourteen

"That makes no sense." Parker knelt in the cold for a better look at Eckard's back, aided by the battery-powered camping lamps he and Dan had brought. "He clearly used a small knife. Probably a pocketknife. But since Eckard's throat was ripped open, I'm guessing Marc didn't have possession of the knife until after Eckard died. So it was probably Eckard's knife. Why on earth would he mutilate the body?"

"He wouldn't." Marc had respect for the dead. Even the dead bad guys. And I had no doubt that if he'd had the strength to dig into frozen ground, he'd have buried Eckard. But even with the additional clothes, Marc was injured and suffering a grave loss of blood, as well as the dangerous temperature. Burial hadn't been an option.

"Why didn't he take the phone?" Dan pointed to a slider cell phone, lying in a pile of leaves a foot or so from Eckard's head.

"It's dead." Ethan picked the phone up to confirm what Kevin had said on Eckard's answering machine. He pressed and held the power button, and when nothing happened, he nodded and slid it into a pouch on his backpack. Hopefully later we could charge it and search it for relevant phone numbers and messages.

"Any reason to keep the body?" I glanced from Ethan to Parker for an opinion, and both toms shrugged in the muted, clean white light.

"Not that I can think of," Ethan said.

"Okay, let's put him to rest."

We only had three shovels, including the one Eckard had brought to dig Marc's grave, and since I was the slowest digger—I'd had the least practice—I got stuck searching and wrapping the body while the guys worked on the hole.

Eckard's wallet contained no surprises, and I slid it into my back pocket to be incinerated later. Other than the ruined throat and the slice on his back, he had only one other injury: a gash across his right forearm, which I examined with my flashlight. The wound stank faintly of metal, and I deduced that he'd been slashed with the screw sticking out of a broken piece of Marc's furniture. And that the resulting wound had provided us with the blood sample Hooper Galloway had identified.

When I was done with the body, I relieved each of the guys in turn, for a water break. Digging graves is hard work, even for a werecat. Even in cold weather. And while I dug, standing in a mostly dark three-foot-deep hole, working too hard to talk, I had nothing to do but think.

At first, I thought about our next move—how best to find Marc, who seemed to be injured and lost in a national forest. But that led to questions and other thoughts I didn't want to think.

Marc had obviously walked away from the fight with Eckard, but where the hell was he? How long could a seriously injured man survive in below-freezing temperatures? He was obviously in human form—based on the fact that he'd taken Eckard's clothes—which meant he was too hurt to Shift immediately. So why hadn't he headed back toward the road? Eckard's car was beyond functioning, and Marc couldn't hitchhike and risk passing out with a human who would take him to the hospital. But he could have followed the road from the woods, and eventually have reached civilization.

Then again, having lost so much blood, he probably wasn't thinking clearly enough for that, especially if hypothermia had set in. He could have been wandering the woods, lost and disoriented, for more than a day.

Despair crashed over me and I staggered into the wall of the grave, steadying myself with a handful of frigid earth. Marc didn't really stand a chance.

"Faythe?" Ethan stopped digging and reached out for me, planting his shovel in the ground. "You okay?"

"I hate not knowing." And I hated my own doubt even more.

Ethan took my shovel and handed it to Parker, then hauled himself out of the hole and pulled me up with him. "That's deep enough," he said, and gestured for Parker and Dan to bring the body.

"What if you're right?" I whispered, letting Ethan fold me into his arms, treasuring both his warmth and his comfort. "What am I going to do if he's gone?"

"You're going to slaughter every motherfucker involved—and I better get a piece of that action—then you're going to move on. There's no other choice." Surprised by the bitter vehemence in his voice, I stepped back to find him watching me in his own quiet wrath, as uncommon an emotion for Ethan as docility was for me. "Now let's bury this bastard before Kevin comes looking for him."

I nodded, still numb and stunned by the thought that I might live the rest of my life without Marc. Then Ethan's last words sank in, and I froze. "Oh, shit."

"What?" Dan asked, gripping the corpse's plastic-wrapped feet at waist height.

"Ethan's right. Kevin will realize Eckard's missing

soon and come looking for him. And when he figures out Marc got away, he'll be looking for him, too. What if he finds Marc before we do?"

"He won't," Parker said, sidestepping toward the grave in unison with Dan. But his calm, sober expression said he didn't think Kevin was much of a threat. Parker still thought Marc was dead, and the search for a body didn't carry as much urgency for him as the search for a missing man.

"He's out there, Parker. Marc may be hurt and cold, but he's alive out here somewhere, and if Kevin finds him first, he's as good as dead."

"Kevin won't find him," Ethan insisted, shooting a censuring glare at Parker, while Dan looked on in concern and confusion. "We won't let him."

After we'd buried Eckard, we hiked back to the cars, and the equipment we carried seemed infinitely heavier and more cumbersome than it had on the way *to* the body. As did my thoughts.

After a brief conference, and a consultation with our Alpha, we decided on a course of action for Eckard's Explorer. The front of the vehicle was wrapped around the tree he'd hit, and it could not be driven. Not even a little way. So, working quickly in case of passersby, Parker retrieved the five gallons of emergency gasoline from his trunk and doused the inside of Eckard's vehicle, concentrating mostly on the bloodstained rear portion.

Then, after Ethan and Dan had turned our function ing vehicles around and parked them on the opposite side of the road, a good fifty feet from the Explorer, Parker lit a match and tossed it into the car, then raced across the street and slid into his own passenger seat as Ethan and Dan both drove away from the scene of our crime.

To my relief, the Explorer didn't explode. But it did go up in a huge ball of fire. Even if the vehicle wasn't melted beyond recognition, the flames would easily destroy the DNA evidence of our existence. It was a drastic measure of caution, and one we'd never tried before. But we'd had no choice.

I watched the fire until I could no longer see it flickering through the rear windshield. Then I watched the reddish reflection of the flames in the sky. Within minutes, sirens raced toward us, and I held my breath as the fire truck passed, followed immediately by two police cars. But we weren't stopped.

With the immediate evidence taken care of, I called my father back, staring at Parker's rear bumper as it bounced down the highway in front of us.

"Hello?"

"It's done." I sighed, closing my eyes briefly. "Do you still have our toms patrolling the border?"

"Yes." My father's pitch rose with curiosity, as Ethan glanced at me with one brow raised. "Why?"

"I need them here. We have to find Marc before Kevin does, and I need every available body out there searching. We'll head back out ourselves as soon as the cops get done with Eckard's car."

I thought he would say no. His silence was a virtual guarantee, so I was all ready to argue when he said, "Okay. You'll have ten new men in three hours."

"Really? Just like that?" I couldn't help my smile.

"I want him back, too, Faythe."

"I know." My grin grew in relief, and I leaned forward to aim the heater vent away from my face. "But I thought you'd say we were past the point of urgency."

"No." My father exhaled slowly. "We will never reach that point."

My vision blurred with tears, and I wiped them on the back of my still-cold hand. "Thank you, Dad."

"Don't thank me. Just find him."

I clenched my jaws tightly, denying my doubt a voice. "I will."

* * *

We went back to Marc's house while we waited for the authorities to finish with Eckard's car, and Parker threw together a huge pot of confetti spaghetti, while I sliced and buttered garlic toast. I'd just put the bread in the oven when my phone rang, and I jogged across the kitchen to snatch it from an end table in the living room, hoping for news from my father about the reinforcements.

It was Michael.

"It's all over," he said, his voice heavy with exhaustion.

"Already?" Manx's trial had only lasted a few days. Was that a good sign or a bad one? "What's the verdict?" My pulse spiked, blood pounding in my temples as if it were trying to burst free from my veins.

"Guilty, on three counts of murder."

Oh, shit. My chest seemed to constrict around my lungs, and my next breath was difficult to suck in.

But as disturbing as it was to hear aloud, the verdict wasn't really much of a surprise. Manx had killed three toms, and technically the danger to herself was only perceived. Still, because of the extenuating circumstances—the severe and prolonged trauma leading up to her crimes—I didn't think she deserved to die. Apparently everyone else agreed.

"The sentence was unanimous," my oldest brother continued, as Ethan emerged from the bathroom and leaned against the hallway door frame, watching me and listening in. "They'll spare her life. But they're going to take her claws."

My head spun, and the room seemed to tilt. I sank onto the couch, my free hand gripping the upholstered arm until reality went still again. But, consumed with simultaneous horror and relief, I could think of nothing to say.

Manx was going to be declawed.

On one hand, that was good. Better than the alternative, anyway. Des would not be an orphan. Manx would not die for crimes she committed as a result of brutal, long-term trauma and a debilitating fear of men.

But on the other hand, being declawed is every bit as horrific as it sounds.

The pain is unbearable. Which is why ripping out a person's fingernails has long been a recognized form of torture in some countries. Obviously, modern Prides perform the procedure in a sterile environment, with the victim/ convict heavily sedated, or even unconscious. But the recovery would be no romp through the woods.

Even worse, Manx wouldn't be able to go out in public again without wearing gloves. Ever. In order to keep the claws from growing back, the surgical procedure actually snips off the very tip of a cat's toes. Shifting a couple of times will accelerate healing the wounds, but will not make the claws—or those lost bits of nail bed—grow back.

Being declawed in cat form was one thing. Aside from the obvious inconvenience, the deformity would hardly show beneath the fur on her paws. But in human form, the mutilation would be conspicuous, and as difficult to explain as it was to hide. She'd be missing her fingernails and cuticles. All ten of them. And the flesh they'd once covered would be puckered and scarred.

When I was in junior high, my father ordered a stray—a three-time offender—to be declawed. Dr. Carver performed the procedure at our ranch, and before the stray left, I caught a glimpse of the result. I've long since forgotten what his offense was, but I'll never forget the sight of that tom's malformed hands, which established my own deep-rooted fear of losing my claws.

"Faythe?" Michael said into my ear, drawing me out of my thoughts. "You okay?"

I laughed bitterly. "Not really? You?"

For a moment he was silent, too, and I wondered how similar his thoughts were to mine. "I...well, I can't say I agree with the sentence, but neither can I justify them letting her off entirely. She committed three very serious crimes, and if they let that go unpunished, they're setting a very dangerous precedent."

But I could have cut my finger on the cold, sharp edge of politics in his voice. He was trying to emotionally divorce himself from the issue and view it with no bias. It was a skill I envied, and sometimes I was certain I'd never be able to pull off. I couldn't even emotionally divorce myself from the boxers versus briefs debate, much less Manx's cruel verdict.

"I know, but her *claws?* How's she supposed to hunt? How can she possibly defend herself or Des?" But I answered my own question before he had a chance to. "She's *not* supposed to, is she? That's the whole point, right?"

In cat form, her ability to hunt would be severely compromised. She could still pounce on and suffocate prey with her strong, feline jaws. But she'd no longer be able to grip with her claws. Or to climb in search of upwardly mobile prey. Or defend herself, should the need arise.

She'd be dependent on others—likely men—to provide and care for her. And that blow was even more devastating for Manx than it would have been for anyone else, because her independence was all she had left. That, and her baby. For years she'd been dependent on the meager mercy of the men who'd abused her and held her prisoner. Now, she'd be at the mercy of every tom she met.

"Well, I don't think that's what *all* of the Alphas had in mind," Michael hedged. "But I have no doubt Calvin Malone holds significant influence over Milo

Mitchell—" Kevin Mitchell's father, who'd headed up the tribunal "—and I would not be surprised to hear that the sentence was actually his idea. Or something cooked up between them."

I had a strong suspicion my brother was right; declawing a tabby was exactly the kind of thing Malone would suggest. It was an irreversible indignity to Manx. A blow to her self-worth. And an obvious political maneuver from two Alphas who were probably patting themselves on their collective back for putting one more tabby *in her place.* The bastards.

My pulse spiked just thinking about it, and if I'd had claws of my own in that moment, they'd have ripped right through the faded upholstery of Marc's used sofa. Though what they really wanted was to sink into Calvin Malone's flesh.

That rotten bastard wouldn't rest until he had every eligible tabby in the country barefoot and pregnant, married off to one of his easily manipulated sons, making him the most powerful Alpha on the Territorial Council.

"Damn it!" I snapped as Parker joined Ethan in the doorway, probably drawn by the sharp tone of my voice. "If someone doesn't stand up to him, we're gonna wake up one day and discover that we need Calvin Malone's permission to take a piss in our own territory." Michael sighed over my crude phrasing, but I ignored him. "How long is he going to get away with this?"

"As long as he's able to retain the appearance of the moral high ground. He couches everything he does in the letter of the law, so we can't even argue about his less-than-honorable intentions."

Michael was right, of course, and that was the whole problem. Malone hadn't actually broken any rules—not that we had proof of, anyway—so there was nothing we could do to stop him until he messed up. In the meantime, *we* seemed to be handing him screwup after screwup, and an uncomfortable number of those instances could be laid at my paws.

"Well, that's gonna change. He's going to make a mistake sooner or later, and we're gonna hang him with it." Assuming he didn't get his hands on our noose first.

I sighed, and stood when the oven timer went off. "When are they taking Manx's claws?"

Parker scowled as I passed him. He must not have heard that part of the call.

"Tonight," Michael said, as I slipped a thick mitt over my free hand and pulled open the oven door, flooding the room with the scents of butter and garlic. "Bert's doctor is coming to do it, and we're leaving for the ranch in the morning. Dr. Carver will follow up with Manx there."

I pulled an aluminum baking sheet from the top rack and set it on a towel I'd spread over on the countertop.

"If you haven't found Marc by then, Vic and I will join the search."

"Thanks." I wanted to insist we wouldn't need them by then, but I didn't want to jinx our efforts.

I hung up as Parker scooped huge piles of pasta onto paper plates, but when I sat down in front of my dinner, I couldn't help wondering when Marc had last eaten. And as I picked at my noodles, aimlessly twirling a bite around my fork, one thought kept chasing itself through my head.

"We can't kill Kevin. We have to find him and turn him over to the council." Chewing ceased around the table as the guys' attention shifted from their food to me, surprise clear in each expression. "We have evidence against him." The tape we'd taken from Eckard's ancient answering machine. "And there's no way the council can refuse to convict him once they hear that."

"Where there's a will, there's a way," Ethan muttered, and I frowned at him. But he had a point. "If you hand him over to the council while Malone has so much pull, they'll find a way to let him go. Especially if Malone's the one he's working with. He and his allies will be thrilled if Marc shows up dead, and they'd rather reward Kevin than punish him. And Kevin *has* to pay for this."

"I know, and personally, I'm ready and willing to pull his heart right out of his chest, Temple of Doom style." My brother nodded eagerly, but I pressed on. "But, Ethan, Michael's right. If we kill Kevin in anything other than self-defense, we'll be hammering another nail in Daddy's political coffin." And that might happen even if it *was* self-defense, because lately, we never knew who the council would agree to hear testimony from. Or whether they'd believe what they heard.

Because Kevin was now a wildcat, jurisdiction for his crimes technically belonged to the council at large, and if our Pride, or any faction of it—namely me and Ethan—acted without the council's permission, my father would pay the price. Probably with his position on the council.

"We have to let the council handle this. But I don't see any reason we can't be the ones to turn Kevin over to them. And if he resists capture and must be beaten into submission, so much the better." I lifted my brows at Ethan, and he answered with an eager grin.

Unfortunately, the larger issue would be much harder to prove: that Kevin was working for one of those very council members who'd be sitting in judgment of him. Assuming we were right about that, surely the Alpha responsible wouldn't have left evidence of his own connection to the crime. That way he could let Kevin take the entire fall, if necessary. And while I was more than willing to give Kevin that last big push, I wanted his coconspirator to go over the edge with him.

"Any idea how to find him?" Parker asked, a forkful of spaghetti near his mouth.

I glanced at my watch. "We still have at least a couple of hours until we can head back into the woods. Why don't we go utilize our resources?" My focus shifted to Dan, who'd listened in silence up to that point. "Didn't you say Ben Feldman was trustworthy?"

He nodded, and speared a slice of bell pepper on his plate. "Some. But that doesn't mean he'll help you."

I shrugged. "It can't hurt to try."

We devoured the rest of our dinner, me included, because I knew I'd need the energy if we spent the entire night hiking through the woods in search of Marc. Then we piled into Parker's car and made our second trip to Feldman's house in less than twenty-four hours.

This time he was home.

It was twenty minutes after nine when we pulled to a stop in front of Ben Feldman's house, two small towns and nearly forty-five minutes from Marc's driveway. A well-kept ten-year-old Toyota sat in front of the single-car garage, and the minute Parker cut his engine, the silhouette of a head appeared in the front window of the house.

Feldman knew we were there.

"Okay, I know I'm one to talk in this regard, but we can't let this one go down like it did with Yarnell," I said from the backseat, unbuckling my seat belt. "Another incident like that won't do much to convince the stray population that we're not out to get them."

Parker nodded in agreement. "We play nice this time."

Dan looked relieved, and I could tell he really respected Feldman—a rarity among strays, who typically spent very little time in one another's company. Though Dan was shaping up to be an exception to that rule.

When we stepped out of the car, the head disappeared from Feldman's window. We crossed the tiny brown lawn with me and Dan in front, Parker and Ethan close at our backs.

The front door opened before we could knock, and Ben Feldman appeared behind the storm door, backlit so that his face was a shadowy compilation of wide planes and rugged angles. Feldman was so broad he took up the entire glass panel, and so tall I couldn't see the top of his head. He wasn't quite as big as my cousin Lucas, but was easily the largest stray I'd ever seen.

And he did not look friendly.

"Painter? What the hell are you doing here?" Feldman's voice was like granite—smooth, hard, and beautiful. A pleasant surprise in all three respects.

Before Dan could answer, I stepped forward and smiled my brightest, friendliest smile, determined to win Feldman over, rather than fighting him. We couldn't afford to make an enemy of every stray we met, and based as much on his confident stance as on his size, this tom would be a formidable opponent. "I asked him to introduce us. I'd really like to talk to you, Mr. Feldman, if you have a few minutes."

"And you are…?"

More smiling. My jaw was starting to ache. "I'm Faythe Sanders." I paused to see if he would react to my name.

Feldman's dark eyes widened almost imperceptibly, but the flaring of his nostrils was much more noticeable, as he verified from my scent that I was indeed who I said I was. Or at least that I was a tabbycat.

But rather than returning my smile, or ushering me inside, both of which I'd expected from a tom who'd probably never met a female of his species, he pressed his lips together in a frown. "What can I do for you, Miss Sanders?"

"May we come in? I have a few questions, and it's pretty cold out tonight." I rubbed my arms through my jacket for emphasis.

Feldman's frown deepened, and he crossed bare, dark

arms over a pale button-down shirt. His eyes focused over my head on Parker and Ethan, then he scanned the yard slowly, inhaling deeply.

"It's just the four of us," I assured him, impressed that he'd thought to check for backup. I used to forget that one a lot myself.

After another moment's hesitation, he pulled the screen door open for us.

I stepped inside with the guys at my heels, all of us relieved by the warmth of the small room, but before he closed the door, Feldman took one last glance and sniff outside, to verify that we were alone. "Sit." He waved one arm at a tan couch. The sofa was by no means new, but it was cleaner than anything in the guesthouse back home, and it matched the armchair in one corner, against which Feldman leaned, facing both us and the front door.

"Thank you." I sank onto the cushion farthest from our host, and all three guys squeezed in with me, intentionally avoiding the aggressive backup stance. On the coffee table, a fat, hardbound book lay open next to a spiral notebook covered in neat, slanted writing. One glance at the book, and I nearly choked on my own surprise. It was a textbook anthology, open to *Antigone.*

"Are you in college, Mr. Feldman?" I asked, eyeing him in interest as I flashed back to my own days as an English major. Feldman looked to be in his midthirties—a little old for an undergrad, but not unheard-of.

His dark eyes hardened, and thick, brown hands smoothed his shirt as he settled into the armchair. "Is that what you came to ask me?"

Okay, he wasn't exactly approachable, but at least he hadn't kicked us out. Or tried to kill us. Yet. "Um, no. I was just curious."

"Then no, I'm not in school. I teach Classical Humanities at the junior college in Natchez. Mostly night classes."

"Oh." *Ohhh.* I felt my face flame, and I glared at Dan, irritated by the lack of background information on our host. He only shrugged and, to my further embarrassment, I thought I saw amusement flit across Feldman's face, softening it for just an instant.

"It's late, Miss Sanders, and I take it this isn't a social call, so why don't you get to the point?"

"Of course." I crossed my legs at the knee, hoping to look competent and official. "This is Parker Pierce and my brother Ethan." I gestured at each tom in turn, without taking my eyes from our host. "We're enforcers for the south-central Pride, and personal friends of Marc Ramos—"

Feldman's thick eyebrows arched. "The way I hear it, regarding your relationship with Ramos, that's a bit of an understatement, Ms. Sanders."

I blinked in surprise, and when I met Feldman's gaze again, I saw challenge in his eyes. He knew exactly who I was and what I wanted, and he was daring me to drop the pretense and stop wasting everyone's time.

So I did.

"Yes." I uncrossed my legs and leaned forward with both elbows propped on my knees. "Mr. Feldman, Marc is more than a friend to me. More than a boyfriend. There's nothing in the world I wouldn't do to find him."

He nodded, acknowledging that I'd met his challenge, though his stony expression did not soften.

"Yesterday, three tomcats broke into Marc's house and attacked him. Two of the toms died, but injured Marc severely in the process. The third hauled Marc off." I was *not* going to reveal that we'd found Eckard, and that Marc had escaped, because if the strays didn't yet know he'd survived, I wasn't going to tip them off. "We know Kevin Mitchell is in on this somehow. I'm here because rumor has it you have your ear to the ground and might be able to tell me where to find Kevin."

Feldman simply watched me for several seconds, letting me stew. Or maybe trying to judge my sincerity. He had the upper hand, and he damn well knew it. Then, finally, he blinked, and leaned back in his chair, digging something from his right hip pocket.

"Yes, I can tell you were to find Kevin Mitchell. Or at least where he lives. But I'm not going to do that. Not now, and not ever. Because of this."

Feldman's thick fist swung forward, and I jerked back from the blow to come, as the guys shot to their feet, ready to defend me. But Feldman's blow never landed. Instead, he slammed his hand palm down on the battered coffee table, and when he withdrew it an instant later, he left something on the laminated wood surface.

A clear, rounded cylinder, half the diameter of my smallest finger and no longer than the first joint. Inside the cylinder was another cylinder made up of tiny green and black parts I couldn't focus on without a microscope.

"What *is* that?" I asked, leaning forward to squint at it, as the guys mimicked my motion.

"That," Feldman spat, glaring across the coffee table, "is the microchip I dug out of my own back last week."

Fifteen

"A microchip?" Parker reached for the tiny cylinder, but Feldman snatched it back, holding the object up where we could still see it between his thick fingers. But we couldn't touch it without taking it from him. Which would not fit into our playing-nice approach.

"Yes." Feldman eyed us closely, each in turn, obviously studying our reactions.

"That was in your back?" An image of Eckard's corpse flashed behind my eyes, complete with the precisely slit skin between his shoulder blades.

Feldman nodded, frowning at my obvious surprise as I made the connection.

"Your *upper* back? Just to the left of your spine?"

"Yeah." Feldman lowered his hand into his lap, fist wrapped around the tiny device again as excitement made my heart beat faster. Eckard had had one, too—until Marc had cut it out of him. But how had he known it was there? If Marc knew about the microchips before he was attacked, he would have told me.

"First of all, that's weird," Ethan said as he caught my gaze, silently telling me he'd made the connection, too. Parker and Dan nodded; we were all on the same page. "And it doesn't look like any microchip *I* ever saw."

"Me, either." I smiled to thank him for keeping the tone light. Whatever these microchips were, we'd stumbled onto something big, and we couldn't afford to piss Feldman off before he told us what he knew. I met the stray's gaze. "Though admittedly, my familiarity with chips is limited to the guts of my cell phone. So enlighten me, please. What does it do?"

Feldman frowned, eyes narrowed in suspicion. "You really expect me to believe you don't know what this is?"

I blinked at him in genuine surprise. "Why would we? I've never seen anything like it."

"So you have no idea how this got under my skin?"

"None." I met his eyes boldly, letting the truth shine in mine.

"Holy silicone suppository, Batman!" Ethan said, grinning. Dan snorted, Parker coughed to disguise a laugh, and I glared at them all. "What?" My brother shrugged defensively. "That's what it looks like."

Un-amused, Feldman ignored Ethan and focused on me. "Then how did you know where it was implanted?"

Crap. My mind raced. I had to answer, to keep him talking, but how much could I say without revealing that Marc had survived? "We, um..." I hesitated, glancing at the guys for advice. Dan shrugged, clearly at as much of a loss as I was, and Parker gave me a slight nod, telling me to say *something.* But as little as possible.

I took a deep breath and continued. "We found a body with a small hole in his back. Just big enough to implant one of those." Or remove it. "But we didn't know what that hole meant until now." *Please, please don't ask whose body we found!*

Fortunately, Feldman was too preoccupied with the chips to waste questions on tangential issues. "And you don't know what this is?" he repeated, his face a tense mask of suspicion. We hadn't convinced him yet.

"No clue," Ethan said, with no trace of a smile.

"It's a digital tracking device." Feldman still scrutinized our reactions. "So whoever's monitoring it can know where I am all the time. Or at least where the chip is."

"They can do that?" Parker stared at the clear capsule in amazement. "Track people with something so small?"

"No. Not officially." Feldman sat back in his chair. "There's nothing this advanced available to the public. Not that I've been able to find, anyway."

"Sounds like supersecret spy shit to me." Ethan grinned, but his eyes held little humor. He knew how serious this had just become.

"Not quite." Feldman rolled the chip between his thumb and forefinger, and his jaw tightened in anger. "It's a high-tech *pet* tracking device, designed to find rich-bitch poodles that wander too far from their gated communities," he said. "But it's still in the prototype phase. We're being tagged like apes in the wild, using a technology that hasn't yet been approved for dogs, and should *never* be used on people."

Indignation shined like inky flames of fervor in Feldman's coal-colored eyes. Not that I could blame him. "And yet you're surprised when we don't welcome your boyfriend with open arms…"

What? Was he blaming Marc for the microchips?

"Mr. Feldman, Marc had nothing to do with this," I insisted, my stomach clenching around the lump of apprehension lodged in my gut. "A violation of privacy like this stands to benefit him no more than it does you. Quite the opposite, in fact. So why would he participate in it?"

Feldman shrugged broad shoulders. "I assume he's following orders."

Adrenaline scorched my nerve endings, and I glanced at Ethan to find my dread mirrored in his expression. They thought our *father* had ordered strays illicitly tagged and monitored?

"You're wrong," I said, fighting to remain calm. To slow my racing heart. "My dad would never do something like that, and neither would Marc."

"That you know of." Feldman leaned forward, studying me carefully, looking for a lie in my bearing or the race of my heart. Then, apparently satisfied, he exhaled softly. "I believe that you knew nothing about this." He widened his gaze to include the guys. "But that doesn't mean it didn't happen. And I'm holding the proof that it did." He held the chip higher for emphasis.

"Why?" Parker asked with his typical quiet composure, drawing all eyes his way.

Feldman frowned. "Why, what?"

"Why are you still holding the proof?" He gestured at the pill-size capsule. "You could have crushed that thing like a bug. Why didn't you?"

"Because then whoever's monitoring it would know I'd found it. They'd know we're onto them."

"We, who?" Dan asked, his eyes narrowed in concentration. "Who else has one?"

"I don't know. Kevin Mitchell knows about the chips because I told him, but as far as I know, I'm the only one who's actually found one. And we agreed to keep it quiet to avoid panic and public outcry until we've decided what to do about it. With Marc out of the picture, that should be a little easier."

Fury scalded my cheeks and Feldman watched my face, but he seemed to get no pleasure from my reaction. He was stating facts—at least as he saw them—not trying to get a rise out of me.

"For the last time, Marc is not…" *Dead.* "Involved," I finished, avoiding the tactical error at the last second. I closed my eyes, thinking. Kevin knew about the chips. And Kevin had arranged the attack on Marc. He was the only thing bridging the gaps in our understanding.

Now, if we could just figure out how he fit in.

Dan shifted on the couch cushion beside me, and I looked over to find him frowning, a mixture of guilt and loyalty highlighting the tired creases around his eyes. If he didn't let go of that misplaced guilt soon, he was going to drive himself nuts. "She's right, Ben. Marc had nothin' to do with this. I'da known about it."

Feldman eyed him in both pity and scorn. "You think he told you everything he ever did? Every man has secrets, Painter."

"I know." Dan dropped his gaze and cleaned grime from beneath one fingernail with another. "But he wouldn'ta done this. Marc doesn't have that in him."

"Bullshit!" Feldman's voice rose, and he scooted to the edge of his seat, his fists hanging over the coffee table between us. "Ramos is neck-deep in this! He's been taking us one at a time for weeks. Some of us never return, and some come back with chips in our backs—" he held up the microchip as evidence "—and no memory of what happened."

"If you have no memory of it, how do you know what happened?" Parker asked softly.

Feldman's angry gaze found him. "I discovered a scar I couldn't account for, and there was a little lump beneath it. Almost too small to feel. And I dug this *thing* out of my flesh. At first I couldn't figure out how it got there. Then I remembered a night a couple of weekends ago. I went out drinking with some colleagues, and I stayed a while after they left. I woke up in my own bed twenty-four hours later, with no memory of going home, or what I'd done since. I assumed I'd partied too hard."

"Do you do that often?" I interrupted, and he scowled at me.

"No. But nothing else made any sense, since I woke up with both of my kidneys in place." The acid in his tone could have melted through flesh, but I couldn't resist a small smile, in spite of the seriousness of his accusations.

"I didn't put it together until I found the chip."

"Why didn't you notice the wound?" Ethan scratched the dark stubble on his chin.

"Because there was no wound. I'd have noticed stitches and a bandage, but there was nothing but a fresh scar, which I didn't notice for another week. Now, how they managed that, I have no idea."

But *I* did. They'd forced his Shift—possibly several times—to accelerate healing, so that when they let their tagged tom go, he had no pain to clue him in to the procedure.

I looked from Ethan to Parker and knew at a glance that they'd come to the same conclusion. The bastards behind this were well organized and smart. And efficient. They'd carried the whole thing off in only *one* stolen day of Feldman's life.

Our host continued, having evidently missed our silent communication. "But at least I made it home. Some of them don't come back at all. Maybe the procedure goes wrong. Maybe the victims wake up and remember what happened." Feldman shrugged. "I don't know. But there are too many toms missing for this to be a coincidence."

"Yes, including Marc!" I couldn't filter anger from my tone. "Marc didn't take those toms. He's *one* of them! Kevin Mitchell sent three strays to his house to take him, and that's exactly what happened with the other toms. I think they were trying to tag him, but something went wrong, just like you said."

Feldman shook his head, his jaws clenched in irritation. "Kevin Mitchell has *nothing* to do with the chips. He probably sent those toms to *kill* Marc. For his part in *this*." He waved the chip again, like a patriot's flag.

"No." Parker shook his head, still sitting serenely on the couch, as if we were having a friendly chat with a trusted friend. "Pete Yarnell said Eckard *accidentally* killed Marc, and called him an idiot for it. They were supposed to take him."

Feldman huffed in bitter amusement. "Kevin didn't orchestrate this. Strays and wildcats have neither the funding necessary to get our paws on so many commercially unavailable devices, nor the organizational network needed to implant them. This is Pride work. No way around it."

"Well, it wasn't *our* Pride!" I snapped, glancing at the others for support. Then I froze as what I'd said truly sank in. Ours wasn't the only Pride out there. Nor was it the only one Kevin had connections to.

"Please, Mr. Feldman. Help us find Kevin." I leaned forward, shamelessly begging, because if we caught Kevin Mitchell and brought proof before the council, my father's case could be infinitely strengthened by a show of our Pride's competence. "I swear to you that he's responsible for the microchips."

Feldman raised both eyebrows. "Can you prove that?"

I sighed. "No."

Feldman stood slowly, staring down at me until I felt obligated to stand also. "Ms. Sanders, I would think that as an enforcer, you would have *some* understanding of the concepts of loyalty, truth, and consequences. Kevin Mitchell has given me no reason not to trust him, and I will *not* hand him over to you without solid proof that he deserves it."

My mind raced furiously, but I couldn't think of any way to prove my claims. Yet. "Fine. I'll get you proof. But in the meantime, may we borrow the microchip? I want to show it to my Alpha. He's our best chance at ending this, and he needs to see what's happening."

"No." Feldman wrapped his fist firmly around the chip and stuffed it into his pocket. "For all I know, you'll stomp it to bits on my front porch, to destroy proof of your Pride's involvement."

My heart sank into the pit of my stomach. "No! We wouldn't do that. We're trying to *help* you!"

The stray's gaze hardened. "It sounds more like you want *my* help." Feldman stomped toward the front door, and the floor shook with every step. "You should go now, before I lose my temper." His voice was gravelly with a deep current of anger.

I walked slowly toward the front door, the guys at my heels, when what I really wanted to do was take the microchip I desperately needed as proof to the council that someone among their ranks was egregiously violating the civil rights of random strays in the free zone. And if that someone turned out to be Calvin Malone, his case against my father would die a blissfully violent death.

But I did none of that because something told me that though Ben Feldman didn't yet trust me, I could trust *him* to do what he thought was right, once he had a clear view of the big picture. And that he would be a very dangerous enemy to have.

I stepped onto the porch and turned back to face Feldman as the guys brushed past me into the cold, disappointment and frustration obvious in their clenched jaws and fists. "I'm sorry. This didn't turn out how I'd hoped. But thank you for talking to me. And I *will* get you that proof."

Feldman looked surprised for an instant before his face went carefully blank. Then he shut the door in my face and slid the dead bolt home.

"Hi, Dad." My cell pressed to my right ear, I sank onto the weight bench in the tiny third bedroom Marc had turned into a minigym. There was barely enough room to turn around between the bench press and the punching bag—which he'd obviously bought used—and I wondered how he could exercise without becoming claustrophobic.

"I was about to call you." Leather creaked over the line, but there was no squeal of springs. He was in his armchair in the office. "Seven of our men made it into the woods along highway 563 about an hour ago, as soon as the fire crews cleared away the wreckage of Eckard's car. You'll have three more toms out there before midnight."

"Thank you." Those two words couldn't possibly convey the depth of my gratitude, but at the moment I couldn't think of how better to say it. "Thank you so much. We'll be heading out with them in a few minutes."

We'd stopped at Marc's for more supplies, and to change into heavier clothes. The current temperature was twenty-two degrees. Too cold for even our natural fur coats to keep us warm. So we'd go out in human form, bundled to twice our normal sizes.

I slowly spun one of the round weights on its bar, trying not to think of how sick and weak Marc would likely be when we found him. "But before we go out, I owe you an update. We figured out why Marc cut a hole in Eckard's back."

My father's armchair creaked again. "I'm all ears."

"He was removing some kind of high-tech digital tracking device."

For a moment, there was only silence over the line. "Someone was tracking Adam Eckard? You're serious?"

"*Dead* serious. And he wasn't the only one. We just spoke to Ben Feldman, and he had one, too. He took it out of his own back, if you can believe that. And he says it's happened to several of the toms here. Daddy, someone's been taking strays one at a time and putting these tracking things under their skin, then they wake up the next morning with no memory of it. If they wake up at all."

"The missing toms…" my father whispered, clearly catching on much faster than I had.

"Exactly. We think something went wrong with a few of the implantations, and those strays just disappeared."

"Feldman told you all this?"

"Some of it. And we pieced together the rest. Unfortunately, Feldman thinks Marc's involved in this, on *your* orders, and that the attack on Marc was an attempt to stop the whole thing. But you're never going to guess who's *really* doing it."

More leather creaked as my Alpha rose from his chair, and I heard his footsteps on the office floor as he paced in thought. "Kevin Mitchell. Though he's probably working with his father. Or maybe Malone."

It was my turn for surprised silence. "We're almost sure. How did you know?"

My father chuckled. "I've been doing this a while, Faythe. Kevin's the piece of the puzzle that doesn't fit. And you've already established that he's involved in the attack on Marc."

"Oh." I leaned against the wall and my free hand rubbed the cracked bench pad aimlessly.

"So, Marc's out there injured and alone, with evidence of a Pride plot to tag and monitor strays without their knowledge."

"Yeah, that about sums it up." Another rush of gratitude flooded me when I realized my dad was assuming Marc was still alive. "And he's probably trying to bring us proof."

"How did he know the chip was there?"

"I haven't figured that out yet. But I hope to be able to ask him soon." My heart pounded fiercely over the possibility, and I stood, ready to start the search immediately. "I'll keep you updated."

"Good." My father's footsteps paused along with his words, and I sensed a less pleasant change of subject. "Michael and Manx are on their way home, and they're going to drop Vic off on the way to help with the search."

Well, that was good, but… "Is it…*over?*"

"Yes. They took her claws."

My whole body suddenly felt heavy, and I sank back onto the bench press, devastated by the weight and permanence of such a…tragedy. Manx would never be the same again, and I couldn't decide whether I should be happy that she'd survived, or sad for what she'd lost, and the juxtaposition of those two emotions left me feeling confused and off balance.

"Faythe…there's more."

My heart dropped into my stomach at the dread echoing in my father's voice. If he didn't want to say something, chances were good that I wouldn't want to hear it. "What's wrong?"

"I need you to come home."

"I will. As soon as we find Marc. I want to bring him to the ranch to recuperate. We can't leave him here with the strays trying to kill him. And I don't think the council is in any position to say no to that, considering what one of your fellow Alphas has been up to lately. I can't wait for *that* load to hit the fan—"

"No, Faythe, you have to come home *now.* Kaci's getting worse. She passed out this afternoon."

A groan began deep in my throat, and my hand clenched around the metal bar. "You mean passed out, like 'fell asleep at the table,' right?"

"No." My father exhaled heavily. "She fainted in the hallway and hit her head pretty hard on the tile. She felt a little better after dinner, but then she fell asleep at seven-thirty. She's getting weaker, Faythe. If she doesn't Shift soon, she's not going to have the strength to do it at all. And you know what Dr. Carver said."

Yes, I knew. The doc thought we should force her Shift, but I had no doubt that if we did, she'd never forgive us. Never forgive *me.* She'd never trust me again, and she *needed* to trust *someone.*

"I can talk her into Shifting." I hoped I sounded more confident than I felt. "But, Dad, I can't leave until we find Marc. I *can't.*"

My father sighed, sounding every bit as conflicted as I felt. "I know how you feel. But the guys can look for Marc without you, and you're the only one who can help Kaci." Because everyone seemed to agree that I had the best shot of convincing her to Shift on her own. "But I'm not going to order you to come home. I can let Dr. Carver monitor a forced Shift, if you think she'd make it through okay. He's coming for a look at Manx's hands anyway."

I was pretty sure Kaci'd be fine, physically, after a forced Shift. But not psychologically. She needed to *want* to Shift, or we'd be in the same position a few weeks later. Only she'd no longer trust me to talk her through it.

"It's your decision," my father continued, and my heart beat so hard my chest actually ached.

My head fell against the wall at my back. Less than a year earlier, I'd whined about never being allowed to make my own choices. What the hell was I *thinking?* I couldn't choose between Marc and Kaci!

My dad cleared his throat to recapture my attention. "Faythe? What are you going to do?"

It was strange to hear that question coming from the man who, in the past, had simply told me what I would be doing.

"I don't know," I said, and immediately hated the sound of what had to be the weakest sentence I'd ever uttered. "Kaci clearly needs me. But I *need* to be here when we find Marc." The weight room swam as tears formed in my eyes, and I rubbed them away roughly, silently scolding myself. Tears wouldn't help Marc. Or Kaci.

"What would Marc say, if you could ask him?" my father asked gently.

I closed my eyes, wiping away more moisture. "He'd say that he'll be fine without me, but *she* needs me, and I damn well know it."

"And would he be right?"

"Yes." My next exhalation seemed to deflate me completely. "But I'm coming back as soon as she Shifts."

"Of course."

"I'll be there as soon as I can." I flipped the phone closed and glanced up to find Dan watching me from the hall, barefoot and naked from the waist up, a clean shirt in one hand. "How much of that did you hear?"

"Enough." He smiled sympathetically.

"And?"

His smile grew, even as the sad wrinkles around his eyes deepened. "You're doin' the right thing. Parker and I will be here for Marc. And he really would want you to go."

He was right. "Thanks."

Dan nodded, and turned to pull his shirt over his head, but as he lifted his arms, light from the dusty bulb overhead shined on something I'd never noticed. A small, smooth white scar right between his shoulder blades.

"Dan, wait!" My pulse raced, and I flipped my phone open, autodialing my father again.

"Faythe, what's wrong?" he asked in lieu of a greeting, as Dan raised one brow at me in question.

"Dad, can you have Dr. Carver leave for the ranch now? I think I just found the proof we needed."

Sixteen

We made it home by four-thirty in the morning with no trouble, and I actually managed nearly three hours of sleep while Dan and Ethan took shifts behind the wheel. They'd insisted I wasn't alert enough to drive, and I wasn't going to argue.

In spite of the early hour, my parents were both up when we walked through the front door, my mother wrist-deep in a colossal pile of shredded potatoes, while grease warmed in two massive cast-iron skillets on the stove. She was making hash browns to go with the huge platter of bacon already fried and ready to eat. Next would come eggs, and I knew by the scent of the entire house that homemade biscuits were already baking in the oven.

"Mom, you didn't have to do all this." I sank onto the closest bar stool and crossed my arms on the countertop, trying to hold my head upright though it felt about ten pounds too heavy from exhaustion.

"Kaci needs the energy, and from the look of the rest of you—" her gaze flicked over my shoulder to where Ethan and Dan had followed me into the kitchen "—so do you." My mother set down her shredder and rinsed her hands at the sink, then dried them on a clean towel hanging from a drawer handle. "You must be Mr. Painter," she said brightly, rounding the end of the peninsula with her arm extended.

Dan nodded and shook her hand. "Nice to meet you." I'd never seen him look so…bashful, and I was just plain amused by the amazement with which he watched my mother. And for a moment, I saw her through his eyes: pretty, petite, nurturing, and efficient, with a surprising strength in her handshake and a bright gleam of intelligence in the Caribbean depths of her eyes.

I smiled and waved the guys toward the remaining bar stools, then swiped a slice of bacon from the platter.

"You made fantastic time," my father said from the doorway, and I turned to see him frowning. "Which means someone drove entirely too fast."

I pointed at Ethan, and he smacked the back of my head, but his grin never faltered.

"Mr. Painter." My father stepped forward and extended his hand toward our guest, as Dan slid off his stool. Apprehension flitted across his face for a moment before his blank look settled into place—another lesson well learned from Marc. He shook my father's thick hand, and I couldn't help but contrast this greeting with the less enthusiastic welcome he'd gotten the last time he'd been on the ranch, when he was interrogated about the time he'd spent with Manx during her crime spree.

It felt like my entire world had been spun off its axis in the four months since then. Everything had changed, and not for the better.

"May I see this scar?" my father asked, and Dan turned and pulled his shirt off to present his back for examination under the bright fluorescent lights.

I smiled at the strange sight, while Dan flushed. I could sympathize. My partial Shift had been perfunctorily examined many times, and I hated being presented like a show horse. But Dan was a good sport about it, due in part to his agreeable nature. Though I assume he was also equally eager to have the foreign implant removed from his body.

I sympathized with that, too.

"I'll be damned..." my father mumbled, removing his glasses to squint at the short, smooth white line on Dan's back. "This is the strangest thing I've encountered in more than thirty years as an Alpha." He looked up and locked gazes with my mother, who had paused in the process of scooping shredded potatoes into the first skillet. "Things are changing, Karen."

She nodded mutely, the slight dip in the thin lines of her forehead the only indication that she shared his mounting concern with the state of the world. But that was plenty for those of us who knew her.

My father stood, his mouth tugged into a deep frown, and motioned for Dan to put his shirt back on. I knew what he was thinking. How could he possibly keep up with rogues committing crimes aided and inspired by technology he didn't know existed?

"Dr. Carver's running late, but he'll be here within the hour. We'll eat, then he can remove the chip from Mr. Painter's back." My Alpha's gaze found me as I snagged another piece of bacon. "And when Kaci wakes up, you *have* to talk her into Shifting."

I could only nod and chew my bacon, hoping Kaci was ready to get it over with.

Ethan went to the guesthouse to wake up Jace and Brian, and by the time they'd showered and dressed, Owen had joined the rest of us in the dining room. We were careful not to wake Kaci—though I couldn't resist peeking into her room to check on her—because in her weakened state, she needed all the sleep she could get. And because we didn't want her to hear about what had happened to Manx or Marc, or the possibility—however slim it was in my mind—that he might not be found alive.

She would have to know eventually, of course. But not until she'd Shifted and could regain her strength.

Dr. Carver arrived as we were sitting down to a huge, hot breakfast. My mother set another place at the long dining room table for him, and Ethan and I introduced Dan and caught everyone up on what had gone down in Mississippi. Including our suspicion that Kevin Mitchell was working for either his father or Calvin Malone, the two Alphas most outspoken about the "stray problem" and least concerned with violating the civil rights of a segment of the population they had no use for anyway.

I was on my third helping of scrambled eggs when soft footsteps whispered from the hallway, and Kaci stepped into the doorway, long brown curls tangled from sleep. She clutched the door frame with one thin, white hand, her huge eyes taking in all the new arrivals at once.

"Kaci!" I smiled and stood, cutting Ethan off in the middle of an off-color description of Eckard's corpse, hopefully before the tabby had heard too much. All eyes followed my gaze to the doorway, and my mother rose immediately to fill another plate, while I shoved Jace's empty chair over to make room for the one he had taken from against the rear wall.

"Why didn't you wake me up?" She lowered her frail form onto the chair between mine and Jace's, glaring at me with accusation swimming in her eyes. "I didn't even know you were coming home."

"It was a last-minute decision. Mr. Painter—" I gestured at Dan, by way of an introduction "—needed to see Dr. Carver for…a checkup. So Ethan and I brought him."

She wasn't buying it; I could tell from the firm, straight line of her mouth. But she'd learned enough diplomacy in her months with us—in spite of my sometimes less than perfect example—to know better than to call me out in front of everyone else. So Kaci just frowned and accepted the plate my mother handed her with a whispered "Thanks."

I'd been gone for less than forty-eight hours, but I couldn't believe the difference in her. Her eyes were dull, and looked bigger than they should have, while the rest of her seemed to have shrunk. Her skin was so pale I could clearly see the veins peeking through the dark smudges beneath her eyes, and her arms were all sharp angles, thanks to the too well-defined bones of her wrists and elbows.

While I watched her push eggs around on her plate, the table went quiet. No one seemed to know what to talk about, now that Kaci's arrival had put an end to the update on the search for Marc.

When everyone was finished except for Kaci, who'd finally donned a small smile as she watched Jace and Ethan spar with the last two sticks of my mother's homemade biscotti, my father gestured for me to follow him and Dr. Carver into his office. He shut the door behind us, and I sank onto the leather couch as if I hadn't just dozed through most of the drive home.

I *had* slept, but I hadn't slept well—not in several nights—and both the physical and emotional stress were getting to me.

Carver lowered himself onto the couch next to me, clutching a steaming mug of coffee in both hands while my father settled into his armchair. "I need to get Kaci out of the house until Dr. Carver has finished removing Dan's microchip. We don't want her to overhear any of that, for obvious reasons."

I nodded, but my gaze remained glued to the mug I was seriously starting to covet.

"What do you think, Danny?" my father continued, and I tried to tune back into the conversation. "How long will this procedure take?"

Carver shrugged and somehow avoided spilling his coffee. “Half an hour, at the most. It’s very simple. Local anesthetic, a short cut, pull out the microchip, then some sutures.”

“Do you think Kaci can handle a half-hour walk in the woods?”

The doctor nodded. “I don’t know that she’ll feel like walking the whole way, but if someone is willing to carry her when she gets tired, the fresh air might actually do her some good. Assuming she’s properly bundled.”

Fortunately, the cold front had already passed over Texas, so it was nearly ten degrees warmer at the ranch than it had been in Rosetta.

“I’ll take her.” I stood, intending to pour coffee into a travel mug before heading back into the great outdoors.

My father frowned, templing his hands beneath his chin. “I want you to stay here and rest. You look like hell.”

“Um…thanks?” But I sank back onto the couch, partially relieved. I couldn’t remember ever being quite so tired.

“Jace and Ethan can take her,” the Alpha continued. “She seems to enjoy their company.”

“Yeah, that’s because she has ovaries.” The wonder twins were chick magnets, plain and simple, and Kaci was not immune to their powers. But if anything, that strengthened my father’s argument. She’d enjoy a walk in the woods with two handsome, older men. And we could trust them to watch her carefully.

The Alpha dismissed us both, and the doc went to set up his stuff in Manx’s room, currently the only unoccupied bedroom in the house.

I headed into the kitchen for some coffee, but I got there just in time to see Jace pour the last of it into a clean mug. I groaned in frustration when he added sugar and cream, then began to stir. I’d hit that odd point of exhaustion at which I could no longer function without caffeine, but I was too tired to make a fresh pot of coffee. It was like being too hungry to eat, or too tired to sleep. Only worse.

"Damn it, Jace," I moaned, opening the cabinet over my head to pull out a five-pound bag of coffee beans.

He smiled and took the bag from my hands, replacing it with the mug. "I've already had two cups. This one's for you." Then he turned to the coffee grinder and dumped the beans in before I could reply.

"Thanks." My heart thumped harder when his hand brushed mine as he reached up to replace the bag of coffee, and I stepped back, confused and startled by the spark. I sipped from my mug and forced my pulse to slow. "Hey, can you and Ethan take Kaci for a short, predawn walk in the woods when she's done eating? To get her mind—and her ears—off of Dan's... *checkup.*"

At the sound of his name, Ethan looked up from the table in the dining room, where he was entertaining Kaci with impersonations of Owen during his single, disastrous semester as a 4-H roper, chasing terrified calves around their pens.

"No problem." Jace leaned against the counter next to me, and from the dining room, Ethan nodded, though his consent wasn't really necessary; the okay from one of them was assumed to go for both. It had been that way for most of their lives.

"Don't take her too far, and pick her up if she gets tired. We only need her out of the way for about thirty minutes, and we want her energized but not exhausted. At least, no more so than she already is. And I'll make sure she dresses warmly."

Jace smiled. "We'll take good care of her."

Fifteen minutes later, I watched through the back door as Kaci—bundled like an Eskimo in the arctic winter—

walked across the dark expanse of the backyard between her two favorite toms. She'd asked about Marc while I helped her dress, but I'd avoided specifics, telling her only that Ethan and I would return to help with the search after Dan's checkup. Jace was coming with us, too, since Michael would be back to help out on the ranch later that afternoon.

As soon as Kaci and her escorts disappeared into the woods, I took my refilled mug into Manx's room, where Dan had taken off his shirt and was now lying on his stomach on Manx's bed, which my mother had thoughtfully draped with black plastic. The patch of skin surrounding his scar was rust-red from iodine, and a clean white towel had been draped over the back of his head, to keep his hair from getting messy.

Carver was using a local anesthetic only, so Dan would be conscious and coherent the whole time, and thus able to answer questions during the simple procedure. Which would conveniently kill two birds while our thirteen-year-old stone was out of earshot.

"You have no memory of the implantation?" my father asked, from an overstuffed armchair opposite the bed. I leaned against the end of Des's crib, since there were no more seats.

"Uh-uh." Dan started to shake his head, then remembered there was a syringe poised over his back and froze. He flinched as the needle slid into his skin, then continued talking, as if to distract himself from the procedure. "I wouldn't've believed anything was in there if I hadn't seen the scar myself in the mirror."

Which I'd held for him. The placement of the microchips was genius; how many people study their upper backs in the mirror on a daily basis? Assuming there was no discomfort from the procedure, the strays would have no reason to suspect a thing.

Dr. Carver gave Dan another shot, and again the stray

flinched. Then the doc sat on the edge of the bed, waiting for the anesthesia to take effect.

My father cleared his throat. "Do you have any idea when this happened? Any lapse of memory?"

"Just one." Dan shrugged, an awkward movement, since he was lying facedown. "I went out drinkin' after work one night—I think it was a Thursday—and woke up the next mornin' with the worst hangover I ever had. I couldn't even stand up without getting dizzy, and I puked on the floor by my bed. I had to call in sick for work, and to this day I have no idea how I got home, or what I did before I got there."

"That seems to be the pattern," I said, then sipped from my mug while my father nodded. Then a new thought occurred to me. "Dan, has Marc ever seen that scar?"

"I don't think..." His eyes closed then opened almost immediately, and he raised his head awkwardly from the bed. "Wait, yes, he has! He asked me about it a couple of weeks ago, but I didn't know what scar he was talkin' about, 'cause I couldn't see it. I forgot all about that!"

I turned to my father in triumph. "That's how he knew! Marc had seen Dan's scar, then when he took Eckard's clothes for warmth, he noticed an identical mark on his back, and knew that was too weird to be a coincidence!"

My father nodded thoughtfully, and I could practically see the gears in his head turning.

When everything was ready, Dr. Carver chose a scalpel from the tools laid out on a clean towel over Manx's nightstand, and with my mother there to soak up the blood with a sterile white cloth, the doc made his first incision.

It was a lot easier than I'd expected. Just a single cut, then Dr. Carver used a special pair of tweezers to remove the chip—which was right where it should have been—and sewed Dan back up.

Dan felt no pain, but claimed he could feel weird tugging sensations, so he lay as still as he could, with his eyes squeezed shut.

"There." Dr. Carver sat up straight and handed his curved suture needle to my mother, who set it on a metal baking tray she'd brought in from the kitchen—at-home medical care at its finest. "Let's get you all cleaned up, and you'll be as good as new."

I stared at the tiny, blood-coated microchip lying beside the scalpel on my mother's tray. "Do you think we could trace a serial number from it, or something like that? Find out who—"

But the rest of my sentence was lost forever, swallowed whole by a sudden, urgent cry from the backyard.

"Help!" It was Jace, shouting with more fright and rage than I'd ever heard in his voice. "Someone help me with her!"

A jolt of adrenaline raced through me. My heart pounded. My hands clenched around the mug and it shattered in my grip, raining hot coffee and chunks of ceramic all over me and the floor. I was out of the room in an instant, and Owen's boots clomped on the floor behind me, where he'd emerged from the office. But my father was already halfway down the hall.

We burst through the back door almost as one. At my first glimpse of Jace—a deep shadow in the predawn darkness—my feet froze on the porch, and my breathing quickened with shock. Owen ran right into me. He would have knocked me down all four steps if my dad hadn't caught me.

My father paused only long enough to right me, then raced across the backyard with the speed of a much younger man.

Jace was halfway between the tree line and the back

door, jogging unsteadily, his arms held awkwardly in front of his chest. When he stepped into the light from the guesthouse porch, I saw that he carried Kaci in both arms. Her head bobbed limply near his right shoulder, her hair brushing his hip with each step. Her legs dangled from his other arm, one foot bare. Blood dripped steadily from either his right arm or her head, staining the dead grass with a trail of fat, red drops.

Owen grabbed my arm on his way down the stairs, hauling me with him. Two steps later, I'd come back to myself and was running of my own accord. We were still fifty feet from Jace when I caught the first whiff of the blood.

It was his, not hers. Thank goodness.

Still, my pulse spiked as I closed the distance between us. Why was he bleeding? Why was she unconscious? And where the *hell* was Ethan?

"…think she's okay," Jace was saying when I pulled close enough to hear him over my own ragged breathing and racing heart. "She just passed out. Here, take her." He held Kaci out to me and I took her without a second thought. "Gotta go back…"

Jace turned toward the trees, but my father stopped him with a single heavy hand on his shoulder. "What happened?" he asked, as I ran my gaze over Kaci's face and shoulders, then down both arms. Jace had said she was fine, but I had to verify that for myself.

Jace shook his head as if to clear it, and I could smell adrenaline pouring out of him and into the air. Mixing with the scent of his blood. Now that I held Kaci, his wound was exposed. The right sleeve of his coat was shredded, and his arm was ripped open from wrist to elbow, the skin dangling in several places. The bone exposed.

He'd been mauled.

My arms tightened around Kaci involuntarily, and a

moan escaped my lips before I could press them together. But incredibly, Jace didn't seem to have noticed his own injury.

"Four toms. Quarter mile southeast of the bend in the creek. Three Shifted. Alex is on foot."

The only Alex I knew was Alex Malone, Jace's half brother—the second son born to his mother and Calvin Malone. And if Alex was more than two years out of high school, I was Thomas O'Malley, the alley cat.

"Cal sent them for Kaci. Said not to come back without her." By the time Jace's mouth closed on that last word, his eyes had glazed with shock. He'd lost a lot of blood, and it was still flowing.

Owen's shirt hit the grass, and the guesthouse porch light glinted off his bare back in the cold. My father's face had grown grim, his eyes blazing in equal parts fear and fury. "Where's Ethan?"

Jace stumbled, and Owen put a hand out to steady him. "Stayed to fight. Told me to get Kaci home."

"Good." Dad took Jace's right hand and gently pulled his arm forward to inspect the injury. "Go in and let the doc get you fixed up," he said, as Kaci moaned in my arms. I hoped she'd wake up, but she only turned her head toward me. Her eyes never opened.

"I have to go back for Ethan," Jace insisted, even as he wobbled again from blood loss.

The Alpha scowled. "Go inside. That's an order." Jace closed his eyes briefly, then his jaw clenched in frustration, but he turned toward the house.

Owen stepped out of his pants and pulled off his socks.

My father's eyes met mine, and my heart beat so hard, so urgently, it actually hurt. "Take her to your mother. If she's sure Kaci's stable, you Shift and follow us. Understand?"

I glanced down at Owen, who'd just dropped onto all

fours. "Daddy, I'm faster. You know it." I could outrun any of the guys, and when I really concentrated, I could Shift in under two minutes. Owen couldn't do that.

The Alpha hesitated for a single heartbeat. Then he nodded and pulled Owen up by one arm. "Take Kaci inside and make sure Jace doesn't fall. Then Shift and follow us."

Before my brother could protest, I handed Kaci to him and tore my shirt open. Eight buttons flew into the dark, and cotton hit the grass an instant later. I shoved my jeans and underwear down together, then ripped the hooks right off my bra.

I dropped to the ground so hard my knees bruised, and my palm was cut open on a tiny pinecone. I Shifted faster than I ever had in my life, forcing the transformation in spite of the agony in every bone and joint of my body. A minute and a half later, I took off toward the creek on four paws, without bothering to stretch.

My cat-brain categorized sounds as I ran, classifying them as wind, insects, or small animals—all of which I dismissed. My ears rotated on my head like miniature radar dishes, and suddenly I picked up a collection of snapping twigs, hissing cats, and abbreviated roars that betrayed the fight still in progress.

At least for the moment. But Ethan couldn't hold off four cats by himself forever.

I'd only been running a few seconds when I heard my father behind me, huffing with exertion like a tiger. He was putting everything he had into this, and he would pay for it later. But hopefully not until we'd run off or disposed of the trespassers and gotten Ethan home safely.

Please, let us get Ethan home safely....

I ran silently now, slipping between trees and soaring over brush, focused only on getting to Ethan quickly and unannounced. The sounds of the fight grew louder. A solid thunk. A low, feline moan of pain. A hiss. Then

Ethan shouting, "Stay the hell back, you Benedict Arnold motherfuckers, or I'll bash your fucking skulls in!"

My heart leapt at the sound of his voice. Ethan was alive and shouting. And apparently holding his own by some miracle.

I zigged around a broad cedar and zagged around a fat clump of evergreen shrubs, and there they were. I had a single instant to absorb what I saw in the cold, predawn glow. Then I shoved off against the earth and went soaring.

My front paws hit the nearest cat. He fell onto his side. I clamped my jaws over his throat, squeezing but not puncturing. An enraged growl trickled from my throat, channeling my fear, fury, and triumph into the most primal sound I'd ever uttered in my life.

An instant later, my father leapt over a fallen log to pounce on the other cat, pinning him with little effort.

Between us, Alex Malone stood in jeans and a thick down jacket. He held his arms out in a defensive posture. His eyes went wide with surprise as he glanced from me to my father, then back again.

"'Bout time." Ethan's tone was light, but his eyes were serious and his jaw bulged with tension. He held a huge, gnarled branch no human could have lifted alone. Swung by a werecat, that branch could kill a man with a single blow. Which was no doubt how he'd managed to hold them off until we arrived.

"Alex, your dad has just made a *huge* mistake, and he's taking you down with him. You have a choice. You can scurry on home and tell Daddy you've failed—and you've just pissed off the biggest Pride in the country. Or you can tuck your tail, ask my father's forgiveness, and beg him to take you in. Because that's the only way you won't go down for this along with your Pride-mates."

Ethan glanced at our father, who was watching him

just like I was, with his jaw still clamped around the intruder's throat, his eyes rolled up almost painfully to keep my brother in sight. "What do you think, Dad? Do we have room in the cage to throw all three of them…"

But that's where my thoughts trailed off. *All three.* Jace had said there were four. So where was the missing werecat? Had Ethan already gotten one?

"We could lock them in together. Let them rip each other to pieces. What do you—"

A black blur dropped from a limb above, a soaring shadow I never had the chance to focus on. His front left paw hit Ethan's chest. His right batted away the huge branch. My brother landed on his back. The cat fell on top of him. Ethan's breath exploded from his lungs.

He reached to the side, left hand scrambling for his weapon. And before I could blink, the cat reared back and swatted him. Across the throat.

Blood poured from Ethan's neck. He gurgled, and his eyes went wide. They found mine, and his lips formed silent words. "Faythe. Help."

I roared and shoved myself away from the cat beneath me. But my father was already there. He knocked the cat off Ethan and onto the ground. His muzzle clamped over the bastard's esophagus and he jerked his head back without hesitation. My father ripped the tom's throat wide open.

The cats we'd pounced on took off into the woods, with Alex Malone on their tails.

Daddy turned his back on the dead tom and whined, nudging Ethan's head with his nose, licking a spray of blood from the line of his jaw.

Anguish washed over me, and I suddenly felt so heavy I could barely move. My chest seemed to constrict around my heart. My limbs wouldn't cooperate.

I crawled on my belly across five feet of cold earth, whining the whole way. I couldn't make it stop. Sounds of grief poured from my throat as blood poured from Ethan's. I sidled up next to him and laid my head on his torso, blinking through tears as his stomach rose and fell beneath me. Twice.

He blinked at me, his eyes the exact shade of green as my own. His mouth worked silently, opening and closing, as if he were trying to breathe. It was horrible. But then his mouth quit moving, and that was even more horrible. *Unbearable.*

Ethan's stomach stopped rising. He blinked one more time, then his eyes lost focus.

My father roared.

I cried.

Ethan was gone.

Seventeen

Cockleburs cut into my heels. Twigs poked between my toes. Branches slapped my bare stomach and arms, drawing blood. I walked naked through the woods, my vision oddly blurred, turning here and there out of habit, like a plane on autopilot.

Goose bumps covered my skin, and moisture froze on my face. I felt it, but I didn't really *feel* it. And I couldn't smell my blood at all. I could only smell Ethan's.

My father walked in front of me, bare shoulders shaking. He sobbed and choked, and my heart broke a little more with every sound. He held Ethan like a baby, my brother's head limp over one arm, his feet dangling over the other.

I don't remember Shifting. I don't remember much of anything after Ethan died, until the walking. I remember walking in the woods. My hair was tangled and my hands were bloody. Ethan's blood. I must have touched him.

But my father carried him. All the way home. At least half a mile.

Owen met us in cat form, about halfway there. He cried and roared and moaned. He tried to get Daddy to stop. To let him sniff Ethan and nuzzle him. But our father didn't stop. He didn't speak. He just walked.

We emerged from the woods into the backyard near the guesthouse, and had only gone a couple of steps when Dan burst from the back door of the house, still shirtless from his minor surgery. He ran toward us, but stopped when he saw Ethan. When he understood.

He shook his head. "Oh, no," he whispered. But we all heard him.

My mother came next. She pushed open the screen door and came out wiping her hands on her apron. Then she saw us. Saw Ethan.

"Nonononono...!" The anguish echoing in her screams broke my heart all over again. She ran toward us, apron clutched to her chest. My father walked on, even when she got in his path, clinging to him. Stroking bloody locks of hair from Ethan's face. "My baby boy..." She sobbed. Then, "Nononono..."

As she screamed, a shadow fell over the back door from inside. Dr. Carver stepped onto the porch, his face frozen in a mask of shock. Jace followed, his right arm wrapped from elbow to wrist, the blood soaking through his bandages highlighted in the harsh glow from the porch bulb. He moved slowly, his face already pale with pain and blood loss. But when he saw Ethan, he paled more.

"Jace..." I said, but my voice cracked on that one familiar syllable.

He stood frozen on the top step, staring. He blinked and his jaw bulged rhythmically, as if he were trying to unclench it but couldn't. Then he jogged down the steps and past us, tears glinting in the moonlight as they trailed down his cheeks.

A second later, the guesthouse door slammed shut, and I flinched.

With Jace's abrupt departure, grief flooded me, settling into place like sand sinking through water, anchoring me to the ground where I stood. Tears flooded my eyes and spilled onto my cheeks, burning my skin through the deep winter chill. My chest tightened unbearably, and I hugged myself to ease a numbing cold originating from within me, rather than from the January freeze.

Dr. Carver put one arm around my mother and fell in line behind my father, guiding her toward the house with Owen padding at his side, Dan bringing up the rear. I watched the door close behind them, but couldn't make myself follow.

Instead, I backed away from the main house, my head shaking slowly in denial. The sharp points of several holly leaves pricked my bare back, and distantly I realized I'd reached the side of the guesthouse. I sank to my knees, the grass bitterly cold on my naked legs, the holly catching in my hair.

The cold soaked into me as great, hiccuping sobs shook my entire body. I gasped for breath that seemed to freeze in my throat, to numb my lungs. My thoughts took no form. There was only a massive, horrible storm of pain and sorrow, slamming into me over and over again with an almost physical force. Grief threatened to drown me, and I made no effort to stop it.

"Faythe…" I looked up slowly to see Dr. Carver through my own tear soaked lashes. "Are you ready to go inside?"

"Not yet." I sniffed. "I need just one more minute." A minute to get myself together. To exorcise the worst of the tears, so I could rally my family instead of making them cry harder.

"Well then, let's at least get you dressed before you freeze." The doc knelt to grab my clothes from the ground where I'd dropped them when I Shifted, then hauled me up by both arms. He was right. Tears had formed little ice crystals on my eyelashes, and if I stayed out much longer they'd freeze right there on my face.

I stepped gratefully into my underwear and jeans, but my shirt and bra were ruined, so I could only put my arms through the sleeves and cross them over my chest to hold the material closed. Then Carver put a comforting arm around my waist and I let him lead me back across the yard and inside the main house.

At first, the heat was a blessing. It took the worst of my chill bumps and eased my chattering teeth, though it didn't even touch the trembling that had set into my limbs. But as my body began to recover from the cold, a large part of me wished I could remain frozen. Numb. Because the ache in my chest was unlike anything I'd ever suffered. It was like something gnawing me alive from the inside out, leaving a dark, empty cavity where my heart had once been.

It was unbearable, and every time I tried to rise above it, to bring reality into focus and concentrate on what lay ahead, I found myself sucked back into that mire of grief, from which I simply could not rise.

And the truth was that I didn't really want to. Not yet.

Because that would mean it was true. It had really happened.

But it couldn't have. Not to Ethan. If any of my parents' children should have lived forever, it would be Ethan. He was fearless. And in the end, that was the problem. He'd sent Jace and Kaci to safety while he'd stayed behind to keep the enemies at bay.

He had to know his chances of survival were slim, but he did it anyway.

Ethan, why did you have to play the hero? But the truth, though Ethan might not even have known it, was that for once, he wasn't playing.

In the hall, Dr. Carver paused at Kaci's room, where she still lay unconscious on the bed. Then he stopped us by the open bathroom door and waited while I washed Ethan's blood from my hands and rinsed my face. When

I was done, his hand closed around mine and I squeezed it, thankful that he was there. I'd rather have been comforted by Marc, but his absence was just one more entry on a long list of things that were currently irrevocably *fucked up* in my life at that moment.

When I had myself under control, we continued down the hall to the living room, where everyone else had gathered, and my father passed us on the way out. He walked stiffly down the hall and into his room. Seconds later, water ran in his bathroom, but over that, I heard him crying. Not the gentle, quiet tears he'd shed in the woods. Great, trembling sobs. Angry sobs, that spoke of imminent action and grim consequences.

Dr. Carver stopped in the doorway. "I have to go check on Kaci," he whispered. "Then I need to see what I can do for Jace's arm."

I nodded and he squeezed me one more time, then let me go.

In the living room, Ethan lay on the sofa, his head hidden from sight by the armrest. Someone had tucked his arm in at his side, and my mother sat on her knees in front of the couch, one hand stroking Ethan's hair back from his face. What little blood still dripped from his neck soaked into the cushion, then the front of her apron.

Owen sat on the floor, tail curled around himself, with his furry chin resting on Ethan's thigh. His eyes were closed, and if not for the occasional mournful whine coming from deep within his throat, I might have thought he was asleep.

I curled up in an armchair, glad I'd washed the blood from my hands. The couch was already stained, but I had the absurd thought that if I smeared blood on the white chair, everything would be worse somehow. That blood on satin would make it somehow more real. More gruesome.

Make Ethan more dead.

As I watched my mother, wondering what I should do to help her, my heart throbbed with every painful beat. With that suffocating grief. A never-ending ache I knew would soon morph into a rage unlike anything I'd ever experienced.

But for now, it was only bitter sorrow.

A door opened down the hall and my father was back, dressed in clean cotton pajama bottoms and his favorite blue robe.

"Karen." His voice was rough, like he was speaking through shards of glass. He cleared his throat and tried again. "Karen, you have to get up."

But she refused. She didn't even look at him, so my dad picked her up and carried her just like he'd carried Ethan. He put her in a chair opposite the couch and waved me over to sit with her. When I stood, wondering if it was even *possible* to comfort a woman who's just lost one of her children, my father crossed the room to sit in a chair in the far corner, where he leaned forward and buried his head in his hands.

"Mom?" I approached slowly, and she went stiff when I put one hand on her shoulder. "Let's get you cleaned up."

She looked at me then, and I had to close my mouth to stifle a gasp. She was covered in Ethan's blood. *Smeared* in it, like she'd hugged him. As soon as I thought it, I knew that's exactly what had happened. I had to get her out of those bloody clothes. My father acting distant and morose was unsettling. But it was even worse to watch my mother's quiet anguish.

My father was the front man. The obvious authority. But my mother was the steel backbone of my family, and without her standing tall and strong, we would all start to bend and wither.

I couldn't let that happen.

"Come on, Mom." I took her arm, and she let me help

her up. Then she surprised me—and frankly scared the *shit* out of me—by clinging to me. Her arms went around my neck and her head found my shoulder, instantly damp with her tears. Her weight went almost limp in my arms and all I could do was hold her tight while she cried, each sob shuddering through both of us.

When the tears slowed, I squeezed her and gently loosened my grip until she was supporting her own weight. Then I stepped back and met her eyes as she wiped her face with both hands, streaking Ethan's blood with her own tears.

Her eyes were red, her face swollen and splotchy, and her usually perfect makeup was now a distant memory.

"How 'bout some hot tea?"

"Of course." She stood straighter and squared her shoulders. Her head kind of twitched, as if she wanted to glance back at Ethan but had stopped herself at the last moment. "What kind would you like?"

"No, I was going to make *you* some tea."

"Don't be silly, Faythe. You've never made a pot of tea in your life, and I'm not going to be your first-brew guinea pig. I'll make it." Her eyes wandered down to my shirt, where blood from her clothes had soaked into mine. "But first, I want you to change clothes. I can't stand the sight of any more blood today."

That made two of us. "Mom…" I didn't know how to tell her without triggering more tears. "You, too." I glanced pointedly at the front of her ruined cashmere sweater, and her gaze followed mine.

Her face paled. "Oh." She turned and walked not quite steadily into the hall.

Owen followed, hopefully going to Shift and dress. Which left me alone with my dad. And with Ethan, of course.

My father stood at the living room window now, staring out at the sunrise just then lightening the front yard, a short, clear glass in his hand, empty but for a few drops of goldish liquid. I knew from the scent that it was Scotch. The good stuff he kept locked in his bottom desk drawer. But now the bottle sat on an occasional table against the wall, its lid off, its contents flavoring the very air.

My dad didn't seem to realize everyone else had gone. I crossed the room toward him, achingly conscious of my stained clothing, of Ethan's scent all over me. "Dad?"

"Hmm?"

But I hadn't thought the rest of it through, and had no idea what to say. Finally I decided to look forward, because my memories had nothing to offer but heartache. "Do we have a plan?"

He nodded, and when he turned, I saw that the pain in his eyes had been almost overtaken by a toxic, seething rage. I could see it churning just beneath the surface of his expression, his anger mounting with every passing moment. And I knew that when the pressure became too great, he would explode, and I could only hope I wouldn't become collateral damage.

"Yes, Faythe, we have a plan." His jaw tightened, and his gaze seemed to burn through me. "We will repay in kind."

"We're going to fight?" A vicious chill clawed its way up my spine, part grim satisfaction, part eagerness, and part fear. My dad wasn't talking about just any fight. Malone's men had killed the son of an Alpha on his own land. If we responded in kind, we wouldn't be finishing what they had started. We'd be starting something much bigger.

We'd be going to war.

"Of course we're going to fight. It is now obvious that Calvin Malone plans to be head of the Territorial Council no matter what it costs him, or anyone else. I wouldn't be surprised to find out he intends to have me assassinated next, and if that's his plan, so be it. He's welcome to try. But I will *not* stand by while he invades my territory and slaughters my children. He's going to pay in full for what he's taken from us."

Damn right! My fingers were tingling, eager to Shift into claws and get going on the retribution. "What can I do?"

He hesitated, his eyes still aimed at me, but unfocused. "Nothing yet. I need to think. Go get cleaned up."

I made my way to my room in a daze. My legs felt heavy, and dimly I noticed that my abused feet were leaving bloody footprints on the tile in the hall. I passed the dining room, where Dan sat at the long table, staring blankly at the wall, then the kitchen, where my mother was crying. But these were the soft, controlled sobs of acceptance. Terrible in their own way, but much easier to deal with.

In my bathroom, I stripped and stepped into the shower, letting my tears fall with the water as I watched blood—both Ethan's and mine—swirl down the drain.

Afterward, dry and dressed in clean clothes, I stared at my ruined shirt and jeans, wondering what to do with them. I'd never be able to wear them again, even if the blood came out by some miracle. Still, I couldn't bring myself to send them to the incinerator. In a weird way, they were the only part of Ethan I had left, and I wasn't ready to destroy that. Not yet.

So in the end, I left them where they lay, fully aware that I'd have to do something with them soon.

On my way back to the living room, I stopped to check on Kaci. She lay on the bed, on top of the quilted purple-and-pink comforter, her chest rising and falling rhythmically. Shallowly. At a glance, I thought she was simply sleeping. Then I realized she was still unconscious. Her socks and one remaining shoe lay on the floor at the foot of the bed, a heartbreaking reminder of how she'd lost the other one.

"How did it happen?"

I jumped, and looked up to find my mother standing beside me, in Kaci's doorway. I hadn't heard her approach. She wore a clean apron, and though her eyes were glazed, like she couldn't quite bring the world into focus, she sounded…okay.

I sighed, reluctant to talk about it so soon. But she had a right to hear how her son had died. "Jace said they were attacked a quarter mile from the stream by four of Malone's toms, including Alex in human form. The others were furry. Kaci passed out, which is no surprise. They probably scared the crap out of her, and she was already weak to start with."

"Damn that man," my mother muttered sharply beneath her breath, and I blinked at her in surprise. But then, I suppose if she'd ever had reason to use profanity, this was it. "He won't be happy until he pushes the whole council into full-scale war. And this may have done just that." She shook her head, then stepped into Kaci's room to take up a post in the chair beside the bed.

"How is she?" I followed her for a better look.

"Dr. Carver says she's okay, considering. Her pulse is weak, but no more so than it was last night. I think Jace is right, she just fainted."

Relieved, I exhaled slowly. I wasn't ready to really think about Ethan yet. Nowhere near ready. Focusing on Kaci was easier.

"She needs to Shift, Faythe," my mother said softly, arranging the tabby's hair over one shoulder.

"I know." That's why I had come home. But now life—and death—had gotten in the way.

I was in the kitchen starting another pot of coffee when my dad started shouting. "What I *want?* I want to know who the *hell* authorized an invasion of the south-central territory!"

We'd all heard my father yell before, of course. Usually at me. But I rarely heard him swear, and *never* with so much raw anger.

I rushed across the hall in my socks and hovered in the office doorway in shock, my mouth actually hanging open. My father stood behind his desk with the office phone pressed to his right ear. His face was scarlet with rage, his left fist pressed into the leather desk blotter. His eyes were dry, and his expression had shifted from insufferable pain to unquenchable anger.

"Surely you're exaggerating, Greg," a coarse, elderly voice said from the other end of the line, so soft I could barely make the words out. "I hardly think a diplomatic envoy could be considered an invasion."

"Envoy my *ass!*" my father shouted, and I almost choked on my own tongue. "Diplomatic envoys don't sneak onto private property in feline form. In fact, it's pretty damn *hard* to be diplomatic without the use of *speech.* It most certainly *was* an invasion, Paul, and I want to know how the hell this happened. Were you in on this? Did Malone call for a vote, or did he simply drop his men off at the border and send you a memo after the fact?"

Oh, shit. He was talking to Paul Blackwell. As the oldest member of the council, Blackwell had been chosen to lead it until either my father was reinstated or someone else was appointed to take his place.

So far, Malone was the front-runner. But for the moment, Councilman Blackwell was in charge, and it was never wise to piss off the head of the Territorial Council. Even the *temporary* head.

But then again, it was never wise to piss off Greg Sanders, either.

A door opened down the hall, and Owen and Dan appeared, both looking every bit as surprised and wary as I felt. They came toward me silently, and though Dan hung back, Owen and I hunched together to peer through the doorway at my father, as I'd never seen or heard him before.

"Of course there was a vote," Blackwell insisted evenly. "Did you think the council would fall apart without you here to run things?"

Our Alpha ignored that jab from the elderly councilman—whom my father himself had once called the most impartial man on the council—and when he responded, his voice had gone soft with hidden danger. "Why would anyone vote in favor of breaching a territorial boundary?" He paused for a moment, frowning in thought, then continued before Blackwell could answer. "Rick would never vote for such an injustice. Neither would Bert Di Carlo."

He was right. Neither Uncle Rick nor Vic's father would ever have voted to let Malone breach our boundaries and attack us. Beyond that, neither of them would have kept such a plot secret from my father.

"No..." Blackwell said, and even over the line I heard the reluctance in his voice. "Neither of them was called to session. It was a closed vote."

Oh hell.

A closed vote meant Malone and his men were openly positioning themselves in opposition not only to my father, but to all of the south-central Pride's potential allies. It was as close as we'd get to a declaration of war until the first blow actually fell.

Or until my father declared himself out for Malone's blood.

Eighteen

"A closed vote?" My father's voice was as cold and hard as steel. His rage charged the air like an electrical current, and I half expected to see his fingers spark where they held the phone.

"What's a closed vote?" Owen whispered, and I glanced at him in surprise. Then I realized he had no reason to be familiar with such an unusual political maneuver. I only understood because our father had been training me to take over for him my whole life—though I'd had no idea that's what he was doing until recently.

Since Dan was obviously also clueless, I addressed my whispered answer to them both, backing away from the door a bit to keep from being overheard by my father, who hadn't noticed us yet. Normally I wouldn't have revealed the inner workings of the Territorial Council to a stray, but Dan had already witnessed a lot of private happenings, and keeping a secret in a house full of werecats is next to impossible.

And, in my opinion, he'd already earned our trust, by fighting alongside us, and from all he'd done to help us find Marc.

"The council needs a simple majority vote in favor of a motion before it can be approved." Which even Dan probably already knew. "A closed vote is a way to get approval for something important without alerting certain members of the council. What you'd do is call for a vote only from those Alphas you're sure will vote in your favor. But it only works if there are enough of those to overrule the nays, assuming everyone not called would vote in the negative."

Dan looked confused, and if Owen had understood the concept before I started talking, he didn't now.

I took a deep breath and approached it from another angle. "In this case, Malone probably only called on the Alphas who are siding with him against Dad. Since Dad can't vote in a matter concerning himself, there were only nine possible votes, which makes five a simple majority. Malone obviously called on Paul Blackwell, and he probably also snagged Wes Gardner and Milo Mitchell. After that, he'd only need one more."

"So, if he can get enough surefire votes in his favor, he never even has to *tell* the Alphas who woulda voted against him?" Dan asked, brows raised in question.

"Exactly."

He frowned and shoved both hands in the pockets of his jeans. "Doesn't sound fair to me."

"Me, neither." In fact, I was getting angrier just thinking about it. "In an open vote, those who vote nay would have a chance to make their case, possibly convincing others to change their minds. But you don't get that in a closed vote. Which is exactly what Malone was counting on."

"So, who's the fifth vote?" Owen asked.

I shrugged. I hadn't heard another name mentioned, though we'd very possibly missed that, thanks to my bumbling explanation of Malone's slimy political tactics.

"Don't care what he *said* he was going to do. What he *actually* did was send four cats—three armed with claws and canines—onto the back of our property to try to take that poor, traumatized kitten by force. And when my son fought to protect her, they killed him."

Whatever Blackwell said next was too soft for me to hear, but his tone came through loud and clear. He sounded shocked and dismayed. Maybe even a little disillusioned, which struck me as a strange emotion coming from a man well into his seventies. At twenty-three, I wasn't sure I had many illusions left to lose, and I couldn't imagine how Blackwell could have attained such an advanced age with even a shred of naiveté still in place.

While Blackwell was speaking, my father's eye caught mine briefly and I stepped into the office, pulling Owen in with me. Dan followed—hesitantly, until I waved him in—and we all sat on the couch in a row, hardly daring to breathe for fear of interrupting.

"Ethan," my father said, answering a question I hadn't heard. He sank wearily into his chair, as if the act of speaking his dead son's name drained some vital bit of energy from him. "And no, it could *not* have been an accident. I was there. Malone's tom pounced on him from above and slashed him right across the throat." His voice broke on the last word, and my hand clenched around the arm of the couch.

"Greg, I'm terribly sorry for your loss," Blackwell said, but I could hear the *but* coming. "But if you had cooperated when you were asked to turn Kaci over, none of this would have happened. We had her best interest in mind."

"Bullshit!" my father roared, shooting up from his chair, and I actually jumped. "If you'd had *her* interests in mind, you would have asked me personally to give her up, rather than delegating that responsibility to Milo Mitchell, who's already declared his opposition to me."

Ahh, so he'd been talking to Kevin's father when he refused to give Kaci up.... Small world.

"You could have chosen to place Kaci with a neutral third party, rather than with Calvin Malone," my father continued, acid practically dripping from his words. "You can't tell me you actually thought I'd turn her over to him without a struggle. And I'd bet my future on the council that *he* never expected me to. He was counting on a fight. He probably already had his men in place and ready to move before I ever even got the call about Kaci.

"Hell, if you *really* cared about her, and if you were *really* convinced she's in danger here, you'd have arranged to take her in some manner that wouldn't put her at further risk. Malone's men frightened her so badly she lost consciousness. So don't try to tell me this is my fault. I've *been* in your position, Paul. I've been head of the council for nearly fifteen years, and I have never *once* let my own ambition get in the way of the common goal." Survival of the species, of course. "And that's *exactly* what Calvin Malone is doing."

For a moment, there was only silence but for the anxious heartbeats and shallow breathing around the room, and I wondered if the other Alpha had hung up.

"No, you would never let ambition impede us," Blackwell replied finally, sounding so calm and collected that I wanted to grab the old man's cane and beat him with it. "I have little doubt of that. But you *would* let your *daughter* get in the way of the common goal. Did you really think we'd let you raise another young woman to turn her nose up at her duty?"

That wrinkled old bastard! I was actually on my feet for nearly a second before Owen pulled me back down.

My father turned around so fast his chair rolled backward to smack the display cabinet behind him, rattling the glass in its frame. "My daughter is *none* of your business!" he roared, so loud I could swear I saw pencils shake in the marble jar on his desk. On my right, Owen was breathing hard, and Dan's pulse was racing.

Our Alpha was throwing large doses of anger and aggression into the air, and we were breathing it in like secondhand smoke. The buzz was just as addictive, and every bit as dangerous.

And if it didn't stop soon, our high would end in a serious case of community bloodlust.

But even with his face violently flushed and his fists clenched, my father seemed unaware of the tension building in the room. "And you know damn well that if it weren't for Faythe, both Abby Wade and Carissa Taylor would be dead by now. Or worse."

Was I the only one who felt like applauding?

"That may be," Blackwell conceded softly. "And I'm sure I speak for everyone when I say how grateful we are for the tabbies' well-being. But that doesn't change any of this, Greg."

My dad inhaled slowly, obviously trying to regain his composure as his colleague continued.

"The fact remains that two days ago, five members of the Territorial Council met and decided unanimously to remove Kaci Dillon from your care. That decision was based on your own most recent report on her deteriorating health. We sent her with you in the first place because she seemed to have bonded with your daughter, but if that bond cannot keep her healthy, we would rather see the kitten placed with an Alpha who can be counted on to raise her in accordance with the ideals of the council."

My father's next words were menacingly soft, and I recognized the current of danger running through them. "Kaci is getting the best *possible* care here, Paul. Faythe is sure she will Shift very soon—*today*—and Dr. Carver assures us that once she has, her health problems will clear up almost immediately."

Blackwell sighed. "I'm sorry, Greg, but that's too little, too late. We've already voted to remove her."

"Did you vote to kill my son in the process?" our

Alpha demanded, and the tension in his office ratcheted up another notch. I couldn't help wondering if Councilman Blackwell could feel it from his end of the line.

"Of course not. And Calvin will be reprimanded for his entire approach."

"Reprimanded?" I squeezed Owen's hand when he took mine to quiet me. *"Ouch,"* I whispered furiously, half hoping Blackwell could hear me. "Careful you don't slice him open with your sharp *words!*"

"Don't bother!" my father snapped into the phone. "I'll deal with Calvin Malone myself. And let me tell you something else, *Councilman...*" Daddy's words dripped with venom, and as badly as I'd wanted to see him confront the other Alphas over the past few months, I couldn't shake the certainty that threatening the current head of the council wasn't the best way to go about that.

But as usual, my opinion was unsolicited.

"Malone has obviously decided that full-scale war is the most expedient way to put himself in charge of the council. Maybe he's hoping the threat alone will be enough to make me bow out, or maybe he truly believes the rest of you will fight with him. I'd like to think you all understand that fighting amongst the North American Prides will only show our neighbors to the south that we have neither the time nor the resources to deal with the threat they represent."

My father sucked in a deep breath and closed his eyes briefly before continuing. "But if I'm wrong, if you've bought into Malone's propaganda—his vision of the council as his own person kingdom, with him on the throne—then heaven help us all."

He paused, rubbing his forehead as if to stave off a headache. "The time for diplomacy has ended, Paul. Now is the time for *action,* and if a war is what you want, the south-central Pride can *damn well* deliver."

With that, my father hung up on Paul Blackwell,

dropped the phone back into its cradle, and sank into his chair so wearily he seemed to have no bones left to support his weight.

"Damn…" I whispered, watching as our Alpha wheeled his chair forward and propped both elbows on his desk, burying his head in his hands. He sat like that for several seconds, and I was about to ask if he was okay when he suddenly launched himself from his chair. His hand shot out almost faster than I could track its movement, and a moment later his marble pencil holder slammed into the concrete wall above the bar.

The jar broke into three uneven chunks, raining pens and pencils all over the bar. One piece of marble shattered the glass in which it landed. Another knocked a half-empty bottle of Scotch to the floor, where it remained miraculously unbroken.

Owen rose to clean up the mess, but I couldn't tear my gaze from my father. Until my mother spoke.

"Greg?"

I turned to find her standing in the doorway, wearing a fresh blouse and pair of slacks, as if it were two in the afternoon, rather than seven-thirty in the morning. She stared at my father for a moment, and when his eyes met hers, something passed between them. Something I couldn't understand. Something born of thirty-three years of marriage and more shared crises than I could remember, or even imagine.

"Could we have a moment please?" she asked in as reasonable a tone as I'd ever heard, yet there was no question she expected to be obeyed. I headed across the hall into the kitchen, and Owen and Dan followed me. The office door closed softly behind us as I settled into a chair at the breakfast table, suddenly hating the floral-print tablecloth for no reason other than that it was cheerful when I wanted to cry. Or break something.

Owen sat next to me, and Dan took the seat across

from him. "Damn," Dan whispered, rubbing one hand through his thick brown hair. "Do your Alphas always fight like that?"

"Lately? Yeah."

Owen sighed and set his cowboy hat on the table, which he would never have done in front of our mother. "You think he was serious?"

"Without a doubt." I was starting to wish I'd snagged a bottle of something strong on my way into the kitchen.

"So...what happened to Ethan? That had nothing to do with Kevin Mitchell, and Marc being missing. Right?" Dan's eyes pleaded with me to confirm his assumption, as if a connection between the two tragedies would have made the whole thing entirely too complicated to deal with.

"Not that I know of. I think this was just about Pride politics. Calvin Malone trying to gain control of as many tabbies as he can."

Five minutes later, my mother emerged from the office, leaving silence in her wake. She crossed directly into the kitchen and pulled the teapot from the stove. I thought I was the only one who noticed her hand shaking until Owen rose to take the pot from her, dropping his hat in his chair on the way.

"I'm sorry, hon," she whispered, stroking his arm as he set the pot on the tile countertop. I think she just wanted to touch him. To reassure herself that he was real. Because Owen was now her youngest son.

When she stopped shaking, my mother served us tea in tiny china cups that looked like toys in the guys' huge hands. I sipped something spiced with cinnamon, but the ten minutes it took for me to drain my cup were pure torture. Dan kept glancing at the doorway, as if he wanted to leave but didn't want to be rude. And didn't know where to go. And it occurred to me then that he was stuck there with us, an outsider in our private hell.

My mother and Owen stared at the tabletop, occasionally wiping their eyes with a tissue from the box she'd put in the middle of the table, apparently content to suffer quietly.

I couldn't take it. I could do silence on my own.

When my first cup was empty, I set it in the sink and announced that I was going to go check on Jace. No one even looked up.

My father was still alone in his office, staring down at his desk blotter, sipping from another short glass. Jace wasn't in either the dining room or the living room, so on my way to the back door, I checked the room Ethan and Owen had shared, just in case. It was empty, thank goodness. I wasn't sure I could handle being in there just yet.

I also checked on Kaci, who seemed to be sleeping now, rather than truly unconscious. She was even snoring lightly, and had turned onto her side, while Dr. Carver dozed in the chair beside her bed, his mouth hanging open. Now that I knew the kitten was okay. I couldn't help hoping her nap would last a little while. I had to get myself under control before I could explain Ethan's death to the thirteen-year-old he'd died defending.

I headed into the backyard, where the frozen grass—stubbornly resisting the weak warmth of the winter sun—reminded me that I'd forgotten my shoes. Instead of going back for them, I raced across the yard toward the guesthouse. The frigid air and bright morning light were invigorating, but did nothing to alleviate the black mood that had enveloped me with Ethan's death and showed no sign of fading.

The rough wood planks of the guesthouse porch were a relief to my feet after sharp, icy blades of grass, and I paused to gather myself before going in. But my thoughts weren't clear enough to truly organize, so I opened the door and stepped inside anyway. I'd have to wing it.

The door creaked and gave away my presence, but Jace didn't look up. He sat on the floor, leaning against the beat-up couch with his knees bent in front of his chest, his heavily wrapped right arm draped over them. His head hung low, as if his neck would no longer support it. His shirt lay on the floor against the opposite wall, where he'd obviously thrown it after the doc had cut it off to tend to his injury.

In that moment, for the first time in my life, I wished I was older. Wiser. I wished desperately for the words to comfort us both. But I didn't have them. I had only my own misery, and the willingness to keep his misery company.

The door squealed again as I closed it, cutting off the icy draft, and I crossed the scarred hardwood to sink cross-legged to the floor next to him. "Hey."

"Hey." His voice was gruff, as if he had a cold. But he didn't look up.

I inhaled deeply and nearly choked on the scent of tequila, though a glance around the room revealed no bottle and no glasses, other than the usual sticky, half-empty ones standing on cheap, scarred end tables around the room. But when I leaned forward and looked around Jace's legs, I found a bottle of Jose Cuervo, a third of the way gone, no lid in sight.

"How's your arm?"

"All sewn up, but even after Shifting twice, it looks like chopped sirloin. Still hurts like hell, but this works better than the doc's big white pills." He held up the bottle briefly.

"You probably should have taken the pills."

"They only work on my arm," he whispered, and I didn't need to ask where else he hurt. The doctor's pills couldn't touch a broken heart. I knew that better than most.

I sighed and leaned against the couch, forcing my

gaze back to my brother's lifelong best friend, who was hurting every bit as much as I was. "Pass the bottle."

He finally looked up, frowning. "You hate tequila."

"I hate this more." Surely a drink would quiet the incessant buzz of angry questions swarming my head so I could concentrate on one at a time.

Or so that maybe—for just a little while—I could think about nothing.

He passed the Cuervo with his good hand, and I guessed by the absence of a glass that we were drinking straight from the bottle. I turned it up without hesitation and made myself swallow twice. The alcohol burned bitterly going down, but if anything, it seemed to bring feeling back to my insides, which had been numb for the better part of the morning.

Jace took the bottle back and gulped from it, besting me by at least three swallows. This time he set it between us and met my gaze. Brown waves fell around his forehead, framing reddened eyes that blazed bright blue, shimmering with tears. "Why the *hell* would Calvin risk all-out war to snatch Kaci?"

I let my head fall back against the couch and stared at the opposite wall. "Because my dad wouldn't hand her over peacefully." And because he was probably *counting* on all-out war. But I didn't want to mention that possibility to Jace just yet.

"What?" His eyes widened, and his hand clenched around the neck of the bottle.

"I heard him on the phone with Milo Mitchell, and Mitchell was clearly speaking on your stepfather's behalf. He said that because of the allegations against my dad, and Kaci's failing health, several of the council members voted to remove her from the ranch."

"That's bullshit."

"Yeah." I took the bottle and tipped it back again. "Hardly matters now, though, does it?"

Jace didn't answer, so I lifted the bottle one more time. I took three more swallows of tequila and knew I was done. I wanted to be numb, not drunk, and if I kept drinking so fast, even with my enhanced metabolic rate, I'd be risking impaired judgment.

But Jace took another long drink. "Why did he do it, Faythe?" he demanded, and I knew we were no longer talking about Calvin Malone. Jace put the bottle down and covered his eyes with one hand, his jaw trembling with the effort to hold back tears. If he cried, I'd begin all over again.

I started to tell him I didn't know. But I *did* know. "Because that's who he is." *Was,* my brain insisted, but my heart rejected the internal edit. "Ethan lived larger than life, and it kind of makes sense that he'd die that way. Protecting someone else."

But it did *not* make sense that he'd die at twenty-five years old.

Jace nodded but looked less than convinced. He stared into my eyes from inches away, his focus shifting from one to the other, as if he were searching for some great truth deep inside me. But whatever that truth was, I didn't possess it, and finally he gave up looking. He blinked, and when his eyes opened again, they were full of tears, magnifying the rings of cobalt that made up his irises.

"What am I going to do without him?"

My heart broke, not just because of the words, but because of the earnest despair with which he spoke them.

I inhaled deeply, and when that didn't help, I reached for the bottle again. One more wouldn't hurt, and I couldn't stand the pain in his eyes without it. So I took a long gulp. Then another, just for good measure.

It didn't burn so much that time. Which was probably a bad sign.

"You're going to do the same thing I'm going to do,"

I said, trying to project strength I didn't feel. "The same thing we're all going to do. Today, you're going to cry, and scream, and hit things if you need to. Let it all out now. Because soon we're going to make them pay, and for that, we'll need everyone in top form."

Especially with so many of our men out looking for Marc. Our forces were split, and our numbers were dwindling faster than we could replace the missing members. And the truth was that we didn't *want* to replace them. We wanted them all *back*. Including Marc. I wouldn't be able to stand losing him so close to losing Ethan.

"Count on it." Jace closed his eyes briefly, as if whatever he had to say next would be especially painful. "I'll have to go after that. After we make Calvin pay."

"What? Why?" I sat up too fast, and the entire room spun around me, my pulse racing in alarm. Would he really desert us when we needed him most? When we were already crippled by a double loss?

Jace frowned, like his logic should have been obvious. "I'm here because of Ethan." He raised the bottle again, as if those very words hurt. "He's more of a brother to me than my own brothers, and he was the only one who ever really gave a damn about me after my dad died and my mom married Calvin. He got your dad to take me on as an enforcer the day I turned eighteen, to get me away from Cal. But now Ethan's gone, and it's my stepfather's fault. You think Greg's still going to want me around? To remind him every day of how his son died?"

He gulped from the bottle again, and I was shocked to see that it was now more than half-gone. How much had he had? How much had *I* had?

"Okay, give me that." I took the tequila, and he let me because he thought I was going to drink from it again. Instead, I reached back to set it on the nearest end table. But the table seemed to tilt away from me, and I almost missed.

"Listen to me, Jace," I began, but by then his eyelids were heavy and his eyes were starting to look glazed. It was too late for much real listening on his part, and soon I might be past the point of rational speech. But I had to try.

"*Look* at me." I held his chin, short stubble rough beneath my fingers, and made him meet my eyes. "Daddy's not going to kick you out. He wouldn't let you go if you *tried* to. And neither would I. We *need* you." My own eyes filled with tears, my recent losses threatening to overwhelm me. "Please don't go. I can't handle losing you, too."

Jace blinked and his expression shifted, his focus narrowing on me, as if everything else had ceased to exist. On his face, I saw only pain and need, and I dropped his chin, nearly scalded by the look in his eyes.

His good hand rose slowly, and when his fingers touched my cheek they were warm. *So* warm. "You're all I have left."

Oh, *no*. He would never have said that if he were sober. He might have *thought* it, but wouldn't have vocalized.

But before I could respond—and I had no idea what to say—his hand slid back to cup my head, and he kissed me.

Nineteen

Jace's mouth was soft and warm, and damp with tequila. He tasted like the numbness I craved. Like comfort, and shared pain. I could have become mired in that kiss like quicksand—unaware I was sinking until it was too late to fight. And for a moment I was. I got lost in mutual, inarticulate grief and the promise of a temporary respite.

And I kissed him back. Simply because it felt good. Everything around me was falling apart. Ryan was missing, Manx had been declawed, and my father was being impeached. Kaci was slowly killing herself, and Ethan was dead.

And Marc was gone.

But Jace was right there, and kissing him felt *good,* when I really needed *something* to. That kiss was the only thing in my life that didn't hurt, at that moment. Though if I'd thought it through, I would have known that in the end, it could hurt as badly as any of those other life-wounds.

But I wasn't thinking. I was *feeling.* I was feeling Jace's mouth on mine. His scent surrounding me. His hand in my hair. I was feeling how badly he wanted this. How badly he wanted *me,* and needed to know that someone still loved him. Especially now that Ethan was gone, leaving a huge wound in both of our hearts. A wound begging to be healed…

We couldn't heal it. *Ever.* A small part of each of us had died along with Ethan, and we could never get those parts back. The best we could do was bandage the wounds.

He kissed me again, and I was no more prepared the second time around. But *he* was. That second kiss started out gentle, but built quickly when I didn't pull away. I *should* have pulled away. But I didn't, and the next thing I knew, I was pressed between the front of the couch and the front of Jace, his hand on my waist, his tongue in my mouth. His grief feeding my own.

His mouth sucked at mine desperately, his lips soft but insistent. His left hand tilted my head gently, giving him a deeper angle, and when my fingers found the curve of his good arm, his pulse spiked. He inhaled sharply, but his mouth never left mine.

I pulled away, confused as a wave of dizziness washed over me. "Wait…"

"I've always loved you," he murmured against my ear, his words slurred but earnest. He kissed me again, and whatever resistance I'd felt before melted away like sugar on my tongue. My hand trailed from his arm to his chest, lingering on the smooth, hard lines, and I found myself deepening our kiss, sucking on his lower lip as he moaned into my mouth.

His fingers traced my hair down my back, then followed my lowest rib around to my stomach, where he lifted my shirt slowly, trailing his fingers along my skin.

I groaned when his hand found my right breast through my bra, and his tongue dipped deeper into my mouth. Then, suddenly impatient, he pulled the material from my skin and lifted my breast, squeezing gently.

My heart sped up until I thought it would break free from my chest, and I closed my eyes as a surge of vertigo crashed over me, liberally laced with an intoxicating dose of need.

Jace pulled away from me just long enough to tug my shirt over my head, careful with his injured arm, then his mouth found mine again quickly, as if to cut off any protest I might utter. His hands went around my back, and an instant later my bra gave way, leaving my breasts bare and heavy. I let the material fall to the floor, as his good arm slipped around me again, angling us both sideways as he gently lowered me to the floor, propped on his right elbow, as if he felt no pain from his injured limb.

The hardwood was cold against my back, but I only had a moment to notice that, because in the next, he'd tugged the button at my waist free from its hole, and was pulling my pants down, one-handed. My jeans landed in a heap on the floor near my head.

Jace was undressed in less than a heartbeat, and his warm, firm weight settled onto me as his mouth found mine again. He throbbed against my stomach, hot and hard. His hand roamed slowly down my side. He gripped my hip tightly and groaned against my jaw as his lips trailed toward my throat. I curled my hand in his hair and he shifted carefully to one side, pushing my underwear down, gripping my backside as the material slid over my skin.

He sat up on his knees then and fumbled for his pants with both hands, flinching when his bandaged arm brushed the couch. Plastic ripped, and I had a moment to wonder if he always carried a condom in his pocket. Then he was back.

Pleasantly dizzy, I let my fingers wander his back as the muscles bunched and shifted with each movement. My spine arched as his tongue wet a path from my throat to trail between my breasts. He lifted my left leg, then settled himself between my thighs.

My pulse spiked, and I felt my legs wrap around his waist. They tightened around him involuntarily when his hand moved between us. His mouth closed around my nipple, sucking gently as one finger slid inside me, testing. I clenched around him, and he groaned again, withdrawing his finger slowly.

My head swam, and I tried to close my eyes. But he took my chin in hand until I looked at him. Then he entered me gradually, as if each centimeter should be treasured individually. I couldn't breathe until he was all the way in, filling me with an unfamiliar thickness. For a moment, neither of us moved.

His eyes burned into me, blue flames of pain and longing, blazing in spite of the tears threatening to douse them. Then he moved within me, and I arched up to meet him with each stroke, my fingers trailing over the familiar planes of his body—lines and muscles I'd seen a million times but never truly experienced.

His eyes never closed. Not even at the end, when everything tightened around an intense spiral of pleasure, uncoiling within me. Within us both. My hips arched to meet his, seeking more friction, faster contact. And finally he shuddered from head to toe as my legs clenched around his hips, holding us tightly together.

I let my eyes close, and my body relaxed onto the floor, allowing the cold surface of the wood to leach some of the heat from our union, mercifully cooling my overheated body.

"Faythe..." he said, running one finger down the damp line of my chin, angling my face toward him. I opened my eyes to find the cobalt in his sparkling brighter than I'd ever seen it.

But that blue wasn't right. I should have been looking into *brown* eyes, sparkling with tiny flecks of gold. *This is all wrong!*

"No. Oh, *no.* Jace, I..." I planted both hands on his

chest and pushed him away, guilt and confusion shredding my heart like claws through cotton. What the hell had I *done?*

Tears filled my eyes, mercifully blurring first his bewilderment, then heartbreak. Then horror. He scrambled off me, banging his bad arm on the sofa cushion and leaving me cold and empty. And miserable.

"Faythe…?" The tremor in his voice broke my heart. Then understanding surfaced, and his tear-filled eyes searched mine desperately. "No. *No,*" he whispered through clenched teeth. "This was *not* wrong. It's the only thing I've done right in months. Don't you *dare* regret this."

"Jace, I'm sorry…."

"Damn you, Faythe." He choked on the words, holding back his own sob. He grabbed my arm, holding me in place when I tried to stand. "I'm not going to let you do this to yourself. Or to me. No matter what happens next, we've done *nothing* wrong. We were there for each other. That's it."

I nodded, but I knew better, and my heart felt so heavy each beat actually hurt. "I know. But this…" I gestured back and forth between us. "We can't do this. I'm with Marc. I *love* Marc." And the real bitch was that I'd still love him even if he never forgave me for what I'd just done. Which was a virtual guarantee…

Fresh tears trailed down my cheeks, scalding me as I looked at Jace. Hating myself. Weren't things bad enough already? How did I always manage to make everything worse?

Determination glinted in his eyes, and was set in the firm line of his mouth. "This isn't about Marc. I *know* you love him, and he'd move the earth to be with you. We *all* know that. But I love you, too, and we could be missing out on something great." His sudden fortitude shocked me. Scared me. "Faythe, don't push me away. You're *all* I have left."

I squeezed my eyes shut and took several deep breaths, trying not to smell Jace in front of me, not to taste him on my lips. But it was useless. In that moment, Jace was *everywhere.* He was in my mind, he was in my heart, and he was in my memory. He smelled good. He tasted good. And the blissful aftershock still throbbing in my most sensitive places felt wonderful, when everything else in my life was an obstacle to be overcome.

No! That's not *fair.* I shouldn't feel pleasure and comfort from someone else while Marc was out there suffering somewhere, trying to get back to me.

"Don't do this, Jace," I begged, because the truth was that I wasn't sure I could put this behind me, if he wasn't willing to do the same thing. I opened my eyes to find him staring at me in heartrending vulnerability backed by resolve the likes of which I'd never seen in him. "We can't do this to Marc."

Jace shook his head, and a fine, hard edge of irritation peeked through his expression, as if he were tired of having to explain such simple concepts. "I'm not asking you to leave him. I'm just asking you not to leave *me.* Don't count me out."

What? My heart tripped, and my stomach pitched in anticipation. "What are you saying?"

"I'm saying that I can wait. For now. But when things get back to normal—assuming that ever happens—I want my shot. We can make each other happy, Faythe. I know it. And I'm done walking away from things I want just because they don't come easily. You're worth the work."

Oh, now, *he decides he's Alpha material…*

The front door opened on my left, and cold air swirled inside to douse the heat we'd built. Jace whirled around and swiped the back of one hand across his mouth, as if that would hide what we'd done.

It wouldn't, and neither would covering myself, yet I

pulled my shirt from the pile of discarded clothing and clutched it to my chest, as if it could also cover my guilt.

Dr. Danny Carver stood frozen in the entry, one hand still on the doorknob. His face was carefully devoid of judgment, but in the werecat world, that only meant he was thinking things he didn't want us to see. "Um...Greg wants everyone in his office."

"Sure." Jace stood and scooped up his pants in a single, graceful movement no human could have managed. Though in that moment, I probably couldn't have managed it, either. "Let me get a clean shirt." His eyes were still red, and the doc's gaze softened when he saw that. He thought he knew what had happened; I could see that in his face. He thought we were comforting each other the best way we knew how. And he was right. But he had no idea it went beyond that. Maybe way, *way* beyond that.

Jace was gone in seconds, his heavy steps echoing up the stairs, and a moment later, water ran from the shower. But his eyes burned into mine from my own memory, long after he was gone.

I pulled my shirt over my head and stood to step into my underwear, gripping the arm of the couch for balance. I was dizzy, and I didn't know whether I had Jace or the tequila to thank for that.

"You okay?" Carver closed the door and reached for my arm to steady me, but I waved him off as I pulled my pants back on. "I'm fine. Well, as fine as everyone else, anyway."

He nodded and lifted the mostly empty bottle of tequila from the end table, amusement glinting in his eyes. "Faythe, this is only to be used under the supervision of a *responsible* adult. And for the record, Jace Hammond doesn't qualify."

But he had no idea how much growing up Jace had just done.

I sighed, dreading what I had to say next, but knowing it had to be said. "Dr. Carver, Danny, *please* don't tell anyone…." I let my eyes plead for me and, to my horror, they began to water, and suddenly the doc swam in a swirling pool of my own regret and confusion.

"About you and Jace?"

"There *is* no me and Jace," I insisted, wiping away tears with the heels of my hands. *There* can't *be*….

"That's not what it looked like."

"Doc—"

But he held up one hand to cut me off. "It's none of my business." That was an attitude no one else seemed to share and part of me thought it would be easier if he'd just start yelling. I knew how to handle yelling.

The doctor shrugged and tequila sloshed in the bottle. "You're both upset, and when people aren't thinking straight, shit happens." Bending, he picked up the lid and screwed it on before setting the bottle down. "And we all know Cuervo's good at making shit happen. Just tell me you know what you're doing and promise you won't have any more of *this,* and I'll forget I saw anything."

I sighed and sank onto the couch, my head buried in both hands. "I've got that second one covered. No more tequila. But the truth is that I have no idea what the *hell* I'm doing."

Carver smiled sympathetically. "Well, until you figure it out, I suggest you take a shower. You smell like Jace."

Twenty

"Put your father on the phone *this instant,*" my dad shouted, stomping the length of the Oriental rug, then several feet onto the hardwood before turning. "You do *not* want to get mixed up in this, Brett. I don't care where he is or what he's doing. Find him. *Now!*"

I flinched when he shouted, and my hand clenched around the arm of the leather couch.

"I'm sorry, Councilman Sanders," Brett Malone said over the phone, but judging from the rage on my father's face, he could never be sorry enough to make any difference. And he got no bonus points for referring to my father as a councilman in spite of his tenuous position on the council. "But my dad's not here right now. I don't know where he went, and I don't know when he'll be back."

My father blinked in blatant disbelief. "It's nine thirty in the morning, and he works from home."

"Yes, sir." Brett sounded truly miserable—and scared shitless—and I almost felt sorry for him. He hadn't *chosen* to be born to Calvin Malone, and what little contact I'd had with him in the past had convinced me he did not see eye to eye with his father. It was thanks to Brett that we'd had a heads-up about my dad's impeachment a couple of days in advance.

But my father was beyond logic, and I couldn't really blame him.

"You can't tell me he doesn't have a cell phone!" Our Alpha stomped back across the rug toward his desk this time. The floor shook with each step, and I ran both hands through my shower-damp hair to keep from fidgeting.

I'd thought I would enjoy this—seeing him jerk a much-anticipated knot in Malone's figurative tail. But instead, I dreaded every moment of it, because each word my dad spoke reinforced my certainty that he was losing control.

He wasn't acting like an Alpha. He was acting like a *father.* A devastated, enraged father.

"Yes, sir, my dad has a cell phone," Brett mumbled miserably. "Unfortunately, I'm standing here looking at it. He, uh, must have forgotten it."

My father stopped pacing long enough to slam one palm flat on his desk. The entire surface bounced, overturning a stapler, a paperweight shaped like a cat, and a paper-clip holder, which rolled to the floor and spilled its contents all over the floor.

Owen was there in an instant, scooping paper clips up by the handful, but our Alpha didn't notice.

"Give me the number," he demanded, whirling in a precise about-face to head for the wet bar on the other side of the room. "I'll leave him a message." But we all knew he would do no such thing. He'd keep calling until he got an answer, even if it took all day.

"I'm sorry, Councilman, but I'm not authorized to give out his personal phone number. He uses the one you called for Pride business, and it's the best way to reach him."

"Yet he's not there."

"No, sir. Not at the moment."

"Aaaaggghhhh." My father's fist clenched, and the

wireless phone exploded, showering him with electronic shrapnel. "Get me another phone!" our Alpha roared, and I flinched as Dr. Carver dashed into the hall.

My dad sank into his desk chair and leaned forward with his head in his hands, elbows resting on the blotter. It was a closed posture and strongly suggested that he did *not* want to be bothered, but with Jace watching me from the love seat across the rug and Owen still on the floor picking up paper clips, I felt I had to say something.

"Dad?"

"Hmm?" He lifted his head to glance at me, but there was no real interest in his eyes.

"Do we have a plan?"

"Yes. We make them pay." The cold determination in his voice chilled me worse than the January wind, and deep in my gut I knew I should try to talk him out of immediate action. He was obviously not thinking clearly, and rash decisions were rarely well thought out. He'd taught me that himself—that whole thing about revenge being best served cold.

But I couldn't do it. I wanted Malone to pay as badly as my dad did, and frankly I was glad we were finally on the same page.

I took a deep breath and nodded. "How?"

"Immediate retaliation. The numbers are to our advantage—" because our Pride had the largest population of any in the country "—and I meant what I told Paul Blackwell. If Malone wants a war, he's *damn well* going to get one. I'll call in every tom in the territory."

Oh, hell.

I stood, trying to keep my hands from shaking as I crossed the room toward his desk. "Um, nearly a quarter of our toms are still out looking for Marc."

"I know." He sighed and rubbed his forehead. "The men who are already out can keep looking, but I can't spare anyone else."

"Daddy… I have to go back." I righted the overturned stapler on his desk, then picked up the cat-shaped paperweight and turned it over in my hands. "There's nothing I can do for Ethan, but Marc needs me."

From the corner of my eye, I caught the glance Owen and Dr. Carver exchanged—part pity, part resignation. They didn't believe Marc was alive.

My father stared at me for a moment, as if trying to concentrate on what I'd said. What I was *trying* to say. Then he nodded, and bowed his head for a moment in thought. "Of course he does." I saw my own confliction reflected on his face. He took the stone cat from me and set the paperweight on a stack of papers. "After Kaci Shifts, Jace can drive you and Dan back to Mississippi. He'll have to come back, though," he said, gaze shifting briefly to Jace. "We can't afford to have our resources spread so thin right now."

I nodded, numb. How the hell could we handle all of it at once? There weren't enough of us to find Marc before the strays did, avenge Ethan against Malone's Pride, and protect Kaci from the council's scheming. Not even if we called in every tom we had.

None of our opponents had to fight on so many fronts simultaneously.

"No problem." Jace's voice cracked on the first words he'd spoken since we'd…been summoned to the office. "I'd be glad to take her."

Startled by the double entendre I hoped no one else had caught, I glanced at him before I could stop myself, and I found him watching me intently. His tortured gaze held mine captive, and my heart thumped harder in response to such boldly intimate contact in the midst of an official Pride gathering.

I struggled to slow my pulse before my father heard it. Fortunately, my dad was so devastated and distracted by the recent tragedy that he hadn't noticed the sudden tension in the room, or the physical signs of stress I was waving like white flags.

But Owen noticed. He shot me questioning glances, but I avoided his eyes. Carver thought he understood what had happened between me and Jace, but Owen wouldn't even come close. And as much as I loved him, as much as I wanted to be physically close to him to mourn our brother together, I couldn't explain it to him. Not then.

Maybe not ever.

I'd just lost the one brother who *might* have understood.

My father cleared his throat and blinked, as if refocusing his uncharacteristically scattered thoughts. "I need to start making calls." He motioned to Dr. Carver with one arm extended, hand open. "Bring me the phone." The doctor complied, and as my father dialed, he glanced at me again. "I called Michael first, about an hour ago. He's as upset as the rest of us, but insists he's okay to drive. But he'd already dropped Vic off with Parker. Would you mind telling them about…all of *this?*"

I nodded reluctantly, my chest tightening as I dug my phone from my pocket. I was not a very good bearer of bad news.

"Hi, Rick," my father said into his phone, and I scrolled through the names in my own call list while he spoke to my maternal uncle. "I'm sorry to call so early, but I, uh… I have some bad news." My dad paused and forced an awkward laugh, rubbing his forehead as if he were trying to wear the skin from his skull. "That's probably the biggest understatement I've ever uttered."

Another pause, and distantly I heard my uncle ask if my father was okay.

"No, I'm not," Daddy said. "Ethan's dead, Rick."

And that was all I could take. I hurried into the hall, ostensibly to make my call in private. But mostly to avoid hearing that horrible sentence uttered again.

"Hello?" Vic said into my ear, his voice crackly from the poor reception and hoarse with fatigue. He was still out in the woods, looking for Marc.

I passed Kaci's room on the way to my own and saw my mother in an armchair next to the bed, asleep with her head fallen to one side. Her face was still red and swollen from recent tears. "Hey, Vic, it's me," I whispered as I passed, hoping not to wake my mom.

Over the line, leaves crunched and a twig snapped, and his next words sounded much more alert. "What's wrong? Is it Kaci?"

"No." I stepped into my room and closed the door, then leaned against it. "It's Ethan." I sniffled and closed my eyes, determined not to cry again. I'd never get through the phone call once the tears started.

The crunching footsteps stopped, and a heavy quiet settled over the line. "How did it happen?" I heard comprehension in his voice. Vic may not have known the specifics, but he knew the outcome.

"He and Jace took Kaci for a walk in the woods," I said, and the tears came anyway. "They were attacked by four of Malone's toms. Jace made it back with Kaci, but Ethan stayed to hold them off." By the end, even I could barely understand what I was saying, but Vic seemed to have no trouble.

For a moment after I finished speaking, there was only silence, broken by the occasional sound of nature over the line. Then Vic sighed, a sound pregnant with grief, and anger, and finally acceptance. It irritated me that he experienced no obvious denial. I wasn't mad at Vic himself, of course. I was angry that he—that *we*—lived lives in which violence and death were so common that we accepted them with a weary sigh and a grim frown.

Brutal death shouldn't be so easily accepted. It should still be an occasion for tears and hysteria and, at the very least, an interruption of daily life. Routine should not continue in the face of such a loss. It should be shattered like silence before gunfire. It should shake everyone it touches, and we should *demand* an end to it.

Yet even as those thoughts flew through my mind—so fast I could hardly catch them, so bitter my lip curled in distaste—I knew that the reality was somewhat different. Violence was as old as our existence, and we could not stop it. The best we could do was harness it for our own use. For justice for Ethan.

And we *would* have justice.

"Why would Malone breach the boundary?" Vic asked, and I heard no disbelief in his words. Only bewilderment and anger.

"They wanted Kaci, and we refused to turn her over." Of course, we suspected Malone was after much more than just the tabby, but I didn't want to be the one to bring up the topic of war.

"Why does he want her?" Then, before I could answer the question, he answered it himself. "Because he who controls the tabbies controls the toms."

I pulled out my desk chair and dropped into it. "That's much prettier than I would have said it, but basically, yes."

"That's *repugnant,*" Vic spat.

"Welcome to my world."

"Damn, Faythe, I'm so, so sorry. I can't believe this." He paused, and I filled the silence with more sniffling. "How's your dad holding up?"

"He's ready to mount Malone's head on his wall." I twirled a novelty pen on my desktop, absently watching the feather-topped lid swirl against my palm. "He's speaking in terms of revenge rather than justice, and that just isn't like him."

"Not that I can blame him." Vic sighed. "What about your mom?"

"She's upset, but I think dealing with Kaci is helping her deal with Ethan."

Distant footsteps crunched over the line—probably other toms combing the forest. "So…we're going to retaliate?"

"Yeah. Jace is taking me and Dan to Mississippi to continue the search for Marc, and you and Parker can ride back with him, if you want. My dad hasn't mentioned any specifics yet, but I'm sure he'll need you both for whatever he's planning."

"Okay. Wow."

"Can you tell Parker? But don't spread the word, other than that. We don't need the rest of the world catching wind of our vulnerability."

"No problem."

"And, Vic?" I already knew the answer, but I had to ask. "Any luck yet?"

He exhaled slowly, and the sound was frustration given voice. "Not so far. But we'll find him."

"I know. We will." Yet when I hung up, tears blurred my vision. I folded my arms on my desk and let my forehead rest on them, wishing I could close my mind as easily as I'd closed my eyes. But there was no way to turn off the doubt settling into my stomach like stones weighing me down, or the fear burning through my heart like acid.

"You okay?"

I jerked upright to find Jace standing in my doorway, his good hand still on the knob. Damned sneaky tomcats…

"Not even a little bit. You?"

"About the same." Jace's ubiquitous smile was gone, and I could *not* get used to the sight of him without dimples.

I turned in my chair to watch him as he crossed the room to sit on the end of my bed, carefully distancing himself from me physically. Not that it mattered. Just seeing him sent a jolt of adrenaline straight into my heart, and I couldn't decide whether that was due to guilt, genuine heartache from the very real connection we'd established, or some involuntary, eager muscle-memory from my traitorous body.

"Will it get any easier?" I asked, my hands clenching around the back of my chair.

"You mean Marc, or Ethan?"

"Either. Both."

"I don't think so. Not until we find him, anyway." Meaning Marc, of course.

"Dr. Carver thinks he's dead."

Jace's frown tightened instantly, miserably, and I can't explain my relief upon seeing that. He truly wanted Marc found alive, even after what had happened between us. How could things possibly be so complicated? Was there any way to untangle the threads without breaking any of the ties?

Jace's good hand clenched around the post at the foot of my bed, his injured arm lying carefully still on his lap. From his posture, I decided he'd sacrificed comfort for clarity and had refused more painkillers. "Did he say that?"

"He didn't have to. And he'd know better than anyone, right? About Marc's chances?"

"No." Jace started to get up to comfort me, then thought better of it and sank back down on the edge of the mattress. "*You'd* know better than anyone. You know his strength and spirit, and his determination to get back to you. Carver doesn't know any of that."

"Thank you." I smiled in gratitude, but my heart throbbed harder when my gaze met his. And though I tried, I could not stop my pulse from racing. I couldn't fend off the memory of his hands on me, his lips on mine.

Sleeping with Jace hadn't changed my feelings for

Marc. Nothing could have done that. I still loved Marc desperately and couldn't imagine life without him. Jace was…something else. Something I could feel but couldn't articulate. Something I wanted, and hadn't been able to resist in my grief-weakened state.

He was something that would have to wait. I couldn't handle that kind of drama with everything else going on. So I forced my eyes away from his, to keep him from recognizing his part in the heartache currently defining my existence.

"I can't believe Cal did this." Jace wiped the back of his unbandaged arm across damp, reddened eyes, bringing us back to the topic at hand. "I know he's ambitious, but what the *hell* was he trying to accomplish, other than pissing us off?"

"He wants a war." I snatched a tissue from the box on my desk and wiped my face. "And when Daddy refused to hand Kaci over, Calvin thought he'd picked a fight the council would approve of. The real bitch is that he may be right. He called for a closed vote and snagged enough Alphas to get permission to breach the boundary."

"Well, if war *is* what he's after, he got what he wanted." Jace's gaze intensified, as if he were searching my face for something specific. "Greg's sending us in tomorrow—"

"No!" I moaned, and he looked oddly relieved by my reaction. "If Malone was *looking* for a war he'll already have his plan in place and his players in motion."

Jace nodded bleakly. "We'll definitely be without the element of surprise. And we don't have our full forces available."

I closed my eyes and took a deep, slow breath before meeting his gaze again. "It'll be a slaughter."

"Well, it certainly won't be pretty." He fidgeted with the edge of the wrapping around his right arm. "But we still outnumber them, even without the toms looking for Marc."

"Oh, yeah? There's no way—" I stopped when footsteps from the kitchen reminded me that privacy was nonexistent in a werecat household. Standing, I closed the door softly, then continued in a whisper as I crossed the room. "There's no *way* Malone would have picked this fight without at least a couple of allies at his back. Mitchell and Gardner, I'm guessing. And they'll have sent men in support. If Dad sends us into Kentucky, Malone's toms and allies will be there waiting for us."

He nodded again as I sank cross-legged onto the bed opposite him. "And the ranch—and Kaci—will be completely undefended."

Fuck.

I ran a hand through my hair, studying one possible solution after another as they ran through my head. But only one offered hope, without sacrificing our stand in the name of justice. "Before he sends us in, Dad needs to find out who's willing to stand with us in this. You can't fight a war without allies."

"I know. Don't get me wrong—" Jace's eyes widened in earnestness "—I'd rip Calvin's throat out myself, if he were here right now. But sending more toms to their deaths wouldn't be avenging Ethan. It would be failing him. We can't afford to go in there armed with nothing more than righteous anger."

I stared at Jace in surprise. Where had that come from? I was devastated and confused by my brother's death, but his best friend was stepping up. Finding courage and purpose in his determination to avenge Ethan—the right way.

The quiet intensity in Jace's gaze swelled as his eyes held mine, and suddenly it occurred to me that we were sitting a foot apart, alone in my room. On my bed. I dropped my eyes and picked at a ball of fuzz on the comforter between us, dragging my thoughts back on topic. "Daddy would never act this rashly if he were thinking clearly."

"You have to talk him out of it, Faythe." He ducked to catch my eye. "Get him to think it through first."

"Talk him *out* of it?" I leaned back against the headboard and let my head fall so that I stared at the ceiling. "When was the last time anyone talked my father out of anything? He rarely listens to me on the best of days, and this certainly isn't one of those."

"So *make* him listen to you. He's still planning to turn the Pride over to you someday, right?" Jace edged forward and took my hand, and though his face was all business—from the sad crinkles around his eyes to the firm line of his mouth—my fingers tingled like I'd just stuck one of them in an outlet.

"Yes. As far as I know." *Damn, damn, damn.* My heart ached, and my pulse pounded, and I was sure he could hear at least one of those. Fear and dread and confusion, and a tiny spark of excitement all raged within me, threatening to blow me off my foundation. And something told me that once that happened, I'd never regain my balance.

"Then he'll have to respect your opinion, if you stand firm," Jace said, oblivious to my inner chaos as his warm fingers tightened around mine. "If he's planning to go in there with nothing but brute strength, he's not thinking clearly, and he's putting everyone in danger. You have to say something. But privately."

Because to question my Alpha's decision any other way would be disrespectful. Even if he didn't listen to us, my father would lose face in front of his other enforcers, and that would be disastrous to morale. Especially in the middle of the current crises.

So I would tell my Alpha—and father—that he was making a huge mistake. No big deal, right? After all, I'd argued with him thousands of times in my twenty-three years. Of course, he'd rarely taken me seriously in the past.

But this time, he couldn't afford not to.

Twenty-One

I snuck into the office quietly, hoping to avoid my father's notice. I shouldn't have bothered. The Alpha was pacing back and forth between the far wall and the love seat, the living room phone pressed to his ear. He was completely absorbed in his call, but to my relief, he looked somewhat calmer than when he'd spoken to Paul Blackwell.

Dr. Carver sat hunched over behind my father's desk, digging through the bottom filing cabinet drawer and occasionally swearing beneath his breath, evidently confident that in his current state of agitation, the Alpha would never notice.

He was right.

I had let Jace go on ahead, and he now sat on the love seat, watching me closely, feeding me courage with the confidence in his gaze. Dan sat straight on the cushion next to him, watching everything that happened around him, obviously surprised to find himself in the middle of our Pride crisis. Owen was on the couch opposite them, his cowboy hat on the end table, beside a short glass still damp with whiskey. He sat with his elbows on his knees, his head cradled in both hands. He looked lost and alone.

I sank onto the cushion beside my third brother and he looked up, his face swollen and red with tears. He spread his arms, welcoming me not with a smile, but with an expression I understood much better: shared anguish.

I turned sideways on the couch and scooted back until my spine touched his side. His left arm wrapped around me, and my head found his shoulder. He smelled like clean sweat, earth, and the mild aftershave he'd used since he was seventeen. They were familiar smells, and I loved them. But beneath them all was Owen's personal scent, at once comforting and heartbreaking for its similarity to Ethan's.

As if he knew what I was thinking, Owen squeezed me tighter, and I settled against him, closing my eyes for a moment.

When I opened them, they fell on Jace. He glanced at my father, then nodded at me encouragingly. I nodded back. I would talk to him as soon as he got off the phone. But first, I'd listen in on his call and try to get caught up.

"What'd I miss?" I whispered to Owen.

"He's talking to Uncle Rick."

"Still?" It felt like I'd been in my room for an hour, but a glance at my watch told me it had been less than a third of that.

"Yeah. Uncle Rick's bringing Abby, Aunt Melissa, and most of the guys for the funeral, on Saturday."

Ethan's funeral. In three days.

Of *course* there would be a funeral. I'd known that. I'd even thought of it in passing moments earlier. But I hadn't really considered what that would mean. Dozens of people, Alphas, dams, toms, even the occasional tabby or child. All there to comfort us, to mourn, and to say goodbye to Ethan.

But I didn't *want* to say goodbye to Ethan. I wasn't ready, and deep down, I knew I never would be.

"What's he doing?" I nodded toward Dr. Carver, still searching for something in the filing cabinet.

"He *was* getting the Pride phone directory, but I think he found that a few minutes ago," Jace said, twisting to glance at the doc. "Now he's trying to find Ryan."

Of course. Because Mom would be crushed—possibly beyond repair—if Ryan didn't make it to Ethan's funeral. I didn't know that Ryan was actually her favorite, though that's probably the easiest way to explain their relationship. But my mother had a soft spot for her second-born, probably because he'd seemed to need her longer than any of the rest of us had, either for encouragement, comfort, or money.

A soft beep drew my attention to my father as his phone call ended, and he set the receiver on the bar. "Carver, hand me that list. Everyone takes a page. Start at the top and work your way down. Call them all in—everyone who isn't looking for Marc." A strong undercurrent of danger hummed through my father, thundering in each step he took, echoing his every word.

Dan shifted nervously on the love seat, and I shot him a small, reassuring smile. Then I swallowed thickly, clenching my hands together to hold them still as I looked for an opportunity to interrupt my father.

"I want them here by noon tomorrow," he continued, oblivious to my nerves. "Keep it brief. Ethan has been attacked and killed on our own land by as yet unidentified assailants." Because some of our Pride members were born into other Prides that might be loyal to Malone. News like what had *really* happened to Ethan would be delivered in person, so my father could watch the reactions carefully. "If you have to leave a message, just give my private number and instructions to call back immediately."

Dr. Carver straightened and rolled his chair back to the front of the desk, where a three-ring binder lay open on the blotter. He popped the rings open and began pulling pages from the notebook.

"Daddy, wait." I patted Owen's knee and he lifted his arm to let me up. "Can I talk to you for a minute?"

"Not now, Faythe." He took the pages Carver handed him and gave one to Jace. "Most of these are cell-phone numbers, but since some of them are patrolling in cat form, you may have to leave voice mails. Make a note in the margin for each tom, to indicate whether you spoke to him or left a message."

"It's important." My pulse racing, I stood, forcing my father to notice me.

He stalked around the love seat and held out pages for both me and Owen. "*This* is important."

"I know, but…" I took the paper he handed me, because there was no other choice. So much for a *private* intervention… "I think charging in with our guns a-blazin' might not be the best way to handle this one."

My Alpha's face hardened in an instant, and he suddenly seemed to take up much more room than his actual physical bulk should have. His nostrils flared, as if scenting the air for the stench of my fear, and I have no doubt he found it. I'd just stepped into the inferno blazing inside him, and could practically feel my flesh smoldering.

Everything went still and silent around me. The guys knew better than to move and attract his attention, except for Jace, who nodded at me almost imperceptibly. I'd picked a very bad time to question the Alpha's authority. But I'd had no choice.

"If we wait, we won't have the element of surprise," my father said through clenched teeth, his fist crumpling the pages he still held.

"We don't have it *now,*" I insisted, trying to bolster my courage with the knowledge that I was almost certainly right. That my father wasn't thinking clearly, and that if I couldn't make him see that, more cats would die.

"Faythe, you have no idea what you're talking about. And beyond that, this is not a democracy!" my father roared, so deep and loud I had to fight the urge to cover my ears, afraid the sudden movement would trigger something even worse. "I am *still* the boss here, no matter what the rest of the werecat world seems to think. I am your sire and your Alpha, and *you will respect me!*"

Startled, I sank onto the couch, and Owen flinched beside me. Dan's breathing had quickened noticeably. The tension in the room felt like an electrical charge, and I was afraid that if I moved, I'd be shocked by the air itself.

"Yes, Daddy," I said, because he seemed to be waiting for an answer from me. I'd never seen him like that before—in the grip of so many conflicting emotions. On the surface was the expected pain and rage over Ethan's death. But below that, there was frustration in the line of his jaw, guilt in the slant of his eyes, and determination in the hard, straight slit that his mouth had become.

I wanted to leave it at that. A large part of me wanted to pull my cell phone from my pocket and start dialing the numbers on the list, just to keep from further upsetting him. Questioning my father's judgment—even for a very good reason—felt like a bitter betrayal, especially when his fellow Alphas had already cast such serious public doubts about his abilities.

However, letting him take the wrong road this time would only lead to more doubt and mistrust when our invasion failed. So I spoke again, trying to calm my heart so the obvious sign of fear wouldn't set him off.

"But going in now—"

My father had started to turn away, but when I spoke, he whirled on me, so angry I barely recognized his face. His lips were curled back from his teeth, and his eyes blazed with anger. In fact, they looked a little strange.

His pupils weren't round anymore; they'd started to take on familiar points at the top and bottom.

Son of a bitch! His face was starting to change! He was well into a partial Shift, with no instruction at all, and no warning.

My mouth snapped closed and I stared at him in surprise for a moment before realizing I could hear a very feline growl coming from deep within his throat. Was it Shifting, too?

Shit. My pulse spiked. It was not the time to admire his accomplishment. His temper had given him feline attributes for a reason, and soon he might have teeth to match his eyes and voice. And while I was sure he would never, under any circumstances, actually hurt me, he *looked* ready to eat me alive, and I wasn't taking chances.

I had to talk him down. Quickly. There was no time for pulling punches.

"Look at us!" I spread my arms slowly, avoiding sudden movements, to include Jace, Dan, and Owen. But I was unwilling to take my eyes from the enraged Alpha. "Do you want all of us to die, too?"

My father blinked those increasingly catlike eyes and froze. I took that as my signal to forge ahead.

"Because if you send us into Malone's territory today, that's exactly what will happen. He'll be expecting us. He's manipulating yo—" *Oops.* It's never wise to point the blame at an Alpha "—us into attacking him, and he'll be waiting with reserves in place to slaughter us all. Then you'll have at least a dozen more corpses at your feet, and a *bunch* of funerals to plan."

Had I gone too far with that last line? I thought so, but my father seemed to be listening, at last.

"She's right, Greg," Jace said calmly, firmly, and I almost choked on my own surprise. "We should think it through before we rush into anything."

My father whirled on him, growling again, but to his

credit, though Jace did drop his eyes out of respect, he didn't take back anything he'd said. Nor did he apologize.

"You have two minutes," our Alpha growled, turning slowly to pin me with his feline gaze.

Okay, here goes nothin'. I took a deep breath, then launched into my argument, leaving Jace out of it to protect him in case my stand ended badly.

"I think it would be wise to wait and talk to the other Alphas first. Everyone who wasn't in on the closed vote. If we're going to retaliate in full for this—and personally, I think we *should*—" all over the room, heads were nodding in agreement "—then we're going to need allies. And allied *troops.* Malone will have backup from the Alphas who support his bid for leadership of the council, and so should we. Our vengeance for Ethan should also be a stand in support of *you.*" I hesitated, daring a small smile. "You know—two birds, one stone?" And *lots* of backup…

My dad was obviously listening, but only seemed half-convinced. "Even if they hadn't killed anyone, invading another Pride's territory is a declaration of war," he half growled, taking two slow steps backward, toward his armchair. His movement out of my personal space was as much a sign of his concession to logic as was his suddenly reasonable tone, and I dared a soft, low exhalation of relief. "If we're slow to respond, I look weak, and I can*not* afford to look weak right now."

"I know, Daddy, but…"

But he wasn't done yet. "And because they *did* kill someone, a prompt response is even *more* important. Failing to avenge Ethan's death dishonors his memory, and I will *not* be party to that."

Knowing he would take it as a challenge, I resisted the urge to stand again and, instead, leaned forward on the couch, trying to convey the urgency of my position.

I was rewarded when my father finally sank into his armchair, in control of his temper at last.

"He *will* be avenged, Daddy. I want that just as badly as everyone else." I rested my elbows on my knees and clasped my hands together. "But going in too soon and losing to Malone would be *dishonoring* Ethan's death, and getting a lot of people killed unnecessarily. And how does more death honor Ethan?"

"It doesn't." My father's eyes closed in thought, and he leaned back in his chair. When he looked at me again, it was through normal, human eyes. "We will bury Ethan first. We will deal with our grief and our loss, so that when we face our enemies, we have nothing left to confront but anger and retribution. We will gather our allies around us and fight as a united front, to show our foes that we are not prey. We will *not* be picked off one sick little girl or one lone defender at a time."

I sighed in relief, and Jace gave me a small, respectful nod.

My father's eyes closed again, and his templed hands found the end of his chin. "But first, we will mourn our dead."

"Well done," Jace whispered from across the kitchen peninsula, and his gaze seemed to burn right through me, hotter than my first sip of fresh coffee. "You're going to make a wonderful Alpha someday."

"Thanks." But my small triumph was bittersweet, in that it followed Ethan's death but *not* Marc's miraculous appearance. *Nothing* felt very good in the shadow of our Pride's one-two punch.

"They're going to find him, Faythe." The weight of Jace's gaze strengthened as his eyes held mine. "And I'm going to help."

What? "No." My eyes narrowed as I studied him, looking for the motive behind his offer. "You need to stay here and rest. *Heal.*" I glanced pointedly at his freshly wrapped arm. Dr. Carver wanted to monitor another Shift or two before the end of the day, to help accelerate his healing, but Jace would still be injured, and if he wanted to fight his birth Pride, he'd need all the rest he could get in the next few days.

"Faythe, no matter where you and I go from here, I don't want Marc dead or suffering. And I swear I won't so much as hug you while we're out there." His voice dropped even lower on the last word, but I glanced around anyway, to make sure we weren't overheard. My father had enough on his hands without having to worry about my personal problems and how they'd affect the rest of the Pride.

Fortunately, we were alone in the kitchen, and the connecting dining room was empty, too. Not that that meant much, considering a werecat's phenomenal hearing…

"Jace…"

"Don't say it." He cut me off with a firm look. "Let's just find Marc and deal with Calvin. We can sort the rest of this out later. Okay?"

I hesitated, for once at a complete loss for what to say.

"Okay?" he repeated, and I found myself nodding, because he was offering me an easy way out. Procrastination and I were lifelong friends, and our reunion was pleasant. If not exactly welcome.

"Faythe!" My mother said from the doorway, startling me so badly I sloshed coffee onto the countertop. For a moment I thought she'd overheard too much, but then I realized she looked worried, not mad or even remotely critical. Her gray pageboy was mussed, her clothes wrinkled from sleeping in a chair, and her normally perfect posture was now slouched, as if the weight of the world rested solidly on her shoulders.

My pulse tripped in alarm. "What's wrong?"

"Kaci's heart is racing, and she's just thrown up everything she had for breakfast. She needs to Shift now, Faythe. Though I'm not sure she has the strength left for it."

"Damn." I blinked, trying to set aside my other problems and focus on the kitten in need. "Okay." I would talk Kaci through her Shift, then, when I was sure she was okay, Jace, Dan, and I could leave for Mississippi. I glanced at Jace, then at my mother, and spoke in as low a whisper as I could manage. "Does she know about Ethan?"

My mother shook her head gravely, gray hair bobbing. "No, and I don't think she should until she's Shifted. She doesn't need to worry about anything but her own health right now."

For once, my mother and I were in perfect agreement. Jace and I followed her across the hall into the bedroom that had once been Michael's.

Kaci looked like hell.

I sat in the chair my mother had occupied for the past couple of hours, leaning with my elbows propped on the mattress, one hand holding Kaci's. Her palm was damp and hot, and sweat was beaded on her face and darkening her hair. She watched me through listless eyes, shivering even with the covers pulled up to her chest.

I couldn't believe the change in her. Hours earlier she'd been walking—okay, she was mostly carried—through the woods, and now she looked like she might vomit again, if she had the energy.

Mom was right. She had to Shift. Immediately.

"Kaci, how do you feel?" The answer seemed obvious, but I needed to know if she could handle Shifting on her own, or if we were going to have to let Dr. Carver force her Shift.

"I feel like crap. How 'bout you?" She smiled weakly, and that one little upturn of her lips did more than her words to convince me that she could handle what was coming. "What happened?" she asked, and it was all I could do to keep her from seeing the truth in my face. "Who were those other cats?"

I inhaled deeply and met her eyes, willing myself to tell her the truth. Some of it, anyway. "They were enforcers who work for another Alpha. Do you remember Calvin Malone? You met him in Montana."

Kaci nodded, and her eyes grew huge and worried. "Jace's stepdad? They were his cats?"

"Yes." I saw the next question coming and answered it before she could even ask. "Calvin thinks you might be better off living with him and his family."

"You're sending me away?" She sat straight up in bed, and what little color remained in her face drained from her like water from a sponge. For a minute I thought she might pass out again.

"No, of course not!" I propped her pillow against the headboard and gently pushed her back to lean against it. "We're not sending you anywhere. Malone can ask all he wants, but the answer will always be no."

She smiled then and seemed to relax, but her pulse still tripped unevenly, which scared me so badly I struggled to blank my face. "I don't want you to worry about Malone anymore. But you know what you need to do now, right, hon?" I asked, and Kaci nodded solemnly. "Are you ready?"

"No," she said. I started to argue, but she lifted one pale hand to stop me. "But I can do this. I have to, don't I?"

I nodded. And though my mother stood twelve feet away in the doorway, next to Jace, I could almost feel her relief. It echoed my own.

Kaci's eyes bored into me, studying me more intently than I would have thought possible considering her weakened state. "I'll be all better when I Shift into cat form? Stronger?" I nodded again, and frown lines appeared in her forehead. "You won't let me…hurt anyone?"

"Of course not." My heart was breaking, and in that moment I was so close to tears my eyes burned. Tears for Kaci, and for Ethan. For Manx and the loss of her independence. For Marc, and me, and Jace. Everything had gone so very wrong, but if Kaci could Shift and reclaim her health—if just that one thing could be fixed—I thought I could make it through everything else. And so could she. "You're too weak to hurt anyone right now, and even if you weren't, we can protect ourselves. Even my mom knows how to lay down the claws when she needs to."

I smiled at my mother, remembering how she'd come to my rescue in cat form several months earlier. She smiled back, but only with her mouth. She was too worried for anything more than that.

"I know." Kaci shifted on her bed, trying to sit up, so I put one arm behind her and gently pushed her forward. "But I want you to Shift with me." She stopped to catch her breath, winded by mere speech. "Alone. Just in case. I can't hurt you if you're in cat form, and I can't get out if the door's closed, right?"

"Probably not…" I hesitated to admit. The doorknob was the plain round kind, which cat paws can't manipulate easily. "But, Kaci, that's really not necessary. You're not going to hurt anyone. You're probably going to be so exhausted you'll fall right back to sleep for several more hours." Though she'd need a good meal as soon as she woke.

But she was standing firm on this one. I could see that in the hard line of her jaw, a strange sight alongside the exhaustion evident in her posture, and the breathless way she spoke. "You Shift, too, or I won't."

There was no more time for arguments, so I nodded

decisively. "Okay, let's do this." I stood and peeled off my outer shirt on my way to the door.

"I don't like this, Faythe," my mother whispered, and for a minute, I thought she'd refuse to leave the room. Over her shoulder, Jace looked equally unconvinced.

"I know." I reached down to pull my shoes off one at a time, dropping them just to the left of the threshold. "But she needs to know she's not going to hurt anyone, and right now she trusts a closed door more than she trusts herself." I stepped into the doorway, forcing my mother back slightly by sheer proximity, as Jace scooted to make more room.

"But what if she can't Shift on her own?" She took another hesitant step into the hall, but only because I was pulling my tank top off and she had to either back up or get hit.

I lowered my voice until I wasn't sure there was actually any sound coming out of my mouth. "I won't completely Shift until she's gone too far to back out. If anything goes wrong, I'll call you. But don't come in unless I do call. In either form."

We can't vocalize specific thoughts in cat form, but my mother would recognize distress in my voice, no matter what shape I took.

"Okay," she said finally, and I smiled to reassure them both as I closed the door.

I unhooked my bra as I turned to face Kaci, and to my surprise, she already had her T-shirt halfway off, though it looked to be caught on her head. "Here, let me help." I dropped my bra and took the hem of her shirt in both hands, lifting it gently until it cleared her skull, and her hands fell from the inside-out sleeves. Kaci was shivering when her face came back into view.

"You okay?" I asked, hoping she was just cold, in spite of the sweat drying on her face and in her hair.

"I should have done this before now," she whispered,

refusing to meet my eyes, as if she were ashamed. Or embarrassed. "A long time before. I think I'm going to throw up again."

Spinning, I grabbed the big metal mixing bowl from her nightstand and set it on her lap, just in case. But after a full minute of deep breathing and closed eyes, she nodded and I removed the bowl. The urge had passed.

I finished stripping and helped her out of the rest of her clothes and onto the floor, where we knelt, side by side. I'd put her close to the bed, so she'd have something to hold on to in case she started to fall over, which looked to be a definite possibility.

"This is just like the last time, right?" she asked, her teeth chattering.

A jolt of surprise shot through me, tingling even after I remembered that she'd only voluntarily Shifted once before, and that was into *human* form. Her first—disastrous—Shift had been brought on by a merciless onslaught of hormones, during which her inner cat practically ripped its way free from her human body, with no regard for her physical or mental well-being.

I was suddenly glad all over again that we hadn't told her about Ethan. His death would *not* help convince Kaci that her own cat could be controlled.

"Yeah," I said, trying to keep my thoughts from showing on my face. "This is just like that, only in reverse. You need to visualize your cat-self. Your fur and the pads of your paws." I intentionally avoided mentioning her claws and teeth to keep her from thinking of her cat-self as dangerous.

Kaci nodded and lowered herself carefully so that her palms were flat against the floor.

"Picture your wrists and ankles lengthening, and your tongue growing tiny barbs. That's what makes it so rough." I knelt with her, still talking as I watched her body tense, arching viciously.

I was a little surprised that she seemed to be flowing into the Shift so quickly, if not exactly serenely. But it made sense. Her body craved the Shift as badly now as it had that first time, back in Canada with her family. She'd only been able to hold out so long this time because she knew she had that option. That first time, she'd had no idea what was happening to her, or that she could control the Shift, rather than letting it control her.

But this time, she didn't need to worry about control. I wanted her to let it come. To just let the cat take over, because she'd feel so much better once it had. And once she'd seen that she wasn't dangerous.

As I watched, still speaking to her softly, listing the body parts in the order they were most likely to change, her feet began to bulge, her ankles and wrists buckling. I felt a mirrored pain in my own legs as my Shift began, and still I spoke, almost crooning to her now.

Kaci's arms and legs started to twist, and a high-pitched keening leaked from between her almost closed lips. Her eyes were squeezed shut, and fresh sweat was beading on her forehead. But this sweat had a clean, healthy scent, and I knew then that she would be okay. That Doc Carver was right—Shifting would go a long way toward restoring her health.

When my own Shift reached my head, speech became impossible. My teeth grew pointed and curved backward, my nose and jaw elongated into a muzzle, and whiskers sprouted on both sides of my nose, growing with the eerie speed of time-lapse photography.

On my left, Kaci shuddered, and I watched as her spine stretched beyond the end of her back and became a tail clothed in pale, bare flesh. Next, fur began to ripple across her sides, and her brand-new claws dug into the carpet. She clenched her long jaws against the pain, then yelped when her canines lengthened in a sudden short-term growth spurt, forcing her teeth apart.

My own ears traveled up the sides of my head—a decidedly odd feeling—and felt kind of pinched as they drew to points at the top.

Two minutes later, it was all over. For both of us. Kaci lay curled up on the floor by the bed, her tail wrapped around her body, as if she were giving herself a hug. She blinked at me, tears standing in her eyes, which looked more green than hazel in cat form.

But her tears didn't fall, and that was a very, very good sign.

I stretched, raising my rump and waving my tail lazily, relishing those first few minutes in cat form, when everything felt new and different. All my senses were heightened, most noticeably my sense of smell, and I could now make out scents my human nose had been blissfully unaware of. Such as residual vomit in the metal bowl and the sick-sweat that had soaked into Kaci's sheets.

But Kaci herself smelled fine now. She was still breathing a little quickly, and her pulse was racing, but I was confident those would both even out soon. They might even have been caused by the stress of the Shift.

I crossed the scant foot of carpet between us and Kaci raised her head. Our eyes met and she whined, asking me wordlessly if everything was all right. If it was okay to relax.

I nodded and rubbed my cheek against hers, reassuring her. She rubbed back against me once, then stood and hopped onto the bed, only wobbling slightly. I jumped up beside her and curled up at her side, sniffing her to reassure myself that she was fine.

And she was.

So I groomed her until the fur on her head and shoulders lay flat. Then I fell asleep beside her.

Twenty-Two

I woke up some time later to find afternoon light streaming through the slats in Kaci's blinds. I turned my head toward the clock on the nightstand and frustration sparked my temper. Two-oh-four. They had let me sleep for nearly *two hours!* I didn't have *time* for a nap!

But I'd certainly needed one.

Shaking the bed as little as possible, I stepped onto the floor and gathered my shirt and underwear into a pile so I could pinch an edge of each piece between my teeth. Then I padded to the door, which someone had kindly left open for me. Probably my mother, when she'd checked on us.

I Shifted in my own room to keep from waking Kaci, then put on my shirt and underwear and grabbed a fresh pair of jeans from my dresser, since I hadn't been able to carry the other pair in my mouth.

Dressed and as well rested as I was going to get, I headed straight for the kitchen in search of...anyone who could tell me what I'd missed during my nap. But the kitchen was empty. In fact, the house was quiet all around me, and only when I stood still and listened closely did I hear my mother's calm, even sleep-breathing from my parents' bedroom. But I heard nothing from the guys. They must have gone to the guesthouse—including Dan.

But they'd left half a pizza on the countertop, still in its grease-stained box. *Huh.* My mother hadn't made lunch. Not that I needed her to. However, it was unusual for her not to insist.

I grabbed a slice and ate it cold while I brewed fresh coffee. The fifth pot of the day, by my count. And as my coffee brewed, soft music drifted into the kitchen from across the hall, and I realized my father was in his office. Alone.

When there was enough coffee in the pot, I paused the production and filled two mugs, then carried them into the office. My father sat in his rolling chair with both elbows on his desk, his head in his hands. The stereo on the shelf behind him was broadcasting Mozart softly, several green bars tracking the pitch and tempo of the music as it played.

I set one mug in front of my dad, then lowered myself onto the couch without a word.

"Thank you," he said, without looking at me. His voice was rough and very deep, but not with anger.

He'd been crying.

"Are you okay?" I asked, relieved to hear my question come out with a gentle, empathetic tone. I sounded like I'd been crying, too, yet my throat was actually raw from holding tears *back.* The few I'd shed were nowhere near enough, and the rest would have to fall eventually, I knew. But not now.

"Is there any other option?" My father raised his head to meet my eyes, and his were bloodshot, as if he'd been drinking heavily. An empty bottle of Scotch sat on one side of his desk, but he'd finished it long before I'd Shifted with Kaci, so alcohol wasn't the cause.

"You need some sleep, Daddy." I wasn't sure he'd been to bed at all the night before, and knew for a fact that he'd had no more rest than I had over the past few days.

"Yes, I do." He nodded matter-of-factly and picked up his mug. "But every time I close my eyes, I see Ethan. Or Calvin Malone. Neither of those thoughts seems to usher in sleep."

"I know." When I closed my own eyes, images passed behind my eyelids so fast I could barely focus on them. I saw Marc, and Jace, and Ethan, and Manx, and Kevin Mitchell. A slide show of everything that had gone wrong in my life in the past week—my mind bursting with energy, while my body hovered on the edge of exhaustion and collapse no two-hour nap could avert. But there was no time for more sleep, or true rest. "Dad, Kaci's Shifted, and I have to go back to Mississippi. I have to find Marc."

A weary sigh slipped past my father's lips as he pushed his chair back. "I know. Michael and Manx should be back any minute. I want you to brief Michael, then when Dr. Carver has pronounced Kaci fit, you can go."

As he stood, I glanced at my watch. *Two twenty-five.* If we left by three-thirty, we could be there by nine. Just in time to take a freezing, after-dark shift searching the woods. "Any word yet from Vic and Parker?"

My dad sank into the armchair at the head of the gathering of furniture, one hand cradling his coffee mug like a lifeline. His free hand curled automatically over the scrolled arm. "They haven't found anything yet, Faythe."

I closed my eyes for a moment, clutching my own mug. "We will." I opened my eyes and stared at him, daring him to tell me the truth. "You believe that, don't you, Dad?"

"I..." But before he could finish—before he *had* to finish—an engine growled softly from the front of the property, and I recognized our old van's labored rumble.

"Michael..." My father smiled apologetically at me, then rushed past me into the hall and out the front door. I followed him across the porch and down the steps just as the van rolled to a stop.

Michael was out in an instant, and he barely paused to meet my eyes, his own bloodshot and red rimmed behind the useless lenses of his glasses. Then he turned to slide open the side door and bent into the van to fiddle with something. When he faced me again, he clutched Des carefully to his chest, the baby wrapped in a tiny blue blanket my mother had knitted for him.

For a moment, I stared at him in surprise; Manx *never* let anyone but my mother handle her son without permission. Michael shifted the baby into a careful, one-handed football hold, like he'd been juggling infants all his life. Then he reached back into the van to help the young mother from the vehicle, his hand supporting her elbow. And that's when I understood: Manx couldn't care for her own baby. She probably couldn't even lift him safely, because her hands were wrapped in thick bandages, from fingertips to wrists.

When she nodded in thanks, he let her go—she still didn't like to be touched—and turned to hand me the baby. But suddenly my mother was there, carefully lifting Des from Michael's arm and cradling him gently.

"Come inside before we all freeze," she said, her voice high and tense, as if she had to force the words out through an unwilling throat.

I followed them all in, staring at Manx in shock. They'd really done it. They'd taken her claws. She'd never be able to fend for herself again, and until she'd fully healed, she wouldn't be able to feed, clothe, or bathe herself, much less her child. She was at the mercy of people she hadn't even known four months ago, and she would have to endure our touch just to survive.

And the dull, hopeless glaze of her eyes said she damn well knew it.

They had killed her spirit. And my inner Alpha-bitch wanted someone to pay for that.

I pulled the front door closed behind me and followed everyone into the living room, where Manx sank carefully onto the couch, Michael's hand on her elbow to steady her. My mom sat beside her, to keep the baby as close to his mother as possible. But Manx looked miserable, being so near her child yet unable to touch him. Her eyes never left the infant's face, calm and relaxed in sleep.

I paused in the doorway, watching Michael. I'd never considered his resemblance to our youngest brother before, mostly because while Ethan and I had our father's green eyes and dark hair, our other three brothers had our mother's blue eyes and the light brown waves she'd had in her youth. But now, watching my oldest brother hover over the injured tabby, waiting to see if she'd need any more help, I realized that though their coloring was different, behind the glasses and beneath the perfectly styled lawyer haircut, Michael's face was shaped just like Ethan's, from his strong jaw to his high, smooth forehead and faint, sparse sprinkling of freckles, lending them both the perpetual look of youth.

Tears blurred my vision, and when I reached up to wipe them away, the movement caught Michael's eyes. An instant later I was in his arms, surrounded and supported by his quiet strength, squeezed so tight I thought my ribs might snap. My head found his shoulder, and the tears came faster when I realized how well it fit there; he and Ethan had been the same height, and I'd never even noticed.

"Shh…" he whispered into my ear. "Don't upset Mom."

Nodding, I clenched my jaws and squeezed my eyes

shut, denying my grief an outlet one more time. There would be time for tears later, when Marc was there to mourn with me. I could wait that long.

I straightened, and Michael looked at me through his own damp eyes, wiping my tears with his bare fingers. "You did everything you could," he whispered.

But that wasn't true. If I'd remembered the fourth tom sooner, I could have warned Ethan. And if I'd insisted on taking Kaci myself, Malone's men would never have resorted to violence in the first place. They would have been more careful with the life of a tabby than they were with just one of the many toms we had to spare. Either way, Ethan might have lived.

However, there wasn't time to indulge my self-pity, so I nodded and squeezed his hand briefly before following him to the main grouping of furniture, where everyone else had gathered.

"How do you feel?" my mother whispered to Manx, rocking side to side on the couch with a motion so natural it must have been a reawakened maternal habit. Had she rocked us like that when we were babies? Did we sleep so peacefully in her arms, secure in the inarticulate certainty that nothing could hurt us?

"I feel like this will never be over," Manx mumbled, her accent thickened with pain and grief as she watched her son comforted in another woman's arms. She held up her heavily bandaged hands for all to see. "Des and I will never live peacefully on our own."

"Probably not." My father settled into his armchair and met her tortured gaze. "But you are both welcome here for as long as you want to stay. Forever, if you like. You are under my protection."

For what little good it does, I thought, the fracture in my heart widening with the private admission that my father was no longer invincible, his protection no longer a venerated guarantee. After all, Kaci was under my father's protection, too, and look what had almost happened to her. And the price Ethan had paid to protect her.

My mother dared a small, comforting smile. "And you're not without choices. Umberto Di Carlo called this afternoon to extend that same offer from the southeast Pride."

He had? I must have slept through that.

"No strings attached," Michael added, making it clear that he'd already known the offer was coming.

Manx's beautiful features twisted into a frown at his idiom. "Strings?"

"It means he won't expect anything from you in return," I explained, impressed by Di Carlo's generous offer. "You don't have to marry one of his sons. Or even sleep with any of them."

Michael scowled at my coarse phrasing, but since Manx's comprehension of English didn't extend very far into colloquialism, I thought it best to speak plainly. And when she nodded in understanding, I shot my brother a mild look of triumph, the most I could muster in the face of so much tragedy.

"I must thank him." Manx placed her bandaged hands awkwardly in her lap and stared at them. "His Pride was very kind to me and to my son. We will accept his offer, after the service." *For Ethan.*

Sinking into an overstuffed armchair, my brother opened his mouth to speak, but before he could, the back door opened, and several sets of footsteps clomped into the central hallway. Moments later, Dr. Carver appeared in the living room doorway, with Owen, Jace, and Dan at his back.

Owen and Carver greeted Michael with brief hugs and sympathetic thumps on the back—more masculine versions of the somber greeting I'd gotten, while Dan stood back awkwardly, not sure where he fit in.

"Manx." Dr. Carver's gaze found the young dam immediately. "May I take a look at your hands?"

The tabby nodded and stood, then looked to my mother when she rose, still holding the baby. "Would you put Des down for his nap?"

"Of course." She followed Manx into the hall, but I called out to the doctor before he disappeared around the corner.

"Doc, when you're done with Manx, could you give Kaci a once-over?"

"I'd be glad to." He smiled gently, and I knew he understood my hurry. "And, Dan, if you'll come with me, I'll take one more look at your back."

Dan followed the doctor reluctantly, and when they'd disappeared into Manx's room, Michael glanced at those of us remaining. "Anyone else need a drink?"

My father nodded gravely, then led the way into his office, where the small bar stood against the far wall. "Scotch, please," he said, when his oldest son headed straight for the collection of bottles.

Michael opened a new bottle and poured an inch into several glasses, then distributed the first two to Dad and Owen. "So, do we have a plan?"

I handed a glass to Jace, then took a seat on the sofa.

"We go in after the funeral." My father followed his decree with a long sip from his glass, as if such a statement required a little fortification.

"How many of us?"

"Everyone who isn't looking for Marc." I shook my head when Michael offered me a glass of Scotch. I couldn't afford to compromise my judgment again. Not after what had happened the last time. "Unless we've found him by then." I resisted an urge to glance at Jace, and kept my gaze trained on my brother instead. "And Parker, Vic, and Jace will go in with you either way."

Jace nodded in confirmation of his part. He would

help search for Marc as long as he could, but he wouldn't give up the opportunity to avenge his best friend's death. And I hoped desperately that neither of us would have to choose between the two.

Michael sipped from his glass. "Any leads on Marc yet?"

"Just this." I dug the microchip from my front pocket, sealed in a snack-size plastic bag, and tossed it to him.

He caught it one-handed and held it up to the light. "What is this?"

"It's a GPS locator chip Dr. Carver removed from Dan's back, and it's just like the one we think Marc dug out of his kidnapper's body. It looks like he found the scar on Eckard's back when he was taking the corpse's clothes, and recognized it from the one he'd seen on Dan." Michael's eyes narrowed and his mouth opened, but before he could ask a question, I held up one palm to stop him. "Wait, it gets weirder. Ben Feldman, one of the strays we questioned in Marc's disappearance, showed us an identical chip he'd found in his own back. And he has no idea how it got there."

"You're serious?" Michael glanced from face to somber face, and when we all nodded, he sank back onto the love seat opposite me, slack with surprise and confusion. "Who did this? And how on earth were they implanted without anyone knowing about it?"

"We're sure Kevin's involved." I reached for the now-lukewarm coffee I'd brought with me from the living room.

"And we're almost certain he's working for either Calvin Malone or his own father," my dad added.

"And as for how they were implanted…" I continued. "The strays were taken one at a time. Sedated, then probably implanted under general anesthesia, which would explain why they don't remember anything. And that also reinforces the theory that Kevin's working with a Pride." Because we didn't know of any stray physicians, but each Pride employed at least one doctor.

"We also think they were forced to Shift a couple of times, to heal the wound before they were released. All of the implanted strays are missing at least a day's worth of memories. But no one ever put it together, because none of them knew anyone else had suffered the same memory loss."

"Wow." Michael glanced at the microchip again, now balanced on his palm in its clear bag. "So, Kevin's helping someone on the council spy on strays in the free zone? After what happened in Montana, I'd guess they're tracking individuals and monitoring gatherings. And if Malone's involved, I would assume the goal is ultimately either some sort of police state or extermination."

My stomach churned at the thought.

"And we think Marc thinks he's the only one who knows about it. He's probably trying to get back to us with evidence—the chip he cut out of Eckard."

Michael's thunderstruck expression darkened into a look of doubt, tinged with pity. "How long has Marc been missing?"

I glanced at my watch, but Jace beat me to the proverbial punch. "Almost fifty hours."

"Two days?" Michael eyed me now with gentle concern. "Faythe…"

"Don't say it." I glared at him, daring him to contradict me. "He's alive. I'd *know* if he were dead."

My father cleared his throat, and all eyes turned his way. "We're assuming he's alive, at least for the next ten hours. After the sixty-hour point, Dr. Carver says his chances drop dramatically, considering that he's alone, injured, and has lost a lot of blood. And that the temperature has yet to rise above freezing."

My mouth went dry, and my first attempt at speech failed miserably. So I tried again. "And after sixty hours?"

My dad looked down. He actually avoided my eyes, for the first time that I could remember.

"Daddy, what happens after sixty hours?" I demanded, scooting to the edge of the couch, trying to pin him with my gaze.

My father was exhausted, and devastated, and beyond angry at the world that had taken his son, and might yet take Marc from us. But he was still the Alpha. And finally, in true Alpha form, he looked up, pain and pity swimming in his eyes while his features held their usual firm acceptance of the inevitable. "After sixty hours, we assume we're looking for a body."

I couldn't breathe. My hands shook, and cold coffee sloshed over my fingers to drip on my jeans. Then the mug was lifted gently from my hands, and Jace's scent washed over me.

"It's okay," he whispered, setting the mug on the end table to my left. "There's still time to find him. And people assuming Marc's dead doesn't *make* him dead. How often does Marc hold to the status quo?"

"Not very often." I could barely hear my own voice, but Jace heard me, and over his shoulder, I saw my father and brothers watching me in varying degrees of grief and sympathy.

Jace nodded, smiling briefly. "So why should death be any different for him?"

I smiled back, and thanked him silently with a squeeze of his hand. Jace was right. Just because they *thought* we'd be looking for a corpse didn't mean we *would* be.

He stepped back when I nodded, telling him I was okay. "Fine." I looked up, and felt my gaze harden as it traveled over the faces watching me. "We'll do it your way. But in the meantime, we can't do anything about Kevin and whoever he's working for without proof that they're involved." My focus shifted to my oldest brother.

"Michael, do you think you can do anything with that chip?" I gestured to the bag he still clutched. "Ben Feldman says it's not commercially available yet, so we need to know where it came from. And who bought it, if possible."

"I'll see what I can do," he said, when our father nodded in support of my request.

Part of me felt guilty for taking their thoughts away from Ethan in the immediate aftermath of his death, but the rest of me knew that—like me—they were better off with something constructive to take up their attention. Something to work on. Some way to impose order on the world, even as it seemed poised to crumble beneath us all.

"Good." I nodded, satisfied for the moment. "If we can prove that trail leads back to Kevin, Feldman will tell us where to find him, and the council can't refuse to indict him. Not if they still claim to be honorable, anyway."

Michael opened the plastic bag, already on his way to the computer on our father's desk, mumbling about serial numbers and credit card receipts.

I stood, struggling to hold back tears as the weight of Dr. Carver's deadline finally truly hit me. "Now, unless you have something else for me to do, I'm going back to Mississippi to find Marc."

"Of course." My father stood and folded me into his arms, holding me so tight I could feel his heart beat against my cheek. "And you know I want him back alive just as badly as you do, don't you, Faythe?"

I nodded, and my face rubbed his shirt, my jaws clenched against the sobs trying to break free.

"If I really thought we were looking for a body, I'd send someone else in your place."

That time I heard the truth in his voice. My father still believed. At least for the next ten hours, we were on the same page.

After that…all bets were off.

Twenty-Three

On the way to my room, I passed Manx's open bedroom door, and saw my mother and the doctor hovering over her. Mom held a tube of antibiotic cream, and Dr. Carver held a brown pill bottle. I paused in the doorway and caught a brief glimpse of Manx's unwrapped hands, and immediately wished I'd kept walking.

The ends of her fingers were an angry, swollen red, still oozing blood, and not yet scabbed over. They looked horribly painful, yet Manx sat still on the bed with her hands in her lap, staring at the far wall as if she felt nothing.

As I watched, Dr. Carver sat next to her, and physically turned her face by her chin, until she faced him, gesturing with the pill bottle as he spoke. "Take these as needed, no more than two at a time, but if you don't need them, don't take them, because they'll make you sleepy and make your thinking fuzzy, both of which will make it nearly impossible for you to take care of Des."

As would the open wounds on each of her fingers.

But the doctor continued, still directing his instructions to the young tabby, though surely he was counting on my mother to actually remember and apply his directions. "Keep your hands elevated and take naproxen four times a day to minimize swelling. You should Shift as soon as you're able to support weight on your hands, because that will accelerate healing." He paused. "Manx, are you listening?"

She made no reply, so finally he turned to my mom. "If you see any sign of infection, start her on these." The doc twisted to show her another, larger bottle of pills on the nightstand. "Twice a day, with food."

My mother nodded, then looked past him when she noticed me in the doorway. "Are you leaving?"

"Yeah." I crossed my arms over my chest and leaned against the doorway. "Jace is coming with us, but we'll be back on Saturday..." For the funeral. "No matter what we find." Then, if we hadn't found Marc, Jace would join the offensive push into his birth Pride's territory, and I'd return to Mississippi to search for Marc. And I would not stop until he was found, one way or another.

Dr. Carver stood, and looked from me to Manx, then back at me, as if he were trying to make an important decision. "I think Manx is okay here with your mother, and I'm on my way to check on Kaci now. But I'd like to get another look at Jace's arm after he Shifts, and you'll need me if you do find Marc alive." The doctor flinched when he heard his own frank doubt, but I waved off his apology before he could voice it. He had a right to his own opinions, and could hardly be expected to put aside years of medical training to indulge my emotional optimism. "So anyway, if your dad says it's okay, I'll go with you."

Gratitude swept through me, easing the ache in my heart like balm on a bad burn. Marc would have a much better chance of survival once we'd found him, with Dr. Carver there to care for him. "Thank you." I spun around to head for the office, but my father spoke up softly before I'd gone three steps.

"It's fine, Faythe. But be careful, all of you."

"We will, Daddy! Thanks!"

I turned toward my room and the bag I'd already packed, and nearly jumped out of my skin when I found Kaci staring at me from the hallway outside her own door, her tail twitching with displeasure. She watched me silently, accusing me with her eyes of abandoning her again.

I sighed and motioned for her to follow me, but she only shook her head and ducked back into her own room, nosing her door shut. I scowled and started to go after her, but stopped when I recognized the pained grunts and rapid breathing that ushered in a Shift. She was Shifting on her own, and would come talk to me in a few minutes, when she'd regained the ability to complain with an articulation especially well honed in adolescents.

In my room, I double-checked my duffel to make sure I wasn't missing anything, then threw in another pair of jeans and underwear, just in case. Moments later, Kaci shoved open my door, still buttoning her jeans beneath the hem of a tee she'd put on backward. "You're leaving again!?"

"I have to find Marc, Kaci." I zipped my bag and settled it over one shoulder. "You don't want me to leave him out there all alone, do you?"

She shook her head slowly, but her angry expression conceded nothing. "Jace is going with you? What about Ethan? Is everyone leaving me?"

The accusation in her tone broke my heart, but the ignorance in her question scared my soul. No one had told her about Ethan. She needed to know, but I didn't want to upset her right before I left. And if I didn't tell her, she'd know soon that I'd lied to her by omission, and she'd never trust me again.

The sigh that slipped from me as I sank onto the bed seemed to empty not just my entire body, but the whole room, leaving nothing for me to breathe. I let my bag slide to the floor and patted a spot on the mattress next to me.

"What's wrong?" Kaci watched me warily as she sat, and I could almost see the armor go up behind her expression.

How the hell was I supposed to tell her my brother had died defending her?

"Kaci…" I stopped, blinking to deny fresh tears. "Ethan got hurt in the woods this morning. Hurt very badly. My dad and I tried to help him, but there was nothing we could do." I swallowed thickly, staring into the denial rapidly forming on her face. "He died, Kaci."

"Ethan…?" She shook her head, curls bouncing around her shoulders, eyes wide and pain filled. "The toms who tried to take me *killed* him?" I nodded, and her head shook harder. "*No.* I just saw him. He told Jace to take me back to the house, and he had a *really big* stick. And he knows how to fight…."

"It's okay to be upset. It's even okay to be really, really pissed. We all are. This should never have happened." My tears blurred my vision, then fell to scald my cheeks. As did hers.

"Why didn't anyone tell me?"

My arm slid around her back, and I squeezed her tightly. "We didn't want to upset you."

"Where is he?"

I blinked at her for a moment, surprised by a question I hadn't expected. "He's, um, in the barn." Where the temperature was low enough to preserve him until Dr. Carver could tend to him with his primary area of expertise. Because Ethan would be given a proper, if private, burial.

Kaci wiped moisture from her face with the tail of her shirt. "Can I see him?"

I shook my head slowly. Ethan's was not a peaceful

death, and she should not have to see it. "Not until the funeral on Saturday. We'll all get to say goodbye to him then."

"Except Marc." She frowned, bothered by the sudden realization. "You have to *find* him. He should be here to say goodbye to Ethan."

My chest seemed to constrict around my heart, and dull pain echoed throughout my body. Kaci had only briefly met Marc in Montana, before he was exiled, but she'd been with us long enough to understand the bond between enforcers, especially those who'd served together as long as ours had. They were closer than brothers, and the loss would affect all of us deeply, even the guys who weren't related to Ethan by blood.

"I will," I said, able to think of nothing to comfort her better.

"*We* will," Jace corrected, and I glanced up to find him watching us from the doorway. "And we should get going. Dan's waiting in the car."

"Are you okay?" Kaci asked him, her hazel eyes narrowed in concern, and I was impressed all over again by her perceptive nature and occasional moments of true maturity and empathy. She was quite a kid.

"I will be." Jace smiled softly at her, and when his gaze flicked to mine, I was staggered by the range of emotions swimming behind his eyes. "We all will be, because we have no other choice. We'll find Marc, then mourn Ethan and avenge his death."

Kaci frowned, and fear flitted across her face momentarily. She didn't want to think about vengeance or violence of any kind, and I couldn't blame her. But what she didn't understand was that if we let Malone run all over us this time, he wouldn't stop, and she was bound to lose as much because of that as any of us. Maybe more.

I stood and retrieved my bag, then wrapped my free

arm around the tabby. "I need you to go let the doc give you a once-over. Then you can ask if Manx needs any help with the baby while I see if Mom can come up with anything for you to eat. 'Kay?"

Though her face didn't lighten, a spark of interest flashed behind her eyes. Kaci loved Des. He was the first baby she'd ever held, and she treasured rare opportunities to help with him. Now she'd find her services more in demand than ever.

I escorted her to her room, where the doctor waited with two packed bags, while Jace stopped in the kitchen to fill my mother in on what we'd told the tabby. Five minutes later, after another round of goodbye hugs, we were on the road, and after another five-and-a-half-hour drive, I didn't care if I never saw another highway. We didn't stop for food at all, and only made one bathroom break, so by the time Jace pulled into Marc's driveway, I really had to use the restroom, thanks to the three twenty-ounce Cokes I'd had on the drive.

Unfortunately, when I paused in my mad dash through the front yard to dig my ringing cell phone from my pocket, Jace gained the lead and beat me to the bathroom, though he'd never been in Marc's house.

Growling in frustration, I glanced at the display on my phone, then flipped it open on my way back out the front door to help Dan and Carver with the bags. "Michael? What's up?"

"You owe me so badly you may as well just hand over your firstborn." The satisfaction in his voice sounded almost foreign to me; I hadn't expected to feel anything even *remotely* related to joy until Marc was safe and sound.

"What'd you find?" I smiled at Dan in thanks and took my duffel from him, then made my way back inside.

"After five solid hours of hunting and nothing stronger to drink than coffee, I not only found the manufacturer of the microchips, I cracked their database and got you the electronic invoice."

"Seriously?" My heart thumped painfully as I dropped my bag on the bare living room floor, and Carver's eyebrows shot up as he listened in on my call.

"Yeah. I'm sending it now. Go check Marc's e-mail."

"I'm on it." I rushed down the hall, pausing to bang on the bathroom door to hurry Jace up, then plopped into Marc's rolling desk chair and punched the power button on his computer. "It'll take a while to boot up, though, so fill me in while I wait."

My father's desk chair squealed over the line, and I pictured my oldest brother leaning back, his hands crossed over his stomach as he demonstrated his own brilliance. "Basically, Ben Feldman was right. This kind of technology isn't commercially available in the U.S. yet, though the military evidently has something similar in the works. The microchips come from a security company in Mexico that started out designing GPS systems to track down stolen cars. But now they're into some truly next-level shit."

"So I gathered." With Marc's desktop loaded, I opened his browser, then cringed when the crappy phone modem dialed and squealed repeatedly, struggling to connect to the Internet. Each page took at least half a minute to load, but evidently there was no better connection available in Middle-of-Nowhere, Mississippi.

No wonder it took him so long to reply to my e-mails.

The irony of that did *not* escape me. How odd was it that Marc's sidekick had been implanted with a microchip capable of tracking him all over the world and transmitting a remote signal, while Marc's computer could barely access the Internet?

When the screen prompted me, I typed in Marc's e-mail password. It was my first name: Katherine. Not exactly secure, but definitely flattering. "So these chips were actually designed to track humans? Not find lost pets?"

"Yeah. Originally they were supposed to help find millionaires kidnapped for ransom."

"Won't Feldman be thrilled to find out he actually has more in common with Bill Gates than Benji?" I said, my voice dripping with sarcasm, but Michael didn't notice. He was on a roll, as excited as if he'd *invented* the microchips, rather than merely researching them online.

"You pay a small fortune up front for installation and service, then, if you're snatched off the street a few years later, the cops can find you with no trouble. In theory. But the battery is only guaranteed for five years. I have no idea what Mitchell—it's his name on the invoice—was planning to do after that. Maybe he plans to have eliminated all the strays by then."

"I doubt he was thinking about the long term." I clicked the in-box tab, and Marc's messages began filling the screen. On top was the e-mail Michael had sent from our father's account. "I can't even stomach the thought..." I clicked to open Michael's e-mail, and there it was: an electronic invoice from the Seguridad Corporation, based in Mexico City, with Milo Mitchell listed as the buyer. The dumbass was stupid enough to use his real name.

But Calvin Malone's name did *not* appear on the invoice. If he was involved—and I found it hard to believe he wasn't—he *hadn't* been dumb enough to leave evidence. He'd probably conned Mitchell into getting his paws sticky by promising him favors once Malone took over the council.

Of course, that wasn't going to happen, and the invoice on Marc's screen would help make sure of that.

Down the hall, the bathroom door creaked open, and I rose. But then footsteps clomped on the recently restored hardwood, and the door slammed shut.

Scowling, I dropped into the chair again, and moments later Jace appeared in Marc's bedroom doorway—a truly odd place to see him—smelling of hand soap and the Coke he'd had on the drive.

I waved him in, and Jace sat on the only remaining chair in the room, an old orange wing-back badly in need of new upholstery. "So, how far does the signal carry?"

"Nearly a hundred miles," Michael said, then slurped a drink of something, right in my ear.

"How do you track the signal?" Jace asked, and my brother heard him easily in spite of his distance from the phone.

"There's a handheld receiver with a small display. You type in the serial number from whichever chip you want to track, and it'll locate the chip and give the location either with a street address, or longitude and latitude coordinates. It even shows a map."

"Wow," Dan said, and I glanced up to find him watching me from the doorway. "Too bad Marc was never implanted. If he hadda been, we could probably find him with no problem, huh?"

I had to admit that my bladder was screaming in that moment, and I was already on my feet, ready to kick Dr. Carver out of the restroom. But before I'd even tossed the phone to Jace, so he could continue the conversation in my absence, I froze as what Dan had said sank in.

"Son of a bitch!"

"What?" Dan's forehead furrowed, and he arched his eyebrows expectantly.

"Marc *does* have a chip! We're all a bunch of idiots!" I sank back into the desk chair and swiveled to face them both, the phone still pressed to my ear.

"Speak for yourself," Michael said, following another gulp of whatever he was drinking. "I had no *idea* Marc was implanted."

"He wasn't." I glanced at Jace to see if he was following, and he was right there with me.

"Marc has Eckard's chip," he said, a smile turning up both sides of his mouth. And finally his dimples peeked out at me for the first time during the longest, most hellish day of my life.

"Hell, I forgot about that," Dan said, as Michael groaned over the phone. We'd *all* forgotten about that.

"So, if we had one of those signal readers, we could track him?" Dr. Carver asked, edging past Dan and into the room.

"Or anyone else with a functioning chip," Michael said.

Jace stood, looking almost as excited as I was. "Assuming Marc didn't destroy it."

"He didn't." There was no doubt in my mind. "He's trying to bring it to us as evidence, so he'd keep it intact."

"I hope you're right," Michael said into my ear, and over the line springs squealed as he rose from the desk chair. "And I hope you know where to get your hands on a handheld tracker. Because they cost eight thousand dollars, and require six to eight weeks for shipping."

I frowned, but Jace only grinned. "Surely Kevin Mitchell has one. If he's the one implanting strays for his father, he'd need to be able to test the chips to make sure they're working."

"Let's hope." I spun around to face the desk again and powered on Marc's printer, then poked the Print Screen button on the keyboard. The printer hummed to life, then scrolled a blank sheet of paper through the slot. "Thanks for the invoice, Michael. Hopefully it'll be enough to make Ben Feldman talk. And I'm willing to bet he's going to want a few words with the tom responsible for the illegal body-tapping." I paused, already heading for the hall, and the bathroom. "Can you fill Daddy in? Tell him I'll report after we talk to Feldman."

Michael agreed, and I flipped my phone closed, then shoved it into my pocket.

"Jace, give Vic a call and catch him up. We're leaving in five minutes." With that, I jogged into the bathroom and kicked the door shut at my back.

"Well, I didn't expect to see you again so soon." Ben Feldman watched me through his screen door, his gaze flicking only momentarily to Jace and Dan over my shoulder. Dr. Carver had stayed behind to get everything set up to treat Marc, now that his return looked more probable.

I smiled and did my best to look affable. Which wasn't hard, considering the miraculous lead we'd just stumbled upon. "What can I say? I'm stubborn."

"As am I." Feldman scowled. "My answer hasn't changed. I won't hand Kevin Mitchell over to you without proof he's involved in the microchips."

My smile widened as I pulled a folded piece of paper from my back pocket. I unfolded it patiently, then pinned it to the upper glass half of his storm door with my entire palm. "Look at the name of the buyer."

"Milo Mitchell…" Feldman read, then leaned to one side to meet my gaze around the paper. "I assume this Milo is somehow related to Kevin?"

"His father." I folded the invoice again and slid it back into my pocket. "And Alpha of the northwest territory."

Feldman's eyes closed briefly, and the muscles of his jaw bulged. Then he met my gaze again and nodded. And opened his door.

"Thank you." I stepped into the warm living room, but the guys had to edge past him carefully, because the stray refused to back up to give them more room—an Alpha move if I'd ever seen one. I couldn't help smiling. Feldman was a good tom to have on our side.

When he closed the front door behind us, after a quick glance and sniff outside to be sure we were alone, I gestured to Jace with one hand. "Ben Feldman, this is Jace Hammond, one of my fellow enforcers, and another friend of Marc's."

Feldman nodded curtly at Jace, then waved a hand at the couch. I claimed the same cushion I'd occupied last time, and Jace sat next to me, while Dan perched on the arm of the couch. I opened my mouth to speak, but Feldman cut me off.

"Just because his father's name is on that invoice doesn't mean that Kevin has anything to do with the microchips."

I nodded. "Especially if you believe in massive coincidences. But I don't. Let me give you a little background on Kevin Mitchell. He was a member of our Pride for nearly a decade after losing a job as an enforcer to Marc. Then, a few months ago, he was exiled for breaking a very serious Pride law. He applied to be readmitted to his birth Pride, but his father—Milo Mitchell—was humiliated by his son's disgrace, and refused to take Kevin back. So Kevin's been here—exiled and humiliated—ever since. And I think he'd do anything to regain his place in Pride society. Especially if that anything included bringing misery to Marc, whom he's hated for the better part of ten years."

"Circumstantial…" Feldman said, but I could tell he was listening.

"Yes," I agreed, elbowing Jace gently when it looked like he might interject. He had built no rapport with Feldman, and would better be used as silent backup until he had. "But enough to warrant a little investigation, don't you think?"

Feldman nodded hesitantly. "What do you have in mind?"

"A joint effort for solid proof. If Kevin's involved, there will be evidence in his house."

"And if he's not?"

I grinned, but my pulse raced. "Then we owe you a huge apology. And as a gesture of our good intent, we'll give you everything we've found out about the company that manufactures these chips."

"But by then you'll already have gotten what you wanted—Kevin—even if you were wrong."

I nodded, momentarily at a loss for how to reply. Fortunately, Dan was not.

"We're not wrong, Ben." He held Feldman's gaze, and I was impressed with his nerve. "There was one o' those chips in my back, too. And think what you want about Marc—he'd never do that to me, even if he was gonna do it to everyone else. He's saved my ass a bunch a times. Why bother, if he was just gonna hand me over to the Prides anyway?"

Feldman studied his fellow stray for a moment, taking in his every movement, and likely his scent, as he judged Dan's honesty. Finally, he was satisfied. "Fine. Tomorrow we'll go to his house together. But if there's no evidence that Kevin is involved, I don't ever want to hear from you people again."

"Fine. I promise." I nodded eagerly. "Except for one thing. We have to go tonight."

"Why?" Feldman frowned at me in suspicion. "What's your hurry?"

I glanced at Dan and Jace in turn, seeking their opinions, and when they both nodded, I sighed and met our host's gaze again. "Mr. Feldman, there's part of this whole thing we haven't told you yet."

Feldman nodded, with no hint of surprise on his strong, dark features. "I gathered…."

I hesitated, then plunged forward, as if the words burned my tongue. "Adam Eckard didn't kill Marc. It happened the other way around."

Feldman went stiff in his chair. "What the hell are you talking about?"

I inhaled deeply, then continued. "Remember me saying we'd found a scar like yours on another stray's back? Well, that stray was Adam Eckard. We found his body in the woods. Marc wasn't dead when Eckard took him, and we're not entirely sure how it happened, but Marc killed Eckard and it looks like when he took Eckard's clothes for warmth, he found the scar, which he'd already seen on Dan. He put the pieces together and dug the chip out of Eckard's back with his own pocket-knife."

Feldman blinked slowly. "Adam Eckard is dead?" I nodded, and he continued. "And Marc Ramos is alive, carrying Eckard's microchip."

"Yes." I nodded again. "And we need Kevin's GPS tracker thing to find Marc."

"And once we have, Marc can tell you exactly what really happened," Jace said.

Feldman's eyes went hard, and for a moment I thought he'd kick us out without another word. Instead, he stood, digging his keys from his front pocket. "Let's go. I'm driving."

Twenty-Four

We wound up taking two cars—Jace's and Feldman's—because Jace and I did not know Feldman well enough to close ourselves into such a small space with him, and he felt the same way about us. Which was perfectly understandable, considering his general distrust of Pride cats. And the fact that he'd probably already heard what we'd—okay, *I'd*—done to Pete Yarnell by then.

So I rode with Jace in his Pathfinder, following Dan and Feldman in a white, late-nineties-model Camry across two small, neighboring towns. It was ten-thirty by the time we pulled onto Kevin's street, and for the most part, his neighborhood already seemed to be sleeping.

Dan called from his cell when we turned onto Kevin's street, to give us the address, and both vehicles made a slow, quiet first pass, taking everything in.

Except for the house number flaking off the curb on the right side of his short, cracked driveway, Kevin's house was virtually indistinguishable from its neighbors. White clapboard with black shutters. Four foot square concrete porch, with no rail and no plants. Small windows, tiny lawn, neat but bare. There was no garage, and the carport was empty. Two cars were parked on the street across from the house, but neither was the car I'd last seen Kevin driving four months earlier.

"I don't think he's home," Feldman said over Dan's open phone line, flicking his right blinker on as he came to a four-way stop a block past the house. "Wanna get a closer look?"

"Absolutely." We drove around until we found a neighborhood playground two streets over, where we parked both vehicles side by side beneath the lone streetlight. Then we headed down the walking trail in the direction of Kevin's street. If anyone stopped us—and that wasn't looking likely; the whole town seemed to be sleeping peacefully—we'd say we were out for a little late-night exercise.

We snuck between two houses, then crossed the road quickly, as far as possible from the nearest streetlight. After tiptoeing past a sleeping cat in a fenced-in rear lawn, we could see the back of Kevin's house, two lots down. Trees provided excellent cover in the dark, and we stepped carefully into Kevin's backyard less than ten minutes after we'd parked at the playground.

All manner of normal family racket came from the house to the east: television violence, loud country music, the soft hum of a dishwasher. Kevin's house was silent—a very good sign—but we went carefully anyway.

Jace and I went right and Dan and Feldman went left, checking each window. Most of them were covered by miniblinds, but all of those blinds were at least a decade old and had gaps through which we could easily see. There were two bedrooms, a living/dining combo, and a kitchen. I assumed there was also a bathroom, but that one had no window.

"Well?" I whispered when we met again beneath a tree in the backyard.

"Nothing." Feldman shrugged, and when he stopped

moving and talking, he faded so thoroughly into the shadows I could easily have overlooked him. "He's not here."

I agreed. "Let's go in."

"Will the lock be a problem?" Dan asked, and I shook my head. It was just a knob twist-lock—typical security for werecats. We had little reason to fear intruders, because even if the potential thief had a gun, chances were good that a werecat could disarm him before it went off. Humans are slow and noisy.

Of course, in Marc's case, that theory had backfired….

I hesitated briefly, well aware that if we were caught, we'd get arrested. It was the possible consequence that gave me pause, not the moral dilemma of the act itself. I was *sure* Kevin was working with his father—and possibly Calvin Malone—on the microchip conspiracy, which was more than enough to justify a little breaking and entering. "Okay, let's do it."

Jace popped the lock on the back door with one quick twist of the knob. The screen door wasn't even locked. We were inside in under two seconds. While most werecat characteristics carry over in human form to some extent, on two feet, our eyesight is our weakest sense. Fortunately, Kevin had left several lights on, so we could see pretty well without having to flip any more switches.

Obviously, Kevin would know we'd been there the moment he got home, from the broken doorknob and our scents lingering on everything we touched. Though by the time he got home, a little B and E would be the least of his worries. But at least this way no curious neighbors would cut our little snoop-fest short. Or call the police.

"What a slob!" Jace whispered, eyeing the sticky countertop and sink full of dishes.

"Like you're one to talk." The guys *could* sterilize an entire house from carpet to ceiling in less than an hour.

But they rarely put forth so much effort unless it was truly necessary. Not that I could blame them.

We snooped quickly, opening drawers and reading mail, pawing through Kevin's fridge, his trash, and his one file cabinet as carefully and as quietly as possible.

The first bedroom held a bed, dresser, and a chest of drawers with a twenty-four-inch television on top. The bathroom was…too gross for words. But the room off the hall, the one that should have been the extra bedroom, held a computer desk and chair, with all the usual complements: printer/scanner/fax combo, telephone, external hard drive, etc.…

But there on the desk, in front of the flat-screen monitor and to the left of the optical mouse, sat a palm-size device with a short, thick antenna and a two-and-a-half-inch display. My heart began to gallop as I sank into Kevin's desk chair, and it bobbed briefly beneath my weight. Could we really be so close to locating Marc?

"Think this is it?" I picked up the device and turned it over while the guys gathered around me. It was thicker and broader than my phone, but weighed about the same, and would easily slip into a good-size pocket. There were three buttons on the sides and top edge of the machine, but none on the face. It was a touch screen.

"It has to be." Jace reached around me, and his arm brushed mine as he pressed a flush-set button on the side of the device. The tracker beeped, then the screen blinked to life, showing a logo I didn't recognize. A couple of seconds later, the logo dissolved and a start screen appeared, in full color, asking for a five-digit tracking code. "We need a code," Jace said, reading over my shoulder. "It looks like each chip has its own tracking number. What's the dead guy's name again?"

"Adam Eckard." I turned to see Dan already heading for the filing cabinet. "Look for a code associated with Adam Eckard." On second thought… "Pull anything with the name Calvin Malone, too." Just in case. Because we'd have to be able to prove the connection to make it stick.

Feldman stood completely still in the center of the room, his face frozen in an angry scowl. "May I see that?"

I spun in the chair and handed him the tracker, watching his reaction closely. He examined the device, turning it over in his huge hands and finally pressing a couple of on-screen buttons. Then he handed it back and met my eyes. "You were right. I apologize for not believing you."

"Don't." I hoped he could see the sincerity in my eyes. "You had no reason to believe us, and I'd have done the same thing in your position."

He shrugged broad shoulders. "Still, I'm sorry. And when I find Kevin Mitchell, I'll kill him."

"Um. We kind of need to take him alive," Jace said, laying one hand on the back of the chair I sat in. "Especially if we don't find proof that any of the other Alphas are involved. We'll need his testimony. And we don't have permission to execute."

Feldman's frown deepened and he started to reply, but Dan spoke up from a squat beside the bottom file drawer. "Speakin' of proof, there's nothin' here."

"You sure?" Jace crossed the room toward him as Dan stood.

"Nothin' but a bunch of old receipts and check duplicates." While they went through all the papers again, I turned back to Kevin's desk and searched the cubbies in the hutch over the computer monitor. I found staples, rewritable CDs, a box of business envelopes, a stack of printer paper, some empty manila envelopes, and an unopened printer cartridge. The drawers held various computer cables and wires. But I found nothing with any kind of five-digit number on it, much less a convenient list of strays' names and corresponding codes.

"Maybe he took it with him," Feldman suggested, turning from the small closet he'd been searching when I threw my arms up in frustration.

"Why would he take the list, but not the tracker? What good would the numbers do without it?"

Dan shrugged and dropped an old check register into the top file-cabinet drawer. "Maybe this one's an extra."

"An extra eight-thousand-dollar piece of equipment?" I held the tracker up for emphasis. "Kevin works in retail. At least, he did last I heard. There's no *way* his pockets are deep enough for redundant systems."

Jace shoved the bottom drawer closed and pushed himself to his feet. "His pockets aren't even deep enough for primary systems. But we're not talking about *his* pockets. We're talking about his *father's* bankroll. Because even if Cal is involved, his *money* probably isn't. Stingy bastard."

Jace's stepfather was not exactly rolling in cash, even though he required the highest Pride dues of any Alpha in the country—a full quarter of each of his Pride cats' earnings. My dad only took ten percent, *all* of which went to pay the enforcers and to cover the expenses we incurred in the line of duty. I had no proof that Calvin Malone was misappropriating funds, but I would not have been surprised to learn that was true.

Milo Mitchell, however, had no reason to bother—he was high up in the executive ranks of a medical sales company in Washington State. He wasn't fabulously rich, but his mid-six-figure annual salary no doubt generated enough cash to cover the cost of a few extra state-of-the-art GPS tracking devices with which to subvert the civil rights of an entire population of strays.

Which only supported my opinion that money is most often wasted on the wealthy.

"Okay, so he might have an extra tracking device. But only the one list he took with him?" I sighed and let my hands fall onto the arms of the swivel chair. Had we wasted twenty minutes of Marc's life searching for a list that wasn't even there?

"Surely he's not the only one with a copy of the codes," Feldman said, leaning against the back wall with his arms crossed over his chest. "If Kevin's really working for his father, wouldn't this father have a list, too?"

"Probably." I spun slowly in the chair, my eyes closed, thinking. "Unfortunately, Milo Mitchell lives in a suburb of Seattle, so our access to his filing cabinet is kind of limited."

Feldman cleared his throat pointedly, and I opened my eyes to see him smiling, one brow raised. "Kevin's access would be just as limited, right?"

I nodded slowly. Then more eagerly, as his point sank in. "So Kevin would have e-mailed the list…" I spun the chair around and caught the corner of the desk with one outstretched palm to halt my turn, then punched the power button on Kevin's CPU. His computer was newer than Marc's and his Internet connection was much faster, so in under a minute and a half, I had Kevin's browser up and running.

And that's when we caught a couple of big breaks in a row. First of all, Kevin's in-box was set up as his homepage, so we found his e-mail account with no problem. Beyond that, the computer was set to "remember" him, so we didn't have to mess around with guessing his password. If I'd known he was that careless, I'd have checked the computer first.

Unfortunately, his in-box was empty, except for four messages that had come in that morning. Two were spam—porn, based on the subject lines—and the other two were advertisements from *Popular Mechanics*, which made Kevin sound smarter than he was, and a video-game site. He clearly kept his in-box cleaned out pretty well.

Not so with his Sent folder and his virtual trash can. Among the messages Kevin had recently deleted, I found one from his father, dated three days earlier. I opened it and scanned the contents, while all three of the toms read over my shoulder. It was in response to an e-mail Kevin had sent his father several hours before—along with a Word attachment titled "Updated tracker codes."

Jackpot.

I opened the attachment while Jace turned on the printer and checked the paper tray. I printed four copies—one for each of us—then forwarded the message to myself, my father, and Michael, just to make sure that the evidence of Milo Mitchell's involvement was well disseminated, in case something went horribly wrong and none of us came out of the hunt for Marc alive.

"Shit, Dan!" I glanced at him with both eyebrows raised, the paper still warm in my hand from the printer. "Your name's top on the list. They implanted you first."

Dan frowned and started to say something. But then Jace cut him off. "Eckard's fifth from the top," he said, and I skipped down five entries on the list. And there it was. Adam Eckard—tracking code 44827. I rolled forward in the chair and reactivated the tracker, which had gone into power-save mode, then typed in the five-digit code. Within seconds, information flooded the screen, including the current longitude and latitude of Adam Eckard's GPS microchip.

At the bottom of the screen was a virtual button reading Map View. I pressed it, and a satellite image map appeared, showing a densely packed forest surrounding a glowing green dot—presumably Marc, carrying Eckard's chip.

"There he is!" I shot up from my chair with the tracker in hand, and was already halfway to the hall—eager to get going now that we had a target to shoot for—when

Jace called me back, his voice oddly strained, as if his throat wanted to close around the words as he spoke them.

"Faythe, look at the last name on the list."

Irritated by the delay, I pulled my folded copy of the list from my back pocket, where I'd hurriedly shoved it, and skipped to the bottom of the page. The final entry read: Marc Ramos—tracking code 44839.

Shock raced through me so fast I got light-headed, and the edges of my vision darkened. "Marc's been implanted? When? If they could track him, why would they try to kill him?"

Feldman shoved an empty duffel bag back into Kevin's closet with his foot, then closed the door and leaned against it. "Maybe something went wrong. Marc woke up in the middle of the procedure, or he remembered too much afterward and figured out what they were doing, or something like that." He pointed at a name on his list, and I glanced at my copy to follow along. "Look at the third entry. It's been crossed out." Using a strike-through font effect. "And he's the first of the toms to go missing. There are three more entries like that, and I haven't seen any of those toms in a while, either."

I nodded slowly as understanding surfaced. "So the toms who made trouble were killed and buried. Only Marc didn't die as planned—he killed Eckard instead. But if Marc knew he'd been implanted, why bother to take Eckard's chip?"

"I don't know." Feldman shrugged, and gestured toward the display I still clutched in my right hand. "Where does that thing say Marc is?"

"Just a second." I typed Marc's code into a box at the top right corner of the screen, expecting the device to show his little green glowing circle overlaid with Eckard's. But instead, the map disappeared and new coordinates appeared, along with another button promising me a map view. I pressed the button, and a new map appeared, this one displaying the satellite view of a small, neatly laid-out neighborhood, with the streets labeled.

Weird. The green dot on the new map was on the south side of a street called Magnolia Drive. "Guys, aren't we on Magnolia Drive?" I asked, glancing around the room at the other faces, my eyes narrowed in uncertainty.

"Yeah, why?" Feldman said.

"Because according to this, Marc's *here.*" But that couldn't be right. If Marc were in Kevin's house—even if he were no longer breathing—we'd have smelled him the moment we'd come in.

"Here, *where?*" Jace stepped close enough to view the screen over my shoulder again, and his chest brushed my back, sending warmth and ill-timed tingles through me. "In this house?"

"I think so." I stepped subtly away from him, disguising the motion as I turned to face the rest of the room. And when I moved, though the dot on the screen stayed still, the map rotated with me. "Wait…" I pressed the plus-shaped zoom button three times, and the image on-screen tightened until it would go no further, showing a thirty-yard span which included a black-and-white view of the roof of Kevin's house, as well as the edges of those to each side.

"Yeah, in this house…." I mumbled. Then I started walking slowly toward the dot on screen, carrying the display with me as I moved into the hall and toward the tiny eat-in kitchen. As I passed the hall closet, the dot on-screen stopped moving, then appeared behind me. I backed up and stopped in front of the closet, and the dot appeared dead center of the screen.

Marc's microchip was in Kevin Mitchell's front closet.

My heart thumped so hard I could hear nothing but the rush of my own blood through my ears, and my throat constricted painfully, cutting off my breathing until I thought to open my mouth and gasp for air.

"Faythe?" Jace's hand landed on my shoulder, and I knew the moment he understood, because I heard his pulse speed up to match mine.

I sniffed the air, just to be sure I hadn't missed something crucial. But I caught no whiff of Marc, or any other biological smell from the closet. Still, my hand shook when it closed over the knob. What if I was wrong? What if my stuffy nose—from too many hours spent out at night—was preventing me from smelling something I should have?

Finally, I sucked in another deep breath and twisted the knob in one harsh motion, then tugged the door open, bracing myself mentally for the worst-case scenario.

But Marc's body did not fall out of the closet onto me. There *was* no body. In fact, there was nothing, that I could see, but a couple of winter coats and a vacuum cleaner that hadn't seen much action.

"I don't get it," Dan said, finally breaking the tension, and I could have kissed him. "There's nothing in there."

"Thank goodness," I mumbled, reaching up to pull the chain dangling from a naked bulb in the closet ceiling. Dim light flooded the closet, illuminating the only thing I hadn't been able to see before. On the floor, in the back right corner, sat a white cardboard box, like the kind medical supplies are often shipped in. At one point, it was taped shut, but the seal had already been broken, so I knelt and lifted the lid.

Inside the box were row after row of small, clear plastic tubes, like test tubes except they had flat bottoms and were closed with plain white plastic caps rather than rubber stoppers. The tubes were separated by a grid of cardboard spacers, like repeating tic-tac-toe boards, the first three rows of which were empty.

"Is that what I think it is?" Feldman asked, peering at me over Jace's shoulder.

"Unused microchips." I handed Jace the tracker and stood with the box in hand, then pulled the first remaining tube from its slot. "Somebody read me Marc's tracking number."

Dan glanced at the paper he still clutched in his right fist. "Four-four-eight-three-nine," he said, as I stared at the number printed on the side of the tube.

"Bingo." My smile was huge—I could feel it. "He was never implanted, though based on this list, I'd say that's the reason they took him. Obviously something went wrong."

"Yeah." Dan rolled his eyes, as if the problem should have been obvious. "They fucked with *Marc.* I could 'a told 'em *that* wouldn't work out too good."

Though it hardly seemed possible, my smile grew when I met the stray's eyes, pride for Marc practically bursting inside me. But that was followed quickly by fear, along with the realization that he was still out there somewhere, probably in the worst shape of his life.

Rather than trusting the "locate previous code" option on the tracker, I typed Eckard's number in manually, then glanced up to find all three toms watching me. "Okay, are we ready?" I headed toward the kitchen and the back door without bothering to return to the office and power down Kevin's computer. He'd know we'd been there the moment he walked into his house, by the scents we'd left behind on everything we'd touched, so I saw no reason to waste time putting everything back where we found it.

"You guys go ahead. Go find your boyfriend." Feldman's gaze met mine, his eyes shining in sympathy and regret. Then a flash of anger swallowed those weaker emotions. "I have some calls to make."

"What?" Jace's eyebrows arched high onto his

forehead, and suspicion edged his voice. "Who are you going to call?"

Feldman held up his copy of the tracker code list for all of us to see. "Other than me, Marc, and Adam Eckard, there are eight other toms on this list, at least four of whom I assume are still breathing. They have a right to know they're being illegally and maliciously monitored by the 'Big Brother' faction of your Territorial Council."

Oh, shit. Even if most strays living in the free zones hadn't yet found reason to come together in opposition to council authority, they *would* once Milo Mitchell's conspiracy came to light. And they were no more likely to recognize the distinction between good Pride cats and bad Pride cats than most of the council was between friendly strays and hostile strays.

The ugly cycle of conflict would be perpetuated, all thanks to one or two Alphas' arrogance and complete lack of ethics.

"Ben, please don't do that," I begged, glancing at Jace to see if the repercussions had sunk in for him yet. They had. I could tell by the tension in the line of his jaw. "This—" I gestured with the box of microchips "—is the work of one or two of our *worst* examples of leadership. Please don't let the entire council—the whole Pride-cat society—pay for the incredibly bad judgment of those few."

Feldman sighed, and for a moment he looked blessedly conflicted. But then his expression hardened. "I see what you're saying, and I sympathize. And I'll do my best to assure them that your family was not involved in any of this. But these toms have been violated, and they don't even know it. They have a right to know what's been done to them."

Unfortunately, I couldn't even argue with that, no matter what the ramifications of full disclosure would be for my Pride. So I nodded, clutching the half-empty box to my chest like a life raft. "Okay. But please, as a gesture of goodwill between the affected toms and the south-central Pride, offer them our doctor's services. Dr. Carver can quickly and safely remove the chips, and give them to you on the spot to be destroyed."

"Miss Sanders, I don't know that they'd trust a Pride doctor to do that. Considering that it must have been a Pride doctor who implanted the chips in the first place."

"But not *that* Pride doctor," Dan interjected. "He took my chip out with no problem. I trust him."

Feldman studied Dan for a moment, then nodded again, and met my eyes. "I'll extend your offer. But I make no guarantees."

I forced a smile. "Thank you." That was all we could ask of him. All we had any *right* to ask. And though I'd played no part in the microchip debacle—other than trying to sort it out—I felt guilty by association, for simply *knowing* Milo Mitchell and his hell-spawn son. I hated that feeling. And suddenly I understood how Jace felt about his stepfather being the driving force behind the effort to have my father removed from the council.

When I looked up, I found Jace watching me, as if he knew what I was thinking. Or as if he *wanted* to. But he knew better than to ask in front of anyone else.

"Okay, let's go." I slid the lid back onto the box and shoved the tracker into my front pocket, then marched for the door, confident that at least two of the toms would follow me. "It's not getting any earlier out there. Or any warmer."

Twenty-Five

Jace, Dan, and I parted ways with Feldman at the playground where we'd parked, and as we turned left coming out of the lot, I glanced back at Feldman to see him gripping his steering wheel with white-knuckled hands, his face twisted into one of the fiercest scowls I'd ever seen. He reminded me of Marc in that moment, because of both the stress he clearly took out on his vehicle, and his fierce determination to see justice done. I couldn't help but respect his motives, even if his actions would oppose mine in the end.

"Hey, Dan?" I twisted in my seat as Jace swerved smoothly onto the on-ramp. "Could you turn around and make sure we have everything we need? I'm hoping this thing will shorten the length of our hike—" I held up the tracker "—but we need to be prepared for the worst."

"Sure." Dan unbuckled and stood on his knees to peer over his seat back into the cargo area of Jace's Pathfinder, then reached up and pressed a light panel in the ceiling to illuminate the area. "Looks like we have a first-aid kit, four bottles of water, a shovel, some tools, and a couple of flashlights. And Marc's coat." Which he lifted from the backseat to show me.

"Good. Thanks." While Dan turned the light off and

rebuckled, I watched Jace's profile lighten and darken as shadows cast by a series of highway lights passed over him. "We have to stop by Marc's house," I said, a supply list running through my head. "We need more water, something quick to eat, and some more caffeine. And a restroom. And we need to cover all that very quickly."

Jace nodded, and flicked on his blinker when our exit approached. Six minutes later he pulled into Marc's driveway, and we all raced into the house. The guys gathered supplies and filled Dr. Carver in on what he'd missed while I used the restroom, all in under eight minutes.

But that still felt like too long. I felt like we'd been looking for Marc forever, and that even though we finally knew where he was—in theory—every second was still crucial.

I was zipping up my coat on the way to the front door, a newly loaded backpack over one shoulder, when my phone began to ring. I didn't recognize the number, and only vaguely noticed that the area code was the same as Marc's, so I didn't expect to know the caller. But he definitely knew me.

"Faythe?"

My insides went cold, and I spun to face the guys, one finger pressed to my lips, warning them to be silent. *Kevin Mitchell,* I mouthed.

Jace scowled and Dan's eyebrows arched in surprise, while the doctor simply nodded his acknowledgment.

"Yes?" I said into the receiver. "Who is this?"

"You know damn well who this is," Kevin snapped, and I wondered if he already knew about our little B and E. "And I can tell you have company by the sudden silence in the background. Do you have them holding their breath?" I rolled my eyes but made no reply, so he continued, unflustered. "Are you still in Mississippi?"

"Are *you?*" I only realized I was pacing when I

reached the kitchen table and had to turn around. He knew we were at Marc's house earlier because Yarnell had found our scents when he'd come to clean up the bodies we'd already disposed of. But did Kevin know we'd made a trip to the ranch? And did he know *why?*

"Where else *could* I be?" he huffed in irritation. "You may recall that I'm restricted to the free zone now."

"That does sound familiar…." I couldn't keep anger from bleeding into my voice. I was desperate to find Marc, but couldn't afford to hang up on Kevin. We needed him in custody, in order to bring him before the council.

"The real question is what are *you* doing here? Other than making a bonfire out of Adam Eckard's car?"

"There was a fire? Ohhh, too bad I missed that. I never pass up an opportunity to make s'mores." I shrugged at Jace, wondering if it would be stupid of me to talk to Kevin from the car, on the way to find Marc.

"I missed it, too." A soft suction sounded over the phone, then a low-pitched hum met my ears. Kevin had just opened a refrigerator. The bastard was having a *snack* while he taunted me!

Did that mean he was at home? Did he already know we'd been through his stuff and taken the tracker? Was he just stringing me along? I shot a desperate look at Jace, but he only shrugged. Either he didn't know what I was thinking, or he didn't have the answers to my unspoken questions.

Kevin continued, oblivious to my silent panic. "By the time I got there this afternoon, there was nothing left but a burnt patch of grass on the side of the road. But then I noticed a break in the tree line, like several people had stomped through the woods."

"*Weird.*" My coat was too thick to be worn indoors, and I was starting to sweat, either from the warmth or from nerves.

"I know!" Kevin exclaimed too brightly, and suddenly I was tired of our role-playing, and ready for him to cut to the proverbial chase. But Kevin liked to hear himself talk. "And it gets weirder from there. I found blood on the ground near that break in the trees, from two different strays. I assume you know whose blood I found?"

I threw my hands in the air. "Kevin, this is stupid. Cut the shit and get to the point."

Jace groaned and let his forehead fall into his hand; evidently he would have handled it differently.

"Who's with you?" Kevin asked, and I glared at Jace for giving away their presence. "It's Jace, right?" Kevin guessed, and I inhaled sharply in surprise. How the hell had he known that? "Obviously it's not Ethan. I hear the youngest Sanders tom met with an unfortunate end this morning."

This morning? Had it really been less than a day? It felt like forever since Ethan died, yet each second seemed to slip away from me faster than the last, time sliding rapidly through my fingers like a rope burning my palm. Hearing my dead brother's name spoken in Kevin Mitchell's irreverent voice made me want to reach through his stomach and pull his intestines out inch by excruciating inch.

A growl rumbled from my throat before I could stop it, and on the edge of my vision, Jace's fist flew. An instant later, his travel mug hit the wall, leaving a cup-shaped dent in the Sheetrock and splattering still-steaming coffee over the wall and floor. Obviously furious and hurting, Jace suddenly seemed to take up more room than he should have, like a cat whose fur is standing on end. It was an angry-Alpha pose, and I would have been impressed if I weren't just as pissed and wounded as he was.

Kevin laughed into my ear. "Tell Jace I said hi."

"What do you want?" I demanded, and had to make myself loosen my grip on my phone before I crushed it.

"I just wanted to extend my sympathy for what happened to your brother—*so sad*—and to assure you that nothing so tragic has happened to Marc. Yet."

What? Shock jolted through me, and my heart hammered against my sternum. "You're bluffing." But my voice came out weak with doubt, and we all heard it. I cleared my throat and tried again, pacing quickly now to burn off the fury racing through my veins with each beat of my heart. "You don't have Marc. Pete Yarnell said he was dead." And hopefully Kevin would think I believed that.

"And that's what we truly thought at the time. Until I followed that trail of blood through the woods and discovered Adam's lonely, unmarked grave. And I suspect the trail was even easier for *us* to follow than it was for *you,* thanks to the path you broke. What'd you do, march an elephant through there?"

No, just four werecats in sturdy boots.

"You *disinterred* your own…friend?" Or fellow henchman. Or evil sidekick. Or…whatever. Shivers of disgust raised chill bumps all over my arms and legs, in spite of the winter coat I still wore. The only task worse than burying a body was unburying one.

"You didn't leave us much choice. We had to verify that it was really Adam in that hole. And it was, as you know, which means Marc was still out in the woods somewhere. Fortunately, finding him was easier than I expected. Remind me later, and I'll explain to you just how we did that."

My eyebrows shot up and a satisfied smile bloomed on my face. Kevin didn't know we knew about the chips, much less that we could track them! Which meant he wasn't at home. But he'd figure all of that out the minute he stepped into his own house. So we couldn't let that happen.

"Why don't you tell me now?" I asked, stalling for

time as I pinned the phone between my shoulder and my ear, then dug the chip tracker from my pocket. I typed Eckard's code into it again, this time from memory.

Kevin chuckled. "How 'bout I show you instead? Meet me at my house in an hour, and—"

"No!" I shouted, as the screen in front of me disappeared, only to be replaced a moment later with a progress bar and the word *Loading*…

Damn it! I hadn't meant to be so obviously opposed to the meeting place. The gears in my brain whirred to life louder than the rush of my own pulse, scrambling for a good cover. "Someplace public. There's no way we're giving you home-field advantage."

The loading screen dissolved, and new coordinates appeared, but I could tell nothing from the longitude and latitude, so I pressed the Map View button, and the progress bar appeared again as the new page loaded.

"You're right." Kevin chuckled again, and I was starting to truly hate the sound of his laughter. "Because you're coming alone. If you don't, Marc's dead."

Nooooo! I could *not* come so close to getting him back—alive—only to have him snatched away from me again!

My heart tried to claw its way up my throat, and speech was suddenly impossible. Instead, a choking sound erupted from my mouth as I dropped the gadget on the table and struggled to draw a fresh breath. Only my hand gripping the back of a folding chair kept me upright.

Jace was behind me in an instant, taking the phone from my hand. *Breathe*… he mouthed, rubbing my back with his free hand.

"Faythe?" Kevin said over the line. Jace put the phone up to his ear, but I snatched it back before he could speak, finally sucking in a deep breath.

"I'm here." I took a longer, calmer breath that time,

and nodded to Jace that I was okay, just as Dr. Carver put a glass of ice water on the table in front of me. "But I want proof that you have Marc. That he's still alive."

"Hmm…" Footsteps sounded over the line, and a rough, scratching sound told me Kevin was covering the mouthpiece. Then he was back. "That's gonna be hard to come by for the moment. He's unconscious."

Damn it. "Is he snoring?" I avoided Jace's wounded gaze. "Or even just breathing loudly? I'll recognize it, if it's him."

"You're serious?" Kevin scoffed.

"As a neutered tom."

Dan flinched at my phrasing, and Dr. Carver grinned—perhaps considering performing such a procedure on the wildcat. But Kevin got my point. "Fine. Just a second." There was more rustling against the phone, then a soft sound met my ears: a strong, smooth inhalation, with just a hint of a rattle.

Tears formed in my eyes, flowing over when I blinked. I'd recognize that sleep-breathing anywhere. One long inhale through his nose, with a slight whistle on the front end, and a little *puh* sound at the end, where he exhaled through mostly closed lips. It sounded like he had a chest cold—hopefully not pneumonia—but Marc was very much alive.

For the moment, anyway.

I choked off a sob of relief as something brushed Kevin's receiver again, then he was back. "Satisfied?"

"Not in the least." I'd just tasted a scrap from the table, when what I really wanted—what I *needed*—was the whole damn feast. "So how's this going to work?"

"A simple trade." I could practically hear the satisfied smile in Kevin's voice. "You for Marc. You show up alone, or we kill him. You show up without fur, or we kill him. You show up ready to play nice, or we kill him. Got it?"

Yeah, yeah. Standard hostage conditions, and about as sincere as a politician's promise. "I got it. Who's *we?*"

"Just me and a friend. I'm serious, Faythe," Kevin warned, and all humor had drained from his voice, leaving it cold and empty. "I have no reason to keep Marc alive, except to exchange him for you. If that trade doesn't work out, he's no use to me."

Kevin had been human once. *Half*-human, anyway. Had exile changed him so much? Or was this desperation to earn his way back into his birth Pride?

"I know." I sipped from the water Dr. Carver had brought me, then turned my back on the toms and closed my eyes. I wasn't sure I really wanted to know, but… "What do you want from me, Kevin?"

Someone else—someone *not* Kevin—laughed lasciviously in the background, until an angry noise from Kevin shut him up. "Information. We just want to talk to you."

Well, that would certainly be a first…not that I believed it. No one had ever expended so much effort before just to get me to talk; usually people worked to get me to shut up.

"So, what? I show up and you let Marc go? How's he supposed to leave if he's unconscious?"

"We knocked him out, and we can wake him up just as easily."

My grip on the back of the chair tightened until the metal groaned. "Damn it, Kevin, I swear, if you hurt him, I'll rip your arms out of their sockets and beat your friend to death with them while you bleed out."

"Oh, I believe you," he said, though the amusement in his voice said that he did *not.* "But Marc was hurt long before we got to him."

"Thanks to another one of your goons. Yet you expect me to just hand myself over and trust you to let him go?"

Footsteps clomped over the line, and that soft refrigerator hum was back, this time followed by running water. "I don't give a shit *what* you trust. He goes out the back door the minute you come in the front. Or not at all. We do this *my* way, or you can take Marc home wrapped in plastic, and have a double service on Saturday."

Fury shot through me like fire in my veins, and all three toms tensed at the rage and adrenaline I was dumping into the air. "You son of a bitch—"

"Save the drama," Kevin snapped. "I've heard it all before. One hour," he said, and this time his voice had the sound of finality. "At my house." He rattled off an address I didn't bother to write down—we knew damn well where he lived. "My watch says 11:07 p.m. If you're not there at 12:07, Marc dies at 12:08."

With that, the line went dead, and I was left staring at my phone. As I shoved it into my front right pocket, already bending for the backpack I'd dropped at some point during the phone call, my gaze caught on the tracker still lying on the table. I'd almost forgotten about it in the excitement of hearing Marc breathe.

"You do *know* they're not going to let him go?" Jace said, as I picked up the palm-size gadget.

"Of course they won't. They'll kill him the moment I walk through the door." I pressed a button on the side to "wake" the tracker, and a map appeared on screen. "Which is why you and Dan have to go in through the back and get him out while I make a fuss in the front."

Jace crossed his arms over his chest while Dan and Carver watched us both closely. "Don't you think they'll be expecting that?"

"Yes." I looked up and met Jace's eyes, showing him the steady determination in mine. "They'll be expecting it in an hour, at Kevin's house. Which is why we're going to hit them twenty minutes from now. At Peter Yarnell's."

"What? Why Pete's?" Dan's eyebrows drew together

in a deep frown. Dread, if I had my guess. If he and Pete had ever been friends in the past, they never would be again, after our little chat with Yarnell the day before.

"Because that's where they are now." I held up the tracker for them all to squint at. "And they won't be expecting Dan, because his microchip is still at the ranch." The guys looked surprised at that little reminder, and Dan even looked a little relieved.

But then Jace frowned and rubbed his forehead with one hand. "That's assuming Kevin has Eckard's microchip with him."

"Why wouldn't he?" I set my bag on the folding chair and dug through it, mentally inventorying the supplies. We wouldn't need most of them, now that we wouldn't be hiking through the woods, but it never hurt to be overprepared. "Kevin has no idea we know about the chips, and he won't until he gets home."

"What if he's on the way there now?" Dr. Carver asked, a can of Coke halfway to his mouth.

"He isn't." I showed him the electronic map again, where Eckard's blip was still sitting pretty at Yarnell's house. "And if he leaves while we're en route, we'll follow them. At the very least, we'll still catch them half an hour early, and hopefully off guard." I zipped the bag and threw it over my shoulder. "But we have to move *now.* Let's *go!*"

"Wait." Jace grabbed my arm, and I would have pulled away from him if not for the naked fear in his eyes. Fear for *me.* "You can't just walk in there. Especially at Yarnell's house. He's out for your blood."

Shit. Ethan must have told him I'd lost control with Yarnell, because I hadn't told anyone. I tugged my arm gently from his grip, trying to soften the gesture with direct eye contact. "Kevin won't let him kill me."

"That's assuming Kevin can *stop* him. And even if he can, they're probably both eager to take you down a peg or two."

"Jace, I can handle myself, and I can take a punch, if necessary. And as soon as you guys get away with Marc, I'll make a run for it, and you can double back and pick me up." I shrugged and smiled, trying to convince him that my plan was brilliant and foolproof. When it was really just desperate. But I saw no other choice. I was *not* going to gamble with Marc's life.

"Wow. How could that *possibly* go wrong?" Jace's words dripped sarcasm, but I only blinked at him.

"It'll work because it *has* to work. And if not, we fight. We've certainly done that before." He opened his mouth to argue some more, but I pressed one finger to his lips, ignoring the jump I heard in his pulse. "Please, Jace. Don't argue with me. Just help me. I can't lose Marc, too."

Finally, he nodded, and I removed my finger, now warm from the heat of his lips. "Fine. But Dan will have to get Marc out, because I'm *not* leaving without you. Even if I wanted to, Marc will kill me if we both outlive you."

I smiled; he was right. "Fair enough. Help Dan get Marc out the door, then stay and fight with me. That'll make it easier for us to take Kevin alive. But for now, please take this to the car and grab the tools from Marc's trunk. Anything that'll work as a weapon. I'll be there in two minutes."

While the guys threw the supplies into the back of the Pathfinder, I stared at myself in the bathroom mirror, trying to find confidence and courage in the face looking back at me. Marc had saved my ass countless times, risking his own life for mine without a second thought. It was my turn to step up, and I would *not* go home without him.

Only mildly fortified by my private pep talk, I splashed cold water on my face, then grabbed my travel mug on my way out the door, dialing Vic as I went. "We found Marc," I said, as soon as he answered his phone.

Vic exhaled heavily in relief. "Where?"

"Kevin Mitchell has him at Peter Yarnell's house." I gave him the address, and hoped he had something to write it on. "We'll be there in twenty minutes. Meet us there as soon as you can. I have a feeling it's gonna get ugly."

"No problem. But it'll take us a good hour to get there, by the time we get out of the woods."

"I know. Just hurry." We hung up, and I shoved my phone back into my pocket as I pulled open the front passenger door.

"You should give your dad an update," Dr. Carver said, as I slid onto the seat and pulled the door closed.

Warm air buffeted me from the vents, and I sipped from my mug to hide my face. "I just did."

"And he's okay with this?"

"No." If I made my dad sound too agreeable to me risking my life, the guys wouldn't buy my story. "But he agrees that there's no better way to play this one. And he says to be careful," I added as an afterthought, hoping they'd attribute my physical signs of stress to the situation rather than to my lie. "He doesn't want to plan any more funerals."

Jace frowned and shifted into Reverse. He glanced at the rearview mirror before twisting in his seat to back down the driveway. "I don't think he'd agree to this if he weren't so upset right now." *About Ethan.* He left that last part unspoken, but we all knew what he meant.

"I know." I stared out the window at the dark, hoping that when this was all over, they'd forgive me for my lie, because this time I wasn't simply rushing in with no forethought, fueled by passion and the delusion of immortality. I'd studied the possible outcomes and had weighed the risks. And I'd decided they were worth taking.

For Marc.

Twenty-Six

This time around, we approached Peter Yarnell's house from the back. We'd actually parked one street over, pulling Jace's Pathfinder into a line of cars parked on the curb, then crept down the dark path between two houses, grateful that neither yard held dogs. The pooch next door had evidently gone in for the night, because Yarnell's neighbor's yard was silent, too.

Dan, Jace, and I hunkered behind a row of overgrown hedges lining the back of Yarnell's property, running along the three-foot-tall chain-link fence. I'd made Dr. Carver wait in the car; we needed him to remain in good health so he could treat Marc, and any of us who came back with injuries.

"Dan, you go in and get Marc. Fight if you have to…." I glanced at the framing hammer hanging from the loop in his carpenter jeans. The loop on the opposite side held a tire iron. "But grab Marc as soon as you can. If he's still unconscious, throw him over your shoulder and run."

He nodded uneasily, but one hand strayed to the head of his hammer like a soldier caressing his gun, ready to go to war.

"Jace, you cover him. Go in first, as soon as you hear

the shit hit the fan. Once Dan and Marc are out, come back and help me. We need Kevin unconscious, but breathing. But if Yarnell becomes a problem, kill him." Because he'd kill either of us if given a chance. Especially once Kevin was neutralized, thus unable to stop him.

I was going to ring the doorbell and go in like an invited guest, then start throwing punches as soon as either Kevin or Yarnell laid a hand on me. My job was to be too much for either of them to handle alone, giving Dan and Jace a chance to find Marc and get him out the door.

Since they couldn't go in cat form—it would be too hard to haul Marc out and knock Kevin unconscious without hands—they were both going in armed. In addition to Dan's tools, Jace clenched a crowbar in one fist. I had no such luxury, other than the folding knife in my pocket; if I came in with an obvious weapon, they were likely to cry foul and kill Marc before my guys even made it inside. But since I'd been in Yarnell's house before, I knew the layout of the front part of his home, and had already pinpointed several potential weapons.

"You guys ready?" I whispered. Dan nodded, but Jace only frowned.

"I don't think you should go in alone."

I matched his scowl, adding a hint of impatience. We'd left Marc's house twenty-two minutes ago, and though Eckard's dot had yet to leave Yarnell's house, it could at any moment. They'd have to leave soon to get to Kevin's on time for the meeting we weren't planning to show for.

"If I don't show up alone, they'll kill Marc."

"I know. I'm just voicing one last protest for the record."

I nodded curtly. "Protest acknowledged." That statement would hopefully keep Jace out of whatever trouble

I got into for leading this unauthorized mission. But however my father decided to punish me, it would be worth it to have Marc back in one piece.

"Okay, we're out of time. Give me two minutes, then sneak up to the back door and wait until you hear me. 'Kay?"

This time they both nodded, and finally Jace put on his game face—a familiar blend of fear and excitement, with professionally empty eyes. Only this game face was heavier than usual on the eagerness. His anger over Ethan's death had to be expended *some*where, and Yarnell's face was just as good a place as any.

I smiled at them each one more time, more grateful than I could ever express that they'd come with me on this maybe-suicide mission, even under false expectations, then stood and jogged hunched over until I reached a backyard two gates away. I turned down the strip of land between the houses without looking back—I couldn't afford to lose my nerve—then ran silently through some stranger's side yard, grateful for the grass beneath my boots, instead of the concrete that could have been there.

In front of the house, I jogged across a broad, flat lawn, sticking to the shadows cast by trees in the lamplight until I emerged in Yarnell's front yard, facing the empty circle of road beyond his house. I took a moment to regulate my breathing and slow my pulse, then I tugged my leather jacket into place and felt in the right pocket of my jeans for the folding knife.

And just as I stepped onto the front walk, directly into the light shed from the porch fixture, Yarnell's front door opened, and Kevin Mitchell appeared, framed by light from within. As if he'd been expecting me.

How on earth was that possible? There was no way in *hell* he had *me* tagged, so I must have been misreading him. He'd probably just recovered from his shock quickly.

"Surprise." I stepped forward slowly, hands in the pockets of my open jacket, hoping I looked like half the badass Ethan had considered me the day before. Because if there was any of that badass left in me, I would need it now.

"Faythe!" Kevin shot me a leering grin, and behind him, a muffled voice went silent, and a door closed from somewhere in the back of the house. "Come on in." He stepped farther onto the porch and held the screen door open for me.

It took a *lot* of control to keep my pulse from racing as I brushed past him into Yarnell's living room, now empty, thanks to the flurry of activity preceding my entrance.

Kevin closed the front door and leaned against it, and again my heartbeat tried to rally. My inner cat hated being caged, and neither the size nor the opulence of the enclosure mattered to her. It was the blocked exit she objected to. So I placated her with a long, satisfying look at the bloodstains on Yarnell's carpet, right in front of the couch.

"I wish I could say I'm surprised to see you here, but that would be giving you too much credit." Kevin crossed his arms over his chest and lied through his canines. "We've been expecting you."

I laughed, letting derision ring in my voice. "Yeah. About as much as you're expecting the tooth fairy." Kevin's gaze smoldered as he tried to burn a hole through my forehead, but I only smiled. "My guess is that you were about to leave for your house. *Without* Marc." Because why bother to haul around an unconscious tom, if they weren't planning to trade him anyway…?

"I *was* about to leave, but Marc's already there waiting for you. You *just* missed him."

"You're lying." My smile grew, bolstered by the uneasy glint in his eyes. "I can smell him." Because unlike *some* people, I took full advantage of my enhanced cat senses.

"That's because he *was* here. Pete left with him about ten minutes ago."

My confidence wavered. Could I really be smelling the scent lingering in his absence? The gadget in my pocket said Eckard's microchip was in Yarnell's house, but that meant nothing if it was no longer in Marc's possession.

"Fine. If Marc's gone, there's no reason for me to stay." I reached out with my left hand to haul Kevin away from the door, my right fist curled around the knife in my pocket. But Kevin shook his head and batted my hand away, holding his cell phone up for me to see, like a grenade missing its pin.

"Sit." He gestured to the plush gray couch. "Or Marc's dead. All it takes is one call to Pete."

I hesitated and inhaled deeply again, trying to judge how fresh Marc's scent was. Had it faded a bit since I'd come in, or was I being paranoid?

"Well?" Kevin arched one eyebrow at me, and the left side of his mouth turned up in a crooked, malicious smile. But his eyes…they were the key. He looked *relieved* by my doubt. Relieved that I appeared to believe him.

Which meant he was lying.

"Okay, let's call Pete…." I smiled and pulled my own phone from my jacket pocket. "Allow me." I'd added his number to my call list from the information Michael had given us before we'd come to Yarnell's house the first time.

Kevin's grin froze as he tried to decide whether or not to call my bluff, but I'd lost patience. I scrolled quickly through my contacts—watching both Kevin and the kitchen doorway on the edge of my vision—and pressed Call when I got to Yarnell's entry.

"It's ringing...." I said merrily, for Kevin's benefit.

His gaze slid to the left, toward the hallway across the room from me. And an instant later, obnoxiously twangy country music rang out from the kitchen. I took one step forward, and the granite-topped island came into view, and with it, a slim black phone buzzing on the smooth surface.

"Oh, no!" I covered my mouth in mock horror. "It looks like Pete forgot his phone."

Kevin growled, and his eyes went hard with anger. "Pete, come get your damn phone," he snapped, but his gaze never left mine. "And *you...*" His voice sharpened when he addressed me, as a door opened down the hall. "You put your *bitch ass* on that couch, or I will *personally* walk back there and stomp Marc's neck beneath my foot."

As Peter Yarnell limped awkwardly into the living room—his good hand holding his injured ribs—I pressed the End Call button and slid my phone back into my pocket. I watched him casually, careful not to tense and clue Kevin in to my intentions. As soon as Yarnell rounded the corner into the kitchen, I leapt into motion.

My feet pounded on thick carpet. I crossed the room into the hall in less than a second. Kevin panted behind me. Grasping fingers brushed my shoulder, then tangled in my hair. I shrieked as a strand pulled free, but kept running.

I dashed through the open door—the last in the hallway—and slammed it shut. Kevin howled as the hollow wood panel hit his face, but I held it closed, bracing my feet against the floor. Tossing hair out of my eyes, I glanced around for something heavy to push in front of the door, just long enough for me to haul Marc out the window. But my hasty plan was born of desperation, not flawless planning, and it depended rather heavily on Marc being *alone* in the back bedroom.

Which he was *not.* Kevin and Peter had backup.

Damn it, Faythe! That's what you get for trusting the bad *guys to tell the* truth!

My heart beat furiously, and despair washed over me at the sight of another tall, thick tom with his back to me, bending over Marc, who lay unconscious on the floor. The assholes hadn't even bothered to put him on the *bed!*

But then I noticed the familiar cut of the tom's jacket and the length of his dark brown waves, just as his scent penetrated my flustered brain. "Dan!" I breathed, as Kevin pounded on the door hard enough to shove me forward at least two inches.

He stood and turned to shoot me a nervous grin. "I think he's okay."

"Good. Help me block this so we can get him out of here." I scooted to make room for Dan against the door as he crossed the room. "Jeez, you scared me. I thought you were one of them."

His uneasy smile faded as his hand wrapped around my arm, pulling me almost gently away from the door. "I kinda *am,* Faythe. I'm sorry."

"What?" Shock numbed me so quickly that by the time I remembered to react, he'd already pulled the door open to reveal Kevin standing in the hall with his fist poised to bang on it again, his other hand covering a nose gushing blood. "Dan, *no!*" I shouted, jerking free from his grip. "Don't do this." Glancing from one to the other, I backed up several steps, and they let me. "You *know* what he's done. He implanted you with a tracking device, so his dad can spy on you whenever he wants!"

Kevin huffed a nasal laugh. "Yeah, he *volunteered* for that—guinea pigs get paid extra."

Shit. That's why Dan was first on the list....

Kevin wiped his nose with the tail of his shirt, then pinched his nostrils shut, lending an odd quality to his speech. "Then he helped lure the others in with massive quantities of alcohol. Do you have any *idea* how much whiskey it takes to get a two-hundred-pound tom drunk enough to believe he passed out?"

"You flea-ridden *bastard!*" I shrieked, fury singeing every nerve ending in my body until it felt like every inch of my skin was on fire. My fist flew before I even knew I was going to throw a punch, and blood spurted from Dan's freshly broken nose—a matched set to Kevin's.

"Hold it down, unless you want to explain all this to the cops," Yarnell said, stomping unevenly down the hallway. "I do have neighbors, you kno—" He appeared in the doorway, and his eyes widened the minute he saw the blood pouring down the front of Dan's shirt, in spite of the stray's best attempt to stanch it. "*Fuck!* My *carpet!*"

For some reason, Yarnell's surreal complaint about the ruined decor shocked me back to myself, and I darted across the room and over the twin bed against one wall. My fingers were scrabbling for purchase on the window latch when Kevin cursed behind me. "*Shit,* Pete, *grab* her!"

Arms wrapped around my waist just as I twisted the first latch open, and I was hauled roughly off the bed and set on my feet with my arms pinned at my back. "Told you I'd see you again soon," Yarnell whispered, his lips brushing my ear. I turned my head and pulled away from him, but he only jerked me back. "And this time it's *your* turn to scream. I had to Shift *four times* just to be able to stand up straight after all the ribs you cracked, and my fingers are as crooked as a country road." He held up his hand to show me bandaged and noticeably bent digits. "And in a few minutes, you'll be begging me to kill you."

"Not likely," I growled through clenched teeth, fury flaming in my cheeks. I moved my weight onto one foot and slammed the other one into his shin, as hard as I could.

Yarnell howled, and jerked mercilessly on my arms as he hopped on his good foot behind me. "Can we tie the bitch up?"

"Please do." Kevin reappeared in the doorway with an olive-colored hand towel pressed to his nose, and tossed its mate to Dan. "Tape her hands and feet and put her on the couch. When we're done with her, she's all yours."

I wanted to ask what they were going to do with me, but I couldn't afford to appear so weak or desperate for information. So I pressed my lips together and began to walk only when Yarnell shoved me forward, viciously twisting my shoulder in the process.

On my way out of the room, I got a glimpse of Marc. Not much, but enough to be sure he was breathing. For the moment, anyway.

"Where's Jace?" I demanded, and as we passed the third door, Yarnell shoved it open to reveal Jace lying on the bare floor of another, smaller spare room, his breathing soft and even, his hands and feet heavily bound with acres of duct tape. Dan had probably knocked him out the moment I was out of sight, and they'd no doubt made it into the house before I'd even gotten to the front yard. Which meant…

"You knew we were here the whole time?" I asked, when Yarnell pushed me into the living room. In one smooth motion, he pulled my jacket off and tossed it over the arm of a chair, then pinned my wrists again before I could swing around for a shot at him.

Kevin shook his head as if our scuffle had never happened, and shot Dan a bitter scowl as he tore a two-foot length from a roll of duct tape. "I had *no* idea until Painter showed up at the back door with your backup slumped on the porch like a rag doll."

Dan shrugged apologetically, still wiping his nose. "I didn't have a chance to call without being overheard."

Kevin sighed. "You know what they say about good help…." He held the first strip of tape out in my direction, and when Yarnell took one hand off me to take it, I twisted from his grip and swung around in as powerful a roundhouse as I could muster.

But Yarnell was ready this time. He caught my foot in midswing with his good hand, absorbing my momentum with a jarring thud of steel-toed boot against bare palm. Then he twisted my leg, and pain shot through my ankle as I lost my balance. I landed hard on my chest, and when my chin hit the floor, I bit my cheek.

I was still struggling to spit out my own blood and draw a breath when Yarnell's weight dropped onto my back. He yanked brutally on my arms again, and my wrists were tightly taped before my double vision merged. My ankles were bound a minute later.

Duct tape is strong, which is why my own Pride used it to bind trespassers resisting removal. But the interesting thing about that particular kind of tape is that, for all its strength, because of its distinctive weave, a single weak point would be enough to start a tear. Which is why we—and evidently Peter Yarnell—used multiple layers. The chance of a single weak point repeating in each layer was virtually nil.

And I didn't exactly have a history of good luck in the first place.

When I was secure, though still thrashing, Yarnell hauled me up by my arms and shoved me down on the couch, my hands pressed into the cushions at my back.

Across the room, Dan caught my eye as he nursed his broken nose. "I don't understand," I said, practically daring him to meet my gaze. "You made a list of strays for us. You fought alongside us in the ambush! And the whole time you were feeding Kevin information?" And suddenly I remembered Dan sitting at Marc's kitchen table, his phone in front of him. The bastard hadn't been playing *Tetris!*

Dan shrugged, but looked distinctly uncomfortable discussing his part in the whole thing. "I had nothing to do with the ambush. Kevin set that up on his own, after I told him you guys would be coming through town. I stopped to make sure Manx and the kid were okay, then it was either fight *with* you or admit I was spying for the other side." He wiped a smear of blood from one cheek, then dropped his eyes. "And I gave you a list of strays I thought knew nothing about the chips. Feldman was a surprise, of course. Just my luck."

"Wow." I allowed myself a small moment to gloat. "You're a piss-poor spy." Except for the fact that he'd infiltrated my Pride's home base—the first successful penetration by a hostile stray. Ever. *Damn it.*

I glared up at Dan, cursing myself mentally for not seeing this coming. And no one even knew where we were, since I hadn't really called my father.

Except for Dr. Carver… How long would it take him to figure out something had gone wrong, and call for help?

"You know, she's right! I don't think you've been pulling your weight around here lately," Kevin said, glaring at Dan as if their conversation had never been interrupted. "Didn't you let her *beat* the living *shit* out of Pete the other day?"

Dan rolled his eyes, looking more than a little irritated. "What did you want me to say? 'Faythe, lay off him. He's my secret partner in crime.'?"

But Kevin continued as if he hadn't even heard. "And they were *not* supposed to be in my house."

"How was I supposed to stop them without tipping them off?" Dan demanded, dropping into one of Yarnell's overstuffed armchairs, his bloody towel hanging limply from one fist.

"You could have at least gotten the tracker away from her."

"She never put the damn thing down!"

"He's right." I shrugged—an awkward movement with my hands pinned behind me—only then remembering that I still had the gadget in my pocket. "I can be pretty difficult to reason with."

"And pretty damn hard to shut up." Kevin crossed the room to stand in front of a mirror hanging over an occasional table against the far wall, turning his head to examine his crooked nose. "Who the hell am I going to get to set this again—" Kevin froze, as what he'd said sank in, and I was pretty sure I knew what he'd just remembered. "*Fuck.* Dan, go get the doctor before he realizes something's wrong and calls in backup."

"Too late for that," I bluffed, smirking at Kevin's newly mutilated reflection. "My dad knows exactly where we are, and he'll have backup here within minutes."

"She's right." Dan glanced back and forth between us, new worry lines bisecting his brow. "She called her dad before we left."

"Did you *see* her call Greg?" Kevin demanded, and Dan shook his head. "Then she *didn't* call him. This little bitch is *known* for insubordination, and her dad would never approve such a risky stunt, for fear of precisely *this.*" Kevin turned to face the room slowly, his arms spread to indicate my unfortunate predicament.

"Vic's expecting to hear from me soon, and if he doesn't, he'll know something went wrong."

"Now, *that* I believe. But how on earth will he find you?" Kevin heaved an exaggerated shrug and pouted in mock distress. Then he dropped the facade and turned an angry look on Dan. "Her father has no idea she's here. And neither does anyone else except the damned doctor. So go get him."

I could have told him that Vic had the address, but I was afraid if he knew that, he'd move us. Then we'd be screwed.

Dan nodded curtly, and jogged through the kitchen toward the back door.

"Don't forget this!" Kevin called, and Dan turned just in time to catch the syringe Kevin had pulled from his pocket. "If you can't con him into coming peacefully, knock him out and throw him over your shoulder."

Dan shoved the syringe into his pocket and slammed the door on his way out, and suddenly I understood why both Marc and Jace were sleeping so soundly.

"Watch the back window," Kevin ordered, and Yarnell wandered into the kitchen as our Pride's most notorious traitor sank into the armchair to the left of the couch, his elbows propped on widespread knees. His eager gaze focused on me, and Kevin opened his mouth. But I cut him off, stalling for time in hopes that Dr. Carver would come of his own volition, thus conscious and able to fight.

True, he hadn't worked as an enforcer in nearly a decade, but hopefully fighting was like riding a bike. Only more painful.

"So, you knew Marc was alive the whole time, and that we knew about the microchips?" I said, cocking my head at Kevin.

He grinned and took the bait, evidently eager to show off his evil *skillz,* now that the damsel was officially in distress. "About the microchips? Yeah. Dan told us Ben Feldman showed you his. But the real irony is that Feldman asked me not to tell anyone else about it!" His smile made me want to puke, but I kept my face blank. "I can't believe he cut it out of his own back. That fucker's *hard-core.* Seriously, Feldman's the scariest damned altruist I ever met. Dealing with him takes real finesse, and getting him implanted was a huge pain in the ass. He was a pretty high priority, though, because he's unpredictable."

So Feldman wasn't in on the microchip conspiracy…

"But no, we didn't know Marc was alive until Dan

told us where to find Adam Eckard's body. But then finding Marc was easy enough, thanks to the tracker. Ironic, huh? He nearly died fighting Eckard before we could get him implanted, then Eckard's chip leads us right to him."

"You really weren't trying to kill him?"

"We were during the ambush. And I can't even *begin* to explain how hard it is to get that many strays to work together, even fighting against a common enemy." Marc, of course.

"I assume it was easier with Dan's help," I spit.

"Nah. He really wanted nothing to do with that. He didn't want the baby caught in the cross fire. I think he feels loyal to Manx, since she didn't kill him when she could have." Kevin shrugged. "But when that didn't work out, the powers that be decided it might be more interesting to track him. See if we could catch him breaking the rules. Maybe sneaking into Pride territory to see his girlfriend." He raised one accusatory eyebrow at me, but before I could argue that that wouldn't have happened, Yarnell called out softly from the kitchen.

"Hey, Mitchell, they're here, and the doc's walking tall."

"Oh, good!" Kevin grinned as he stood, looking giddy enough to bounce off the walls. "Now that the loose ends are all tied up, the real fun begins."

"What fun?" I demanded, but Kevin was already walking away from me.

"Keep her quiet," he muttered on his way across the room.

Yarnell raced in from the kitchen and was on me before I could yell to warn Dr. Carver. He pulled me onto his lap on the couch and shoved the end of Dan's blood-stained towel into my mouth, then clamped his hand over it. My shout came out as a muffled moan, and no amount of struggling could dislodge Yarnell's grip on me, though his still-healing ribs must have been in agony.

Kevin stopped beside another armchair and squatted to pull something from behind it. My eyes widened when I saw the tire iron Dan had been carrying, and I wasn't much comforted when he took the time to wrap his own bloodstained towel around the business end of the tool.

"Shh," he said, eyes wide, one finger pressed to his lips. "I'm hunting *wabbit!* But we don't want Carver dead until he's fixed my nose, now do we?" Kevin stood flat against the wall, where I could see him, but someone coming through the back door would not.

I thrashed harder, but Yarnell's grip on me only tightened until I was afraid he'd break my ribs. Unfortunately, there was no time for a partial Shift, or any other offensive measure.

The kitchen door opened, and Dr. Carver's voice reached my ears. "Where is she?" Then his gaze landed on me, and his forehead crinkled in confusion. "What the hell—"

I screeched wordlessly in warning as he passed through the doorway, but it did no good.

"What's up, Doc?" Kevin swung the tire iron like a baseball bat. The towel-wrapped steel connected with the side of Dr. Carver's skull, and the doctor collapsed onto the carpet with a muffled thud.

Noooo! I screamed in my head, but the audible portion was nothing more than an inarticulate groan.

"Tape him up and toss him into the tub," Kevin ordered, and Dan stepped forward reluctantly, a fresh roll of duct tape in one hand.

Yarnell copped a generous feel of my inner thigh, then shoved me off of his lap, onto the center couch cushion, where I fell over on one side, unable to right myself without the use of my hands. Tears formed in my eyes and ran sideways across my cheeks as I watched Dr. Carver—my last hope for help from the cavalry—hauled down the hall.

"Now…" Kevin said, slinking across the room toward me, the rings around his eyes darkening with each second as he took the towel out of my mouth. "Let's get down to business.…"

Twenty-Seven

"Here's how this is going to work." Kevin stopped three feet in front of the couch, squatting to put himself at eye level with me, my face half-buried in the cushion. "I'm going to ask the questions, and Pete's going to make sure you answer them."

"And let me guess," I said, my words slurred with the left half of my mouth pressed into the upholstery. "If I play nice, you'll let me go, but if I don't, you'll kill me."

"No." Kevin shook his head firmly and hauled me upright by one arm, so fast my vision swam. "You're going to die either way. I can't see any way around that, considering how much you know about all this." His open arms took in the whole room, indicating their little conspiracy.

"Kevin..." Dan began, and my gaze found him slouched in a chair across the room. "You said she'd get to go home...."

"Yeah, well that's before she wound up in the middle of all this! If you'd kept her out of the way like you were supposed to—if you hadn't blown your fucking *cover*—she'd get to go back to Texas with you tonight. But you fucked up, so she has to die along with her collection of adoring tomcats."

Dan flinched and avoided my eyes.

"It's a shame," Kevin continued. "Considering how badly we need tabbies. But when Dan brings the bodies of Greg's Pride cats—including his precious *kitten*—back home, the Alpha will be so grateful for your compassion and so impressed by your loyalty that he'll accept you into the Pride. Hell, he'll *need* you. Which will put you in the perfect position to extract both of the other tabbies, when their guard is down and you've gathered enough intel…"

Shit. Kaci and Manx. Were they the point of this whole operation?

No, they couldn't be. The microchips were implanted long before the council decided to remove Kaci. So maybe they were just *part* of it.

The lines in Dan's forehead deepened, and for a moment, determination flickered behind his dark brown eyes. "Kaci's just a kid, Kevin…."

"Exactly." Kevin whirled on him, legs spread wide to take up as much room as possible in imitation of an aggressive Alpha stance. "And kids need proper care, which she is *not* getting in the south-central Pride. The council's already ruled to remove her, and you have the chance to succeed all on your own, where Calvin Malone's highly trained team of enforcers failed."

"And Manx?" I asked, curious to know how he could possibly put a positive spin on *her* forcible removal.

Kevin twisted to glare at me over his shoulder, then turned back to Dan. "Manx has paid for her crimes. She lost her claws. Do you really think it's fair for her to be stuck in the middle of a war zone—once the fighting starts—when she can't defend herself anymore? Or her baby?"

Damn. I was almost impressed. If Kevin had shown so much potential as an orator while he was a member of our Pride, my father might actually have found some use for him.

Or not. We weren't big on moral ambiguity in the south-central Pride, and that included propaganda. But it was the propaganda itself that caught my attention.

"Fighting?" I tried to keep my voice calm and steady.

"Oh, come on, Faythe!" Kevin stepped back so he could see both me and Dan. "We all know the war is coming, but I don't think even Calvin Malone could have foreseen your father throwing the first punch."

"*Malone* started this!" I shouted, straining desperately against my bonds. I felt helpless, *worthless,* without the use of my hands. "His tom killed Ethan in cold blood!"

"Ethan died because he stood in the way of an *authorized mission.* The official first strike will be when your father invades the Appalachian territory. And thanks to Dan, we know that's exactly what he's planning."

Dan had the grace to look guilty as hell while judiciously avoiding my eyes.

"And when your father makes his move—an *illegal* breach of another Pride's territorial boundary—the entire council will unite against him."

I shook my head with feigned confidence, while my aching heart withered in my chest. "Uncle Rick will never go along with that. Neither will Bert Di Carlo."

Kevin shrugged smugly. "If they side with your father—supporting his treachery rather than the council's authority—they'll be removed from power just like he will, and their territories will be redistributed once the council membership is settled."

"That's not going to happen!" I spat, glowering at Kevin in the most frustratingly impotent moment of my life. "No one but your dad and Calvin Malone will support this war once they hear how Ethan *really* died. He was pounced on from above—murdered in cold blood. My father and I saw it with our own eyes."

"Unfortunately, *you* won't be there to testify, and after

the council hears the intelligence we've gathered against your father, the Alphas won't believe a word he has to say."

My pulse jumped, in spite of my best effort to steady it. "What intelligence?"

Kevin's gaze narrowed on me. "That's where *you* come in."

"Oh, the whole Q and A bit?" I rolled my eyes, trying to look calm and fearless, while my heart raced like a scared rabbit's. "What's my motivation to play along, if you're just going to kill me anyway?"

On the edge of my vision, Dan went stiff, and I took heart from his reaction. He was clearly uncomfortable with the thought my murder—as was *I,* for the record—which definitely gave me something to work with. But should I appeal to his sympathy, or his faltering sense of honor?

"Pain," Kevin said, and I blinked at him in confusion, trying to haul myself back from thoughts of escape long enough to make sense of that one word.

"Huh?"

"*Pain* is your motivation," he clarified. "Pete's looking forward to beating a little compliance into Greg Sanders's infamous shrew before I give him the all clear to take whatever *else* he wants from you. The more you talk, the less opportunity he has to hit you. Is that motivation enough?"

My heart slammed against my chest, and my hands began to sweat against the soft gray upholstery at my back, but I forced confidence into my expression, crowned by two eyebrows arched in challenge. "Knowing that either way, this party ends with my rape and murder? *No.* There *is* no motivation strong enough to guarantee my cooperation."

"Yeah?" Kevin smiled viciously. "Let's give it a shot anyway…."

I shrugged, bolstering myself with bravado, since I had nothing else left to work with. "I'm not exactly new to being threatened. Or punched."

Yarnell's leering grin widened. "Sounds like she likes it rough."

I never said I liked *it that way….*

"Well then, she's in luck." Kevin paced in front of me again, arms crossed over his chest. "Ryan's missing again, isn't he?"

"What?" I was honestly thrown off by his first question; Ryan's was the last name I'd expected to hear from Kevin's mouth.

"Any idea how he got out of his cage?"

No. So far as I knew, no one had figured that out yet. But responding to Kevin's question—even one I had no answer for—could be construed as cooperation, and I couldn't let them think I was capitulating so early.

"So Kevin asks the questions, and Peter likes to hit girls. What's your role in this?" I leaned to my left to peer at Dan around Kevin's arm. "I mean, other than informant and traitor…?" Because he was the only one who could have told them Ryan was missing. My father hadn't reported that development to the council, because technically they had no authority in the matter. And until the larger pile of cat shit hit the fan, we were hoping we could find him before anyone else found out.

So much for *that* idea…

Kevin stepped into my line of sight to block Dan from view, so I leaned the other way. "What are you getting out of this, other than Milo Mitchell's pocket change?"

Dan shrugged, looking miserable. "Membership has its privileges."

"Membership to what?" I demanded. "You were just eight months' probation away from membership in the biggest Pride in the country, and you threw it all away! Why?"

"Because he sees logic, which is more than I can say for *you* recently," Kevin snapped, moving between me and Dan again. "Your dad said he'd *consider* accepting Dan if he could keep his nose clean until September. But by then, the war will be over, and your Pride won't even exist. Dan's smart enough to side with the inevitable victor early on."

"But for what?" I leaned the other way again, already tired of having to fight for eye contact. "You sold us out—sold *Marc* out—for a little cash!"

"No, that was *Pete,*" Dan snapped. "I just wanted out of the free zone."

"Oh…" Understanding finally came, and I almost felt sorry for Dan. *Almost.* "You think they're going to take you in. Did they tell you that? That after you've served as their spy, or their foot soldier, or whatever, that they'll let you play their reindeer games? Because they won't. You *know* that, don't you, Dan?"

Surely he wasn't that gullible….

Kevin growled, and backhanded me so hard I fell over sideways again, the living room spinning before me. I never even saw the blow coming. "My father will stand by his word."

"The hell he will…." I mumbled, my words slurred by shock and the pain radiating through my right cheek. I tasted blood in my mouth, and licked it from my lips as Pete pulled me upright again, probably positioning me for another blow, rather than for my comfort. "He said you could come back, too, didn't he?" I pinned Kevin with my gaze. "How often has he promised? How soon did he say you'd be back home, in your old room? Next month? Next week? Or was it *last* month?"

Kevin glowered at me. "Plans change."

"Wow, you're so *naive* for a bad guy!" I let genuine amusement leak into my tone, then leaned forward to spit more blood on Yarnell's pale, plush carpet before I met

Kevin's eyes again. "He's not going to take you back, and my bet is you already know Dan'll never make it to the northwest Pride. So how's he going to die? In a fight? Or peacefully in his sleep? Or are you going to bait one of us into killing him for you? Either way—" I leaned around him again to catch Dan's gaze "—once you hand over Manx and Kaci, they'll be done with you, and you'll end your existence in an unmarked hole in the ground. Maybe right next to Adam Eckard. Because the truth is that my father's the only Alpha in the country who'd seriously consider admitting a stray into his Pride. The proof of that is lying unconscious in the back bedroom."

Marc, of course.

"Where *you* put him." I glared at Dan, unable to censor my anger and betrayal even if he *was* my only shot at survival. "Were you there when they came for him? Did you fight him? We'd never have known, would we? Since you were the one who reported it, we didn't think twice about your scent in his house."

Dan closed his eyes and gritted his teeth. "I wasn't there. I knew they were going to implant him, but I couldn't help, or he'd know I was in on it. I didn't know the guys they sent, and I didn't even know when they were going to do it. I never touched him."

"Yet he's going to die because of you! What did Marc ever do to you? Other than teach you to fight and welcome you into his home?"

"Enough." Kevin slapped me again, and this time when he picked me up, I spit blood in his face, knowing it would hurt his broken nose to wipe it off. He dabbed at his nose gingerly with the towel Pete had stuffed into my mouth, then dropped it on the floor, fury glowing crimson in his cheeks. "I'm going to give you one chance to answer, then I'll let Pete go to work on you. How peacefully you die is up to you."

I rolled my eyes again, then met his gaze to let him

see the derision swimming in mine. "I may be a girl, but I bet my rear claws I have bigger balls than either of you assholes. Not that that's saying much." Yarnell growled on my right, but I continued as if I hadn't heard him. "I'm not going to answer your questions, no matter what you do to me. So why don't you just save us all the trouble and kill me now?"

Not that I expected them to actually do that. In fact, I was kind of counting on their refusal. And hoping that the madder they got, the more careless they'd get. If I could stall them long enough for one of the toms to come out of their drugged sleep—and Marc was the most likely to wake up, since he'd been put under first—we might have a chance to make it out alive.

Kevin squatted to watch me from eye level, as if whatever he had to say was too important to be spoken at any real distance. "If you won't cooperate, and we can't beat the information out of you, we'll just bring one of your boys in here and let you watch us beat him until you answer. How 'bout that?"

I refused to answer, my jaws clenched shut so hard I thought I heard the bones creak. Taking my own beating was one thing, but I couldn't watch the guys suffer in my stead. No more than I could have watched Abby raped, or Kaci kidnapped. And Kevin clearly knew it.

"Should we start with Marc? I'm assuming he's the one you'd most want to protect. But I don't know…" His voice rose on the end, and he glanced up at Yarnell as if for an opinion. "Jace and the doc have nothing to do with any of this. They're innocent bystanders, of a sort. And I'm guessing you don't want to see them suffer, either. Maybe we should flip a coin…."

"Good idea, dumbass!" I knew smarting off was a bad idea, but I just couldn't help myself. My mouth was the only weapon I had left. "You have a three-sided coin?"

Kevin bitch-slapped me again, and this time my lower

lip split wide open, and blood spilled over my chin. "Go get Marc. He should be coming out of it soon anyway. I have a feeling there's nothing she won't do to spare him pain. Except marry him."

Twenty-Eight

Yarnell clomped off down the hall, and I wiped blood from my chin onto my shoulder, then stared at Dan, begging him silently to look at me. "Dan, don't let them do this! Marc never did anything but help you!"

Dan turned away from me, but his leg began to bounce, his foot rapidly tapping the thick carpet. I was getting to him.

"How can you sit there and watch them beat him for no reason?" Yes, Marc had often pounded information out of hostile trespassers, but Kevin didn't want information out of him. He wanted it from *me,* and we'd *never* hosted a pounding by proxy. That was a line my Pride would never cross. "You can stop this, Dan. You can do the right thing. Hell, you fought *with* us in the ambush. Was that part of your act?"

He shrugged, still avoiding my eyes. "I'm not close personal friends with every stray out there. Besides, I didn't kill anyone. And it's not like I could stand there and watch you all get *slaughtered.*"

"But you can *now?*"

And finally he met my desperate, imploring gaze, silently begging me to understand. "Now, it's him or me, Faythe." His voice was empty. Hollow. Detached. That was the only way he could remain sane, because inside, I knew Dan Painter was a good person. He'd fought alongside us because he and Marc were *friends.* I was sure of that, because Marc was a wonderful judge of character.

But Kevin had preyed on his worst fears and his biggest dreams, convincing Dan that his only shot for acceptance by and protection from his fellow werecats lay in giving them Marc.

"If I help you, they'll kill me." He tossed his head at Kevin, who nodded smugly. "And even if they don't, your dad will. Every cat in your Pride will be after me within the hour, and you know it. I'm sorry, but it's too late. I gotta think about me."

Fresh tears formed in my eyes, and this time the pain had nothing to do with my bruises. Dan was breaking my heart. Killing some relentlessly optimistic part of me that had truly believed Pinocchio would listen to Jiminy Cricket in the end. That good would triumph over evil, as trite as that sounded.

"That's the difference between you and him," I said, as Yarnell backed into the living room hauling Marc with an arm under each shoulder, his feet dragging the carpet. "He'd *die* for you, or for me, or for anyone he cares about. And you're just gonna watch him do it."

Dan's jaw went tight, and he stood silently, then walked into the kitchen without another glance in my direction. Though I could have sworn I saw moisture glinting in the corner of his eye.

Though his eyes remained closed, Marc moaned when Yarnell dropped him on the floor, and I got my first good look at the wound Eckard thought had killed him. There was a two-inch-long gash on the side of his head, crusted over with blood. It was a miracle he'd survived that one. And if Kevin had his way, it wouldn't be for long.

I had to do something. I couldn't watch Marc beaten

to death, but neither could I give Kevin information that might doom my father's quest for allies against Malone. Unfortunately, the only trick I had up my sleeve was the partial Shift, and with my hands and feet bound, cat's jaws wouldn't do me any good unless someone came really close to my face. And trying to fully Shift with my wrists taped at my back would only dislocate my shoulders. Assuming Yarnell didn't kill me when he saw what I was up to.

Now, if I could partially Shift my hands, *that would be another story entirely.* With cat claws, I could slice through duct tape like a canoe paddle through water. But I couldn't Shift just my hands.

Could I?

With a start, I realized I'd never tried. But I'd gotten pretty damn good at Shifting just my face, and my hands couldn't be that different, right?

"Bring him around," Kevin ordered, recapturing my attention while Yarnell headed into the kitchen. Water ran, and a moment later he was back with a large, full glass. Which he promptly dumped over Marc's face.

Marc's eyes popped open, and he sputtered, trying to expel water from both his nose and mouth, even as he blinked it from his eyes. Watching him, and suffering along with him, I harnessed my mounting rage to fuel a partial Shift I couldn't even be sure was possible. I pictured my left hand slimming and lengthening, and fur rolling over my fingers.

"Oh good, you're awake!" Kevin peered down at Marc from two feet away—well within the danger zone, had Marc not been bound as I was. "Your part in tonight's production is that of the whipping boy. If your girlfriend truly can't be motivated by pain, then every time she refuses to answer a question, Peter will break one of your bones. Make sense? Or are you still foggy from the tranquilizer?"

"Leave him alone, you bastard!" I said through clenched teeth as I flexed my hands behind my back.

"Faythe...?" Marc's voice was slurred, yet he called my name with a sense of urgency, of fear, and fresh tears spilled over my cheeks. I was the first thought on his mind, the moment he woke up from an ordeal that would have killed just about anyone else.

"Over here," I whispered, and he twisted toward me at the sound of my voice, one shoulder slanted awkwardly into the floor, the side of his face pressed into the carpet. In my mind, I pictured my nails growing into long, curved claws, and I flexed my fingers to unsheathe them.

"Your face..." he said, and his features went hard with anger on my behalf, in spite of the drug-glaze in his eyes.

I forced a grin to tell him I was fine. "Don't hate me because I'm beautiful." My left hand twitched, and my heart leapt at the familiar sensation. It was working! And suddenly my smile felt genuine.

"Well, now that we're all caught up, let's move on," Kevin said, and Yarnell stalked toward me, ready to commence with the interrogation. "Did your mother let Ryan go?"

"*What?*" For a moment, I couldn't process the sudden subject change, and my partial Shift faltered as my concentration wavered. But then the question sank in, and the possibility flooded me like lead anchoring me to the sea floor.

Had my mother let Ryan go? The truth was that it was entirely possible. I have no idea how Kevin came by that idea when *I* hadn't even thought of it, but it made sense. My mother couldn't stand to see her son locked up, so she would have let him go for the same reason she'd taken care of him, even while he lived in the free zone.

Because he needed her.

Kevin saw the answer on my face, but that wasn't enough for him. The bastard wanted to hear it. Wanted to force me to play his game. "Did she?"

"I don't know," I whispered, because even if my hunch was right, I couldn't tell him. He'd stepped way over the line, going after my mother. Especially considering that she was well respected by most of the Alphas, even those who didn't like my father's politics.

They were trying to get to him through her, and in an odd way, I was disillusioned by that realization. Was *nothing* sacred to these pricks?

At that thought, and the fresh anger it triggered, the skin over my hand began to itch unbearably, and my fingers ached as they shortened and thickened, protective pads covering my palm.

Kevin nodded at Pete and gestured toward me grandly with one outstretched arm. "No bones yet. We don't want her passing out this early."

Yarnell pulled me to my feet by one arm, and I let him, still focusing on the weapon forming at my back. "Answer him."

I could have repeated my reply, and technically it would have been the truth. But the words tasted bitter in my mouth. So I swallowed them.

Yarnell's huge fist slammed into my stomach, dead center, driving the air from my body and folding me in half.

"No!" Marc thrashed as if *he'd* been hit, and I fell to the floor hard, bruising my knees. Several seconds passed before I could draw another breath, and when I finally looked up, agony still radiating outward from my center, Yarnell stood over me, a blissful smile on his face, as if he got actual physical pleasure from my pain.

Great. But the latest blow had so thoroughly pissed me off that my left hand had Shifted completely. Perfectly. That arm now ended in a fur-covered cat paw and claws. Unfortunately, the tape binding my wrists was too far up for my new claws to reach.

Or was it…?

My dewclaw! Cats have an extra claw—like a thumbnail—high up on the inside of their paws, near where the wrist would be in human form. Dewclaws aren't good for much. They don't even hit the ground when a cat walks. But most werecats can flex their dewclaws, and I was no exception. If I could move it enough to puncture all the layers of duct tape, I'd have that weak spot in my bindings I'd wished for earlier.

"Did she let him out?" Kevin repeated, as I flexed my dewclaw desperately, trying not to squirm as I worked.

I glanced at Marc, silently hoping that they'd hit me again, instead of him. Then I met Yarnell's gaze boldly. "I. Don't. Fucking. Know." But instead of hauling me up, he stomped across the room toward Marc and pulled his right foot back, preparing to slam his heavy boot into Marc's ribs.

My pulse raced, and I swallowed thickly. "Wait! I'm serious. Even if she *had* let him out, she wouldn't have told me about it. She wouldn't have told *anyone,* so I can't imagine where you're getting your information."

"Fine," Kevin said, and Yarnell let his foot drop, though it was clear neither of them planned to reveal their sources. "Let's talk about something you do know about. When will your dad move against Malone?"

My heart pounded, and I began to sweat in spite of the cool draft near the floor. I flexed my paw furiously, wiggling the dewclaw as much as I could. And finally that tiny, vestigial claw popped silently through the layers of tape binding my wrists.

I could have squealed with relief, but it wasn't over yet. I couldn't move the dewclaw enough to actually cut the tape, so I'd still have to rip it open the hard way. But I couldn't do that with Kevin watching me.

Exhaling dread and frustration, I glanced at Marc, silently apologizing for what I was about to do. I needed a distraction, and the only thing that would take all eyes off me was putting them all on *him.*

Marc blinked at me and nodded, telling me to go ahead with whatever I had to do. My guilt level skyrocketed at his selfless submission, but I forced the words out anyway, staring at Kevin with challenge written in every line of my face. *"Fuck you."*

Kevin's face flamed with anger, and instead of looking to Yarnell, he turned toward Marc himself, drawing his own foot back. As all eyes focused on Marc, I pulled my arms apart with all the strength left in my body. My shoulders ached. Tape tugged at my recently grown fur. And my pulse spiked with the fear that even though I'd come so close, I would still be too late. Or too weak.

Kevin's foot slammed into Marc's ribs, and his whole body jerked in pain. Then, just when I though it wasn't going to happen, the tape tore open at my back with a loud ripping sound.

All heads turned my way. Kevin's foot was cocked and ready to fly again. I gave my arms one last, violent tug, and the tape pulled free from one arm, taking large patches of fur with it. I grabbed the edge of the couch for balance and was on my feet in an instant, slicing through the tape binding my ankles as I stood.

"What the *hell!*" Yarnell lunged for me, and I leapt to the left, ripping the remaining tape from my ankles with my human right hand. He tackled me a second later, driving us both to the ground. Yarnell tried to force my arms to the carpet, still staring in shock and disgust at my newly furry appendage.

I brought my knee up hard into his crotch, and he groaned miserably. His grip loosened in the face of intense pain, and I tugged my Shifted hand loose. Still wheezing in agony, Yarnell wrapped one hand around my throat and squeezed. Gagging, I unsheathed my claws and swiped them across his arm, shredding the flesh in one pass.

Blood sprayed my face, and I shoved Yarnell, then rolled out from under him. He howled, and clapped his good hand over the injury, trying to slow the blood loss.

I jumped to my feet just in time to see Kevin run at me. I dodged him to the left and dropped to the floor beside Marc. Dan stared at us in shock from the kitchen doorway, making no move to join either side of the fight. I ripped the tape from Marc's arms, then rose into an immediate roundhouse as Kevin dove at me.

My boot hit his stomach, and he doubled over the blow, barely grunting because of the air he'd lost. But he grabbed my human wrist as I tried to run, and jerked me backward so brutally I heard a bone crack, and pain radiated from my fingers all the way into my elbow. His fist hit my back, and an all-new agony slammed into my kidney, so acute I couldn't move. I clamped my jaws shut to keep from screaming and waking the neighbors as I breathed through the pain.

On the floor, Marc sat up and ripped the tape from his ankles. He leapt awkwardly to his feet, but Yarnell rammed him an instant later, dripping a trail of blood on his own carpet all the way across the room.

Marc went down on his back, with Yarnell on top of him. They alternated blows, grunting and wheezing as the fists flew.

Kevin tightened his grip on my broken arm, and I choked on a scream as he pulled his fist back for another blow. I twisted away from him and slashed my paw in a vicious arc. Blood instantly soaked his shredded shirt. He started to shriek, but I followed up with a breath-stealing blow to the gut, acutely aware that too much noise would lead to neighbor—and police—involvement. He knocked my feet out from under me and his weight crushed me to the floor.

Across the room, Marc rolled over Yarnell, still throwing punches. A moment later, Yarnell was on top again. Then he suddenly lunged sideways, and took a punch to the ribs from Marc as he shoved one hand under an armchair. When his arm emerged, he held Dan's framing hammer.

My heart stopped beating, and pain shot through my chest. I tried to shout, but Kevin's hands closed around my throat. Yarnell raised the hammer. And out of nowhere, a denim-clad blur shot across the room toward him.

Kevin forced my cat's paw to the floor. His free hand clenched harder around my throat. I gagged, and on the edge of my vision, Yarnell's hammer thumped to the carpet. He made a horrible, wet, gurgling sound, and I froze, Kevin straddling me. I'd know that sound anywhere, though I'd only heard it once.

I jabbed Kevin in the throat with my free hand, gritting through the pain in my wrist. He gagged and let me go. I twisted my head as far as it would go, just in time to see Marc shove Yarnell off of him. Yarnell hit the carpet on his back, with a crowbar protruding from both sides of his neck, blood soaking both him and the carpet.

Dan stood over them both, his hand still raised from the death blow.

Kevin punched me in the gut. Paralyzing agony clamped around my abdomen. He scrambled off me and across the room, scooping up the hammer Yarnell had dropped. Dan never saw him coming. Kevin swung the hammer in a broad arc. It shattered Dan's skull with a revolting crunch. Gray matter splattered one of Yarnell's suede armchairs.

Dan went down like a felled tree. He was dead before he hit the ground.

Marc was on Kevin before Dan's body even hit the floor. He put one hand on each side of Kevin's face, and one last, sickening crack later, Kevin hit the ground on his knees, then fell onto his stomach, without uttering a sound.

I sank to the carpet in consuming pain and overwhelming relief, clutching my fractured wrist to my chest. The world was rendered one big blur by encroaching shock. Soft grunts and eerie bone crunches played over and over in my head as I forced my bloody paw to Shift back into the left hand I desperately needed, now that the right one was out of commission.

"Faythe?" Marc said, and my head swiveled toward him on its own. He stood over Kevin's body, splattered with blood from head to toe. "Are you okay?"

"Broken arm. Bruised ribs. Sore throat. Busted lip. But I'll live." I tried to force a smile, but his reaction said it looked more like a grimace. "You?"

"Bruised ribs and a hell of a headache. And I suspect a concussion."

"And probably a fractured skull," I added. "You were gone for two days. They thought you were dead." I pushed myself to my feet and limped toward him, eyeing the gash over his ear in the light from the fan fixture overhead.

"I almost was. I passed out in a storage shed at a ranger's station."

I reached out for him, and he folded me into his arms, careful of my broken one, his heart racing. "You probably would have frozen otherwise."

He nodded, and wiped blood from my face gently with the hem of his shirt, which wasn't much cleaner. "I almost did anyway. I've never been so cold in my life."

"How much do you remember?"

"Nothing, from the time I passed out until I woke up with my mouth taped shut, when Kevin and that other asshole threw me into his trunk."

"Bastards."

He grinned, but then his smile faded abruptly as concern wrinkled his forehead. "But that's not all. They have some kind of tracker. I found one implanted in the tom who tried to bury me alive. And I think Dan has one."

I nodded, and put one finger over his lips. "I know. They're GPS chips, and we never would have known a thing about them if you hadn't left that body with a hole in his back."

"You found him?"

I smiled. "Yeah, and for the record, I never doubted you were alive. But once he figured that out, Kevin found you by tracking the chip you took from Adam Eckard. Dan *did* have one, but Dr. Carver removed it. And there's a lot more." I closed my eyes, and he pulled me closer, rubbing my back with both hands while I tried to figure out how to best explain everything he'd missed. But there was no easy way.

"Marc, Ethan's dead." I blinked and wiped away the fresh tears with my good hand. "Malone's men breached the border to take Kaci, and Ethan was killed defending her."

His heartbeat hitched, and he closed his eyes as his arms tightened around me. "We'll get them."

"I know. You're coming back home. Screw the council."

Marc started to protest—or maybe to agree—but then froze when a thump sounded from behind the living room wall. "Shit…"

"Wait!" I grabbed his arm when he reached down for the bloody hammer at our feet. "It's Jace and Carver. One of them woke up." His brows arched in surprise, and he dropped the hammer, then followed me down the hall. "Can you get the doc? He's in the bathroom. And have him look at your head. And his own. He took a pretty good hit with your tire iron."

He nodded and jogged down the hall while I opened Jace's door, warning him with a single look to stay quiet. I peeled the tape from his wrists, then leaned in to whisper in his ear, ignoring the hitch in my pulse as I inhaled his scent.

"We'll deal with this later," I said, and he knew what I meant. "This isn't the time."

Jace nodded, either in compliance or agreement, and unwound the tape from his feet. Moments later, Marc appeared in the doorway, behind Dr. Carver, who looked disheveled and pale, rubbing a big lump on the side of his head. But he was alive. We all were.

But as we waited for Vic and Parker to arrive, I looked around the living room in horror. We'd won this fight, but at what cost? How many more had to die before Malone gave up his bid for control of the council? And would one of us be next?

Because the truth was that though we'd won this battle, the real war was still to come, and I couldn't begin to imagine the cost of such a victory, for either side.

Much less a loss.

Twenty-Nine

"People are starting to ask about you. Are you ready?" Marc asked, and I looked up to find him watching me from my doorway, just like old times. Except that the old times were gone for good, as was the golden sparkle in his eyes, at least for now. With Ethan gone and war on the horizon, things would never be the same again, and at the moment, finding happiness in my new reality looked about as likely as werewolves making a miraculous comeback from extinction in the early twenty-first century.

My only option for moving forward was to patch together my future as best I could with the scraps of my past. Which were looking rattier and less substantial with each passing day.

I smiled sadly at Marc and shook my head. I would *never* be ready for this.

We'd buried Ethan an hour earlier, and now we had to put on stoic faces for our guests, in the aftermath of the most devastating tragedy my Pride—as well as my family—had ever faced.

"Come on." Marc took my good hand, pulling me gently out of the desk chair, and my pulse jumped the moment he touched me. He'd come back to the ranch with us two days earlier, after we'd spent the remaining hours of darkness cleaning up the mess at Pete Yarnell's house. Even with Vic and Parker there to help, it was a big job, and had to be performed very carefully and quietly to avoid waking the neighbors, or being spotted carrying corpses across the suburban backyard.

Since Kevin Mitchell had acted like a criminal, we'd interred him like one. Jace and Carver had buried him in the dark, in the woods, in an unmarked hole in the ground more than a mile from where Vic and Parker buried Peter Yarnell. Which was more than a mile from where Marc and I buried Dan, so that if one of the bodies was ever discovered, its connection to the others would remain buried.

Dan Painter's grave was the hardest one I'd ever had to dig, and filling it in was even more difficult. Yes, he'd made some really bad decisions, and yes, those decisions had nearly gotten several of us killed. But in the end, he'd saved Marc's life, and I couldn't help but attribute that to my certainty that he'd genuinely liked Marc and treasured their friendship, as well as my conviction that he was a fundamentally good person.

Then, of course, there was the fact that I'd made more than my own fair share of mistakes in the past, which had also cost at least one life, and nearly cost several more. Knowing that, and that Dan had died making an important stand, I couldn't help the tears I shed as we tossed dirt in on top of him. And I could have sworn I saw Marc's eyes glisten, too, in the mottled moonlight shining between the bare branches overhead.

At my father's insistence, Marc had agreed to stay through Ethan's funeral. We hadn't bothered to clear the visit with the other Alphas, because anyone who supported my dad would approve, and anyone who didn't would disapprove. In short, telling them would change nothing, so we'd exercised our right to remain silent.

Marc must have known how I felt. He must have seen that I was near my breaking point, because after he pulled me from my chair, he held me close. He was careful of my right arm and its cast, already covered in signatures and inappropriate jokes from every tom I knew. And from Kaci, who'd written her name in flowery letters in a pink Sharpie, in one of her lately-rare moments of levity. When I groaned over the color, she'd even smiled. For nearly five seconds.

I hugged Marc back with my good arm, and fresh tears fell on his shoulder and my black dress, in spite of my best effort to hold them back.

I'd been fine during the service. We'd buried Ethan beneath the apple tree in the east field, with an arched granite headstone. I'd held it together for the entire burial, and had even spoken at the graveside. I'd said the things everyone expected to hear from the dead tom's sister: Ethan was loyal and funny and protective. When we were little, he was the brother most likely to make me cry—and mostly likely to wipe away my tears. He died doing what he loved to do, and we couldn't honor him more than to remember him at his best and lift a glass in his memory.

My voice only cracked once, when I caught sight of my three remaining brothers, all lined up across the grave from me. Michael stood with Holly on his right—a rare appearance at the ranch, and one we'd all been briefed on—and Owen on his left, his formal black cowboy hat held over his chest, his eyes rimmed in red and magnified by tears. Ryan flanked Owen's other side, after a surprise appearance that morning.

Only my mother had looked more relieved than truly surprised.

My father was just as upset as the rest of us, but not too upset to notice that his prodigal son had returned. Again. I had no doubt he would soon find out exactly how Ryan had gotten out of the cage—and how he'd known about Ethan. *After* the funeral.

"Let's get it over with." Marc kissed my forehead, then guided me gently but firmly toward the hallway. We passed my mirror on the way out of my room, and I noticed that the blue bruise-bloom on my cheek was finally fading, and with it, the memory of my fight for my life. And for Marc's, and Jace's, and Dr. Carver's.

Marc looked pretty good, considering how long he'd spent outside in below-freezing temperatures, with no food or water. And that his skull *had* turned out to be fractured. He'd been Shifting at least once a day to accelerate the healing of his head and too many bruises to count.

We stopped in the living room first and said hi to Bert Di Carlo and my uncle Rick, my father's strongest supporters. They stood near the front window, sipping whiskey from short, thick glasses, and the sight of them gave me a nauseating moment of déjà vu. They'd stood in that same spot the day we found out Sara Di Carlo had been murdered.

Of course today's crowd was much smaller than the gathering that day, because thanks to the current Grand Canyon–size division in the council, nearly half of the Alphas had not been invited. But Paul Blackwell, the acting chairman, had made an official visit, and true to character, he'd remained professional and impartial. And unfailingly polite, especially to my mother.

After brief words with my uncle and Vic's father, Marc and I circled the room somberly, greeting the congregated toms in dark suits, then made our way to one corner of the room, where Michael stood with Holly. I could tell from his posture and the tense line of his mouth that something was wrong.

"It's because they're all in mourning," he was saying as we approached. "It has nothing to do with you."

"I don't know, Michael," Holly insisted. Her voice was like honey: smooth, and almost too sweet to stomach. "I don't think they like me. Everyone looks at me like I come from another planet."

Michael smiled tightly and tucked a golden strand of hair behind her ear. "They just don't know how to act around a famous model."

Or a human woman at a werecat funeral, I thought, smiling at him from behind his tall, twig-thin wife.

"Hi, Holly, thanks for coming." I rested one hand briefly on the tan shoulder exposed by her sleeveless black dress.

"Of course. I'm so sorry about Ethan. He seemed so full of life, and twenty-five is so young to die. What was he doing in that tree, anyway?"

"He was just messing around. Just being Ethan."

We'd told Holly that he'd fallen out of our apple tree and broken his neck. We said he'd died instantly, and that there was no obvious pain or fear. The truth was somewhat different, of course, but everyone who really knew Ethan knew he'd died a hero, and that was all that really mattered.

He would be remembered.

"Faythe, what did you do to your arm?" Holly eyed my cast in obvious horror, and I wasn't sure if she was more upset by the thought of a broken bone, or by the fact that my scribbled-all-over cast didn't match my funeral dress.

"I tripped and fell on a hike a couple of days ago. Sucks, 'cause I'm right-handed."

"I'm sure. So, how do you put on makeup…?" Her question faded into awkward silence as her focus moved from my cast to my bruised face, which was bare in comparison. "Oh." Holly wisely brought her cup up to her mouth, likely to avoid shoving her foot back in, and Marc rescued mc—or maybe *her*—by claiming we had to check on Kaci.

As we walked away, Holly's latest question followed us. "These men are your father's colleagues? They don't *look* like architects…."

I chuckled at Michael's weary sigh, then followed Marc down the hall and into my dad's office. Kaci sat at one end of the couch, playing a silent game of chess with Jace. She was beating him. Badly. But then, that was no surprise.

"Hey." She looked up from the board briefly when we entered the room.

"Hey, Whiskers." Marc scuffed the top of her head and leaned against the couch at her side. To my surprise, when we'd returned to the ranch, Kaci had greeted us in cat form, rubbing her whiskers against my leg in welcome. Marc had rarely used her real name since.

I sank onto the love seat next to Kaci, eyeing the pieces on the board. "I think you'll have him in—"

"Three more moves. I know." She moved her rook into place with no hint of a smile. Kaci had sniffled all through the service, then had refused lunch, claiming an upset stomach. But the truth was that she'd seen enough of death in her short life but hadn't yet learned how to deal with it.

Hell, neither had I. Unfortunately, I was fairly certain we'd get plenty of practice in the near future.

Jace watched me while Kaci contemplated her next move, his eyes red from both tears and exhaustion, and the intimacy in that look jarred the breath from my lungs. But he'd kept his word; he hadn't so much as hugged me since we'd found Marc. Not even when they'd lowered Ethan into the ground and covered him with earth, though I know his heart was breaking just as surely as mine was.

He'd stood beside the coffin, jaw clenched, fists curled tightly at his sides, eyes shining with unshed tears. Then he'd met my gaze from across the grave, and the misery in his eyes took hold of my heart with a grip of iron. For several seconds I couldn't breathe. I was stunned by the depth of his need, and scared witless by the knowledge that I could ease the ache in his heart. And that he could return the favor.

Fresh tears formed in his eyes as he watched me across the chessboard. But his grief hid something new. A very *changed* Jace, just waiting to take the stage.

When Ethan died, he'd taken part of Jace with him. The tolerant, even-tempered, jovial part that had made him easy to love but hard to take seriously. What was left was raw emotion and a steel glint of determination in his eyes worthy of any Alpha. Jace wanted only two things out of life now, and I understood that once he'd regained his equilibrium, he'd do whatever it took to attain them.

One was revenge for Ethan's death, which went hand in hand with my father's plans.

The other was *me,* which went in direct opposition to *Marc's* plans.

Marc saw the change, too, and though he couldn't know what it meant for him, I could tell from his grim sympathy that he understood that he and Jace were in much the same position. They had no home to go back to, other than the Lazy S, and no real family to lean on, other than me and mine.

Having both Jace and Marc on the ranch made me feel like I was standing on a smoldering rope bridge over a lake of lava, and no matter which way I turned, I would eventually fall in and get fried.

And we'd just buried the brother I would normally turn to for comfort.

"You're too late," Ryan said, drawing me from my thoughts, and I looked up to find him standing in the office doorway, a frosty can of Coke in one hand. "I'm playing the winner."

I nodded and gestured toward the board. "Be my guest."

Ryan rounded the couch and leaned down to whisper into my ear. "You missed it. Milo Mitchell just called to express his *sympathies.* Can you believe it?"

Unfortunately, I *could.* That's just the kind of prick he was.

As expected, Milo Mitchell denied any knowledge of his son's activities in the free zone, and we expected him to file formal charges against Marc for Kevin's death any day. In fact I looked forward to testifying on his behalf, armed with the invoice Michael had found. As did Jace. As a non-Pride member, Marc wouldn't even be allowed to testify on his own behalf, and neither would Ben Feldman, though he volunteered to verify what we'd found in Kevin's house.

"Where are Mom and Dad?" I asked as Ryan settled onto the love seat across from me.

"Having tea in the kitchen."

My parents had taken Ethan's death harder than anyone, except maybe Jace. My mother had all new lines around her eyes and the silver spots at my father's temples had actually broadened. He'd always said Ethan would eventually make him go gray, and apparently my brother still wielded that power from beyond the grave.

Although now he was attributing a few of those new gray hairs to me, too. My father was *furious* with me for going after Kevin without permission—without even telling him where we were—and though he was grateful for the outcome, his relief did nothing to lessen his anger, indignation, and outright fear over what could have happened.

I was in serious trouble. After all the years of training me, of grooming me to take over from him, when he'd found out what I'd done, he told me—in no uncertain terms—that if I ever disobeyed an order again, I would never sit on the council as Alpha of the south-central

Pride. He would name Marc as his heir, whether or not I married him, consequences be damned.

I believed him. And so did Marc.

And for the first time in my life, I realized how badly I really did want to take over from him. I could lead this Pride. I could protect the cats under my supervision. And I could change things, for Kaci, and for Manx, and for myself.

I would not screw up again. *Ever.* I'd play it by the book from then on.

At least until I was in the position to rewrite the rules.

Kaci captured Jace's queen and set it on her side of the board, while he shot her a distracted scowl. I leaned forward to tell him how best to take her remaining knight, but my words were cut off by a sudden high-pitched squalling from across the house.

Des.

"I'll be right back," I said, and Marc nodded. Kaci and I'd been helping as much as we could with the baby, considering her age and my broken arm, because both of Manx's hands were still bandaged, and my mother was more than a little distracted.

I jogged down the hall, bracing myself for another diaper full of poo—I couldn't *believe* how much excrement a child so small could produce!—but stopped short in Manx's doorway, surprise stealing both my words and my breath.

"He does not like powder," Manx was saying, gesturing with one heavily bandaged hand. "But he seems to like the cream."

"This stuff?" Owen held up a half-empty tube of Desitin, his lip curling in distaste. "It smells like Crisco."

I smiled, leaning with one shoulder against the doorjamb. "I don't think you can cook with diaper cream, cowboy."

Owen flushed, and dropped the tube into a blue-checked lined basket on the changing table. "I was just trying to help...."

"By all means." I smiled, amused by his embarrassment. "But a word to the wise? Desitin stains, so don't get any on your suit."

"Thanks." Owen nodded, and gingerly peeled back the tabs on Des's diaper. He lifted the front flap and peeked inside hesitantly. "Holy shit!" he cried, and I was laughing for the first time in days when I heard the phone ring.

It was a cell phone, playing "She Hates Me" by Puddle of Mudd.

My smile faded, and chill bumps popped up on my arms. *Well, shit.* What were the chances someone else had Angela's dedicated ringtone?

I wandered down the hall, following the song, hoping it would go silent with every passing moment, when the voice mail kicked in. Because I *really* didn't want to take that call. But *someone* had to.

Puddle of Mudd played on, and I found myself standing in the doorway to Owen's room, which he'd shared with Ethan until three days earlier. And sure enough, there was Ethan's phone, bouncing around on his night table, its screen illuminated in an eerie blue light.

I glanced down the hall toward the living room, wondering if I should answer it, or take it to my father. After all, what would I say? Was there a socially acceptable way to tell your dead brother's girlfriend about his demise?

Hesitantly, I crossed the room and glanced at the display screen. My heart seemed to swell within my chest, and I felt my pulse race at the information it verified.

Angela Hasting. The "long-term" girlfriend Ethan had been avoiding all week.

I snatched the phone before I could chicken out, and pushed the Accept Call button. She should know what had happened. Or at least one version of it. "Hello?"

"Hi. I'm looking for Ethan Sanders." She sounded nice. And I really didn't want to ruin her day.

"Um…is this Angela?" I asked.

"Yes. Who is this?" Her voice dipped into the suspicion range, and I flinched, because it was about to get *so* much worse.

"This is Faythe. Ethan's sister."

"Oh, hi, Faythe." Relief was thick in her tone, and that made everything so much harder. "Ethan talks about you all the time. Can I speak to him, please?"

Well, here goes… "Angela, I'm sorry to have to tell you this, but Ethan had an accident three days ago. A really bad one." I hesitated, then made myself say the rest of it. "He…died."

"What? *No.*" She sniffled, and fresh tears formed in my own eyes. "You're serious?"

"Yes. I'm sorry." I sank onto Ethan's bed, wondering if I should offer to meet her for lunch or something, to explain the human-friendly version of his last moments.

"Me, too." The sniffling grew more pronounced. "What happened? How did he…?"

"He fell and broke his neck," I said, closing my eyes, but even as the words left my lips, his actual death replayed in my head, his last words—a plea for my help—haunting me. "Ethan was just being himself, and he fell out of a tree in our front yard."

"How horrible…" Angela's pause felt heavy, as if she had more to say, but I wasn't sure I wanted to hear it, whatever it was. I wasn't up to remembering Ethan with someone who couldn't possibly have really known him. Not with the dirt still fresh on his grave.

But she continued before I could figure how to hang

up gracefully. "I know my timing really sucks, but… well, I need to tell you something."

What, had he left a toothbrush at her place? Snagged one of her T-shirts? Whatever it was, it could damn well wait until we'd at least said goodbye to the other mourners.

"I'm pregnant."